the breadmaker's

Carnival

Andrew Lindsay

ALLEN & UNWIN

This project has been assisted by the Commonwealth
Government through the Australia Council, its arts
funding and advisory body.

First published in 1998
Allen & Unwin
9 Atchison Street, St Leonards 1590 Australia
Phone: (61 2) 8425 0100
Fax:     (61 2) 9906 2218
E-mail: frontdesk@allen-unwin.com.au
Web:    http://www.allen-unwin.com.au

National Library of Australia
Cataloguing-in-Publication entry:

Lindsay, Andrew, 1955– .
  The breadmaker's carnival.

  ISBN 1 86448 808 5.

  I. Title.

A823.3

Set in 11/13pt Plantin Light by DOCUPRO, Sydney
Printed and bound by Griffin Press, South Australia

10 9 8 7 6 5 4 3 2 1

# Disclaimer

Certain details in this book have been altered to reduce the chances of anyone attempting to enact their own 'breadmaker's carnival': thus anyone attempting to replicate Gianni Terremoto's 'tarantellini' will find this book of little practical use. Many details remain verifiable. The usual denials have been made. It is best to regard this book as a work of 'fiction'. It is not an authoritative text on techniques of breadmaking, techniques of olive oil production, the reproductive habits of certain spiders, and so on. It is an 'unnatural history', rather than a natural one, if such may be. Some of the inaccuracies are there for the sheer sensual pleasure of telling lies, or of being inconsistent.

The author apologises to anyone who may share one or more names with any of the characters in this book. They are creatures of fiction, for the most part reprehensible, and certainly not copies of any other characters, living or dead: unless, of course, they are all self-portraits of the author. Rest assured 'you' are not one of 'them'.

The town of Bacheretto, a.k.a Little Italy, should not be confused with the towns of Bachereto and Bacherreto, which are in Italy. As far as we know there is no 'breadmaker's carnival' or similar event in those towns. Whereas in Bacheretto it may be that there is *only* The Breadmaker's Carnival. The Carnival is a world unto itself, and perhaps it's best left that way.

'. . . The most interesting attempts and unlimited experimenting were directed towards the preparation of disguised breads, somewhat hallucinatory and mildly stupefying, like the "poppyseed bread" praised by Ovidio Montalbani . . .'

Piero Camporesi
*Bread of Dreams*

# Prologue: But I Digress . . .

In the town of Igres, a long time ago, they used to make good beer. And once a year they used to make a day of it, a day, a night, they drank till they were blind. And it was a relief to find the sun came up and they could see again. No end of miracles in this life. But because they drank so much, they rambled, and the more they rambled the more they drank. It was a legendary day.

Needless to say the stories spread, and the people of Igres developed quite a reputation as a pack of drunks. Even though they only really drank on this one day. Or so it's said. In the local dialect, to say 'I'm from Igres' you said 'Y D'Igres'. In time the words progressed and it became then 'I digress', meaning of course 'I am a drunk who rambles'. Because they all drank on that day. It was I'd guess a fine precursor to the one and very thing, The Breadmaker's Carnival. But I digress.

# Preface: About The Painting

The entire picture is in code. It shows a church built like a breast, with a stone nipple for a dome. Before this church is a statue of a woman, also in stone. This is Saint Francesca, The Black Madonna.

In the square before the church you can see a number of figures. They are dressed in different guises and disguises. There is a young man riding a goat, his name is Amaretto and the goat's name is Francesca. There is a fat man made entirely out of bread, in the manner of Arcimbaldo. He is a composite of buns, rolls, cakes and loaves of different sorts. One curious detail concerns his sex, for a certain cake the artist places in the breadman's groin gives the impression that his genitalia are female. Unless he's a hermaphrodite, and his male sex organs are merely hidden from view.

A man in the foreground, dressed in red and black and sporting a pair of horns, is flogging a young woman who carries her head upon a plate. Another man is lying in a pool of mud, taking a bath, and is dreaming of an old and gnarled madonna. A woman of middle age stands on one leg, she is singing, and a swarm of wasps have issued from her mouth. These have gathered all around the flogging devil, and complicate his own desire to lash the woman on her knees with her head upon a platter.

A one-handed man is writing something on the ground with a piece of rock. This is Stefano Costa, who, it is said, built the church single-handed.

The entire scene depicts, in the artist's imagination, one version of the events that took place some time ago in the town of Bacheretto, also known as Little Italy. In that year

Good Friday fell on the first day of April, so that the holy rites of Easter collided with what is known as April Fool's Day to some and All Foole's Eve to others.

This painting, which once belonged to my maternal grandfather, is now in my possession.

I am, through the intractable workings of God or fate, infertile, so that the line ends with me. This is why I have decided to leave this record, so that the story of the canvas and the curious history it documents can be preserved, and be passed on.

Up until now this has always been an act of oral transmission, in my case during the last days of my grandfather's life.

Before I tell the story proper, I would like to add just one or two details about the manner in which the story came to me.

I had been travelling overseas, staying predominantly in Italy, where I was teaching theatre and preparing to attend the wedding of some friends, up in the hills of central Italy. I received a telegram from my grandfather asking me to return immediately, as he was dying and urgently needed to transact some final business with me.

For the last days of his life I sat and listened to his story, call it a history if you will. As he himself averred, it's an eccentric tale, at times even bizarre.

It's clear that in its retelling some details have been changed, others embellished. For all its discrepancies, I have chosen to leave it in much the same shape as my grandfather gave it to me. With his consent I recorded the entire thing. One curiosity among many was that he talked for three days, and died at exactly the same time as the batteries of my tape machine, a portable Sony.

Here then is the story my grandfather told to me.

# PART ONE:

# A PHOTOGRAPH OF GOD

# Gloria!

I don't expect you to believe a word of this. These things just happened, that is all. If you do believe, I won't think the less of you. After all, who could believe the facts of life? It takes us years as kids to get the whole thing straight, the idea of the sperm among the eggs—no wonder cabbages make more sense. Let me just tell you then what happened, and the rest is up to you.

Luigi Bacheretti was sitting in his studio, trying to take a photograph of God. No-one's ever tried to take a photograph of God before, thought Luigi. Poor bastard probably feels left out.

That's when the whole thing started. The actual dimensions of the photograph, and what it held within its frame, and what the frame was made of, and all sorts of things that no-one, and least of all Luigi, had thought of in advance, all this and more was about to become the very stuffing of a legend. The name of the legend was The Breadmaker's Carnival.

The name of the baker was Gianni Terremoto. A giant earthquake of a man. Because he ate a lot of rye some said he had the loudest fart in town. That stable doors had blown open with the force of his report, and other unsubstantiated rumours.

He was a big fart of man, that much is true. He used his farts to punctuate his monologue as other men might cough or sneeze. I mention this not for effect but because I'd like to try and set the record straight; you might say it's my commitment to the truth. It's a pity that veracity has no modesty, and no sense of propriety. But where was I?

3

Gianni Terremoto was an enthusiastic drinker, a man possessed at times of a rather grotesque humour, and a fascination for the line between the sacred and the profane. With the hot spirit breath at one end and the hot rye wind at the other it's just as well there was a separation of the powers, or there might have been a terrible explosion.

Perhaps that was the secret of Gianni's death—that Terremoto farted, and being pissed on spirits, spontaneously combusted. One of the wilder theories. Might be the truth. An even bigger worry.

Terremoto's biggest worry was his only child, Francesca, a bursting thirteen year old who was looking like a young fig set to bloom for the first time. She'd soon start menstruating. What should he tell her? Was it better from his lips or those of a woman friend, her mother being absent from this life? He felt the need to consult his good friend Amaretto at the bar. He farted once and felt his head go clear. He was ready for a drink. But first he had some bread to bake.

Francesca had yet to realise just how many revolutions were about to occur inside of her, that she would be transformed. Her ovaries like two hidden eyes that saw things which were foreign to her now.

One longs to say that she became the sacred tree of her own self, but shy of that, let's say instead that the fig had not yet burst, but the waters in her surely had begun to move.

Hard to describe the feeling of betrayal that she felt as she observed the early sprouts of pubic hair, and then the very furze and bush of it. She shaved it off, it pricked at her and then grew back, only hardier, grew more like wire. The more she shaved the wirier grew her hair, as if perhaps a little of the metal of the blade had entered in each time she shaved. No-one had warned her that her hairy hair would sprout. She felt as if something had been taken from her, though this was odd as something had in fact been added to her. Even so, that strange feeling persisted, that something had been taken from her, some very part of her denied. No-one had talked to her about the death of childhood.

4

# La Tarantula

The name of Terremoto's bakery was La Tarantula. Over the doorway was a great hairy black spider, La Tarantula, poised and ready to strike. Six white eggs at her feet, eggs like breadrolls, so fine beside her hairy legs. La Tarantula, such a fine and beautiful creation.

Her venomed bite a kiss to send you out of this world, such potent juice come off her fangs you had to dance to save your life, or end it there all in a spasm on the ground. La Tarantula. An eight-legged creature in majestic black.

Luigi's father was bitten by the mother of this great tarantula. He'd had to dance to save his life, trusting the ancient knowledge of folklore to sweat the poison out of him.

It's an ugly death. Your throat swells up and you can't get liquid down, you'd swear you'll die of thirst. Nor can you get your air down, and you asphyxiate. If you've ever had the mispleasure of watching someone die this way you'll know they twitch and prance, both on the feet and then towards the end just on their backs. Churning the dust into clouds like a snake when it stirs the summer dust. The way the bit one gets to twitch and shake looks exactly like some dance. The nervous disorder called tarantism swept through the south for two hundred years, so many people jiggling on its string, so many died, and the popular belief was that the bite of the tarantula was the sole cause.

After you're bit, there's a funny calm that lasts a little while, call it a fatalism, when you know these coming minutes might be your last. They say that you can feel the poison travelling down your arm and up your leg, filling you up, and when it starts to burn you'd swear this fire comes from the inside, what can you do?

To use the common phrase, you now begin the dance of death.

The great difference between the living and the dead, as far as it relates to the bite of the tarantula, is this: the ones who live are not the ones who sit on a stump and wait for the end to come. The ones who do this soon have what they expect, a most violent release from this fine earth. The ones who live do not wait, instead they take the spider by the fangs, as it were, and straight away they dance. The cure's become a legend, so has the dance of it, the tarantella, and all because that folk cure works.

The emblem of the spider that hung outside the bakery was made by Gianni Terremoto. He was nearly dead from hunger when Luigi's father, Ernesto Bacheretti, crossed his path.

Ernesto had been lying in his bed having an erotic dream, his wife being absent from this life. He slipped his hand under the pillow, the spider bit and woke him up.

Young Gianni was sleeping nearby, under a hedge, having no other place to spend the night. He heard the wild whoopee and yell of Ernesto Bacheretti, and wasn't sure if this was a one-man party, or a calling of distress. Mr Bacheretti, being well versed in lore, knew that to dance straight off could save his life, but the bedroom was too small, and the heat that spread inside him like a fiery whisky he had drunk in through his hand, that spider's venomed whisky called for room. He ran downstairs into the kitchen, still too small though he was dancing now and knocking chairs out of his way, he had to sweat the bastard kiss straight out of him and not by sucking on it, the spider's fangs inject the stuff into the blood, they're well-made fangs.

The first time Gianni Terremoto, starveling, saw Ernesto Bacheretti it was as the bitten man exploded through the front door of his cottage and started dancing in the street, a mad-danced tarantella.

Gianni Terremoto watched Luigi's father dancing and on an impulse he joined in, dancing for the life of Bacheretti. They joined hands and locked fingers, the world blurred and the two men span. At that moment they knew they

A Photograph Of God

would never forget this face that looked and mouth that opened, those eyes that shone; nor forget the wild screaming that came out of their mouths.

They span and span. Extremities of head and neck and bitten hand were racing by, they tarantella'd up and down the street, they slapped hands and backs and ran on the spot, they dared not stop until they could not go on.

There was a dark light of the coming day in the distant sky, and the men were laughing as they lost their feet, falling arse on arse and landing with a bump. They ended in a ditch, dusty grass with brambles, they had not spoken a word and yet they'd danced a night away.

Ernesto Bacheretti felt exhausted but he didn't feel like a dying man. He felt that death was nearby but was not standing over him. The scrawny boy had got in first. Ernie felt a great love and a debt and wondered who this young boy was. They were still and lay together.

It's true the world still span, but slowly now, so that it seemed the stars were fixed in the one place, and their breathing slowed; the heart was not a fish trying to leap and break the surface that its fine skin might find the gleaming of the light up in the sky. They lay, and felt at peace.

Ernie sat up and cleared his throat and spat into the bushes. Then he lay back. He must have dozed, for the next thing he knew there was a hot sun on his face, a fly buzzed up his nose, it woke him.

The starveling lad was sitting there, sucking a blade of grass like another man might suck a straw, to get the liquid out. Then he chewed on it, savouring the sweetness, eating it like a carrot.

He plucked another blade of grass and took time again to savour it, and as he plucked the third blade out Ernesto Bacheretti stood up and said, I think it's time we ate some bread!

The young man sitting across the square wooden kitchen table had an odd look to him. He was so skinny that his skull was clearly visible beneath his face. He looked like death himself, the canny way of it, and the shock, to see a man with a death's head face. Needs feeding up, Ernie thought. He wondered if he'd ever seen such a hungry-looking man in all his life. The young man had not spoken, and he himself had barely said a word.

He set bread and olives and cheese and apples on the table and was waiting for the kettle to sing out that he might make coffee. He felt a mighty hunger coming on, and something more, though what it was he couldn't put into words.

For the moment breakfast was his major occupation. The boy looked uncomfortable in the chair—he lacked the ease he'd had when they were sloughed against the hill, down in the ditch. He'd looked at home there, where now he seemed out of place. The kettle whistle blew and Ernie shuffled over to the stove, lifted up the heavy copper kettle with its burnished beak and poured the steamy water into the coffee pot.

The lad seemed rigid, as if the very bones of him set stiff upon the morn. Have a roll, Ernie said.

The boy licked his lips and looked at Ernesto, picked up a breadroll and held it in his hands. Then he put it down. He began to scratch his arm. He brought the bread up to his nose and breathed it in.

Ernie was intrigued by this display. He picked up a breadroll, broke it with his hands, and stuffed a small piece in his mouth. It felt so good to chew. He was unnerved to note that his companion had still not begun to eat, instead had fixed his eyes on him and was sitting, watching the big man chew.

The bony hands of the bony boy. Almost he'd swear he could see through the translucent skin right to the bone. The lad was so pale and thin, Ernie wondered where he'd found the strength for such lifesaving dancing the night before.

The decision was made: the boy would stay with him, he'd feed him up, this sapling needing nourishment. It was not the only decision that he'd made. Somewhere between the dance and his sleep and waking up a true idea had formed; faced with the prospect of dying he'd glimpsed an image of the man he'd like to be. He was going to be a baker, and this scrawny lad would be his first (and last) apprentice. And so it was. Viva La Tarantula!

# A Regular Customer

Father Pestoso was a regular customer of La Tarantula.
He was an enthusiast of the hot crostoli and cannoli, an admirer of the bomboloni warmed and bloody with raspberry jam. He was a true patrician in his keen faith in Terremoto's almond breads. He preferred them to the wafers he gave out in church, and would have preferred to make a substitution. Perhaps the sweetbread of crostoli would suffice? Jesus was, he felt sure, a man with his own sweet tooth.

All in all, he found La Tarantula a fine House of Temptation, and was often tempted to drop in and engage in a brisk exchange of views with Terremoto. If Terremoto then felt the need to ask his views on the pastries that issued from the baker's oven as they spoke, well, it would be an outright rudeness to refuse.

One thing Pestoso found most comforting in Gianni Terremoto was his girth. Gianni's starveling stature had long since disappeared, as Gianni gorged and his girth inflated.

Pestoso was prone to paunch, it troubled him, the look of it not quite ascetic to his eye. It was not just a paunch but a veritable layer of comfort fat that spread around his frame, girdling each limb, each bone and organ well encushioned. He was not fat but he was padded, and his paunch was the final adoration of his flesh. But Gianni Terremoto made Emile Pestoso feel quite thin, it was enough, and it inspired his affection.

People often dropped into the shop for a little bite of something before the service, a cannoli or bomboloni to help settle the morning coffee before matins and the usual benedictions. Gianni Terremoto saw himself as a spiritual

10

man, but he was a man of the flesh as well, who felt that filling the bellies of the parish faithful was indeed part of God's work. Not that he minded filling the bellies of the unfaithful. He was a man of a most immodest girth but of a moderate opinion.

Terremoto's bakery was in a sidestreet not far from the church and the open square. That heady smell of baking bread would waft inside the church on a Sunday and have the congregation salivating, they'd sing the hymns now with renewed enthusiasm, their spiritual hunger fuelled by thoughts of lunch and the prospect of sitting down with some of Terremoto's baking bread.

Terremoto got on quite well with Emile Pestoso. 'Father,' he'd announce in that hefty voice of his, 'we serve a different hunger but I'm sure they are both sacred in God's eyes! You serve the spirit, myself I serve the belly—stocking up the belly of the parish. After all, they need stamina if they're to serve their own god well enough!'

This sort of talk Father Pestoso found charming in its way. It may be just as well he never asked Gianni Terremoto for more details on the god he served.

# Terremoto's God

Terremoto's god was the god of rising bread. He sat in the baking room, watching the bread slowly rising. His own sense of the miraculous depended on this, the wonder of it, that he lived in a world where loaves could rise out of the thick dough of themselves.

This was his peace, a peace he made with his own baker's god.

I'm a pagan, he thought. A pagan in love with life.

He decided to pay a visit to his lover. Sylvana. It was she who had first told him about The Lips of Aphrodite and the symbol of the fish. But first he had to bake some bread.

Terremoto watched the dough flapping and floundering on the table, sped by his hands, as if it was some finely floured fish, the simple symbol of the Christ. It was true that at times his own opinions, call it a knowledge, had startled the poor Emile Pestoso.

'Emile,' he said, 'did you know that the fish, before it was the sign of Christ, had been the sign of Aphrodite and had no fins? Well, I'll tell you the truth, it was no fish, it was the splendid evocation of the Cunt, God's shaggy mouth, borrowed by the Christians to symbolise the fleshy mouth of God, Our Creator. Later they added on the fins, made it a fish, some new propriety there, as if to clean it up. What could be cleaner and more apt, Mary's cuntfish mouth, its fishy tasty lips, turned into fish? Ah, but the Cunt of Aphrodite, that was the Holy Symbol of them all, the very mouth of God's own Mother! Temple of Life!'

Pestoso said nothing to this, just sucked his mouth and

nodded with a stunned look in his eyes, as if perhaps he
was the fish who'd just been whacked by the great Justicer.
He stuffed a bomboloni in his mouth, the red jam oozing
out as his teeth sunk in, and then he left the shop. Troubled
by this migration of fishes.

The bakery was full of spiders. There was a spider living
underneath the counter, and Gianni didn't want to kill it.
Never kill a spider in the house—his mother's words, she
said it brought bad luck. He had even given the spider a
name, Lola. The spider had stepped out of its skin, as if
it had stepped out of itself. He wondered if this was why
the spider was a sacred animal. Because of its power to
metamorphose and yet remain itself, leaving its old skin
behind.

What were Sylvana's words?

'The female tarantula stings her mate at the moment of
ejaculation. This numbs him, and in this blissful state she
slowly devours him, eating him alive. He feels no pain, as
her sting works like a morphia d'amour, promoting a finale
of euphoria. His flesh will in turn feed that of his offspring.
The male is conscious, though euphoric, as his mate
consumes him utterly. By some quirk of evolution, or
perhaps simply awareness, she always saves the brain till
last. Then the lights go out. I've always thought it must be
quite a way to go.'

# A Difficult Child

Francesca had seen her mother die. Watching as the eyes closed, knowing they'd not reopen, brought its own finality. Something she could not discuss with her father. He became edgy when she mentioned her mother, looking around the room as if he might espy some previously concealed means of escape. And so she'd quickly change the subject, making her own fast exit from her father's spidery kingdom with its noxious airs of the baker's inner gasses. Hanging around at Amaretto's, wondering why she gladly did his menial work when she avoided it so adroitly at her father's.

Amaretto and her father had become friends, despite the difference in their ages. Amaretto had confided to Francesca that Gianni was a better father than his own had ever been. Francesca nodded mutely. Feeling a tinge of jealousy when she saw her father and Amaretto enjoying an animated conversation as they drank, envious of the ease she saw between them. The careless confidentiality they achieved after the second glass, with the third in hand.

Francesca wondered if she'd outgrown her father. A tension between them. She could bring him to the verge of tears at will, just by giving him one of her reproachful looks. It never failed to stop him. As long as she kept staring at him he seemed unable to move, or speak. Yet she felt she had nothing to say to the man.

The smell of bread and rising yeasts held no attraction for her. She had no appetite for bread, preferring biscuits, and rice. If truth be told, she had no appetite at all. 'You cannot live on air,' her father had once said, and she'd replied, 'There are some things that can!' She had in mind

14

the aerial roots of trees, and had forgotten their roots plunged into soil. She felt certain that the air could hold enough nourishment for her.

The fat man Gianni Terremoto, baker to the populace and father to The Breadmaker's Carnival, was near wits' end in the family matter of his daughter. He was scared of Francesca. Something in her confidence made him feel paltry. She reminded him too much of her mother.

It was with relief that he heard her say one morning that she was going to leave his house and take up residence with Pestoso. For all that Gianni knew, the goodly Dawn still held Pestoso's kitchen in her thrall. 'No,' his daughter filled him in, 'Dawn has left town. I have already spoken with Emile, and said that you and I agreed it would be a proper thing, that I should take the place of Dawn and become his new housekeeper. The arrangements have been made. I'm moving in this afternoon.'

Gianni was taken aback. He had felt for some time now he was not equal to his daughter, that she had slowly taken control over him. He felt he had become an odd appendage to the life his daughter led, and wondered what had happened to the life that was his own. It was as if the role of father had consumed the other aspects of his being. He did not feel that theirs was a relationship of health. And of one thing he was sure: Francesca needed to learn some discipline, and if good Father Pestoso could supply it, then so be it.

Trying to make sense of a strange world. So many ways that people find to get closer to God. Pestoso looked at the small knotted whip, the tight hard knots in the hemp strands, and the coiled thongs that bound the handle. He wondered if it were time he showed Francesca the path of penitence. Penitence, and enlightenment as well.

A sacred duty, then. He'd show her how to make the strokes, the prayers that came with the separate strokes, and caution her against excessive zeal in the practice of her devotions.

There are, he thought, so many different ways of serving God.

To his surprise she took to it as if returned to her native habitat. She took the small whip from his hands and brought it sharp down on her back, and then annunciated her clear prayer. The punctuation of the whistling thongs, and then one firmer blow at her Amen, quite sure and quite precise, her own full stop. He had to say she seemed quite deft. Even, dare he say it, she had a gift? A strange gift, perhaps, but there's no end of strangeness in this life.

And what was the gift Francesca made her own? Perhaps, most simply put, that of Renunciation.


Emile did not feel that La Tarantula was a fitting name for a bakery, and had often thought to raise the matter with Gianni. Yet his determination faltered every time he approached the shop. As if the spider's eye could stare him out and force him to deviate from his intention to suggest some more fitting nomen.

He was also stayed in his desire to suggest a change of name by the fact that he could not think of one more fitting. The Osculant's Revenge certainly did not do the trick. The Disciple's Delight had pleased him for the length of an afternoon, but by nightfall he'd collapsed drunk onto his bed, nursing his empty wine bottle, and decided that wine, not bread, was the true delight of the disciple. Such was his personal discipline. But a new name for Gianni's shop eluded him, in a way in which his own true thirst did not. Gianni's Cakehole? Out of the question. He dozed off, and when he woke his head hurt so much he was fit for no other contemplation bar the throbbing in his temple.

# Sylvana

He made the most erotic bread when he thought about Sylvana while he moulded and kneaded the dough.

Rolling her shapes between his hands. She brought desire to his mouth.

Sometimes the loaves looked more like breasts than breads, bread balls instead of rolls, the doughy testicles hanging in the window. Fat cocks of rye and blackbread.

The shop gave you a healthy appetite for life.

Kissing the lips of her vagina was something that he loved. Thought of it as a devotion, part of his own sense of the sacred. The Lips of Aphrodite, the tender mouth of the Creation. The sort of thoughts that passed through him as he nuzzled at the gateway to the world.

The pleasing warmth of her, her oven fired and smouldering, and his hot roll shooting cream like hot cannoli. Don't waste a drop! she'd say, and lick her teeth before she bore down once again, that hot cannoli in her mouth. Ah, life was rich and sweet, and how he loved this baking life.

Her enthusiasm surprised him. He was not shocked, but he knew that not all women liked the taste or the event, and it was with delight that he discovered her own appetite for him. And, both of them knew, this was their mutual appetite, the pair of them hungry for each other. Like an eight-legged hairy spider cavorting in the flour, the hairy spider's mouth, laying her eggs, burrowing into flesh. Coming up for air and then descending once again.

He kissed her shoulder, a kiss that slid and nipped into a bite.

'God, I love it when you come like that. You're sure that's fine for you? It's great for me. Really, I don't want to talk about it. It makes me want to start again, but my cock's rubbed out. Where did it go? You bit it off? Ah, here it is.'

Her lips felt dull and bruisy. Smell of him, the damp hair of his chest, the wet trail of his sweat between his breasts then right down to his belly, and below. That sweet and bitter smell she loved. Putting her head right up into his armpit. God it was good.

Gianni had been making his favourite baker's cream when Sylvana first set foot inside the shop. A combination of mascarpone, egg-whites fluffed into meringue, and yolks beaten with sugar. He'd let Sylvana fold the mix, and watched, intrigued, as she worked the whites in with the mascarpone and the yolks.

This was the delicate part. He'd never seen anyone work the mix so well. You should have been a baker, was all he thought to say.

He dipped his finger in the bowl and licked it. 'That's good!' he said.

He dipped his finger in the bowl again and offered it to her. She refused the offer, instead she dipped her own finger and licked the cream. 'Ooh yes,' she said, 'that is good! That's all it is, those three things?'

'Yes,' Gianni answered, 'the yolks, the whites, the mascarpone. For me that's a baker's trinity. Of course you must add sugar.' There was something he wanted to tell her but he didn't know what. Was he just wanting to impress her?

He blundered over to see how the buns were going, he thought that they'd be ready now to pop into the oven.

He gave her one of the uncooked rounds to hold. It was warm, and the dough felt supple in her hands. Without thinking then she said It feels just like a woman, and Gianni knew he wanted her to stay with him right there and then.

But she had left, and he'd felt nervous, agitated. I need

a drink, he thought, a calming amaretto. But first he had some bread to bake. A minute later she was back. What was she saying?

Telling him a story of Aphrodite.

'The Roman bakers, once a year, would bake a cake in her honour. It was called The Lips of Aphrodite. They used to eat them once a year. Actually, I lie. They were called The Lips of Venus. It was the Greeks who called them Lips of Aphrodite. Made with ripe figs. They were eaten as a prelude to the sacred orgy.'


She was undoing the buttons on her green-and-brown checked flannel shirt. She rarely wore a bra, and the loose folds of her skin as the shirt now opened drove his pulse up higher. Not just his pulse. Her freckled breasts.

He let the flour slowly sift from his fingers in a tiny stream and wash down on her breasts. He kneaded and joked that he'd love to pop her in the fire and eat her whole, and eat her hole.

'God though you're a dirty bugger.' She loved to talk to him like that. Calling him a filthy bastard.

It brought him on, and brought him off, and before they knew it the pair of them were at it once again. Their dozy afternoons of love as the bread cooked slowly in the oven.

She wondered if she'd ever known such happiness in her life, or if she'd ever know such happiness again.

# Blood Pudding

Gianni and Sylvana were a funny pair, like a ripe blood pudding some days, the pudding made from flour and fresh blood.

Before long, he knew, they would start making love among the loaves upon the old wood flour bench. It was nice to have a bit of ritual in your life. Their bodies rolling in the flour like a pair of great loaves come to life. The handy sizing of her breasts, like a pair of sourdoughs. The perfect fit upon the hand. He often thought of her when making buns, the size and shape of her was his mental mould, translated into warm dough which he then fed into the oven. The great bread eaters of the shop found the weight and feel of this doughbread most delightful, and this was true for man and woman, something essential had been handed on. The pleasing warmth of it now cooling from the oven.

Sylvana. One breast was clearly larger than the other, the left breast, the breast over the heart. As if somehow her left breast swelled and fed directly from the heart and in return protected it.

As a child she'd slaughtered ducks and chickens and plucked their feathers, blood was a vital liquid and she was comfortable with it. A man of flour and a woman of blood. They were an interesting couple.

To think that she had just walked in through the door! What kind of mystery was that? As if the great tarantula provided for him still.

'Did you know the clitoris disappeared for six hundred years? It was there for such a long time, where it had always

been—and then, for centuries, no-one could find it. At least,
if you read the medical and other books of the time, that's
the impression you get. Where did the clitoris go? Of course
it didn't go anywhere. But why did no-one talk about that
pleasured point for six hundred years?

'I'll tell you something else. It is no blasphemy to say the
Virgin was no virgin. There's a clear case to suggest the
problem lies in the translation: the word for young woman
and virgin being the same. Mary was a young woman. She
had a child. Did you know that Salome, it says this in the
Bible, stuck her finger inside Mary's cunt to see if it was true
she was a virgin giving birth? The strange idea!'

Sylvana made sure of one thing: even if the clitoris had
disappeared for six hundred years Gianni knew exactly
where to find it.

Sylvana. While he desired her body deeply, the quality of
hers he treasured most was her intelligence.

She'd been a tutor in history at a nearby university, and
had prepared her final thesis on a history of bread. And,
having grown up on a farm, she knew a lot of the traditions
of the country.

Terremoto had looked up from his baker's cream with
some surprise to see a rather beautiful young woman asking
him if she might have a word. He was most happy to oblige,
and they had gone on to have much more than a word
together.

'The history of bread is a history of the world' was a
quote of Sylvana's that he often borrowed as his own. He
had been impressed with her knowledge of his subject, and
it was a simple thing, the way she started spending more
time at the bakery, telling him stories about bread and
bakers, quite strange ideas with a lucid potency, like the
man who'd climbed into a baker's oven to prove that his
elixir would give a monstrous strength to all who imbibed
it. His display had caused a riot, as he'd been slid into the
oven like a mighty human loaf and then popped out again,
his hair was singed but there was no burn or other mark

on his body. Needless to say he'd cleared the whole stock of his wares there on the spot, though none were keen to test their strength in fire.

Some nights the two of them, Gianni and Sylvana, slept warm and naked on the bench beside the fired wooden oven, a large floured pillow of fresh dough beneath their heads. It didn't bother them at all, the flour sticking to them, or matting their hair. They knew another kind of knowledge then, a knowledge they acknowledged as antique.

They were watching the shadows of the fire flickering on the roof above their eyes, a private shadowdancing theatre like a fresco on the ceiling that changed and changed.

'Did you know,' Sylvana said, 'that people once regarded the deceased body of the flesh as something sacred? Or at least something closer than they to the divine? Medicines were made from skulls, and the nectar of the corpse.'

Terremoto shifted. His arm underneath her shoulder had fallen asleep. He rolled onto his ample belly. If his arm had fallen asleep, the rest of him had not been far behind. He hadn't caught her drift at all.

'Sorry?'

'People used to eat the flesh of the ones who died, they believed it would protect themselves from death. It was something sacred.'

'Cannibals?'

'No, not cannibals. Well, maybe just a little bit.'

'How can you be just a little bit cannibal?'

'Are you eating me?'

'No, just nibbling.'

They both laughed then, and he rolled his holy loaf around once more to face her. There was a small light from the fire quietly dancing in her eyes. He kissed the lips of her mouth, her lips responded. Then she bit him hard.

'Ai! That hurt!'

She was over him now, her hands pushing hard so that he was pinioned to the bench, her legs astraddle. Terremoto could not move. A part of him loved this crazy strength of her. Another part felt terrified, an irrational thing, he knew, yet there it was. Sylvana spoke again.

'I thought you said you wanted me to eat you? Didn't you say that?'

'Well, yes, I did.'

'So what's all the noise about?'

Just then there was a loud knock on the door.

Luigi was rather startled to see the pair of them, looking like leopards with white spots from the flour and the sweat. A funny pair, a puddinged Adam and a finer, suppler Eve, all floured up. The gentle halfdark of the baking room with its play of shadows somehow clothed them in a finer thing than night and day. As if the shadows still were fucking, oh so gently, on the roof.

'Oh, he said, I'm sorry. I've just seen Father Pestoso, he asked if I could give a message. Francesca's started bleeding.'

Luigi wasn't sure where to put his eyes. They kept straying to the fine points of Sylvana's breasts but he felt awkward about this so ended looking at the floor.

His message out, he was relieved and quickly left.

'How did you feel when you had your first period? What did your parents say to you?'

'My mother and father were whispering in the hall. Finally my father came into the room and said, "Your mother has something to tell you." Then he left. She told me how to wear a napkin, and to wash myself.'

'That was all?'

'Yes.'

'Was it enough?'

'How could it ever be enough?'

# Luigi's Camera

**B**ut we were talking of some other thing. I was telling you about Luigi Bacheretti's fine attempt to take a photograph of God. This was happening in his studio, The Filing Cabinet. It used to be a stable.

Luigi had been born there, his mother grunting like a heifer. He loved the smell of straw for that reason. So The Filing Cabinet was also a kind of nest.

Even on the sunniest days Luigi liked to stay indoors. He was born at dusk, and wondered if this was why he loved the darker lights, things that lived in burrows, and the life subterranean. The world of shadows and other knowledge that daylight could not reveal.

It might be better not to speculate on the nature of Luigi's god.

Perhaps if I describe the photographic apparatus he'd set up, the features of his god might come out clear. Luigi's god was the god of frogspawn and green slime. Might it be true as well that the kind of camera you create defines the kind of god you'll photograph? Here then is my description of Luigi's camera.

In a corner of the studio, obscured by mounds of junk within which the eye discerned alarming shapes, nests, anthills, and other things more properly conceived of as belonging out of doors, behind all this or else just the logical extension of it stood a large tank, of the sort used for developing photographic images.

This tank was full of frogspawn, tadpoles, green slime, frogs of all sizes, baby frogs with their tadpole tails still in place. On the bottom of the tank was a series of photo-

24

graphic plates and other paraphernalia in a similar state of evolution: the raw materials of creation, so to speak, and the end result. Thus a rock, a photographic negative of the rock, a series of photos of the rock, and next to these a series of treated photographic papers.

Luigi's hoped-for result was the transference of the rock onto the paper through a process of 'image resolution', a process he felt was typified by the transformation of frogspawn to tadpole to frog. The image constantly redefining itself, resolving the tension between its actuality and its possibility. He was hoping that in this way the rock would produce an image of itself on the photographic plates, executing a 'natural portrait'—nature would become her own artist. This image would be a photograph of God.

In the middle of the room, if room is a word that can be used to contain such a proliferation of objects both animate and inane, stood a twisted, burnt-out hulking ruin. A seething fossil of plumber's pipes, organ stops, pedals and so on, congealed with thick ashes like some crazy bizen pot, filled up with gizzards, turned inside out, but the thing had gone awry, if such a thing could ever have been wry. It was huge; even as a meltdown the thing had scale, which served to hint at the former function of the relic and the magnitude of the idea that this machine was built to serve.

In short, it was the mortal remains of The Photoplayer, Luigi's first experiment with photography. Compared to it his attempts to take a photograph of God really seemed benign enough.

The Photoplayer was quite literally a photo player. A black and white photograph was read by a beam of light. The visual pulses generated by the play of light and shade in different sections of the photo were translated into sounds and music. The resulting chords and discords were, Luigi said, 'A revelation of the inner light of the object photographed.'

At the inaugural demonstration of The Photoplayer Luigi invited members of the public to feed their photos into the machine.

A prominent politician on the local scene inserted a family

portrait, executed in the conventional manner of the times. As the light beam scanned the youngest child a pleasing series of high whistles and ululations filled the room. Proceeding to the eldest daughter the tonal quality changed. A harmony that contained the insinuation of a monstrous discord. This chord of division found full voice when the features of the prominent man fell to the scrutiny of The Photoplayer.

The note of doubt was replaced by a terrible certainty. The Photoplayer exceeded itself: great bass-throated ruminations and preposterous assertions combined with a tight-larynxed quality that was punctured by a sudden gash of air as when cotton sheets are torn apart.

The man in question was most embarrassed by this display. But The Photoplayer was not finished. It gurgled and groaned, groaned and gurgled. Perhaps this was prophetic. If a machine might fart, it farted. It drew in a long low breath and held it. Something rumbled, then it clanked and began to shake, rocking itself like an abandoned child who has begun to expect the worst.

As The Photoplayer shook a counter-melody could be heard: the living voice of the man who could no more contain his anger. His grunts of indignation only incited The Photoplayer to greater ecstasies of musical revelation. The machine now quivered and its coils began to writhe as if preparing for some final dissertation.

A sudden harmony prevailed as man and machine chorused in one terrible lament that burst into a roar then whimpered softly. The man of good repute had suffered a cardiac arrest and needed immediate attention. He was luckier than The Photoplayer, which had exploded and was damaged beyond repair.

Some said the whole thing was a prank organised to humiliate the man. Others claimed The Photoplayer was just too accurate, a vehicle of truth that overturned the habit of good manners.

Luigi retreated to the stable and kept the door firmly bolted. Truth is like a bomb, he thought, and like a bomb it can explode.

There was a terrible smell behind the door. Perhaps it

was more truly a terrific odour. Or simply awesome? Is there one smell that puts the fear up God? The smell of rotting eggs. Hard to believe that God could fear a smell, God seems to love the stink and fug of rot and slow decay as much as the scent of any rose or jasmine.

Might this be true—that God's an indiscriminate soul, halfblessed halfcursed with all creation; whether it rots and blooms or blooms then rots, is eaten by worms or just cascades into a slimy molten liquor of tumescence, God doesn't really mind? Though on the face of it you'd build a case for God's love of mud and muck, there seems to be no end of it. Starts with mud, ends with shit, and in between brief flowerings of some fine and elegant thing, like a refrain from an old love song that comes to mind in moments that precede some foul despair or gloom. These were the kind of thoughts triggered by the waft behind the door, that smell of eggs. Yet Luigi grew to love this smell.

The door was big and heavy, an old wooden stable door about three metres high, and two metres and more across. It had a great wood crossbar that latched into place between two metal clamps, and if Luigi decided he was not at home, with his great crossbar in its place, there was nothing left to do except turn and head for home. More often though the door was open and swinging gently on its hinge, like the wooden sail of some boat that's found its true home port at last and come to rest.

Behind this door, if you had the luck or grace or folly to enter Luigi's domicile and domain, you'd hear the clucking sounds of chooks. These were his experimental brood hens. Not only were they partly responsible for the smell behind the door, they were also part of a scheme that was, perhaps, the true precursor of Luigi's attempt to 'take' a 'photograph' of 'god'.

Luigi was trying to reproduce photographic images onto the hens' eggs by a process of 'natural reproduction'. He constructed a special harness for the birds, so that the object to be reproduced—a pencil, or a photograph of an egg on which he had written the word 'egg'—would be permanently fixed in the bird's vision.

He reasoned that the image would implant itself in the bird's total field of consciousness and so be reproduced on the eggshell.

Following this thought to its logical conclusion he later realised that the image would in fact penetrate to the centre of the egg, protected by the shell and thus invisible to the eye. He was sure he had a series of eggs whose insides contained such images. He refused to break them open, as this would destroy the image he had succeeded in preserving.

Though he was fond of counting them, Luigi did not want these eggs to hatch, as that too would destroy the image he had preserved. Instead, the eggs were left on a little ledge behind the stable door. He had thirty-seven of them.

# Francesca's First Period

A great change came over the household on the advent of Francesca's first period. No-one had forewarned the girl, and so she simply walked into the padre's study, hitched up her skirt and showed the good Father her condition. She put a finger to her vagina, at which point Pestoso slapped her face and said Don't be disgusting! Now go and wash your hands and face and say a prayer to the Virgin!

For the moment he didn't know what else to do, and nor did Francesca. Her face felt sore where Pestoso's hand had left a red print on her cheek. She closed the door and walked slowly down the corridor. She was holding in her tears, and felt ashamed. When she reached the bathroom she locked the door and plonked herself onto the toilet. The cold seat contrasted with the hotness in her face. What was happening to her?

What should she do with it? She put the blood-spotted rag down in the middle of the floor, folding it as best she could. Wondering what happened next. Did she flush it down the loo? Bury it in the garden? What about a paper bag, then dropping it in the bin? Surely you couldn't leave it there? Wouldn't it start to smell? What about making a tiny fire and burning it?

She carefully picked the soiled rag up and headed out into the garden behind the house. There was an old apple tree that produced odd sour apples of a small and slightly malformed shape. Good for stewed apple, if you added lots of sugar. Pestoso frankly considered the fruit of this tree quite inedible, and scolded her the times he'd found her underneath the tree sucking the bitter juice. She took a stick and dug a hole in the ground and placed the rag there.

29

She looked around, feeling guilty. She saw the empty shell of a cicada on the ground nearby, and without really knowing why dropped the insect's shell into the hole as well. Then she scooped the earth she'd dug up and firmed it back in place. She tried to rearrange the grass so that no-one would know a hole had been dug, with something planted in the soil. Then she went inside to wash her hands.

She was sitting on her bed again; she'd dropped her panties in a bucket of cold water, left to soak, and enjoyed the feeling of sitting on her bed, her body naked underneath her skirt. The feel of her flesh just as it was, touching the softness of the white quilt on her bed. A funny seeping inside her. She shifted on the bed, and then stood up. A small spot of bright red blood had stained the quilt. Oh no. She'd spoiled the bed. What should she do? She'd have to wash the quilt as well. And where would she find another rag? She couldn't face the thought of asking Father Pestoso. How long would she keep bleeding for? Should she go and see a doctor?

This second rag she just dropped into the toilet bowl, pulled the chain and watched it flush away. With some relief she saw it pass out of her sight.

Pestoso was appalled to stand and watch the bowl as it slowly filled with water. Instead of washing backwards through the pipe, the water level rose and rose, and then it slowly started spilling from the bowl onto the floor, the mix of water and his urine. He stepped backwards but already there was a puddle, he'd fouled his shoes, disgusting mess, he'd have to get Francesca to mop it up, and he'd have to call a handyman. A nice embarrassment that would be, the priestly dunny blocked, as if the bowels of his own house were choked with filth.

Stefano Costa had seen this problem twice before, simple enough, a blooded rag blocking the old and narrow pipes.

He had to dig the pipes and follow them out in the yard until he found the bloated blotted rag choked with water and nightsoil. A smelly job, not that he minded overmuch; he'd skip his lunch though, somehow he found he couldn't eat for quite a while after such jobs. Even a cup of tea or glass of water seemed too much to contemplate.

He told Pestoso what had been blocking the drains and noted with surprise the way the Father's colour rose up on his face. He asked the Father then would that be all? 'Yes', he'd replied, 'that's right enough. Or just one thing—I wonder, as you leave, if you would send Francesca to me?'

Scrubbing the bathroom floor on her hands and knees with an old wooden brush of bristle, the warm suds soaping sloppy on the floor, and the pleasing texture of wet rags. She enjoyed the labour of it. It made her feel like she was cleaning out herself at the same time, a thorough scrub down and a wash, and she liked the work of water on the stubborn grease around the edges of the bath, grunting again with the effort to shift the black mire off the yellowing enamel, making it white again. Smell and the heat of her, working hard at it, catching the sweet and sour wind from off her arms and underneath. She knew how to scrub a bath and get it clean, clean, clean, and even this small satisfaction made her feel she had at least some little worth. Some power in her too, that was the thing she liked the most, the simple hard strong work of it, testing herself, feeling her muscles stiffen and release, feeling the power in her shoulders and in her arms, her muscles bulging. The strength down in her back, and her strong hips, as if just in this act, cleaning the bathroom on her knees, she felt a power in and of her start to grow. Grateful for this, at least.

Emile may not have been haemophobic, but the smell of Francesca's blood seemed to derange him. He could smell her all over the house, and nothing seemed to dim that smell from his nostrils. He had the smell of her on his brain, and it was a strange thing, this smell of her. To him she now appeared to be unclean. Unclean. He could not wash his brain of her, nor remove the foul smell from his nose.

Her smell grew denser. Almost, you would swear, her smell began to have a mass, as if its molecular density had exceeded that which can be borne by any gas. When Emile smelt her now, her smell fell on his back like a shadow, and he tugged at his collar as if someone was poking a finger down his back, or tickling his collar. He was prone to hot sweats when he thought about her smell, and the thought was no preparation at all for the actual scent of her.

The smells of blood high in his nose, the smell of her coming down into his lungs.

When he awoke he swore the smell remained in him, not just on his skin or clothes but deep inside, mingled with the sponge of his lungs, something that he could not expunge merely by breathing out. Why did the smell of blood have such effect on him? Some primary anger, or a confusion?

Francesca made a bonfire out the back and piled up the old newspapers, soiled rags and other detritus of her cleaning binge. In the middle of it all she placed her menstrual clothes. Then she set the thing alight. Another kind of satisfaction.

When it had burnt she grabbed a handful of the ash. It was still warm. An old cork had blackened into charcoal. She picked it up.

On a small shed behind the house that had once held chickens, on a private wall well hidden from the house, she began to draw, without thinking what it was that she'd begun. A caricature of her fat father, his gross flesh hanging off his bones. A cloud of sooty gas burst from his arse. She found a private satisfaction in the game, a power she could wield with just an old piece of burnt cork. Quickly sketching a portrait of Emile in the sooty cloud of her dada's bot. She stood back, admired the work, then rubbed and scratched until its every feature was obliterated. To her surprise this brought another deeper kind of pleasure.

After four days the blood had stopped, and she felt gratitude for this. Was it a sign? A sign of what? She'd had a dream, her mother walking through a field, her mother bleeding, and as she walked and bled each drop of blood had turned a green blade red, until the whole field was transformed. The red blades bending in a gentle wind. What did it mean? She was unsure, and yet she found some comfort in it, this dream of blood and grass gone red.

She looked outside and saw the grass was green. A fat man and a slender, taller woman were walking silently together. Sylvana and her father, come to visit her at last.

She knew the answer before he'd asked the question. The nestling sound of her father's voice inside her ear. Her father looked so worried. 'Would you like to come back home? You know that you don't have to stay here.'

She heard her voice, almost as if it was another who spoke. 'No, no, I'm happy here.' She looked away, and saw the red grass of the field.

In a way that had no words she felt an exile opening up inside her and wondered if this was punishment enough for both of them.

Pestoso standing by the door. She saw the black shoes on his feet, and did not look up. She would not cry, at least she would not weep in front of him. The thought helped cheer her up.

'Would you like a cup of tea?' She shook her head, and watched the black feet walking slowly down the hall.

'Sea sponge is best,' Sylvana said. 'It's soft, you have to tie a little string around the middle, and then you just tuck it inside, with your finger. Look, I'll show you.'

The girl was watching with a great deal of surprise as the older woman now simply gave a little push, the sea sponge gliding upwards, out of sight, a tiny trail of string remaining for the eye to hold.

'When you're bleeding, you leave it there, you'll know when it's time to take it out. Just rinse it in running water, then you can put it back. You'll get used to it and you'll almost forget you've got something in there. I've brought you three or four, some different sizes, so you can find out for yourself. I don't know why your father didn't tell you.

'It's the way a woman's body works. Was there much pain? Mine hurt like hell for the first day and then it eases off. But we're all different. If you want just come and see me any time.'

The girl nodded her head. Sylvana took her hand, then kissed her cheek.

'Pestoso's had a pretty sheltered life, I'm not surprised he's so confused and ashamed. What would he know? The Virgin in the church is made of stone, she's never had her period. It's a pity you blocked the dunny up! I had to laugh when your father told me, and he wasn't half impressed when Pestoso made him pay. They clog up the works. Burn them. There's an incinerator out the back.'

And then she left.

She paused outside Francesca's room, knocked gently on the door and sat down once again beside Francesca on the bed.

'It's called a diaphragm. They're funny things, but they do the job. I don't expect you're going to need this for several years—you're too young, but your body's old enough. You need to go to the doctor, come to me when you think the time has come. For God's sake don't mention it to Pestoso, he'd have a fit and preach a sermon against me about the pornography of the imagination. The doctor will have to fit you with one that's the right size, we're all different sizes, the same as men are with their cocks.

'You'll know when the time has come. The last thing you need is to fall pregnant and have a baby before you reach fifteen, take my word for it. That's all. You're not too talkative today, are you?'

She gave the girl's hand a gentle squeeze and almost leapt to feel the sudden response, the girl's hand squeezing her hard, then pulling at her.

Francesca throwing her arms around and bursting into tears, and then the pair of them sobbing on the bed. Grateful for the sense of company it brought, of something hidden spilling out into the air. They rocked and wept together, and when the storm had passed they stayed just holding gently, laughing shyly, feeling silly, brushing the hair out of their eyes, blowing their noses, wiping away the tears.

As Sylvana walked back home in the falling light of the early autumn afternoon, she thought out loud 'Reminds him too much of her mother!' and sighed. For a moment she thought she'd weep again; instead she felt her body start to run, and loved the feeling of the cold wind that she made rush on her face, a burst of speed, how long since she'd just let herself run free, stretching now, the way her legs reached out and touched and sprang up from the earth. The perfect fluid motor of her hips, dropping her hands right there, just on the joint, the way the thigh joint bulged and surged, the mighty feeling of it, the wonder too, almost a thing too much to contemplate, that it existed in the world. She was running down the hill, watching the small lights of the town flicking on. The yellow warmth of it, the stretching shadow of her running on the ground, stretching ahead. Then she stopped, feeling worn out, slowly easing up till she was walking again, thudding heart still racing. The panting of her now, catching her breath, her slowing down, the sticky heat under her jacket, the cold air of the night and her hot face, hot skin, hot her. The swinging, walking image of herself, swaying soft from side to side as she slowly found her easy way back home.

She was feeling sexy with herself and didn't care to go with any man, was quite content to know this sexy feeling of herself, as if somehow a part of her had come into its own. The simple studded sex of her, and her delight. Touching herself and feeling good, the simple knowledge, that she knew the sexy nature of herself.

She closed her eyes. She hadn't thought to take a nap but there it was, she closed her eyes and promptly fell asleep.

# Sylvana's Reverie On Sex And Violence

Sylvana's mother was a suicide. Sylvana sometimes wondered if she'd follow in her mother's footsteps. The days it seemed a certainty, the question then was merely When? Not If. Those days she told herself If I feel like this on my fiftieth birthday, I'll shoot myself. And so she knew that she would never live with firearms in the house. The sound of her father's shooting rebounding in her ears. Out in the hills, looking for rabbits, perhaps a wild pig. Once he'd shot a young deer. Dragging it home, he could hardly speak from the exertion, dropping the bloodied carcass, his shirt soaked with sweat, and stained from where the deer had bled into the cotton. Swabbed by her father's shirt.

She was sad to see the young deer dead, but ate the meat and found herself eating a second serving of the gamey flesh. Strong flesh makes strong blood, strong bones. Her father's truism.

Sylvana made her living fixing broken plates and china.

Gianni had only slept at Sylvana's once, using the excuse that he needed to keep an eye on the bakery at all times. Sylvana had jibed him then. 'What, you're afraid that while you're away La Tarantula will pick up her flour bags and walk?' The truth was that Gianni didn't like being at Sylvana's. It reminded him of his late wife's own plate-hurling volition. He found it upsetting. All those broken plates made it difficult to relax at Sylvana's. If she moved suddenly he'd flinch and cower before muttering an apology. His body too conditioned by the reflexes of preservation, ducking in time to avoid the skittling plate. Feeling foolish when no plate materialised, instead perhaps a cup of tea as his lover turned from the sink with a breakfast tray. All the guilts still in him. And the fears.

Nor was their lovemaking of the same pitch. True, he'd not stayed at Sylvana's enough for a fair sample to be prepared. But he'd been unable to sustain his erection the one time he had stayed. Perhaps he was used to feeling in control by having the familiarity of his surrounds, the spidery walls of the bakery, well in view. When their roles had been reversed and he'd been the guest, he'd felt diminished somehow. Preferred to think the fault lay with the plates, and the smell of glue. The anxiety this provoked. The fact that their first night at her place he'd been unable to hold his erection had also made him feel ashamed, a stupid thing, perhaps, as if the world might stand upon the supple swollen point of his own organ, a foolish notion.

Foolish as it was, from then on Sylvana's place filled him with a sense of impotence.

Sylvana, after her initial disbelief had turned into disappointment, had been surprised how much she'd enjoyed their lovemaking that time, with no emphasis upon the phallic. The way they'd simply snuggled, holding each other, and the great peace and comfort they'd known. In the early morning, to their mutual delight and surprise, they'd woken to find that Priapus had also woken up: the pair of them would later swear they had both been asleep and had woken to find that they'd begun to couple in their sleep. Each accused the other of taking matters into their own hands, but denied the accusation that they'd started fucking the other in their sleep. Not that they minded, but the truth was simpler, they'd enjoyed the kind of foreplay you only have when you're asleep. Who knows, perhaps they had enjoyed a common dream while sleeping, and their erotic bones and juices had stirred themselves.

Delightful as this was, Sylvana's pleasure had been marred, in retrospect, by the great heaving bulk of Gianni on her. At the time she'd found his vigour pleasing and the pair of them had come with the sweat pouring off them, a heaving and a grinding. Later though, as Gianni slept and she'd retrieved her arm from underneath his flesh, she found herself disturbed by a hint of violence there. That's just absurd, she told herself, there's always an element of risk, of violence, when you let yourself go and really get to it.

But there was more to it, she felt somehow that she'd been had, and not in a way she had enjoyed. Nor could she put her finger on the exact moment when she'd felt . . . she hesitated. What had she felt? Had she really felt abused?

She recoiled from the word. Gianni was not an abuser. And yet, if that were true, why did she feel, in some deep part of herself, that she'd been violated? Had she simply been overwhelmed by the intensity of her sexual power? It was she, not Gianni, who'd instigated the mounting threshold that verged on physical punishment as they banged their bodies hard against each other. She'd locked her legs around him, and dug her nails into his back.

Gianni had squealed then, the image of a great pig riding, and she'd slapped his arse hard and felt his haunches rock right forward as his body rolled with her mighty slap, the pleasure as the shockwaves hit her pulsemeat, and she slapped his great pink arse again and could imagine the great red welt, the throbbing imprint of her hand upon his arse, this second slap of hers had been a harder thing, she'd wanted to leave an imprint on him then that would stand the test of time, wanted to leave her mark upon him, and he'd squealed again and grunted with the shock, and then he groaned and the violence in him now as he thrust so hard upon her, and she dug her claws into his flesh and scraped her nails right down his back, and he hollered then, the great wracking spasm as he came, and the uncontrollable rocking of his hips as his sperm shot out in bolts, and her legs still locked hard on him and her hips banging against his, the pair of them come hard off and screaming out any damn thing they wanted, Oh Fuck Oh Shit Oh Shit, Oh Fuck, Fuck Yeah, the nonsense of it, as if their orgasm obliterated any finer intelligence they may have once possessed, and the animals in them took possession of their brains, but oh, the great and fine sensations. The liberation.

They had slept truly then, and it was only slowly, as

she'd woken, that a needle of discomfit had pricked at her. Trying to find a way through her confusions. She felt shaken by the intensity, even the furore, they'd achieved, embarrassed to think what her neighbours had heard as her mighty slaps rang out like pistol shots to be smothered by Gianni's groans, and their profanity. She was ashamed and delighted by the cruel streak he'd set off in her, she could see the long lines of the weals left by her nails, she'd drawn his blood. What had she thought? Wanting to scar the man for life? Or merely leave her mark upon? She felt as if something had been released, and she was not sure what it was, nor if she was happy now the thing was out. She was not even sure what thing it was—was it her violence? Her savagery? Or had she merely realised the sexual power of her body? Or had it been her mind that had achieved the greatest state of relaxation, and liberation?

She was alarmed by the ease with which her body had thrust all finer sentiment aside, and Gianni too had been pounding her with a force she hadn't previously known. In a way that provoked confusion somehow coupled with delight, she felt uneasy now with the recollection of it. Was it their best sex, or their worst? Or both at once? They'd never had such a good orgasm. Yet the hint of violence . . . she broke her thinking then. Unable to make her peace with the riddle of it, she decided to get up and make some tea.

Gianni seemed quite remote from her convoluted thinking as he slept and snored a little. Yet he too had been surprised, disturbed and delighted. The disturbance had come from an image of Rosemary, his former wife, that had appeared, perhaps it was the slaps, or the fingernails, perhaps it was a violence in him that had been locked away, but as he'd thrust down hard upon and into sweet Sylvana, among the claws that ripped his skin, he'd seen Rosemary all too clear, and the violent thrust he had propelled had been the thrust with which he hoped he might annihilate his ex-wife for all time. Killing perhaps the memories of her in his body, that he would flinch no more inside his lover's house.

The impotence of the evening and the furious liberation of their early morning sex. The confusion that both Sylvana and Gianni had then known. They hadn't spoken much about it, they'd been quiet as they drank their tea in bed. The broken plates in boxes seemed to have once again made Gianni retreat, burrowed somewhere in his mound of flesh. Sylvana asked him if she'd hurt him, and rubbed some skin cream where she'd ripped her nails so hard. 'Oh God,' she'd said, 'did I do that!' Laughing with her own embarrassment. Gianni was belly down on her bed, his face near smothered by her pillow. She straddled him, rubbing the cream into his back, the blubber of his buttocks between her legs, a pleasant sensation. Gianni flinched and she felt something releasing in her, surprised by the curious mechanism, that she might enjoy his pain. 'Sorry,' she said, and continued to rub his great bum with her thighs and fanny, this was an easier sensation, no hint of violence there at all, he had rolled over then and she'd rubbed his belly, his chest, gentle on him as she settled on the great lump in his throat, his Adam's apple, intrigued by the supple fit of it, something that she'd not tried before, the pleasure then of finding something new in the way their bodies made their fit, and moving on, his chin, the jawbone's hardness suited her, and the warmth of Gianni's palms as he lifted up her buttocks and brought her up into his mouth, and their mutual delight as she began to slowly melt in his mouth—He's having me for breakfast, his slushy tongue, Who's having who? Not caring to engage in speculation, losing herself instead in this careless early morning love that had no hint of violence.

Something had shifted in them both that night, however, and Gianni had not stayed again at her small flat with its broken plates and its smell of glue. Their domain was Gianni's oven.

He missed her in the days that followed, half expecting at any time to hear the sound of her fist knocking gently on the door. Sometimes he opened the back door of the shop, so sure he'd heard her knock, and felt a private grief each time he opened up to find the absence of her there.

# Francesca And Emile

Pestoso was born of an Italian father and an English mother. His mother had died in childbirth, a fact for which he never forgave the medical profession. He considered the world of doctors and medicine to be full of charlatans and satanic forces. He never went to the doctor if he fell sick. He believed that all illness had a spiritual cause, and was a blessing, a sign from the Creator that we needed to mend our ways.

Emile Pestoso also insisted on taking cold baths and showers in all seasons, feeling that hot water was an unnecessary and weakening indulgence. This might have made him a man of great strength and health if the Creator had not blessed him with a weak constitution. Consequently he was often confined to bed, or else undertook his rounds with a semi-permanent cough and cold which produced small clots of mucus every few minutes.

Pestoso's house had rising damp, and it stank. No other word for it. There were dark corners whose walls were wet the whole year through, and the place smelt like it had been closed for months, or years. Its musty odour was the first thing Francesca noticed when she arrived there.

Pestoso, however, didn't mind the smell. It had become a part of him, his nose no longer rendering any impression of it—it was the base upon which he inhaled the scented picture of his world. Or perhaps he'd simply given up his life into the service of a musty god? An impecunious god as well, as he was inclined to wander round his rooms in darkness, just so that he might save his candles.

What was his greatest virtue? It might have been his doubt. Is doubt a virtue? It was the needle of his soul. He'd seen the vision splendid, had been consumed, and then recoiled. Baffled as to where his certainty had fled, unsure if what he'd seen had been a blessing or some wild, infernal thing. Something that he could not forget, something far greater than himself, and yet it seemed to him as well something that he could not attain, which caused him grief and great remorse. That vital longing for something yet unattained, and unattainable perhaps in his lifetime. He wondered why he had recoiled, why he'd not been able to grasp that livid moment when he'd seen the face of god.

His sermons were short. Around his sparse words he created a prodigious silence—it was this silence which often carried the force of his pulpitic message. He was a man of a most explosive silence.

As a young man he had once watched a hurricane explode, strapping himself to a tree on a beach and waiting for the hurricane to arrive. The tempest was preceded by green lightning. Emile had never heard of green lightning, and the sight of it surprised him. A disturbing emanation from God's heavens. He was afraid. He wondered if his decision to observe the hurricane breaking was an impulse he'd regret.

This day his own vocation became clear. It was a story that he preached often, and which had become his favourite sermon. It was the crest of his belief, and brought with it the certainty that God had sought him out.

'I was still vain and stupid, and on that day God did not come and whisper in my ear, oh no, God came and slapped me in the face! That day I found God—or should I say that God found me, and He has never let me forget it!'

The young Pestoso had not gone to the beach with the intention of watching hurricanes explode. But in the late afternoon a man had come to warn the bathers at this small secluded beach that a hurricane was imminent, and that they should leave at once or else prepare to meet the storm full in the face. The young Pestoso chose the latter, and with a borrowed rope he lashed himself to a large tree. And then he waited. His parishioners well knew what happened next.

'At first the water's surface was broken by the rippling

of the oncoming wind. Then the sea went dark. When the storm hit it was a revelation. I feared the tree to which I'd strapped myself would be uprooted, yet suddenly the wind died and the world was absolutely still. This was the centre of the hurricane, the place where the conflicting forces of the world were held in a terrible balance, a calm that promised to explode at any moment. This was the moment that God chose to show His face to me.'

The silent force became his pulpitic trademark. His silence was too terrible to bear, and his parishioners had even tried pelting him with questions in an effort to make him speak. His slowness to respond only intensified the dreadful silence with which he suffocated his parish. It was the held breath of the hurricane, suspended, infinite, eruptive. Father Pestoso. The local kids called him The Strangler. This came from his habit, when he patted them on the head or back, of invariably resting his hand behind their neck and squeezing, an odd gesture of affection which cut the circulation off and made the child feel like a young rabbit who was about to be throttled, or with a sudden twist of the head have its neck broken.


Francesca was surprised to find how much she enjoyed the play of charcoals on the back wall of the old shed. The liberty of it, and the freedom of the line that came now off her hand. As if she could seize some essential, vital thing, a key to expression. Call it a vengeance if you will, because her true delight was to wreak her savage portraits of Pestoso and her father on the wall. When the wall was full, she shifted to the abandoned piggery that lay further from the house. Emile avoided these parts of the old church buildings, something in them too primary, perhaps, he found their stink repelled him. He had no love of fug and dung, and so Francesca claimed the old animals' buildings. And it was there that she discovered a wild liberty that was her own, a liberty of line and emblem.

She'd stay in the old piggery for hours, she liked the darkness and that fusty smell of pigs from long ago. The dung dried and gone to dust. The way the sunlight broke in from the window, the window itself covered in dust, and she had no desire to clean it. She liked the patterns of the light, as if the yellowed dust had etched some essential form there. Standing in the old dark barn, her skirt hitched up so that she could bend and stretch, feeling the strong earth underneath her feet.

Then one day she found she'd lost the desire to take her caricatured revenge on those two men in her life, her dual Fathers. Another impulse forming, to her surprise she heard herself announce, 'I'm going to draw myself.' And surprised once more, feeling a new fear in her, she looked at the yellowed wall, its old whitewash gone all damp and crumbly, disturbed to realise that she had no idea how to begin, no idea how to describe the essential features of herself. She left it then and walked outside, sitting on the low step of the doorway. Her back to the barn, the air cooler in there, she squinted in the brighter light of out of doors. Wondering if she might change her name. Calling herself—what name was that? Franny? Fanny? She didn't know. Perhaps, she thought, it isn't such a good idea.

It had never occurred to her before that she had any choice at all, or freedom to choose, and it was then perhaps, with the charcoal in her hand, that the thought had struck her first. But rather than any exhilaration or delight, she felt only one thing, which was appalled. It was not an auspicious beginning for the birthing of her self.

Stillborn, perhaps, at the moment of realisation?

She was not unaware of the power she had over Pestoso. She began to flaunt her sex. She no longer wore a modest dressing-gown, instead she'd bought herself a short black nightie, which she wore all around the house. This to Pestoso's consternation, and his pleasure. He couldn't stand the sight of her, it brought him on, nor could he bear to take his eyes away.

He was sure the girl had begun to taunt him. Francesca knew that it would drive him crazy, and it did.

Francesca also knew how indecisive Pestoso was. She peppered him with choices, questions, so that she might season him with Indecision and cure him with Anxiety. She had sensed his vital weakness, and did her best to undermine him with her traps. Would he like tea or coffee? Would he have sugar today, or milk? What should be done about the broken tiles on the roof? And Emile would feel the seizure coming on, he didn't want to make any decisions, if he could he'd curl up in his cot again, with his bottle. His favourite pastime? Lying in bed with the shutters down, sucking from the mouth of a good bottle of red, feeling his lips against the smoothness of the bottle's neck. Seasoned as he was by Indecision he was not by any means what you would call a savoury man.

Pestoso's indecision extended to the choice of cakes inside the sweet Tarantula. Gianni had only to ask him What will yours be today? and Pestoso felt the itch of his collar growing sweaty with distress. Bomboloni or crostoli? Crostoli or bomboloni? Which one's fresh? Emile, is that a question? They're both fresh, both fresh today, which would you like?

Pestoso's bottom lip trembled, and then his tongue ducked out and licked the small wart that grew just underneath the lip and a little to the left of centre. This wart was for him a constant reminder of man's imperfection, and the extent to which only God was perfect. Father Pestoso was sure that the human estate was the estate of imperfection—as if we were somehow defined by our defects rather than our perfects. His theology was a theology of flaws.

Pestoso loved the red wine of the village, made from the grapes that grew in the hills and undulations outside the town. It was, perhaps, a pagan thirst at times that did possess him.

Each night he drank a bottle on his own, preferring the company of himself to that of others, and having no choice, being a lonely man by disposition and temperament.

As he drank he felt a horn begin to grow inside and then outside of him. The way some things grow hard that start their life first as a liquid. This filled him with disgust, and he drank in part to try and overcome this horniness.

The more he drank the hornier he grew; the hornier he grew the greater his self-disgust, leading in turn to greater drinking and greater horniness. Thus it was through drinking that he assailed new heights of self-loathing. He was a terrible drunk, he always ended pointing in only one direction. This was his hard knowledge of himself. He mused at times upon the possibility of cutting off this horn, but knew it would just grow back, or at least that the root of his disease was not so simple to extract.

Shame. It was a part of his ugliness. It was not the only ugly part, but it was the part that he knew best. He thought of this as he drank the bloodwine of the village. His custom was to drink the first three glasses from a long-stemmed round cup, but after that—the cup was quite a generous vessel—his thirst grew more direct and he swilled directly from the bottle.

Someone was knocking at the door. Francesca.

She was the dumpling of her father's eye. The growing dimples of her breasts. She was grown cheeky too, and more assertive. Prone to sulking. Almost a feline presence in the house. Unsettling him. She stared him down, the arrogance of it. On the fat side. Like her father, hulking huge. What kind of woman would she be? One of those prone to an enormous fatness? What was it called? Puppy fat? She was not thin, that much was true. And she would not be a puppy for much longer. What then? A bitch?

# Pestoso Collared

He loved the feeling of the collar on his neck, a minor mortification. He was reminded of the story of how the mandrake grew, the seed of dead men on the gallows that then shot out of the ground. Chafe of the collar, and the pleasing tightness of the throat. Liked the way Francesca put the stud in at the back. Reaching up to fasten it, up on her toesies, feel her breasts in his back, and then her front rubbing against his buttocks, couldn't help, they clenched themselves, feel of her pushing harder, just from the struggle of her fingers with the stud. Dirty little thing, sure it is she's rubbed her front upon his arse again, the subtle pressure of it, the smell of her now wafting up, another incense in the room. Gamey smell, like venison, strong meat, they used to say strong meat would make the father's semen strong, a strong child born though weak of brain. Ripe little bitch, she'd love to get her hands onto the stud, sure as he'd dance all the way to hell, the gay abandon of it, and fuck her in a trench, he'd like that, yes, such sinful thoughts in a tender girl, no, not a girl, a woman growing as she watched the mandrake root sprooting underground.

Like it, my collar. Gives me a hard-on just thinking. God loves a sinner to repent more than he loves an honest man. Look at Augustus. Dirty bugger, never known to spare the rod, his blessed sainthood come on late to him, but not before he'd come a whole lot more than Our Saviour Who Art In Heaven, He Who Came Twice, no second coming for Saint Augustus, oh no, not him, Sate Augustus more the like. How many women did he have? Dirty buggers both, he and Francesca. She'd love to do it with a man like Saint Augustus, ordinary man not good enough for her, wants to get stuck upon a saint, not just a country cleric, hard word of God is what she wants. God made the lamb lie down, God lit the burning bush, he'd get the friction, all you need, to light her fuzzied tinderbox. How many bastards spawned by hoary Saint Augustus, or did he take that other road, the road that leads to no conception? Hell and damnation and the eternal cup of shame that we all drink, the carnal knowledge that's the worst knowledge of all, what was God thinking of when he made the cock that crows and spouts its heady cloud of juice, not any different to a frog that blurts its spawn into a puddle, God making woman's hairy flesh. Children of copulating cunts and cocks, say that in Latin for Sunday Church, no-one would bat an eye.

Mournful estate, just being human in this life, mixed blessing at best, no end of bestial enterprises, and God made sin, God's way of saying Please Indulge! The very rock of Holy Church, God loves a sinner to repent, God loves a sinner more than any Holy Man. Amen. God though, I swear that I can smell her juices in my nose. At least she's done, feel it again, her front's gone sliding down my bum, there, she's pulled away. Hands on my hips, to catch her balance, could fart right now, that would be a shock, ripe paternoster from the bum. What's that? Brushing the neck hairs out from under collar. Nice touch. Father would kill me if he knew. God though, she's ripe!

I wonder if she's got clean underwear. Seen her washing it, and putting it on the line. Moist as the inside of a fig. Oh Father, Father, please forgive me, I'm a mortal sinner, God though I'd swear that I can feel her breath upon my neck. Must preach a sermon on temptation, lovely theme, need to be firm, stand strange, no, strong, Oh God, you made the prod of man, not with animals though, these bestial thoughts, what's got in me? Father, forgive me. Must try and drink a little less. Muddies me up. Give me strength, oh Lord, give me strength that I might strive to earn your love, and learn to emulate your purity and grace. I am a sinful man, that's true. Take pity on me, You, inventor of the cock and its erection, God's stiffened hand, no, no, that's not a fit thing for a prayer, somehow it seems I've wandered off. Hard with her living in the house. Dear God, I've made a proper mess of it. Forgive me! I am your Emile, you came to me when I was strapped firm to a tree, the storming wind wrapped fierce around my ears and then you shewed your face. Why do I feel like a lost sheep? You made the lamb lie down, why won't you let me lie down too? Am I making sense? Can one man sin too many times in one lifetime and then he's crossed the threshold into hell for all of time? How can I know? Oh God in heaven, heaven and earth, dear God, take pity on my soul!

Succubus. Latin, such a lovely tongue. Always brings a kind of succour to the lips.

Is it just saliva? Really, I shouldn't be so foul. God smells his own farts first, they say it was a joke first uttered from the lips of Saint Augustus. Could do better than that myself. Always wondered if I'd get to be a saint. Can't really go beyond that in this life. Augustus had the thing mapped out. Screw round for years and then repent, turn on a miracle or two. Spent all his life just turning different kinds of tricks.

Jesus knows I'm a foul bugger. Is there one dirty thought I've yet to think? God loves a sinner. Set to become my private catechism. How do you make a miracle? Can it be true he turned the water into wine? Seems a bit much, the Son of God doing party tricks. Walking on water, might not that be the sin of pride? Why not a mud flat at low tide? Sun shining on, you'd get the clear impression sure enough. Feel of the soft mud squiggling in between the toes. Blaspheming now. Can't get that girl out of my mind. Perhaps it would be best to send her on her way. Fault's my own, not hers. Perhaps God means this as a test. Nobody's ever kissed her breasts, her middle name is Olive, a lovely thing, to be a virgin in the world. Never seems to last as long as you'd like. Life presses hard on us. A candle snuff, God's voice in a puff of thick mancloud. Do sperm have souls? What of the ova? Or do they only make one when they meet and join, if so does each sperm then have half a soul?

What if two sperm collide, like sparks perhaps, might they not fuse and make a soul as well? God though, theology's a frightful task. No sooner do you think you've figured it out than God sneaks another finer puzzle into mind. We'll all deserve to rest in heaven if we succeed in making sense of God's Creation. Perhaps that's why God puts us here on earth? He couldn't work it out himself, he's wondering if one of us can make sense out of the world he's gone and made.

Francesca was talking to him, he was having trouble hearing what she said, mesmerised by the curious dancing of her lips, what was it she said? Something about kissing.

She wanted to go to The Kissing? No, my dear, out of the question. The Kissing was no place for a girl. He wasn't sure it was any place for man or woman either.

'I am thirteen this year, and my middle name is Olive. You ask me why I must go to The Kissing, and all I can say is it's the fine imperative of my middle name that beckons. That is all. I will go, good night and good luck to you.'

And then she closed the door. Troubled, left to his silence, Emile Pestoso watched the door close slowly and then shut with a click that was itself imperative, and decided to pour himself another glass of wine.

He was such a coward.

Father Emile Pestoso had never been to The Kissing. He found the whole thing quite disgusting, obscene, and pagan. From the Latin *paganus*, one of the village. He found the whole lot common, though they didn't have a lot in common with him.

That they kept his pantry stocked with oil and wine and good smoked ham hardly redeemed them in his sight.

To redeem this flock he knew would take a miracle. How did miracles come about? He wanted to believe in miracles, though part of him resisted this heady truth. He put it down to faith. But faith in what? In the common mass to rise above its baser pulse? He knew that pulse, it throbbed in him, he was a man, after all, and not just a man of God.

If he could make one miracle before he died—this was the deepest wish in him. He had studied the lives of the miraculous ones, the blessed saints and virgins. He'd abandoned this reading after a while, finding prolonged exposure to such purity too depressing. It was one of the things that had led him in his drinking. He knew as well that those who were not virgins had still been able to bring their miracles about. The Great Augustus. Their achievements seemed the more miraculous for that. Thinking on it made his head swim, and he poured himself another glass of red. The fine wine of the village.

He'd grant them that. The miracle of good wine was one the villagers of his parish had long perfected.

Pestoso was there to tuck her into bed. A childish ritual she felt she had outgrown. She did not want to look at him. She felt the movements of his hand beneath the blankets and knew she was too old for this, yet said nothing, preferring to avert her eyes instead. She felt a hand linger on her shoulder, and heard him snuffling in his nose. She was thinking of her mother, the scared look in her eyes before she died.

'You cannot tell me where I'm going.'

The thin lips of her mother's face, and those last words, and shortly after that she died. Pestoso bending over her. She could smell the wine on him. Closing her eyes, as if in this way she could move to some other place, out of his reach.

He'd hoped that when he became a priest his doubts would clarify and he was right, if by clarify we mean the essence of the thing somehow comes clear. The doubts he felt now as a priest were greater than any doubt he'd known before. So often he felt called upon to justify himself, and would find himself immersed in an eloquent soliloquy as he fended off the harassments of his own self. Why can't I leave myself alone? he mused. Why must I indulge this oddly habit? Why am I prone to so many morbid and erotic speculations?

He remembered the day the sniffling had begun, he'd had this cold for nearly thirty years and often prayed for its relief, and yet to date no relief had been proffered. It had been the day after the hurricane of belief, he'd stayed in bed, taken by cold. He wondered on the voice he'd heard, God's voice that spoke to him, and wondered how he knew. How did he know it was the voice of God and not just the whisper of some other voice inside his head? This was the beginning of his doubt, its birthing seed, and it was then that his nose began to drip, as if somehow God's punishment for Pestoso's lack of faith had come instantly to him. There was a comfort in it, as if the dripping nasal tap of him was the constant presence of the Creator, the nose worried by a hand that might have been a hand of God. He was prone to such speculation and wondered if this cold would ever end, his snuffling faith founded on doubt. He knew that if the day came when he truly did have faith, was free of doubt, on that day his nasal passages would be clear and dry and he would be The Snuffling Priest no more. As if his faith was like a truffle and he the pig who snuffled round, his snouting doubting faith, hoping for the day that ripe truffle would be found.

He could not help but fantasize, the curious reverie of it. He thought of Dawn, who'd kept his house before Francesca, thought of the heat that came off her cheek against his groin, her hands clasped inelegantly around his buttocks. He began to say The Lord's Prayer to himself. He could feel her pressing harder to him. You're Such A Good Man! Such a Good Good Man! Who art in heaven . . . He wondered if he should speak, why did she clasp him so, what would she have of him? Why had she thrown herself down at his knees, what request might she make of him? Did she need money, perhaps a loan? What troubled her? And did he dare suggest she pull her face away, remove her hands, surely she was just overcome, some grief perhaps, or even some relief. He was distracted from this thought by the feeling of her fingers now as they gently stroked his thigh, she was in tears, sobbing to him. Was she hysterical? What should he do? He looked at her looking up at him with shiny eyes, then burrowing her head once more into his groin, So good you are, true man of God. Somehow he'd lost the words of his Lord's Prayer, just start again, Our Father . . . her teeth brushing so light against the flesh, did he feel that? He felt his own response now as he quickened up with blood, certain she'd felt him move, her teeth pressing firmer once again, there was no doubting it, a nibble clearly felt, he was surprised to find a voice in him that said I want to fuck with her! Scent of her hair rising like steam, his hands caressing the soft fibres of her hair, the sculpted feeling of the skull, back of her head, surprised also to feel the confidence of her, no shyness now, when did she learn to do that? No longer talking, no words of what a Good Man Him, be punished yet, God seeing everything, her teeth running slowly down the stem, could feel the whole thing through the cloth, she'd suck him off, she would, the staff of life, another gift of God and fine, could feel the blood inside his heart, his face gone red with shame and desire, the strange confusion of his breath, he wanted it and he felt damned, how could something that felt so good be called a sin? A revelation, more the like, his collar chafing at the veins gorged with blood, his swollen head, her hands so firm upon, his hands held heavy on her shoulders, her own strong back, to take his weight. My child. Trying to speak he finds instead somehow her lips have found . . . her mouth . . . weak at the knees, somehow ascending and descending into heaven, into hell, the pleasure of forbidden fruit. Don't Touch! Don't Touch! Oh god, is good!

He was ashamed. Was it night or day? Dark light of morning, overcast perhaps. What were the limits of the things that he might do? His guilts unhinging him. It was shortly after that the beatings started.

She watched him taking up the belt, standing with the belt now doubled in his hand, and then she got down on her knees. Pleasing contrition, Pestoso thought, and yet his mind was set, he felt the hotness of her cheek pressing his hand, he felt the heat in the water in her eyes, begging him now. He remained firm. He put her up onto the bed, her small clasped hands were a nice touch, he thought, and pushed the sound of her sobbing from his mind. He pulled her knickers down, raising his arm at the same time, poised to strike. Indeed, he thought, we worship at the altar of a hard god. He knew the diabolic force was in him now, and could not rest, and he beat her even as he wondered what possessed him. Into that darkness he went, and kept it up until that force was spent. A curious penitence. He'd sent Dawn on her way, and now he thrashed Francesca to appease his guilt.

Somehow Francesca felt she was at fault. The death of her own mother, what had she done? She had not answered when her mother spoke, instead she merely stood there open-mouthed, leaving her mother dangling between a heaven and an earth, and perhaps some other place. I'm a bad girl, she thought, I blocked the dunny up, glad I did that, he had to stand in his own piss.

When Emile awoke he felt both raw and numb and knew this darker knowledge of himself now mocked him. And yet a part of him felt true and calm. He'd often been perplexed by this deep impulse in his breast, and now at least the thing had been confirmed.

He felt contrite, if yet unsure how to atone. He bowed his sins, and contemplated a simple prayer.

Know Thyself, Love Thyself, Rule Thyself. Wasn't this Augustus?

'Not all animals are good.' Pestoso was talking to Francesca, mesmerised by the movement of her elbows as she did the ironing. He was also watching her behind, and observed with a keen eye for detail the way the fabric of her dress pulled taut and then released over her rear.

'Not all animals are made by God.'

He paused, and cleared his throat. Was it too early for a glass of wine? He suspected not. It was early, that he knew, but not too early.

Yes, he thought, there was something in it. A sermon

there. Quite an insight, really. It made more sense, if he'd been Noah he would have been a little more discriminate, he would have blocked the paths of some beasts.

'God made the dog, but the devil made the flea!'

He liked the sound of it. He snuffed, then swallowed, drank some wine, swallowed again then cleared his throat. A pleasing bitterness on the backside of his palate, mixed with the seeming sweet taste of his bile. Yes, yes, a good line, that, the dog and flea, almost an aphorism, really.

He drank again, trying to keep his eyes off the supple movements of Francesca Terremoto and the shifty moving fabric on her bum. Hardput.

# A Priestly Vision

Emile was sitting in his bedroom, looking out the window. He saw Francesca disappear behind the piggery. Wondered what she might attempt up there, and didn't care to speculate. His head was dull and hurting from the wine he'd drunk the night before. He'd managed to find a stub of pencil and had written on a small notepad his aphorism of the day before.

God made the dog, but the devil made the flea.

Now that was really something. A sermon there. He was thinking about Noah. In his mind's eye Noah looked exactly like Emile. This NoahEmile was dressed in a handsome black costume, with a black headband upon which a single silver diamond had been woven into the fabric. In the middle of the forehead. He held a bent shepherd's crook, the kind Emile had only seen on sentimental Christmas cards and innocent nativities, free of all hint of copulation.

Emile stood erect, a proud and noble man. He was standing in the middle of a wooden ramp that led up to the Ark. He'd just let a pair of dogs on board, white shaggy beasts. He crushed a flea between his forefinger and thumb. Wondering now where he might wipe off the flea. He didn't want to spoil his nice black gown.

There was a light breeze blowing that made his silk gown billow. It made him look heroic, even serene.

How clearly his true self was revealed to him. But what should he do with that dead flea? He didn't want to wipe it on his sleeve, nor put it on his crook. A flea had no place on EmileNoah's ark, dead or alive. The flea mangled on his thumbnail.

Emile felt that his deliberations were of great magnitude.

All future decisions would issue from the decision he now made about the disposal of that flea's corpse. He looked down the wooden ramp at all the beasts of creation. There were rabbits, oxen, geese; there were reptiles, rodents, owls, all the sea creatures out of water; a family of octopuses were making their slippery way towards him, expecting they'd gain access to the ark. An Ark of Excess? An impossibility, thought Emile, that God would create such obscenity.

He still had not managed to dispose of the flea, so now he simply flicked it off his thumb and watched it disappear. Only then, as the flea rekindled its vital spark and hopped away, did Emile notice that his ark was beached on solid ground and not in water. Of course, he said, it hasn't started raining!

He was feeling uncomfortable, his elegant black robe that billowed in the breeze was making him feel hot and sweaty, as if his skin could not breathe beneath it and was slowly choking. He could see, in the middle distance, a lovely black and white cow, chewing her cud. Emile wanted to get this lovely cow onto his ark, but between Emile and the cow was a sea of creatures.

Some swarmed, others scuttled, all of them, he felt sure, were hostile creatures; and he could not leave his post to usher this one nice cow on board. The other beasts would take advantage of his brief desertion to scuttle, swarm and slither onto his ark. As he watched, the cow lifted her tail and dumped a cascade of liquid nitrogen onto the earth. The octopus family was at his feet, and had begun to climb upon his shepherd's staff and up his gown. Emile was feeling queasy and afraid. He blinked then, and saw Francesca walk out of the piggery, her hands were black and she was exhaling a final puff of cigarette out of her mouth.

He looked down at the page. God made the devil but the dog had made the flea. No, no, not that. There was a lesson in it, but for the nonce it quite eluded him. He felt somewhat defeated, and his head was throbbing. Perhaps a glass of milk? No sooner did he think of milk than he thought of octopus, and felt quite ill. Some water, then.

He walked down the hall. At the end of the corridor,

standing at the entrance to the kitchen, Francesca was waiting for him. She had already changed so much since she'd arrived.

'Emile,' she said, and Emile grew afraid. She had a physical confidence that he lacked. He had no power over her. He wished her self-possession were something he could own himself. He wished he could get away from those strong eyes. But her eyes held him in place, even as he wished he could escape into the sanctuary of his bed.

'I've moved my things into the piggery. I need a hand to get my cupboard and the bed.'

Emile could only nod.

'Now,' she said. 'I want to do it now.' He followed her into her bedroom, and then together they hauled the heavy wooden chest up to the pigshed. But she would not let him inside. They put the cupboard down. She blocked his way so that he could not see inside.

'Just leave it here,' she said, and once again Emile complied. 'I'll drag it in myself.' She stared him down, and he turned to walk away. 'Emile,' she said, stopping him. 'Thank you. You needn't bother with the bed. I'll pull the bed apart and bring it here myself.'

Emile felt that he was now dismissed, and as he walked back to the house he felt alone. He felt she'd just said her goodbyes, and there was no turning back.

Francesca watched him go, then pulled the cupboard down over the single step onto the earth of the piggery. Home. The cupboard just fitted through the door. She dragged it across the dirt and pushed it up against a wall. The legs had ploughed deep grooves into the dirt. She smoothed this ruffled earth with her foot. When she reappeared in the doorway of the piggery she could see no sign of Emile. It was almost dark.

And so the piggery became her sanctuary. A crude domain, but it was at least her own.

Sitting on the bed in her new home, she stared at the wall with its curious designs of her father and Emile. She'd brought a large pitcher of water up from the house. She poured some of this water onto a rag. Then she erased the charcoal features of her father and Emile from the old yellowed wall. Ducking the rag into the water. She liked the way the wall was slowly coming clean.

Once she'd finished she sat back down on her bed and admired her nice clean wall. It was a start, she thought. If not an end, then at least it was a clear beginning.

There was something else Francesca knew: that whether Emile liked it or not, she was definitely going to The Kissing. Would Amaretto be there? She felt sure he'd go. She couldn't say why she felt attracted to him. She'd heard him singing after work some nights, in the cafe, when she was young. Or was that just last year, six months ago, when she had been her daddy's darling? Sitting with her father, her father tired after work, falling asleep and snoring while Amaretto sang and did the washing up. She'd sweep the floors. He even offered her a job. Gianni's girl, he'd called her, and she felt embarrassed. Or was she angry? She was no longer Gianni's girl. And she hoped and wondered, she might even pray, that Amaretto would be at the olive grove, there for the kissing.

# PART TWO:

# THE KISSING

# The Infant Francesca

The Kissing always brought with it a tremor of regret: it was the end of autumn, and the only certainty now was winter.

The Kissing had once been a huge event. There were stories of fevered, slimy copulations where men and women swam through oil, aspiring to a total immersion in each other. But The Kissing had become a small affair, where small groups of men and women made a simple offering to the god of olive oil, if such a one exists. A farm labourer's thanksgiving.

Terremoto kneaded, warped and gently thumped the dough on the rounded wooden bench. Fondling it into shape. Years of bakers slapping dough had produced the gentlest hollow in the wood. How he loved to be a baker! He thought about Francesca and the dough stopped dancing in his hands.

He was worried, knew these loaves would never rise. He wiped his hands on his apron, dusted the flour off his sleeves and arse, and hung his apron on its trusted metal hook.

Gianni slept in a small room out the back, beside the storeroom. When he and Rosemary were together they'd slept upstairs, and Francesca had her cot up there as well. When Rosemary left and Francesca was older Gianni moved downstairs, and Francesca had the large room to her self.

He hadn't yet decided what to do with the room upstairs. Francesca had taken her bed when she moved into Pestoso's.

Gianni sat on his narrow bed and closed his eyes. He and Rosemary had slept in single beds, pushed in together to make their marital domain. But the separate nature of their beds had underlined the separate nature of their lives.

I should have bought a double bed, Gianni was thinking. Though he knew their problems would not have been solved by a larger mattress on a bigger bed.

He could not help thinking about Rosemary and The Kissing. Hers was an unconventional beauty, her tight jaw and narrow mouth. Her mouth was often pursed. Francesca had inherited this trait from her mother, it made her look stern at times when she was merely thinking. When Gianni saw Francesca he saw Rosemary's mouth, and almost expected to hear the shouting start. To see the plates being hurled. She was too much like her mother for his comfort.

Sitting on his bed, Gianni felt quite sure that, were he to see Rosemary again, as younger man and younger woman, he'd still want to kiss that mouth. Perhaps the oil had tricked him, he'd been taken in by her slippery lips? Such labial lubricity. It had been her eyes that drew him in the first time they'd met. The Kissing was not an invitation to an orgy, it was an invitation to good oil. It got them talking. After the oil was drunk there was wine and food, music and laughter. They'd wandered off, wanting the chance to lie somewhere and hold each other. It had been a warm day for autumn, and then the wind came up. They huddled closer, and rubbed each other's hands to bring some warmth. She looked at him and said, 'For a big man, you're still quite handsome.'

An awkward compliment, he'd taken it awkwardly. Charming her with his affection. She placed her hand then on his neck, it was clear that he was going to be kissed. He closed his eyes, they kissed again, and he was quite surprised to find, later, that they'd made a child.

When they woke up the fireflies were dancing in the olives. They had both grown nervous of scorpions, and left. Nine months later Francesca had been born. They had thought to call her Olive, yet felt reluctant to draw attention to the moment of the child's conception. So they called her Francesca, and Olive was her middle name.

The next year Gianni, Rosemary and Francesca Olive had attended The Kissing *en famille*. Francesca had been rubbed with olive oil from head to foot. A suckling babe. Unfortunately, in his excitement, Gianni had dropped her.

'She was so slippery,' he exclaimed in his defence. 'Like a little piglet!' Francesca had become a squally baby after that, and Rosemary always said the fault was his.

'Put your baby girl to sleep,' she'd say. It was always his baby girl, never hers, or theirs. 'Your daughter's crying again, pick her up, put her to sleep, give her a feed.'

He hadn't minded changing nappies and washing them by hand. Something about mushroom and truffles, though he did his best not to inhale.

And they had argued.

'If you hadn't dropped her we'd have a normal baby still.'

'She is a normal baby.'

'It isn't normal for a baby girl to cry that much. The only time she doesn't cry is when she sleeps, and she doesn't sleep enough. Not like other babies.'

'All babies cry.'

'Not like that. She's got a soft spot on her head from when you dropped her. Babies aren't like your breadrolls, you don't pick them up and dust them after you drop them. You don't drop babies. You've already ruined her life, and she's little more than one year old!'

'That is a terrible thing to say.'

'It was a terrible thing to do.'

Gianni was no match for Rosemary, and that was that. And when she started throwing plates, Gianni was the one who went to pieces.

Rosemary never let Gianni forget his moment of disgrace at their second Kissing, and their habitual fights had started out of this. In time they forgot how the fighting began. They didn't need to remember, it became their new habit. On sight, they didn't wait to hear each other speak, preferring to try and score the opening shot.

Rosemary started spending a lot of time at her sister's, out of town. Gianni was spending all of his time at the bakery, with Francesca bundled up in bandages and hanging on a strong metal hook behind the door separating the baking room from the front of the shop. The baking room was warm and cosy. Perhaps that's why, in time, Francesca found the bakery so stifling.

It was a common practice to bind your baby up and hang them somewhere safe. Out of the grasp of jumping dogs, out of accident's way. And the bandaging made the infant's limbs grow strong and true. It was a boon for the working parent, as the swaddling helped to pacify the child. Gianni had not discovered the joy of swaddling bands until Rosemary had gone away, and there were times he was glad she'd gone just because he'd stumbled on the ancient trick of it. The swaddled Francesca now slept most of the day and all of the night. So Gianni was able to get on with his work.

He kept her swaddled for much longer than was usual, however, and had to install a special metal bracket on the door to hold her weight. Gianni hadn't realised that his daughter had outgrown swaddling bands until Luigi remarked one day that his daughter had turned into a mummy.

Francesca was consequently slow at learning to walk, and never managed the art of running. When she began to run she had an unfortunate tendency to fall over. She was also terrified of dogs, perhaps because they could move so much more quickly than she could.

Rosemary finally left him for good, her stays away becoming a season unto themselves, her return visits lasting a single day. She said her sister Gina was gravely ill, and needed curing.

The truth was that Rosemary and her sister's husband were having an affair. There were rumours that they were poisoning Gina. The simpler truth is that Gina's health got worse the longer Rosemary stayed to mend her.

If ever Gianni hinted that Rosemary might like to take Francesca with her, he was quickly rebuked.

'Don't you love your daughter? I'm putting my life at risk just setting foot inside that house. You're a disgraceful father. You'd kill us both, Francesca and me.'

She'd work herself up into such a righteous frenzy she'd

start smashing plates, and Gianni would beg her to stop. Rosemary would keep throwing plates until she had him on his knees, in tears, and Francesca would be bawling too.

'See what you've done, you human worm. I risk my life for my only sister, and you can only think about yourself. Pathetic!'

She'd make an ostentatious display of picking up Francesca and nursing her until she settled down. Then she'd say to Gianni, 'I'm sorry darling, but Gina really does need me.' Then she'd hand Francesca to him. 'Olly will keep you company till I get back.'

She'd give him a moist kiss on the forehead, pause at the back door, wink once, blow a kiss and leave.

It wasn't much of a family life. Whether Rosemary really did hasten her sister's departure from this earth we'll never know. When Gina died Rosemary stayed in her sister's house, 'taking care of the arrangements'.

The funeral came and went, but Rosemary did not come home. She stayed dressed in mourning, and it was rumoured that she and Bing, her sister's American husband, who had a private income and had never done a day's work in his life, that she and Bing now shared one bedroom.

And then, within a few years, Rosemary too was dead. There were many funerals in those days. Pestoso could not believe his luck—he was a man who found a funeral more uplifting than a wedding.

Rosemary had been out of town when Gianni learnt that she was pregnant. She sent him a postcard with the message 'Congratulations. You're having a baby.' The card made him scratch his head. It was a picture of an old woman carrying a huge bundle of sticks upon her back. The woman supported herself with a wooden staff and she looked like a hunchback with a hump made out of wood.

Gianni had gone to Amaretto's and asked if he would like a drink. What's the occasion? I've just found out I'm going to be a father. Amaretto poured him a whisky. The whisky burnt his throat in a pleasing way, and Amaretto filled his glass once again. Gianni sipped his second drink more slowly and felt a supple warmth down in his belly, like a baby's gentle hand that opened slowly in him. He was glad, and felt like crying then, as he stood and sipped his whisky at the bar.

Sitting on his bed, lost in reflection, Gianni knew he'd never go back to The Kissing.

# Cramp Bark

Sylvana had never been to The Kissing, and had been looking forward to it for weeks. But now, feeling betrayed by her body upon waking, she was lying on her back chastising herself for not getting up, yet unable to spark herself into action. Her period had come early, she was exhausted and crampy. So drained of animation she swore she was bleeding from her kidneys.

Her mother had always been most depressive when she bled, and something of this disposition had passed to Sylvana. Haranguing herself as she lay inert on her bed, feeling a weight of failure in her. Telling herself she was wasting her abilities: she could have been teaching history at a university, or some school, instead she was holed up in a remote town mending broken plates and poking around the bakery with her fat Gianni. Yet she'd found that her studies of history so easily provoked her worst humours, as she stumbled on fresh accounts of human villainy and disaster. Tales of famine; cruel deaths by diseases; women sealed up in walls; old men and women beaten to death by their families, having outlived their usefulness; people who ate their own arms from an excess of hunger. Wishing she could read of such things with a greater equanimity.

She'd hoped to reinvent herself by moving to Bacheretto, and felt despondent to find that, in essence, she was the woman she'd always been. She hauled herself off the bed, stumbled into the bathroom, rummaging around for something to ease her cramping. She found a small bag of herbs, Chaste Tree, Cramp Bark, and False Unicorn Root—she'd forgotten these, she'd meant to give them to Francesca.

Wondering then if she'd been much help to the girl, feeling negligent and guilty. She'd gone to visit Francesca three more times, and each time found no-one home. Glad that Pestoso had not been there, yet worried that she'd not seen Francesca. After the third failed attempt she found she was less willing to make the walk. Wanting to leave some note or gift, yet in the end doing nothing more than walking home alone.

Her negligence made her want to go and see Francesca at once, but she knew she didn't have the strength, her cramping abdomen and legs would never make the distance. Making herself an infusion of Cramp Bark, she headed back to bed

Her mother had told her about Cramp Bark. Used by monks to reduce their sexual desires, and so some people called it Monk's Pepper. In women it could help with conception, though it could also ease the pain when blood was falling.

Lying back, settling her hands on her belly, feeling she was ebbing away. Remembering a time when she had straddled Gianni in the bakery and been surprised to find Francesca staring, wide-eyed, at their performance. Wishing she'd noticed the girl earlier, rather than at the moment her father began to come with an urgent theatricality. Fumbling for their phrases then. What did it mean to say this was how a man and woman showed their love for one another, when their grunts and wilder exclamations sounded like they were trying to kill each other?

Sylvana heard herself groan in her embarrassment and confusion. Wondering if her concerns for the girl were prompted more by her guilts, or a desire to rectify those things she'd felt were spoiled in her own girlhood. Had she already overstepped the mark, talking of diaphragms and cocks? Did she have the right to impose such knowlege on the girl? Did she have the right to withhold it? Telling herself that Francesca would come and visit if she needed help, or company. Perhaps all Francesca needed was the chance to find her own way in the world, without being pestered by her father's girlfriend?

Wishing she could turn her thinking off, feeling her brain had become a hammer she used to bash into herself. Trying to convince herself she'd done her bit to help Francesca, yet not quite succeeding. Her infusion of Cramp Bark was now ready to drink, and as she swallowed the slightly bitter water she almost felt glad for the pains and lethargy, they made it easier to put her obligations on hold, feeling as she did so utterly incapable of useful action. She pulled the sheets over her head, willing herself to sleep, forgetting all about The Kissing, and disinclined to dwell upon what she was missing.

# The Kissing

Stefano Costa was making a mound of rocks, out of which he'd soon construct a wall. He followed his father in this trade, though in later life his father had gone from making walls to tiny rock mosaics.

Costa was lost in thoughts of rocks as he picked them up and felt their weight. The curious way rocks had of fitting back together, as if the mother rock from which they'd come was slowly reassembled in his hands.

There always came a point when he knew there was just one missing rock. It was the key, the navel of the wall he was building. The canny way the drystone wall would fit together. Sometimes the hardest thing was looking for that navel stone, sure that it was near at hand, lying buried just out of sight. He'd scrabble in the earth, the hard earth tearing his fingers, the soil clogging underneath his nails.

His fingers had grown hard as those rocks. There were days he'd bathe his hands in a mix of wine and oil and lemon juice, it seemed to be the only way to get them clean and it washed the wounds as well.

He heard voices calling yet didn't hear. He was submerged in the terrain of his wall's design.

Costa looked up and saw a small group of people standing in the olive grove. They were calling out and waving to him.

An old woman was playing a hand drum while a younger man danced before her. Others were singing as they clapped their hands. They were getting ready for The Kissing. An old man played a tarantella on his accordian.

No-one remembered when The Kissing had begun. It

was just one of those things, an old tradition. Each year as the first of the new oil was pressed they'd gather round and drink from an old wooden bowl that passed from hand to hand. The bowl was carved from olive wood, its diameter the length of an arm.

Everyone drank. It was part of the legend of the place, just as you never slept in an olive grove because of scorpions. Why did scorpions like to live in olive groves, Costa was wondering to himself as he wandered over to join in and pass the bowl around. It was considered a lucky thing, to drink the fresh oil of the first pressing. Costa didn't know about that but he was certainly quite partial to the kissing.

They stood in a small and quiet circle, passing the bowl, the green oil a little murky, almost a thickly yellow hue. In turn they drank a sip for health and luck, and rubbed some oil onto any part that ailed, a ricky knee or a pinchy joint, then rubbed their forearms, their faces and their hair. They were a glistening lot.

As olive harvests go it had not been the best of years. We saw no portent in it. The olives the year before gave their all, and so the fruit this year were small and paltry. To make things worse a sharp frost in the hills had killed many of the trees, some of them hundreds of years old.

Costa licked his lips. The taste of oil on his lips and tongue. A pleasing slickness. It was called The Kissing, this day that celebrated oil, because after even a short draught of virgin oil there was no pleasure greater than that of kissing, oily lips to oily lips, and well-primed tongue to tongue. Costa licked his lips again, enjoyed the taste, enjoyed as well his anticipation of what lay ahead. Looking around their little group to see who he might kiss. In this he was not alone, his eyes met eyes, other tongues licked lips in preparation for the game. The sudden exclamation of a metal shutter falling, and the grunt of a man with all his air knocked out brought The Kissing to an end however before the kissing had begun.

Luigi's studio was a catastrophe, Luigi's sense of order revolving around the degree of chaos he could create at any time. He was convinced this mess had a mind of its own.

Luigi was lost in contemplation. He was sitting on a small wooden stool trying to read the mind of God, but he kept drifting off. Or was he simply reading the mind of God at a moment when God's attention too had drifted? Did God have daydreams, get lost and wonder off the point? If God was all knowing—point of some conjecture and contention—there must be a lot of trivia in His mind. Name of the first submarine? Aquascutum.

Luigi burped, and enjoyed the aftertaste of breakfast sausage in his mouth. Did God taste everything? What of olfaction? Luigi was disconcerted to speculate that God might sniff his farts, whether in bed or out. Though even the humble fart was a part of God's creation. If God made the whole world, God made it naughty bits and all, God made it vulgar and obscene, violent, cruel and tender. God made the fine scent of the hay bale and the ploppy sound of horse dung as it hit the stable floor. Luigi shifted on his seat and cast his eyes around the room, his beloved Filing Cabinet.

A low rumble in his guts suggested that his bowels were about to move. Thus he was distracted from his photograph of God.

Luigi's throne room was also a fume cupboard, a ventilated enclosure used for experimenting with chemicals with harmful vapours. The precise nature of the experiment depended on the nature of his diet—lentils, beans or cabbages, for example. He was reminded that the ancient Greek for beans also meant 'the voice of God'.

He sat there, musing. The smell of shit and the smell of flowers: are these not the same smell? Just as the high leaf and the root are parts of the one tree, *creazione in extremis*?

The tendency of gasses to escape or expand is defined by a mathematical equation and is one of the concerns of thermodynamics, but Luigi wasn't thinking about the fugacity of his farts. His attention had been captured by the sight of a young brown lizard crawling up the wall onto a window ledge. It lifted its head and revealed a flash of soft white skin speckled with black spots. A fine black line traced the edge of the brown cowling of its head. The lizard turned its head to take him in, the pair of them immobile, joined now in their silence.

A beak that flashed as fast as eyes could blink disturbed his meditations. The lizard's tail bitten off by a fast blackbird. And yet the lizard had not moved.

The sounds of people shouting, their shouts mingled with the sound of someone screaming, broke through this simple moment. He was scrabbling with his pants, and already he was running. Out the door, trying not to stumble as he fumbled with the belt, he fell and rolled and stood up straight. He hadn't yet secured his belt, he stopped and swore and fixed it then. So lost in thought he had forgotten about The Kissing and the oil harvest, but it seemed that had been overtaken now, replaced by the sound of disaster in the voices that he heard. Running to join them in the olive grove.


The old accordionist was trapped beneath a heavy metal shutter in the pressing room, where he'd snuck off for a quiet sip of homemade amaretto.

The wonder was the man was still alive. Amidst the confusion of the kissers' shouts, his vital groans and the sharp points of his screams cut through the cold air of the room.

The shutter was too heavy for the man to lift. They gathered round, their fingers searching for a point of purchase. Some were swearing while others swore at those who swore. Costa yelled through this confusion a giant 'Ready?' and counted to three. At three they lifted, the broken man hauled free, the weight of the heavy shutter held in air by oily hands—the strain of it, as Costa now began his count again, their signal to drop the mighty weight.

Luigi could never later explain satisfactorily to himself

why he chose to do so, but he let go of the heavy shutter before Costa had counted up to three. He was thinking, I didn't wash my hands. This thought distracted him. He let go when he heard two. Unfortunately, so did everyone. Everyone, that is, except Stefano Costa.

For a moment, Costa had the impression that he was singlehandedly holding up the massive weight. It was a prescient thought. A moment later the shutter crushed this illusion, he slipped as it fell yet managed to flick his right hand out of the way. However his left hand was severed instantly.

There was a curious silence then.

Costa, when he thought about it later, realised that at this moment he felt no pain, it was a shock, that was all.

It was as if everything had become still, even, you might say, calm. Or becalmed. No-one moved, they could not credit what had happened, and what they now knew to be true: that an act of collective cowardice had just crippled one of their own. This peaceful state and its disturbing meditation endured for just a moment. Then all hell broke loose, as if a wall of rocks had suddenly come tumbling down.

The hand curled on the ground in a curious supplication.

Without knowing why Luigi, being closest, picked it up. He took the bottle of homemade amaretto and gave Costa a mighty slug to dull the pain. Costa was groaning now, and the pain in his arm was a cruel thing. Luigi pulled his handkerchief out of his back pocket and wrapped the severed hand in it. I didn't wash my hands, he thought again, and doused the hand and handkerchief in amaretto.

The heady smell of bitter almonds filled the pressing room, just for a moment overpowering the fragrance of the olives. The accordionist was being carried by two men holding a blanket by the corners to make a clumsy stretcher. They were walking quickly up to where an old farm truck stood, half filled with tools and produce ready to take into town. Luigi ripped his shirt off and bound it round Stefano's wrist, to try and stem the flow of blood. He was surprised to see Costa stuff one sleeve into his mouth, trying to stem the flood of sound that issued from him. The great pain coming truly now. Someone had started up the truck and driven down to meet the stretcher bearers—the obvious thing, to bring the truck down to the man and not the man up to the truck, but in the heat of such a moment there is a different logic, the logic of panic and chaos. Easy enough to lose your head. Costa's turn now, Luigi bundled him into the old truck's cabin, then Luigi climbed in too and they were racing into town.

The smell of amaretto and the muffled cries of the injured men preceded them down the hospital corridor as they headed off to the casualty ward.

Both men would live. The man under the shutter had cracked his ribs. The surgeons could do nothing for Costa's hand. Costa was kept under observation, and to his surprise Luigi left the hospital with Costa's amaretto'd hand still in his own.

# Francesca And Amaretto

Francesca and Amaretto found themselves alone, both shaken. Walking all the way to town. She felt unwilling to go home on her own.

They started off meandering, but as the sun came down and the cold came on their stride became determined, and they set off for Amaretto's. He was wondering what he'd cook when they got there.

His thoughts had turned to broth, and Francesca lit the fire, the pair of them glad to be busy. It meant they had no need to talk, and held their native shyness at bay.

It was getting warm inside the cafe. The metal stove fired up the place in no time, and the gas rings in the kitchen threw their heat. They had no need of coats and jumpers now.

When he started sweating in the kitchen Amaretto took his shirt off. Francesca liked the way he looked without a shirt. A strong, young body, and he seemed so happy. Sweet-natured. She didn't know about the bitterness he had in him.

Francesca was grateful for the broth, it warmed her chilly innards, and as she drank it down she was also warming to its maker.

Something had changed on the brisk walk home, in the nature of her affections. She was drawn to Amaretto in a way that differed from the girlish admiration she'd once had. If she ever had a girl, she thought, Conception would be such a lovely name, and she blushed when she caught herself out thinking.

Amaretto caught her blush and said, 'What?' He hadn't meant to be so blunt.

'Nothing,' she said, 'I was just wondering if Stefano is going to be alright. She blushed again as she caught herself lying, and was embarrassed to realise that she'd been quite occupied with Amaretto and hadn't given Costa a second thought.

Then the pair of them fell silent, and fell to slurping once again. And so they slurped together. The broth's warmth began to settle through them.

'Let's have some wine,' Amaretto said, and before Francesca could reply he'd darted up and brought a bottle back, with two large glasses shaped like bells. She hesitated long enough for Amaretto to pour the wine, and then decided she'd not quibble about whether she was old enough to drink, nor whether she should be drinking wine alone in the company of this young man.

The wine tasted sweet and warming in her mouth, and the alcohol blossomed on her palate. Drinking broth and wine, she had to say that despite the disasters of the afternoon, at this moment all of life seemed fine to her.

# Sweet Fingers

Everyone called the barman Amaretto. Every year he conjured a wild brew from his homegrown almonds. Always kept a bottle of it underneath the counter. The recipe was secret, held in Amaretto's fingers. It was the jewel of any thirst.

Amaretto had started working at the bar when he was seven, helping out his uncle. He washed the floors and dishes. He was one of those men who have a gentle knack with food.

He'd learnt to make amaretto so long ago he couldn't remember a time when he could not make it. His mother craved it when she lay pregnant with him. The first word that he spoke as a child was 'amaretto', much to his parents' delight and consternation. Since then he'd been known by that very name, as if he had baptised himself. He had sweet fingers.

He'd knock about the kitchen at his uncle's, making them lunch—we had a different idea about childhood, you grew up quick, or else you died. The smell of ripe tomatoes breaking down in a pan with olives, and olive oil, black pepper, fresh basil and red wine—as a boy you'd have to say he had a sophisticated palate, but then he'd grown up with wine, a boy like that soon learns to drink though you will rarely see him drunk.

The smells that issued from the kitchen aroused the curiosity of those who sat at his uncle's bar with their sandwiches and coffee.

It wasn't long before the boy was cooking lunches for anyone who stepped inside: he had the knack, and he had the love.

His uncle had named the place Zio's, but the name never stuck. In no time at all the cafe was renamed. Where are you going? Amaretto's! His uncle could see the writing on the door.

Amaretto's uncle, Andreas, was one of those men who never succeeded. He never did decide what he wanted in this life, he drifted here and there, he bought the bar when it was a rundown affair, one of the many Cafe Sports around the world. He'd thought to build it up but underestimated the work involved—the mopping of floors, the early starts, the late late nights, the food to buy, the cooking to be done.

But Amaretto loved it.

One day his uncle left him the keys and walked out. Periodically he'd turn up and want a feed and drink, and take whatever cash was in the till. One day Amaretto heard that his uncle had hung himself in a town not far away. He closed the bar and helped organise the funeral. The bar stayed closed for a week, and then reopened, a modest sign by the front door, with just one word—Amaretto's.

Amaretto's cafe was a small affair, a twenty-seater, though he'd cram thirty people in, fifty if they stood around pushed up against the walls, with drinks in hand. On a summer's eve they'd spill out into the night, the clientele became quite fluid as they drank his handmade booze. And then, in winter, they'd be cuddled up inside, the place a mess of woollen coats and jackets, the big thick jumpers peeling off and the large window steaming up, as if the glass had started to perspire from the heat of people coming on to one another.

It made Amaretto feel good to see the love and the desire, as if his place fulfilled some necessary function, a point of social lubrication.

# Luigi Makes An Impression

The next morning Luigi woke heavily. It was Sunday. Luigi heard the ringing of church bells across the valley and felt that ineffable sadness that sometimes comes over one, unavoidable and inevitable.

Waking gray and darkly, as if for now the poisons in his body had the upper hand.

Thinking of Costa's severed hand, outstretched in supplication. A kind of prayer. Praying for what? Reunion?

Luigi's father had died on a Sunday. He had come back from the war with a piece of shrapnel lodged inside his head, and from that time had been prone to a great despair.

When he'd gone to fight, Gianni had kept the buns and breadloaves baking. When Luigi's father returned he took control again, but his hands had soured and his breadloaves wouldn't rise. He'd lost the levity his fingers needed to work the supple doughs.

His loaves grew pale; stacked in the window of the shop they looked like piles of dying men. People who for years had come to buy their bread from him now stayed away.

A cerebral haemorrhage killed him.

The scent of bread still filled Luigi with a souring remorse, reminding him of his dying father. As a child he'd always wanted to be a baker, but following his father's death he'd lost the sense of his vocation.

And yet the baker's shop lived still, known to all who came to her as La Tarantula. What was his father's joke? That his business had one body and eight legs.

The straw of the loft that he called his bed tickled his ear. He roused himself, shaking the straw and sleep off him.

Some vague impression nibbling at him from his sleep. Unsure yet what it was.

He had trouble focussing his eyes too early in a morn—just as well he knew his way around the darkness of the place. The darkness brought a comfort to his eye, as if he was still half immersed in his dreaming world. He felt his hand grip the smooth railing of the ladder that ran in an angled line down to The Filing Cabinet. Without stopping to survey the ruin of it he ambled by, out to the throne room. The early morning air bit his ears and nose, he sat on the cold rim of the seat and waited for the piss to come. He enjoyed the meditation of it, the ease with which he let himself go with the flow.

He yawned, involuntarily gulping in the air. At his mouth's widest gape he stopped. His eyes falling on the lizard he had seen the day before. The lizard had not moved. The blackbird's beak had snipped the tail away, and the lizard stayed stock still, perched on the window ledge.

Luigi washed his hands in an enamel basin full of water, drying them on the seat of his pants after running his fingers through his hair. He cupped the lizard in his palm and went looking for a box. He walked back inside, then stopped. What he saw was an arresting sight. Costa's hand was floating in a jar of amaretto in the middle of The Filing Cabinet.

Looking at the lizard's shiny stump he saw how the thing had begun to heal, to resprout.

In the vacant space where the lizard's tail had been an idea formed. It was this, the vague impression formed in sleep he'd been unable to pin down. Could a man not emulate a lizard?

He uncorked the jar that contained Costa's hand, the waft of bitter almonds and another darker smell enveloping him. He was going to make a perfect copy of this hand.

Rummaging around the studio he found a paper bag full of plaster. He bent to pick it up and kicked a battered metal bucket, then thought, The very thing! He headed off to the kitchen, an alcove with a basin and a cold-water tap. He let the water run as he walked outside, broke off a small branch from a berry tree, went back inside and poured the plaster powder into the bucket. He turned the tap off.

He scratched his bum and wondered where he'd left the clay. He wandered round the room, turning over bundles of old newspaper, stooks of rag, and decided to inspect the machinations of the rocks and frogs and tadpoles on the way.

I haven't fed the chooks, he thought out loud, and turned to get some kitchen scraps from the compost heap outside. I'll need some oil. I'll need a razor blade to shave hair off my arm, what else? Feed the chooks.

These materials now assembled on a bench before him, he felt quizzly as he fished Costa's hand out of the bottle. Holding it by the middle finger he gently shook it.

It reminded him of the way his father would wake him as a child, gently clasping the big toe of his left foot then shaking while calling out his name. Gigi! Wake up now! Gigi!

Luigi wondered if he should do the same, softly calling Costa's name while shaking drops of amaretto off the wrinkled hand. He'd bury the hand in clay, then he could make a perfect cast in plaster. He could glue hair from his own arm and touch the whole thing up with paint.

It would take longer to make this new hand than it took to cut the old one off. And, sanded back, the thing would be quite smooth, where Costa's hand was rather coarse.

This new hand would be a finer hand than the one which Luigi gently held between his fingers. He gave it a final shake and set it on the bench, palm down. He dried it off, then coated it with oil.


Taking an old bread knife he deftly sliced around the hand of Costa buried in the clay. He could feel the dual textures of the clay and then the flesh against the blade. Lifting off the clay, the image of Costa's hand preserved inside the mould. He lifted out the hand, streaks of clay on the fingers, and the delicate seams of Costa's palm.

He dropped the hand into the jar of amaretto. A curious specimen.

With great care now he joined the two halves of the clay, the perfect echo of Costa's ruptured hand caught within the mould. He looked again at the hand inside the jar. Costa was a nailbiter. He'd never noticed it before, but the evidence was hard before him now.

He sighed. Pouring the plaster in. Nothing now except to wait. All of a sudden he had to say he felt quite tired.

# Emile, Straightfaced

Emile had no sympathy for Costa's misfortune. He felt that Costa's accident was in the nature of a self-inflicted wound. A divinely provident intervention in a pagan ritual. He wondered if he might mention this in church, and knew he would not. He was a coward, and feared the reaction his words might provoke.

He felt he was in competition with the old oil ceremony. He wanted to stage some kind of revival, bringing people back into the church, rather than malingering in the hills. How could he make his god their star attraction? He'd need to tune a fine pitch.

Looking out from his altared point of view, seeing the empty rows, and thinking about bums on seats. Fixing his beady eyes on his congregation. Preparing to speak, that he might impart his own bold lesson.

'There's not one man or woman here could look at themselves straightfaced, and look into their Eye.'

He paused then. A frog nearby shat itself inside a ditch. Others feeling quite the same.

Feeling a pulse down in his groin.

A cold draught blowing from the rear of the church. Fingers of wind, blowing on a man with no sensation.

# A Primary Dialogue

Francesca never got around to finding out much more about the diaphragm. But she did find out a lot more about sex.

Lying in her bed at night, the sounds outside her window, of animals in the fields. The window open. She slipped outside, and she was walking in the night, a night that ovulated and wore horns.

She saw a figure approaching. Though all she could see was the bouncing whiteness of a shirt, something about the stride made her quite sure the wearer was a male. As he approached she could make out the details of the shape and face. It was Amaretto.

Sometimes there is no need for conversation, our bodies assert a primary dialogue quite free of spoken language. Some wilder, wanton spirit breaks out, and we remember part of us is animal still.

Suffice to say they knew each other, this was their keen intent and pleasure. And nobody was denied and the cock crowed thrice, there was a kiss exchanged. They both slept heavily that morn, and even as they slept alone, their sleeping solitude was sweet and sound, more than a medium for dreams, it was such nourishment you'd almost think it was a solid.

The next night she was waiting for him. This night they were more brazen. A warmth that carried smells from off their bodies. The warmth become a heat. It is true that the earth was soft and the imprints of their feet were soon replaced by the shapes of knees and the gentle curves of bums. Suffice to say they had their fill.

She waited for him on the third night. She waited until

she felt the chill come off the earth, and she was cold. She waited still. And then she walked back to the piggery and climbed in through the window. She was in bed and still felt cold, and closed her eyes but could not sleep. The cold was in her bones, as if it was her lover now, she shivered in her bed, got up and pulled a jumper on. Her feet were cold, she got back into bed and pulled her feet so they too were curled up in her jumper. Like a little chick in a woollen egg. Yet she stayed cold, and still she could not sleep.

Pestoso was alarmed by the changes he now saw in young Francesca. She started smoking openly around the house. She started tying up her hair, or then again letting it fall down across her shoulders, and had started wearing colour on her lips. She was becoming Woman before his very eyes, he had to say the sight of her was most unsettling.

# Il Mano Finto (The False Hand—An Ungrammatical Appendage)

In the days that followed his accident Costa was in shock. He remained in hospital under observation. He muttered in his sleep and woke from dreams where surgeons kissed while sipping amaretto.

Odd, those parts of life that happen in slow motion. Costa thought of this while thinking of his hand. Curious thing, waking with the impression that his missing hand was there. Cruel comfort, though, to clench the fingers of his hand only to find those fingers were not there. Propriokinesis. Was that the word the doctor used? He closed his eyes and remembered how the great metal blade had hovered, a quite strange act of levitation, the weight of it had overwhelmed the muscles of his back and shoulders and his arms and slowly floated to the earth, and in the slowest flash he'd seen he had been crippled.

Costa was lying in bed staring at the ceiling. Trying to distract himself from his grief and anger. What was the funniest thing he could think of?

He'd been repairing the broken slates of the church. After laying the slates he had rubbed earth into the spire, so that moss would grow and the spire and church would look old again. One of the tricks of the trade. From where he worked he had a mighty view of the town. Looking down he could see Amaretto's bar, and Terremoto's baking shop, the outline of the black tarantula just visible to him.

A funny thing. Every time he ascended to the spire he had a great need to piss. Given that it took him half an hour to reach that height, he was disinclined to climb all the way back down to have a piss. He'd discussed this

89

odd phenomenon with friends who worked at heights and found for each of them this thing was true: no sooner had they reached the heights than they'd need to piss.

One night, at sunset, his bladder begging for relief, he let himself dangle like a spider from his safety rope, hanging free in the wind, and let his water stream out into the night. Watching it fall, he'd had to laugh, an idiot giggling on a string. He hauled himself up the safety rope with two strong hands and arms, briefly surveyed the town, and then prepared to make the long climb back down.

It made him laugh to think.

His eyes now drifted downwards from the crack in the yellow ceiling and his laughter stopped as he saw again the stump of his left arm.

He turned away, and as he did his eyes returned to the curious hand made by Luigi. A freakish thing. He picked it up and felt its weight with his right hand.

He sat up in his bed, holding his breath. Gently he brought the curious hand towards the stump. He stopped, lifted it up, and smelt the leather pasted to the stump of the plaster hand. A pleasing smell, old leather, reminding him of horses and a woman he once knew. Their mingled sweat and a coupling by two horses tethered to a tree.

He brought the plaster hand back down and let it nuzzle the stump of his arm, the way a horse might nuzzle a trusted rider's hand. It fitted well, created its own illusion. He snorted out a horsy kind of grunt, a grunt that might have been a laugh.

Luigi had been talking about lizards.

'A lizard grows a tail. Might not a man grow back a hand to replace the one he's lost? Stranger things have happened!'

One of those infuriating things, once uttered, that become hard to put out of mind. Defying all logic, the outlandishness of the proposition becoming part of its magnetism. Lying looking at the crack in the roof over his head, thinking about lizards, dismissing the whole thing as a cruel prank, turning onto his side in disgust.

And yet the damn thing worried at him. Despite his

anger and scepticism he kept returning to it. His eyes would rove around the room, yet in the end his eyes would come to rest upon the plaster hand. The more he tried to put it out of mind, the more he found he couldn't take his eyes away.

It even had a name. *Il mano finto*. The hand he'd lost was *la mano sinistra*. The plaster hand ought not have the same name. And so he called this new appendage *il mano finto*, and even if its grammar was all wrong he hoped some good would come of it.

He closed his eyes. In his nostrils a fleeting smell of amaretto. He wondered if he could ever drink the stuff again without choking on the thought of amputation.

When he opened his eyes Luigi was standing by his bed. Costa wondered what to say. He decided to say nothing. Instead he let Luigi watch as he fitted the plaster hand in place.

'I haven't worked out how to make the fingers wiggle. Now tell me, what did you really have in mind when you made this thing?'

'The lizard in The Filing Cabinet has now got half a tail.'

Costa nodded with a grunt. He was fond of grunting. It seemed to him you could say more with a grunt than with a word.

'How does it fit?'

Costa lifted back the sleeve of his pyjama shirt. It fit so well that there was nothing to say.

'How long can you look at it without blinking?'

'Sometimes I can't take my eyes off it.'

'Good. Let's find out how long. Ready?'

Costa nodded once again, fixed his eyes onto the hand and locked his gaze into place.

After about a minute Costa blinked, though not before his eyes were squinting from the effort.

'Now close your eyes,' Luigi said. 'What can you see?'

To his surprise, Costa could see his missing hand, or, more truly said, Luigi's fine false hand. As if his third eye had seized this vital image and held it fleetingly yet firmly in his head.

At first Luigi's exercises gave him nothing but headaches, and Costa was only half convinced they were not a waste of time. Luigi assured him that the headaches were normal, and would soon pass. He was wrong. They got worse. As the headaches intensified, the pain gradually extended from Costa's head all the way down through his shoulder and arm to the stump of his wrist.

Despite the pain, he persisted with his meditations on Luigi's false hand. To his surprise he found that he was able to retain an image of *il mano finto* in his mind's eye, and to manipulate this invisible hand inside his head. He discovered in the movements of this false hand a subtlety and grace he had never known with his real hand. Or so it seemed to him then. He could spend hours each day, sitting in bed, manipulating this phantom appendage.

The stump of his arm had healed and sealed. No new hand had yet sprouted from the stump. Even so, Costa was intrigued by the possibilities as he performed exquisite ballets for one hand in his mind.

# The Darkling Features On The Wall

Francesca had spent the morning gathering firewood and enjoyed the sweaty work. She'd found a large fallen log in the overgrown orchard behind the piggery, had dragged it back, and chopped the log with a blunt axe she knew Emile had never handled.

The axe was in the musty storage shed behind the house. Emile never went in there. She'd never seen him do anything that resembled physical labour, and wondered if he'd known the joy of working his body hard enough to get the sweat out on his skin. She'd need a big supply of dry wood to keep her warm right through this winter. There was a lot of kindling in the orchard, and once she'd chopped the log into five pieces she spent an hour gathering twigs and small dead branches from the trees. She had enough wood for the night, perhaps even two or three days.

She'd also found an old and rusted metal stove in the storage shed. While the day was warm for winter, she lit her fire then. The flue leaked and the smoke crept into the piggery.

She could make do with that, and didn't mind the smoky smell. The old stove had held the remnants of the last fire lit in it; she'd cleaned the ash and lifted out the charcoal from the grate, putting the charcoal to one side for later use.

When she'd hauled the log and chopped it, she'd been surprised by the strength she found in her own body. It was this strength she wanted to communicate to the wall. Unsure how to begin, she decided to cover the entire wall with charcoal. This took her hours to achieve. Once done she started rubbing at the wall with her fingers, so that white spaces opened up among the field of charcoal. Before she knew it she'd drawn her father once again, and a strange hybrid of Emile, with a wine bottle for a body.

Each time she thought to attempt some likeness of herself she stopped, as if a hand came from the wall and held her own immobile, so that she could not complete, nor yet even begin, a primary self-portrait. She was dismayed to find that her supply of wood had already burnt, the afternoon now spent, and the prospect of a cold night without wood the most she could look forward to. She wondered if she should move back into the house, the comfort of it. And yet she would not. Nor would she move back to her father's.

There was always Amaretto's. The warmth of his cafe, and the room above the shop where he slept. There was no room for her, she knew, but the thought of Amaretto's was more appealing than a cold night on her own inside the piggery. She decided to walk into town, pay a surprise visit to her young man, perhaps she'd eat and leave, perhaps she'd stay the night. She did not care, she had a plan of action that would take her through the sunset and help her navigate the first half of the night, that was enough.

She left the smoked-out piggery and felt the comfort of the earth beneath her feet. She wore her old black woollen coat, the bristly feeling of the wool against her legs reminded her of the prickly feelings that had come when she'd first shaved her hair. There was little comfort in the memory, she picked her pace up then, and the clear intention in her was all she needed to feel at peace in her own world.

When she arrived at Amaretto's she found him cutting carrots for a large bowl of soup that slowly steamed on the stove. The great lid of the pot clinking as the steam forced its way out of the pot, pushing the lid up for a moment before it clinked back into place.

'You're just in time,' Amaretto said. 'Are you hungry?'

He didn't wait for her reply, but gathered two bowls and with a swift scoop of a ladle filled them to the brim. Holding a round loaf of bread, her father's own, Francesca sliced a large slab for Amaretto and, being hungry, decided that she'd cut one for herself. She had resisted the temptation of Gianni's bread for so long she was surprised to find her hunger overcome her lingering distaste for all things connected to her father. And then they sat, and ate their soup and bread. As she dipped the bread into her bowl and sopped the soup, she couldn't help but wonder how her father was getting on. Was he still seeing Sylvana?

She didn't really care. She felt she had already changed from the girl she'd been, and wasn't sure she'd recognise herself if she stepped back inside her father's place.

Was she better, worse, or merely different?

She looked again at Amaretto. He had already finished his soup and was wiping out the bowl with his bread. Something in his enthusiasm that displeased her. She felt him distant, as if he was not the same one she had known, and wondered what she might have to say to him.

Amaretto made no effort at conversation. He seemed preoccupied. Or was he merely grown evasive?

She finished her soup, and heard Amaretto rattling in the kitchen, the plopping sound of carrots as they hit the steaming soup, and the sharp, quick strokes he made while cutting chives for garnish. She didn't wait to thank him, nor did she wait to say goodbye. While his back was turned she quietly stepped out of the cafe into the night. Amaretto looked up then, as he heard the door slam shut. Surprised that she had come and gone—he'd thought she'd stay, they'd talk while he served customers, perhaps she'd stay the night. And yet he was relieved. He had already lost interest in Francesca.

# The Bride And Groom Ate Duck

Amaretto had never forgotten the first time he'd killed a goose.

His mother had bought a goose for Christmas, he had to pick it up and bring it home. For some reason he expected the goose would be already dead, but it was a live goose. When he got home his mother said 'Take that bird away and kill it.'

He didn't know how and for reasons he'd never fathomed he didn't ask for her advice. As if he had to prove himself in this. He put the goose under his arm and walked off. Only after he'd walked away from his mother's house and over the hill did he realise that he had no knife. He idly wondered if he'd swing the goose by its neck around his head then dash it on a rock. This seemed absurd, of course, but he was scared because he'd never killed a bird and felt a little nausea at the prospect of this odd crossing he must now make.

He tried to wring its neck, but if you've ever tried you'll know a goose has a most strong neck. And the goose was no passive observer of Amaretto's dilemma, he had to struggle just to keep the bird within his grasp, and while the man who'd sold the goose had been prudent enough to tie the wings, its feet and claws were working hard, and so was he, to defy those claws sharp purchase in his belly. In the end he'd found a stream and plunged the goose's head beneath the water, and held its head immersed right through the spasms, kicks and shivers, until at last the goose was dead. It took much longer than he expected, and exhausted him. He collapsed beside its downy carcass and wept. Then he washed his face in the same stream as the drowned bird's parting gesticulations, and walked home. The bird much heavier to hold now, as a corpse, than when it was a live and flapping thing.

Before they died Amaretto's parents had been universally hated. They owned too many geese. We only ate geese at weddings. A wedding would be measured by the number of geese we ate: 'It was a seventeen-goose wedding.'

You can feed a dozen people off one goose. Or you could eat one all yourself, if you had the capacity and the will. It's a greasy meat, some say it has an unpleasant odour, though others swear the flesh when well prepared is lean and subtle to the tongue and eye.

Amaretto's father made it a point of honour to buy up all the geese in the district. He paid well and became the goose monopolist.

He then refused to sell his geese.

Amaretto's father was planning, at the marriage of his son, to have the greatest slaughtering of geese there'd ever been, and had built up a flock of one thousand birds.

He wanted a veritable massacre of geese, and people started calling him Massacro.

People began to fret: it was essential to serve goose at the wedding feast. This was an ancient custom, the goose has always been associated with the fidelity of the union. We even had a proverb that spoke on this: 'The bride and groom ate duck.'

The duck is not a symbol of fidelity in marriage, and to say 'The bride and groom ate duck' is a gross slander, suggesting both bride and groom will indulge in frequent sexual congress with other partners.

People stopped making plans to marry. Or else they tried to steal some geese, so that the wedding was founded on a theft, a terrible wedding gift. If they married in defiance of the custom that demanded goose, the seed of doubt was quickly planted, and once planted that infidelity would occur, so these unions were clearly blighted.

There were scandalous rumours of alleged infidelities during the wedding feasts themselves, with either bride or groom or both consummating the wedding vows with best man, bridesmaid, and so on.

Massacro was the source of many of these rumours, a strategy to make the goose's presence at the wedding most essential.

And yet he would not sell his geese, and people baulked at serving duck or other fowl, nor was the flesh of goat, sheep, cow or fish considered suitable. The occasion demanded goose. But Amaretto's father was a malign man. He wanted to hold the grandest wedding for his son, with a glut of geese served at the wedding table, to show his worth and to exert some vaster moral authority.

A spurious thing, and a bastard logic. But he was a bastard, born well out of wedlock, and felt the stupid stigma of it, more in his own mind than in the mind of others. With us the tradition was to go to church when you knew the baby was well in the oven, so to speak. Were we backward people?

Massacro had placed a curse on all of us. He wanted the whitest wedding for his son, a wedding that would swim with gooseflesh, and sail upon a sea of white goose feather. Amaretto was no candidate for a wedding. At the peak of his father's mania the boy was just fourteen.

Massacro was a terribly unfaithful husband. When his name arose in conversation people nodded, and then someone would spit and say, 'What would you expect? The bride and groom ate duck.'

A name can be a heavy burden. The weight of it began to tell on poor Massacro. His wife and child also began to bear the brunt of it, becoming known as Massacretta and Massacrino, this last of course for Amaretto. Amaretto Massacrino. A lethal nomenclature. It killed those geese, and it killed Massacro and his wife.

How did Massacro die? It was quite banal. In a bar one night he boasted of his feathered empire. A frustrated groom challenged him, a fight broke out, and for his efforts Massacro received a sharp knife between the ribs.

Massacretta, attempting to avenge the death of her husband, attacked the man who'd stabbed him, and managed to scrape her claws across his face. The killer's wife then grabbed Massecretta by the hair and quickly jerked her head back. Massacretta fell and, in the fall, broke her neck. Her throat was cut for good measure. Thus Amaretto lost both his parents within minutes. Those who knew Massacro and Massacretta best suggested that the boy had known a stroke of great fortune on that day.

# The Whole World Upside Down

Walking home in the darkness, Francesca was surprised how easily she'd turned her back on Amaretto. She wondered why she'd gone there, perturbed that she'd found it easier to take herself to town than stay at home. Without being aware of it, her pace had quickened, as if she was eager for some vital confrontation.

She stopped to gather any larger piece of wood that caught her eye, that she might enjoy the warmth of a smoking fire when she got home. She made a wide circle around Pestoso's house.

The piggery door was ajar. He's been in here, she thought, and looked for footprints in the soft earth.

She lit a candle and could see no trace of Emile, and felt a disappointment. Finding the company of anyone, even Emile, preferable to her own. For a moment she felt that she could cry, but instead she strode with renewed purpose to the cold metal stove, opening the shutter of the stove's belly, hoping to find some sparks among the ash. The grate bereft of heat.

She gathered up a bundle of the smallest sticks, one larger piece of wood, and with her free hand grabbed the candle. The woopsy shadows as the candle travelled with her through the room.

Stacking the twigs in the grate, arranging them to make a pyramid. Lighting the pile, watching the flame now start to take, she blew the candle out. The encompassing darkness of the room brought her a pleasure.

She started drawing as the stove cast its dim light, creating shadows. She was drawing without thinking, and remembered the pleasure she'd discovered when she first scrawled her crude designs.

Her hand swimming among shadow as she attempted her tenuous dawdling toward herself. Stepping out of time, returning to it when the fire burnt low, feeding the wood into the stove's hot mouth, and returning to her dindling. Loving each and every minute.

The piggery was full of a smoky fog, the fire starving her brain of oxygen. Dulling her. Yet she enjoyed the smoke. Stepping outside to get some air. The night sky full of stars.

She could see a pair of legs striding through heaven, and a great sword held high above the head, striking down and cutting through her.

She stepped back and disappeared into the smoky depths of her room. The glowing embers of the fire warmed her hands. She felt at peace, and fell asleep beside the fire.


When Francesca woke she felt cold. Stepping outside, the morning dew made her feet wet. The twigs and leaves she gathered were also wet. She'd persevere.

Her damp socks making mud of the piggery dust. Lighting the candle with her matches. The first match breaking in her fingers, the second flaring briefly before fizzing out. The third match burning truly.

She looked over to the wall. There was Sylvana, and there was Gianni underneath her, copulating in the bakery. There was Emile, masturbating in his bed with a wine bottle stuck up his bottom. Costa was digging in the garden and held her menses cloth for everyone to see. An upside-down tree grew from the roof and spread its branches to the ground. The figures that she drew sprouting like strange fruit among these branches.

Looking away, baulking at further inspection. She lit the fire then, relieved to see the small flames burning.

Lifting the pitcher to her lips, letting water gush into her throat. The water swelling her belly, as if for now it was the only thing she'd need to eat.

She'd turned the whole world upside down and etched its darkling features on the wall.

It was a vulgar work, you'd hardly say it was well drawn.

Etching in the outlines of a world, putting her self in, if only at the margins.

A kind of purgatory she saw. Amaretto she had drawn as a hairless goat. She'd been surprised, around his pubis there had been no hair at all, and she herself had been shaved bare. The goat had a small stiff penis and a leery smile. Francesca stood behind; reaching underneath she milked this young he-goat, and his milk shot out like a whitened stream into a metal pail.

# Zanetti

Costa felt quite lost. Perhaps that was why he persisted with the regime Luigi had imposed.

He began by staring at the hand for five minutes, then closing his eyes while trying to retain the precise image of it in his mind's eye. Over time he was to increase the length of his manual meditations, all the while trying to provoke the idea of regrowth at the end of the stump. He felt alternately hopeful and stupid, yet persevered. He didn't know what else to do.

He had not realised how much of his image of himself was bound to the hand he'd lost. As if part of himself had been repudiated. A violation of his image of himself. This knowledge sat uncomfortably with him as he sat up in his bed and stared out of the window.

He saw a woman's head bob into the window frame and disappear. He scarcely had time to ask himself if his eyes were playing tricks before he saw the head bob into view again, and then a third time, before it disappeared.

It was not unlike the travelling head of a young girl jumping as she walked with a skipping rope, except the head, while small, was not the head of a girl. It was a woman's head. Short black hair. Small ears. Pia Zanetti.

Pia Zanetti had lost her leg while rehearsing for a production of *Aida*—she was one of the extras. They'd been rehearsing one of the big parades when an elephant panicked and knocked over the replica of the Sphinx, which was the central ikon of the set. She'd made the papers: ACTRESS CRUSHED BY SPHINX!

The Sphinx had crushed her leg, which was then

103

amputated. Her leg had started turning black from the toes, slowly continuing along the foot and ankle. Once the blackness passed the knee there was no option, and the doctors had removed the entire leg. Pia also knew Luigi Bacheretti.

Luigi loved picking flowers, and had developed quite a reputation among the people whose carefully tended gardens crossed his path. He couldn't help himself, the ire of gardeners made no mark on him—he would just look and stare until they wondered, Was he deaf? He knew no shame in this. Eloquent of finger, he could pick flowers so quickly from a bush the very speed at which he picked was like a dance that held the viewer captive, or at least it stilled the rage until the deed was done. Luigi was not a man to come and visit empty-handed. He moved around the hospital corridors giving out flowers, and in this way he met Pia Zanetti. She never thought her life would change by meeting an idiot who had come to give her flowers.

He walked into her room, his smile lit up the whole of him, it bespoke a kind of trust. He was holding out a clumsy bunch of red geraniums. She didn't need to ask 'Are these for me?' but she did, and then felt such a fool. Luigi handed her the flowers and was already shuffling out when Pia said, 'Oh, look at that!'

A centipede was crawling up the wall.

'It seems unfair,' she said, 'I've lost a leg and look at her, she's got a hundred.'

With surprise she heard this man who'd given flowers say, 'Not everyone would know the sex of a centipede, you must have seen the nippers at the back. A centipede's a friendly thing, they never bite, at least not one that's ever bitten me,' and then he gently picked it off the wall and placed it on the palm of his hand, that the pair of them might have a closer look.

The young man looked at her, his dark brown eyes the colour of nuts. 'Roll over,' he said.

She did so without thinking. He ran a gentle finger down her spine.

'This was the great invention. How did the worm

become the spinal cord? The thing we have in common with lizards, dogs and monkeys, a part of us that's also part of fish and snake. Somehow the inner water has become a thinking fluid, full of electric pulses that flash with an intelligence. A blinking worm in a bone or armour.

'The earthworm is a monopede. A leg that has taken possession of an entire corpus. It's an extreme idea taken to its logical conclusion. And, as usual when logic is taken to extremes, it no longer makes sense. For the monopede—the "one leg"—cannot walk. It can only wriggle.

'The centipede is the pinnacle in the evolution of the concept of legness. More than any other creature it celebrates the idea, Leg.

'Did the centipede create the leg, or did the idea Leg, existing in some other dimension, summon up the centipede, giving flesh, form and substance to its very idea of itself?'

Pia was speechless.


Pia spun her bum on the edge of the bed like a pivot. It felt funny to have only one leg. She placed her foot on the ground, her toes spreading across the floor as her weight came over the foot. The supple mechanics of it.

The rim of her stump on the bedside disturbed her thoughts. She shifted her weight, wiggling her bum forward. Surprised to find that she could walk on her buttocks. She bumwalked backwards on the bed, then bumwalked forward, like a baby lost in the discovery of her body.

Her foot found the floor and she began to sway from heel to toe. She rocked like a pendulum, swung in the hammock of herself. Her breath falling out of her body as she rocked forward; a moment of suspension, then the air filled her up and carried her back. The air was breathing her, and as she breathed the air gave her a voice.

As if she was rocking herself into a trance, or orgasm, for her sighs now formed with an intensity that came from deep inside her.

As she rocked she observed the moment of suspension

before she rocked back the other way. At that moment time was still, and she was all control, all balance.

She rocked forward once again, then suddenly stopped.

She was standing on one leg, balanced like a stork, the very thing she had been aiming for. It was a different sense of balance, doubled on one leg. But to have caught it now brought her great satisfaction.

She heard herself grunt, and felt the beginning of a laugh trembling like a lover's hand on her belly. With her next breath she took a tiny hop, refound her balance, then hopped again, a sparrow among breadcrumbs.

Slowly she straightened up. She was hopping around the room, a thing she hadn't done before. This strange new balance on one leg. As she moved in tiny leaps she felt some fine thing move inside, as if her insides were dropping and leaping upwards at the same time. She let this feeling go and began to laugh, her laughter threw her off her balance; she banged her head and knee against the wall and hit the ground, still laughing, rolling backward, one legged awkward, holding her knee, her eyebrow bleeding, laughing and then crying on the floor.

I'm starting from the beginning, she thought. Learning how to walk. Strange feeling. Have to listen to myself. Don't know I've done it much before. Always been a raucous bugger. Curious sounds I make. Almost swear it's a new voice to fit with a new body.


It was Luigi who introduced her to Stefano Costa. Costa and Zanetti were a funny pair. Each afternoon they'd walk along the path from the hospital to the rose garden, Zanetti leaning on Costa while she hopped and hobbled on her leg, her arm around his waist.

It was a short walk, perhaps one hundred metres, yet it could take them twenty minutes to cover this ground. Pia found the effort exhausted her.

'The only leg I've got,' she would complain, 'and all it is is flab and bone, no muscle!'

Costa was trying to pick a white rose. His fingers were

clumsy, he bent the stem but couldn't break it from the bush. He tried again, his fingers worrying at the bloom, and succeeded in shaking off the outer petals. Shit and damnation! His fingers pricked by thorns.

He bent forward, bringing his nose to the flower. Its heady scent. Without thinking, he used his thumb to push away two thorns then simply bit the stem, and turned around to face Zanetti, the white rose and its green stalk in his mouth like an unusual roseate cigarillo. He was blushing again. God damn this woman who made him feel a fool. The contrast of the whiteness of the rose against the blooded, hooded redness of his face. Then they were laughing.

'Don't move!' said Pia.

She hopped over to him. She was laughing freely, and there was a charming wicked light that lit her eyes. She brought her face to meet Costa's. He was the taller of the two and she had to place both hands onto his hips to let her rise up on the toes of her one leg.

She placed her lips against the stem of this white flower, and for a moment their lips met before she plucked the rose from Costa's mouth. He held her close and took the rose back from her mouth. Or tried, but she resisted, a thorny tug of war for lips and rose, the thorns cutting the skin, so that the pair of them now found fine cuts in the flesh of the face that looked at them from such close range.

Costa took the rose away with his good hand, and then they were licking fine blood tears from the other's mouth.

'I think it would be a bad idea for us to fall in love.' Pia's voice, falling like a shadow on his face.

'Did you know that the open rose is a symbol of orgasm?' Zanetti, speaking again.

# Sylvana, Swollen

Sylvana was feeling edgy. Walking home from the bakery, her boots pinching her feet. Her feet swollen. She'd spent the morning with Gianni, only to find that she and Gianni had started arguing. They seemed to spend more time arguing than making love these days. He'd reminded her of a time when she'd once said, 'When are we going to make love again? It's already been three days!' This in the blooming passion of their first weeks together. Gianni had meant it as a joke, yet the recollection had unsettled them both. Their lovemaking, now much less frequent, felt more like a habit than a joy. They both made excuses, Gianni more concerned about his baking than lovemaking, where once he was happy to postpone his labours for what he termed his sweeter duties. Sylvana found she was more inclined to talk, or busy herself sweeping floors, than touching up her man. If they lay on the old wooden bench she kept expecting to see Francesca standing in the doorway, ogling them with her mouth open. When she mentioned this to Gianni that morning he'd suggested she lean against the oven, or the floor, convinced the problem was in their choice of location and position. It made Sylvana angry. As she began to raise her voice she was appalled to discover that she sounded like her mother arguing with her father. The thought derailed her, and she had walked out without another word. Her last sight of Gianni had been disconcerting, his shoulders were hunched up and he seemed to be seething with a rage he could not express. As she slammed the back door behind her she was sure she heard Gianni farting with an ostentatious volume, echoing her slamming. Despite her anger, she could not help laughing.

By the time she'd walked home she couldn't bear the pains in her feet any more. Her feet were swollen so she pulled her boots off, glad to be unshod. With her workboots on she was ready to meet the world, now she'd slipped them off she felt a curious vulnerability. Recalling that her first boots had been sewn by her mother, using the hide of an old goat tanned by her father. Her mother stitching the tough hide with bare hands, cursing every time she poked the needle into her hand. She'd never made boots before, but had decided her daughter needed boots. She'd seen three snakes in the hills and it was not yet high summer. The girl could not go scrambling round the rocks in bare feet during such a season. The soles of the boots were made from several layers of goathide glued then nailed together like a stubborn pancake. They were good boots, once Sylvana wore them in and lost the blisters on the back of her heels. The soles of her feet already hardened by her habit of walking barefoot.

She still had those old boots—when she'd outgrown them she didn't want to part with them. They reminded her of some aspect of her mother that she loved, even admired, and helped offset the more difficult memories she harboured.

Sylvana's mother had a strange knack of always preparing for the worst. Convinced that if she did not protect her daughter's feet, the lass would be dead from snakebite before the end of the season. If Sylvana announced her intention to go walking in the hills, her mother would insist on packing a small bag with a waterproof sheet in case it rained, despite the fact that the sky was cloudless and it never rained in the dry season. She'd pack a ball of string, matches, some dried fruit and dried tomatoes, an old crust of bread, a candle stub, believing it necessary at all times to be ready for disaster. Sylvana had learnt that it was futile to argue over this.

Her mother had been born with an erratic temperament and sometimes disappeared for days. Her father saying 'She's got business in town,' though on her return her mother never spoke of it. At other times her father would say 'She's had to visit a sick aunt,' though Sylvana was not aware that such an aunt existed. If she asked for details she was told to stop being bothersome, or dispatched to the vegetable garden to pick zucchini flowers or basil.

It was not until after her mother's death that Sylvana learnt her mother had been periodically hospitalised, or else went on sprees that could last several days, before she came home feeling wearied and disgusted. Cursing her weakness, never quite believing that she was ill.

Her father had spared her some details, yet preferred that Sylvana hear the truth from his lips, rather than learn of it through some stranger's gossip.

'I don't know why her depression fuelled her sexual appetite. When she came out of it she'd feel dazed, wondering why she'd spent the night with two or three men in a cheap hotel. I didn't like it, yet I preferred it to visiting her in hospital. So she ran away three or four times a year and had sex with men I hope I never meet. She didn't know why. Why did I put up with it? Because I was sworn to her in sickness and in health. I loved her, even when I was appalled by her actions, and my inability to help her. What would you have done?'

Sylvana knew her mother could be a creature of alarming honesty at times, seemingly unaware that she'd overstepped some limit of propriety. Sylvana was never sure if this was a virtue or an abberration.

'Every time a man comes it takes a day off his life,' she'd told Sylvana once. 'I think about it whenever your father comes inside me. There goes another day! On our wedding night I took a week off his life. I can't help feeling that the more I enjoy the man, the more I'm slowly killing him!'

The young Sylvana had been so confounded she'd been unable to do anything more than stare at her mother, mouth open, trying not to ogle. Sylvana wondered then if this was the very look Francesca had given her as she watched the pair of them coming on the bench.

# Pietra!

Given that many people in the town already knew Pia Zanetti, and that her unfortunate encounter with the Sphinx had made the front page of the papers, there was great curiosity when word got out that she was about to star in her first solo dance spectacular.

This curiosity was fuelled by the fact that she would only have one leg to dance on. How might this be achieved? Propelled by this speculation the first night quickly sold out. And then the second, and the third. She was a hit before she'd even hopped on stage.

On her way to the theatre for the opening night she saw a sign outside the box office that made her laugh. It seemed quite apt. 'Standing Room Only'.

She nodded to Luigi, who was selling tickets. He gave a thumbs-up sign and called out as she started hopping up the stairs, 'Break a leg!'

She opened the door to the dressing room and turned on the light. It was cold, a draught blew in from an unsealed window. She dropped her things onto the table, threw her bag on the floor and sighed. She was about to sit down when she caught sight of herself in the full-length mirror: she looked pale and tired, quite tense. Was she feeling apprehensive? No, that wasn't quite the word.

She was terrified. Why had she ever let it come to this?

It had seemed such a simple thing. Things at their beginnings, their consequences having no form. She had the runs, which seemed unjust, that her bowels could run when she herself could not. She hadn't thought of it before, that she would never run again. It was not a brilliant way to feel before the start of her show. She was on show. She was afraid. She wondered if she'd dare sneak a quick glimpse through the curtains at the people in the house. She knew that if she did she'd never have the courage to go on.

Zanetti's muscly leg was quite a sight. When she flexed her leg, or stood and hopped along, it was like a rock. She had given her leg a name, Pietra. The female rock, perhaps, on which she'd resurrect the new church of herself.

Thus it came as no surprise that she gave her leg top billing. 'Pia Zanetti presents PIETRA!' Her leg stood out. It was, she thought, the upper case of her own self. As if her leg had become her first and finest creation.

It wasn't just the muscle, or the bristle—she refused to shave her leg. This leg has form, she told herself, as well as content. This leg is the strong leg of a strong woman. It deserves to dance all on its own!

This thought led to what was without a doubt the funniest part of her first show. She had a black box made out of fabric, and in it, out of sight, there was a chair and arm supports and handles, and in the fabric there were slits through which she could disport her leg.

To their surprise the audience could see nothing but a black box on a stage. Then, slowly, just the twinkling of a toe, then all five toes were winking. Out of this modest start Pia slowly built to a crescendo of leggy folly and candour. This was truly a celebration of her leg. A ballet for one leg alone. No-one had seen such a fine and stupid thing, it was preposterous.

Inside her black box Pia smiled at the sound of laughter, then found that she too was laughing—she knew right then the show was a success. That communality of release which laughter brings, and the acceptance. She started improvising new details. Oh my God, she thought, Pietra is a hit! Not only that, she's a show-off too!

Pia finally appeared on stage with her arms firmly by her sides, a pink ballet slipper on her foot, with pink ribbon laces entwined and wrapped around her leg like a festive vine, disappearing underneath a ridiculous pink tutu. Her leg was otherwise bare. So were her arms and head and chest. Her small breasts bouncing as she bobbed and hopped. She looked for all the world like a jumping skittle. Or like a woman who was all leg.

A ludicrous sight. Yet something more than that. For every impulse people had to laugh, there was something else which took their breath away. This was a shocking image, a diva dancing on one leg. And as she danced she sang, but she wasn't singing a song. Her song was the sound she made while moving, as if her leg was talking as it made its odd perambulation round the stage. A sound that tottered, teetered, stuttered then found voice. Long-winded sighs turned into moans.

All the sounds so often bitten off, held back behind clenched teeth, these were the sounds that she released. Each person saw and heard parts of themselves in Pia and that awesome leg, her fine Pietra. Their laughter became another thing, a holding breath that turned to sighs, in the belly a tender impulse flickering and vibrating, and what vibrated was the beginning of a sob.

It was quite a show.

After the first performance she was exhausted. She wondered if she'd overdone it, carried away by the exaltation and the triumph of her dancing one-legged body.

And so it was that Costa piggybacked her home. She clung to him, and he enjoyed the calm weight of her body, her single leg clamped around his thigh. He was surprised how light she felt to carry. Even so, by the time they arrived he was sweating hard.

When they got inside the door, just as he planned to set her down, she said, 'Oh God, I think . . . if you'd be so kind, I'll have to ask you if you'd carry me to the bed.'

One request with which Stefano Costa was most happy to comply.

# What She Fantasized,
## And Why They Stuck Together

It was hard, feeling she was deformed, to be sexually assertive. The ruptured image of her. A part of her felt ashamed, as if through having lost a leg she had violated the essence of her woman's life. So it was with trepidation that she took his hand and placed it on her thigh. Would he be disgusted? She went to turn off the light, then stopped herself. If he could not live with this, the sight of her just as she was, then she wanted no part of him.

At times she'd fantasized about pouring champagne straight from the bottle over her breasts, belly and thighs, in this way quenching the thirst of her lover, busy lapping between her legs. But she doubted this fantasy would come true, and thought perhaps it was best that way.

'Here,' she said, 'I'll pour you a drink,' running a fine trickle of liqueur over her nipple. He drank, smelling her skin, the soft heat of her breast, and the sharp and sweet aroma of oranges came in his mouth. He admired her audacity, and the freedom she had.

Pia licked her bottom lip, and the line made by her eyes down to his crutch betrayed her appetite.

'Have you ever made love to a woman with one leg?'


They were so gentle with each other. This was the thing that he loved best. As if, after the violence of their recent pasts, this was their moment of reprieve, a time of tenderness.

The soft down of her upper thigh, the hairs standing up, a charge of static in the bed. He'd never slept with such a fine and hairy woman. He'd always thought a hairy

114

woman to be coarse, but she was not, this downy creature called Pia. Short for Piacere? Something more than pleasure.

The soft thigh down became a pleasing bed of pubic furze, in which the fingers of his hand entwined, as if from these fine threads he might begin to weave some magic thing, though what could be more wondrous than the thing itself? Her scented hair and the smoothest skin of her flesh below, beneath the nest, and the many secrets of the life inside the body. Pouring himself into the funnel of his love.

She traced a line along the inside of his palm, the thrill of it, and it seemed to him he'd never known such intimacy. She curled her fingers around the middle finger of his hand and gave a squeeze, and he wondered if he was not about to come. He sucked, and felt the soft whole of her breast fill 'up the inside of his mouth.

Her shape conformed just like a fluid. 'Oh God,' he heard her say. Her voice gone deep and rough. If he inhaled the last small part of her breast into his mouth, might he not gag or choke? How much of her could he hold inside him?

Astonished that he could suck all of her breast into his mouth. He heard her breath, its subtle shift, and slowly loosened his grip of air, released her teat, wetslick and slow, could not resist, and sucked the tip back in. Surprised to find it just slid in; the way his tongue admired the hardened dimples.

He loved this game. Giving his head to pleasure. The slippery curd of her, and his saliva. He'd never dared go further than the nipple, but this was a new and fine estate he'd swallowed up, and he wondered what ancient fear had held him from this pleasure in the past.


He saw her fingers fumbling by the bed, watched as she stuck a cigarette into her mouth, blew out some smoke then sucked it back in through her nose. She hadn't smoked for years but she hadn't forgotten any of it, either. The fine plumes drifting up inside her nostrils. He took the cigarette from her, their fingers just touching, then he took a cautious puff, with no thought to mimic the filtered acrobatics she had made.

'What's it like, being a woman?'

The smoke drifting and then lifting like a curtain between them, the dim outlines of their torsos propped on elbows. Pia took the cigarette from his fingers, enjoying a last drag before she stubbed it out, then responded to his question.

'Which would you rather be, man or woman?'

'I'd rather be a woman. And you?'

'I'd rather be a man.'

'You mean we're both inside the wrong bodies?'

'I think yours is pretty nice.'

'I was going to say the same.'

'Thank you, darling.'

They kissed. He heard a noise.

It had never occurred to him that a woman, too, might fart in bed. He wasn't sure of the courtesies involved, goose and the gander, yet what provoked him most of all was something more than smell. The ripened life of the interior? Perhaps it was a simple thing: that there was much more to a woman than that which met the eye.

He was not thinking of her sex, but of those other aspects, the clumsy parts we try to hide.

He couldn't help but make a small laugh through his nose.

'What?' she asked.

He wondered if he dared tell her the truth.

'It's the first time I've had a philosophical intuition triggered by a fart.'

Her mouth was open, she was lost for words, blushing right down to her breasts, he found that most enhancing, this blush that ran down her face and neck onto her breasts. He couldn't help himself, he rolled onto his side, he meant to stroke her, but as he moved he accidentally farted.

'You dirty bugger!' she said, and punched him firmly in the shoulder.

'You rotten bitch!' he answered, and pummelled his fist into the firm flesh of her shoulder, not violently but with a strength of provocation, an understanding of the game. She grabbed him by the balls. He felt rather flushed and wondered if his face was turning white, the ancient fear and apprehension.

'Do that again, I dare you!' Pia said.

He punched again. She squeezed a little harder, he felt his fear relax and something in him stiffen up. Quite an agreeable sensation. A curious trust. He did not mind that she had him by the balls.

'You bastard,' she said. He felt comfortable with this. The violent edge was familiar and somehow easier to accommodate than their intimacy.

'You're a very beautiful woman.'

'Don't think you can wriggle out of this so easy!' and she laughed. 'I'd really like to feel you inside me.'

This was another kind of flight, another miracle of the body. A transcendence, the very nature and the essence of a coming. A coming into what or out of where he did not know.

Pia started laughing gently as she came, a warmth inside her body and her voice unlike any love that Costa had known before. He was infected by her laughter, the pair of them in a funny love-filled tremor that shook the bed with the mirth of their embrace.

Singing the praises of his god as he now came, hearing in her voice a magic that released a fine erotic spring in him.

PART THREE:


# HER CHILDHOOD NOW ENDING

# Making Water In The Church

Emile Pestoso was an unusual prophet. Something had soured in his view. You'd swear that if he looked into a bucket of fresh milk he'd turn it into sour cream, or yoghurt. But perhaps that is a gift. For even as his vision soured, it still captured something quite wonderful. Not many men will tell you they've clapped eyes on God's own Mother. Emile was sure he had. The Holy Mother is more often seen by women, and young girls. She came to Emile early one morning. At first he thought it was a dream. He didn't dare to pinch himself, for the disrespect he'd pay the Holy Mother standing by him, as he lay in the narrow confines of his bed. Needless to say it was a single bed. Surely it wouldn't do, to see the Holy Mother in a double bed. Emile was sleeping soundly, he woke up and there she was—the Blessed Virgin standing by him. It was no dream. And yet, he knew, he had been dreaming.

Around him the masses of his parish had been crawling on their knees, which were lacerated by the ancient stones of the cobbled street. Emile was hanging from a cross, blood ran from the bleeding sockets of his eyes. He'd put them out in the service of his god.

The people sang his name in a monotone dirge. He announced that soon he would annoint himself and restore his eyes to sight.

His flock was growing until it spread beyond the borders of the town. The members of his flock began to cover their faces and flesh with dirt, adding filth to filth. Rough hands of dirt and gravel to lacerate the skin and bring a fine and soothing penitential trance. Like lambs on a muddy bank they were a dirty daggy flock. He had the scissors now to cut their flyblown dags right off.

It was a happy dream. He hardened up beneath the folds of his night frock.

Young lambs with heads of girls and old men leapt into his arms, he raised his scissors and cut their tails and threw them down, they scampered off. One by one he clipped them all, he cut the tail and now an ear, then an old and wrinkled nose, and then a foot.

Beneath him the sacred mound of severance grew like manna. It was turning into bread and he exclaimed 'Eat your fill.' They ate the curious shaped rolls of bread and Good Father Pestoso began to laugh. He annointed his fingers in the blood of his eyes and cried out, 'Now Father, that I might see.'

Just a blackness. He opened his eyes. Through the blinds of his room he could perceive the greyer streak of the first morning light. Pestoso dreamt in black and white. Even then he dreamt but rarely. His narrow bed was sagged and bowed. A constant ache in the lower lumbar was the legacy of the poor condition of his sleep and he swore at the bed. He lifted himself onto his elbows with the enthusiasm of a corpse. It was five o'clock. Another day in paradise.

That's when the Virgin came to him.


Costa wanted to go to church that morning. He was not a religious man, and felt sure that he and Pestoso could not be praying to the same god. Even so, the small stone church seemed to be the place to house his thoughts. It was cold outside, and even colder inside the church. He knelt down in a front pew, the comforting cushion set for prayer beneath his knees. He closed his eyes.

It struck him as odd that he might give thanks for giving up his hand. How could he give thanks for such a loss? And yet he felt himself to be a lucky man.

He closed his eyes, and promptly fell asleep.

When he awoke he was surprised to find the church

was nearly full. It was a small church, and while the church's belly was not packed, it had its belly full.

At the pulpit Emile was wondering what to say. He cast his eyes around the pews. They seemed a savage flock, even those of good intent, and without willing it his eyes replayed in starts and fits the image of his shepherd's dream, the mangy flock before him now. He tried to cast this canny dream out of his mind, but it stuck fast.

He'd thought to raise the point of better heating in the church, but this clear agenda was obscured by a greater text, its words unformed, that he must now express. He clasped his hands around the pulpit, leaning forward and rising slightly on his toes as he drew breath. He was, he knew, a commanding figure, and somehow he never sniffed or coughed while in this pose. One of the miracles of his life, as if just for these moments he attained a deeper access to himself.

His nose and sniffs behaved themselves. He saw the image of the Virgin standing quietly by his bed, heard the peaceful sacred music of her voice, and felt that awe, that fear, of being lifted from the ordinary to the sublime. This was not face to face with God, but God's ambassador at least, and it was certainly close enough to God's own face for him.

He heard his voice, and as the first tones rang around the walls of the stony church, he felt the great relief of the congregation, as if they'd held their breath with him, the whole church stifled, and now that he'd begun to speak and breathe there was a kind of peace there too. This peace quickly disappeared, as the godly import of his message became clear.

'This morning I had a vision of the Virgin.'

He paused. He felt their many eyes on him, and once again it seemed that not one breath now stirred the air of this holy place. He swallowed, and saw a chorus of larynxes and Adam's apples rise and fall with him. If he held his silence now it was not for dramatic effect, but simply because he didn't know if he dared go on. But having announced with such conquering ease his vision, he knew there could be no going back, no time to falter. He swallowed once again then found his voice.

'She came to me as a headless woman.'

He had a great desire to tug his collar, instead he gripped his knuckles hard around the pulpit's woooden rim. A long deep breath. He let the air inflate him from his belly to his chest, as if the air drew him up and made him longer. Imposing. His jaw was firm, quite rigid, and he could feel the indentations of the molars, his solid bite. He heard a small sound, a single whimper, as the straining silence started to push his audience beyond its comfort. He did not know what else to say. Knew he couldn't leave it there. A clearing of throats. Sounds of discomfort. He turned his head, the church stock still. Leaning forward a little, a confidential thing, the awe and wonder of it, the blessed shadow cast by the robes of office, the mysterious priestly duties.

'She said "God wants another child, a girl this time." She said she wanted nothing of it. "I'll not cast my fruit upon the earth and have it trampled by the herd."'

His own confusion and perplexity showed itself now as his forehead conjured up a row of horizontal wrinkles, with a small indentation in the centre, as if it was the well from which his several wrinkles ran. As one he saw the many brows in many pews also wrinkle, as though they had been set a common problem.

'What is the meaning of this dream?'

His voice so quiet, a whisper in the dark. Some voices made their own involuntary refrain, chorus of smallest sighs, the very problem of it so defined and yet so difficult to grasp. Or were they whimpers? The whimpers of some innocent?

'In protest at her role she cut her head off as I watched, and let it fall into a basket. She did not take her eyes off me, let me confess I found this disconcerting.'

He licked his lips, the many tongues in church joining spontaneously in this gesture, the curious privacy of it, each person acting on their impulse, knowing that in this they were unseen, except of course by the one above, who could see all and everything. Watching his flock. Who now continued.

'She said that she was looking for an honest man or woman, someone who lived life in God's truth, whose first miracle would be the reconnection of her severed cranium.'

He wondered if perhaps he'd said enough. A massive sigh spent from his lungs, his belly pushing out its air— almost, he'd swear, he felt a soft breeze on his face, the wind of his own congregation breaking gently, a waft of garlic, not quite unpleasant. Something improved by distance.

He froze. He'd let his eyes roam round the church, taking his congregation in. His eyes had strayed to Costa's stump, plumped on the top rail of a pew in front of him. This stump seemed some kind of signal. At any rate it held him fast. The grip of the missing hand more powerful than the muscles of his eyes.

Prodigious silence, a silence in which the only sound was one of rippling thought, a sound so quiet the ear hears nothing of report. Pestoso felt the great blood in his chest beating, a mighty surge of it roaring in his ears like a pounding wave, his tongue prised free of the jaw bone, and now a quick torrent of words, each one it seemed was fastened to the missing hand, as if a swarm of bees had found their queen and held to her.

'I'll tell you what it is, this mighty thing, this apparition sent by God to speak to us, this faithful vision of the Most Holy Mother of us all.

'Saint Francis cut the hair from the head of beloved Santa Chiara, and she became the first nun of his order. And Saint Francis told us clear we must renounce the fear that binds us to our possessions in this world, compared to them what we'll possess in the world that waits . . .'

He dragged his eyes away as Costa, unsettled by this talk, had dropped his hand and stump onto his lap.

Pestoso's voice had lost its roar.

'How can we say what they might be?'

He'd lost his impetus. Unworldly thoughts crammed in, and worldly thoughts as well. He saw Francesca sitting quiet

in her row, wearing white gloves, and he could not help
but think upon the spotted redness of her menstrual blood.
This disturbed him, and he feared that he'd cough or have
to wipe a running nose on the sleeve of holy office.

'No!'

He was surprised to hear the power of his voice, it
startled him. This mighty negative he affirmed bounced off
the walls like a rock and there were gasps and held-in groans
that now escaped, as if this rock had struck the mortals in
their place, and hurt them too.

'How could we reduce our Holy Mother to this estate?
It is so clear to me, this vision, it speaks to every one of
us! It's not enough to just renounce the worldly possessions
we amass, it's not enough to renounce the many pitfalls of
the flesh, their passions and vast temptation, not even this
much will suffice! The time has come! The time has come
indeed! We must renounce the very flesh itself!'

He wondered what had got hold of him. He felt he was
a man possessed, he saw the crowding, mangy flock of his
dream, and saw again the mighty shears he raised, the scissor
blades making the shape of holy cross.

Costa placed his stump once more onto the pew, and
Pestoso knew he could not stop, though as he spoke part
of him wondered what drove him on.

Costa himself was pondering this, and the way his life
had gone, the giving of a hand. Perhaps he had given it to
divine service? So many things had stemmed from that, as
if the blood that flowed out of his hand had flowed back
into other parts of his life. Costa lifted up his eyes. Emile's
eyes met his.

'One hand can hold much less than the many wonders
of a life.'

It seemed a single vision passed between the two. Emile
looked away, astonished by the power in his own voice.

He was thinking on the warrior priests who would go
to battle on the strength of their own faith. The thought
consoled him.

'How much is any human life worth? And a hand, a
single hand—what is its value? Who dares test the waters

of the greatness that they know is part of them? Mediocrity and cowardice as ways of life are so much simpler.'

There was a common grievance in the church.

It brought a moisture to the eye, some salty thing that baffled, bathed and stung at once and brought more moisture on, in the way that water has, once there's a drop you'll soon find there's a river.

Pestoso trembled as he watched, and he was moved to see his flock brought face to face with the hard knowledge of their god.

He felt that sadness, another member of the straggling daggy flock, and was brought to tears himself. What kind of weight was this, in any life, to be forced to take one's own self seriously?

Costa looked at the dark stone walls of the old church, he noted with surprise that there were rivulets of water, tiny tears in beads, dropping and running down the stone, leaving a shining track in their wake. This is the Very Mystery of It, Costa thought, Even the stones are weeping with us!

Was this some kind of miracle?

A sceptic could have pointed to the influence of so many bodies breathing in the air, and the effects of condensation.

Costa saw the heads beside him turning to look at walls and tiny tears that seeped from stone, he watched and saw a tear fall onto the ground from the ikon of the Virgin by the Rock.

A most strange silence, then. Was there one word for it? If so, that word was Awe. Ancient sound of terror and belief. Even the Virgin wept with them, and they were joined in one great longing, and one great grief.

Then it broke, that pure silence, and was replaced by the sound of men and women weeping, the sound like tiny pebbles being scattered on a wall. They wept, and as they wept they were refreshed.

'Do not be afraid of doing something great with your own life! Who could ask for more? Who would ask for less?'

Emile paused again.

'Who of us knows with certainty what demands that greatness might make on us? Who has never felt the fear of greatness, the remorse of the petty nature of our lives, this gift of God, a life, a thing so fine and great, and who has never wondered why we hold this gift in such disdain? Who could tell us they've realised their gifts, and have not squandered the richness of the life to which they're born?'

Costa stood up. Pestoso was surprised—he'd thought the question was rhetorical enough.

On a common pulse they bit their bottom lips.

'Father . . . I lost my hand in a farming mishap some time ago.'

Pestoso nodded. Costa wondered if he should go on or take advantage of this pause to flee the place.

'Father, since then . . . how can I speak?'

Pestoso nodded once again and then muttered, 'Go on, my child.'

'I lost my hand—and yet, so much of the richness of this world has since been shown to me. I've never known such pain, such anguish, and humiliation. And yet, and yet . . .' He looked at all the heads on necks now craning at him. 'And yet I'd have to say I've never known a greater peace, nor greater joy.'

He flushed a bright crimson and then sat down. He wondered why on earth he'd spoken. In this he was not alone.

'That man is not a saint,' Pestoso said, 'and yet he is to be admired for his courage, and the generosity of his spirit.'

Pestoso felt confused. He was not prone to compliment.

Costa was wearing his plaster hand on a length of rope around his neck like a crucifix. When he'd stood up Pestoso could not believe his eyes. Impossible thing whose truth he could not deny. What was happening in his church? Repository of bad dreams come to life? Knew as he spoke that the ossuary was through the floor under his feet. What was this man doing with a hand around his neck? Something unhinged. Pestoso inhaled and smelt the must inside his cloth, out of the belly of his house.

'One hand is worth one year in heaven. Also one foot. A single hair is worth one minute. That is all. An entire leg . . .'

Here he paused. What was a good leg worth? Half a lifetime? How long was paradise? Was one body quite enough to get there for all time, when sacrificed?

Emile caught a look from Francesca, a subtle thing, the thin set of her lips, the way her eyes were tight and hard. She dared him to go on. How could he refuse this invitation?

He pulled a single thread of his own hair, feeling it go taut, the tiny sting as the single hair came free. He enjoyed the power of it, the confidence and ease with which he had them in his thrall.

To his dismay he observed Francesca stand up and, without hesitation, pull a fistful of hair out of her head.

Was this the way she'd call his bluff? Where he'd had the congregation in the palm of his hand, now that subtle power was held by young Francesca, and the many strands of hair that she clutched in her tight fist were like the single strands of every head in the church.

He did not like the thing at all. How to bring their focus back on him? He closed his eyes and prayed.

Pestoso's hands were lifted up to heaven. He sang one note and then he plunged his fingers in his eyes, and as he did his voice let out one God-almighty scream. With this the church exploded, all screaming then, screaming as one, as if their screaming might have been the birth pain of the first hymn in the world.

# A One Leg Sparrow

When Pia woke her worst fears were confirmed. She couldn't move. Her leg and back felt like one block, as if the whole of her had turned into a wooden leg, most inarticulate of body. She was alone.

Costa had left a note beside the bed, saying simply 'See you soon!' signed with an S inside a circle. Beside her bed, two newspapers. What time was it? She looked outside, the strong light from the street made clear the day was truly started. She could see the town hall clock, it was almost midday.

With a yawning sigh, and preparing for the worst, she picked a paper up. Riffling through until she saw her photograph and name, and with a growing sense of trepidation began to read her first review. Her worst fears were confirmed. They'd spelt her name wrong. Pia Zanelli. Well, perhaps there was some small relief in that.

After the first few lines she skimmed the rest, then threw the paper on the floor. 'Bad news travels fast,' she said aloud, then settled back into the bed. God, she was sore! She needed a massage, a spa, a sauna, she needed to be bathed in oil, she thought of Costa and felt the rawness on her shin from his rude stubble. Part of her wetness spoke to her and she was dreaming to herself, Oh yes I'd really like to fuck that man again!

A small bird pecking its reflection in the window. A symmetry of beak and leg, the single leg of the tiny bird. Beating its wings, a tiny hovering dance to its own image.

Pia drank the glass of stale water by the bed, felt the pleasing wetness as it travelled down her throat into her gut. A one leg sparrow.

The pleasing smells of sex came on her nose, in that half-sleep half-awake state she loved, the mingled scents of her perfumes and his, her lovely stinking man. She rubbed her hand upon her belly and felt the tiny flakes of sperm drift away like lover's dandruff in the bed. The sweet smells of the inside of the body come out into the world, smells at once so tender and obscene.

She slung her leg across the bed, jumping her bum across the rucked up quilt. That's when this whole thing started, she thought, the first time that my one leg hit the floor and I couldn't walk, couldn't stand up.

It was no use. No strength at all in her leg. The muscles seized like a motor that's been run hard with no oil.

Bugger, I'm going to have to crawl across the floor to make a cup of tea. Like a lizard. Better flick my tongue inside and out. God though, he does it good, after I put a pinkie in his bum it seemed to rev him up. Wonder where the energy for it comes from, you're tuckered out yet still somewhere you've got a spark to heat your juice. Amazing thing, the power a little finger comes to have. Smells ripe, though.

The hot tea burnt her mouth and she had to spit it back into the cup. She sipped more cautiously, and picked up the second newspaper.

'Pia Zanetti's *Pietra!* premiered last night. Zanetti redefines dance. She is the human javelin. What she can do on one leg other dancers cannot achieve with two. She throws herself through space, arriving like a dart, transfixed, immobile. *Pietra!* is her triumph.'

The review went on at length and Pia reread it until her tea was cold. A fine strand of spittle floating on the surface. She set the cup down, sploshing liquid on the table, and only then realised her hand was shaking. She didn't know if this review made her feel much better or much worse. In a funny way it terrified her. Was this the second tremor of the terror that she felt before she'd danced, or was this another brand new terror of its own? She wanted to run back down the hallway and dive into her bed and pull the pillows dark over her head, knew she'd never run again and was buggered if she'd go crawling all the way.

131

# Our Lady Of The Piggery

Francesca could not get the image of Pestoso's dream out of her mind, as if she'd breathed it into her body and digested it. She could see her own Madonna with no head. Reminded of the ancient statues with their heads lopped off, their heads, their arms and legs. A whole population of Pestoso's devotees, she thought. Pausing then, scratching her head and feeling with delicate fingers the tender scalp. She'd pulled her hair out, just one fistful. Surprised herself. And Emile. An edge of shock still there, when she thought about his fingers lunging at his sockets, and the great scream that filled the church.

They'd sat quiet then, Emile had flopped onto the altar, she'd wondered if she might go to his aid, yet no-one moved. Then he'd straightened up his body, turned his back, and disappeared into the dark vault of the church. The awkward silence. The embarrassment as they left the church. Their eyes averted. They had wept together, and their eyes were as red and savage as Pestoso's. She'd felt an impulse to talk to Costa, or squeeze his hand. And had done neither. Keeping to herself, walking home. And as she walked she felt Emile's ruptured Madonna walk with her, or within her.

Feeling her feet picking up speed and her body tilting forward. Something she must attempt and must set down, this image of the woman with no head, her head held in her basket.

It was dark in the piggery and she felt a damp chill as she walked inside. The dusty windowlight was quite enough for her. She didn't stop, if she did she'd not be able to go on; instead she walked up to the furthest wall and started rubbing it with dirt. Loving the certainty of the earth, the feel of it between her fingers, the smell that came into her nose. She wished that she could make it stick to the wall, and wondered if she might turn it into mud, that she could build an image large as life, or larger. Turning to the pile of charcoal and burnt sticks, she gripped the largest one, more log than stick, and needed both hands to guide it.

Starting at the neck, rubbing at the wall as the neckline, bust and abdomen came clear. Then the arms and a circular basket. She needed something finer for the face and took a smaller piece of charcoal, like a small burnt rock, she thought, and dashed in a pair of eyes, a nose and mouth, and as an afterthought a tongue that poked out through the lips. Returning to the torso, sketching in the nipples, and a line of shadow underneath the small breasts of Her Lady of the Piggery. She didn't bother with the legs, so that the figure was truncated. With a finer hand, sketching in vaginal lips and pubic hair, and standing back at last.

Walking backwards into the middle of the shed. She could feel an agitation in her pulse, the laboured beating of her heart, surprised that this was so, she would not have said the work was physical. She felt like panting.

Something in the basket caught her eyes, perhaps it was the strange tilt of the brows, perhaps it was the poking tongue, but the disturbance that she felt coincided with a moment's recognition—she saw herself as the woman on the wall, even as she knew the woman was not herself but some great other. The sadness then, that might have been a rage, or was it just fatigue? Feeling a great need to weep, and giving over to it, dropping to the ground, grasping the packed earth in her fingers as she wept. Sitting up when the weeping fit had passed, the wetness of her eyes. That's twice today, she thought Must be a day for weeping.

Her eyes returning to the image on the wall. Something about the woman, which might have been her strength, was slowly making her feel calmer, and even glad.

# One Small Detail

Emile's head was aching so much it was all he could do to lie in the darkness of his bed, drinking wine and trying not to notice the dull pain that began behind his eyes and consumed his full awareness. Trying to ignore the pain and managing only to amplify his knowledge of it.

Emile was dismayed to see the bloodshot ruins of his eyeballs and the deep bruising. He could not go about in public. He felt ashamed.

He had been sure that his vision of the Headless Virgin would produce an exalted stature for himself. Instead, he'd made a fool of himself, and belittled the magnitude of his vision.

Perhaps he had misconstrued the meaning of the Virgin's actions. Did she really say God wants a girl this time?

He felt a need to undertake some great defining adventure. He still longed for his miracle, even as he recognised that he was an unworthy man.

What would my greatest miracle be? he asked himself. To salvage some semblance of warm humanity in myself. Sainted then unto myself, if no-one else.

He felt he'd been deserted by the Great Headless Mother that he'd seen, and he was angry. This great hostility welling in him, and he was glad of it. It gave him some kind of ballast, and took away the empty feeling. Better, he reasoned, to be full of hatred, full of anger, than to be a vacuum. He thought of all the good people in the world and felt an immediate enmity. Why were they good and he not? Surely this was just some accident of conception, that one was full of goodness and the other full of bile? The reasoning steadied him, in an off-balance kind of way.

There was one small detail Emile had not related in church about his Vision of the Virgin. God wants your living seed, she had said to him. You are the One!

He was a marked man, marked by God. And he had trembled with fear, and could not even manage a premature ejaculation, let alone a coitus interruptus. Such was the rapture of his trepidation. His sexual exhilaration was absent, and only later, when he thought on it again, did he feel a longing.

He wished that he could have his chance again, to try his coming, and chance a second one as well. All in his priestly service.

But he'd been afraid. He had been horrified, in fact, and could not sustain even a small erection. Emile, lying in the dark, asking himself the usual questions of his waking life. Was he the One? And, if so, which One was he?

Emile looked a terror with his blue-black eyes, and when they turned purple and yellowy and were still puffed out and misshapen, he look a sight . . . Had he been masturbating all night with the devil? No, surely not. He'd merely blackened them himself when he'd plunged his fingers in the sockets. Glad he'd fumbled his jellies. At least he could still see, even if his two black eyes gave him a most frightening mien.

# Pia's Fresh Disaster

Pia decided to go for a walk.

The sun was shining and the warmth of the sunlight on her skin seemed to warm the whole of her. She felt happy, the liberation of her night with Costa. He's a shy man, she was thinking, not a talkative soul at all. She was of a mind to hurry home in case he arrived. Thought the better of it.

If I go home and wait for him, she told herself, I can be sure he won't turn up. If I stay out, he'll probably arrive and then leave before I get home.

She hadn't gone too far. The weariness she'd felt on waking was with her still. She had a second show to do. Did she really have the strength for it?

She'd only gone round the corner. There was a small staircase. The sun shone on those steps, and there she sat. She watched as three small brown birds hopped and pecked among the cobblestones. She closed her eyes. She leaned her head against the cold stone of the steps and fell asleep.

When she woke the sun had moved, though to be precise the earth had crept along. She woke in shadow and felt a chill in her bones. She tried to stand and found she could not bear to place her weight upon her leg.

Bewildered, she found her predicament somewhat amusing and wondered how she'd get home.

I should have brought a walking stick, she muttered. A despondency then. She could not move. She could feel tears welling up, and the long tide of self-pity.

Down in a heap. Huddled against the wall, she bit her fingernails before she had the time to think, and was surprised to find herself become once more a nailbiter.

136

Perhaps the bitten nails were the last straw. She began to blubber. She tried to scold herself back into action, but was too full of remorse, and her sobbing flowed and ebbed down the darkening street, whose shadows lengthened as they slowly turned to night.

Struggling once again to find the upright mode, she got back onto her foot and scrabbled with her fingers for any purchase she could find. At a break between walls, where a small lane cut across her path, she had to hop, only to collapse against a lamp post. She had to give up all her pride, then, and crawl the last fifty metres home, scraping the skin off her knee as she travelled.

Hauling herself up the stairs. At her front door she made no effort to insert the key, lacking the strength for that. Lying on the floor outside her place. She had a show to do in two hours, she had no idea how she'd manage it, no idea how she'd even make it to the theatre. She finally got onto her knee, put the key into the lock, and dragged herself inside. Someone had shoved a note under the door. 'Called round to say hello, you were out. See you. Love, Costa.'

The paper was worn and smooth, the feel of it between her fingers was a comfort. She brought the paper up to her nose, hoping for a waft of the man himself.

She still had no idea how she would get down to the theatre. Disinclined to move, she stretched herself down on the carpet; she was cold, yet preferred the cold to the thought of moving. And so she lay, staring at the ceiling, wondering what to do, loving the feeling of doing nothing.


She hadn't known that she'd been sleeping until she was woken by a gentle knocking at the door.

'Pia? Pia? It's me.'

I should have given him a key, Pia thought as she stirred herself. Or would that scare him off completely?

'I'm nearly there.' She propped herself up, unlocked the door, glad she didn't have to stand to do so. Costa was standing, looking embarrassed, in the doorway.

'I wasn't sure if I should drop by. You know. The show.' Then he paused. 'You look terrible. Are you alright?'

'Thanks for the compliment. I don't know yet. I think I'm catching a cold, and I feel shocking. I don't think I can walk and I'm meant to be dancing within the hour.'

Costa squatted down beside her. He had thought to kiss her, but that seemed to belong to the passion of the previous night, and now he was unsure what to do. Pia was wondering what she thought of him.

'How are you getting to the theatre?' Costa asked.

'I thought I was going to hop. But it's a bad job. To tell the truth I can't believe I hadn't foreseen this dilemma. I can hardly stand, let alone walk. Pietra is exhausted—she feels like a marathon runner the day after the race.'

'I've got my bicycle downstairs. Why don't I cycle you to the theatre?'

And so they went. He dinked her on his bicycle, and as they rode together she rang his bell, a bright nocturnal emission through the darkening streets.


Pia's disastrous second night seemed, in retrospect, something she should have been prepared for. She'd always known that second nights could be terrible affairs. The deflation that followed the excitement of opening night, and the rigours of rehearsal.

After the show had been halted she had no choice bar speaking lamely.

'I'm sorry,' she spoke into the darkened auditorium, 'but I can't go on. You'll get your money back at the door.'

Costa had helped her to the dressing room. She wanted to cry but felt too despondent, or perhaps she did not have the strength. He wheeled her home, they did not speak, and when they arrived at her front door she slid the key into the lock, still on his back. Costa was wondering where he'd put her down, remembering her request of the night before to carry her to the bed. Could this really have been only one night ago?

The events in church—when had they happened? Only

that morning? They seemed to belong to an ancient past. If that were so, then how antique the loving scenes of the night before?

'Would you like me to stay?'

Pia was not sure. She felt a great need to be alone, and yet felt unequal to the heavy weight of her solitude. Not that her solitude had always seemed a heavy thing, but for the moment she sensed no levity in being on her own.

'Stay with me. God, I feel like a bucket of cold shit.'


Pia and Costa were sitting in her kitchen. She had not spoken, beyond her utterance on cold *merde*, and he was reluctant to provoke her. He felt uncomfortable with their silence and wondered if he should quietly go. He stood to leave but Pia stopped him then. 'Don't go. I'm sorry, it seems I've become maudlin. I don't think I'll be famous company tonight.'

Costa sat down. No sooner had he done so than Pia spoke again. 'Perhaps it would be better if you left. I don't think you'll get much joy from me tonight.'

'I didn't come here to get much joy. I came here so you could get home.' He paused, unsure how to proceed. 'We don't have to bib and tuck.'

He caught Pia's smile, and they laughed together. But their laughter did not last long, and they subsided into a strained silence. They were awkward together. Perhaps an excess of intimacy the night before had left them too exposed?

'Oh well,' Pia said at last, 'one could do worse than be a sparrow among breadcrumbs.' She wasn't sure what she meant and so retreated to a firmer premise. 'Why don't you make us both a cup of tea? Or, better yet, there's whisky in that cupboard above the stove.'

And so they drank, and then they made once more their shy way to bed. They found it hard now, as they undressed together. Costa averted his eyes as Pia started to undress then plonked herself onto the bed, weeping with a liberty that had previously been denied her. Costa sat on the edge of her bed, catching a hint of perfume from the bottles on the bedside table. He took a bottle in hand, unscrewed the lid. Pia was lying face down, sprawled, untidy, as he dabbed the perfume on his fingertips and began to rub her neck. At the first touch Pia stiffened, then relaxed, and he untucked her shirt that he might rub her back. Trying to unclasp the hooks that held her bra he cursed—he'd never had that knack, and now with only four fingers and a thumb it seemed impossible. Pia reached back to help. 'No, no,' he said, 'I'll get it yet!' And did, and with his one good hand he lifted her shirt and poured a trickle of perfume along her spine, and rubbed it in. Pia had stopped crying and her breathing came more regularly, then she began to sob again.

Costa was surprised by the profundity of the sounds she heaved up from her body. He knelt forward, letting his chest and stomach cover her back, and felt the force as her diaphragm contracted, then released, and contracted once again.

Then they were calm.

'I think you'd better tuck me into bed,' Pia said. 'Actually, do you know what I would really love?'

'I've no idea.'

'A cup of hot milky tea. And then I'd love you to massage my leg. Rub my leg with oil, and don't forget my toes, and then, yes, please, I'd love it if you tucked me into bed.'

Three more requests with which S. Costa was most happy to comply.

As he began to rub her leg, Pia flinched. 'I'm sorry. Let me relax.' Pia took three long breaths and let the air sigh out of her, and then Costa began dribbling a stream of oil from thigh to ankle. She had removed her skirt, though he noticed she had left her undies on. He was reminded of the way his mother's furze would bush beyond the line of her bathers.

Costa was surprised by the hardness of her leg. It felt like rock. He laughed—it brought to him the friendly sensation that he'd known when handling rocks out in the field.

'What's funny?'

'Your leg. It's hard as rock. But I like rock.'

'Well then, cut the blather! Oh, that feels so good. Bruisy though. You can go a little deeper.'

And so he did.

Once he'd finished rubbing the front of her leg Pia rolled over and he plied the back of her leg with oil. A hint of rosemary there. The power that he felt in her thigh impressed him. He'd never taken such interest in a woman's leg before, or not from such a muscular point of view. It seemed her leg was comprised solely of muscle. And he admired as well the hair that grew, downy on the upper leg, but from the knee down a vibrant growth of thick black hair.

Costa was disturbed from this reverie by the sound of Pia gently snoring. He paused. He'd been trying hard not to stare at the stump of her thigh, her severed leg, the odd modesty of it; he felt there was a privacy that should be respected. But in the sanctuary of her sleeping, he took the chance to look once more at what remained of Pia's other leg. It had healed well, though there was still a redness that graced the rim. He caught his next thought with surprise, then acted on it, and lifted once again the oil bottle and began to massage the stubby remnant of his lover's leg. Without being conscious of it, the motion of his hand fell into the rhythm of Pia's sleepfilled breathing. Quiet then he raised the sheets and blankets and covered her.

Sitting on the corner of her bed, he felt at peace. He found it hard to believe this was the same day as the day he'd gone to church and listened to Emile's strange dream of a madonna with her head held between her hands. He was thinking on this dream when Pia turned onto her side. He waited for her to speak but the only sounds she made were those of a woman deep in sleep, the air sometimes blowing between her lips and punctuating her rhythmic snores.

He knew right then that he was happy and felt quite unprepared for it. Nor was he prepared for the tears that he could feel welling in him. For a moment he felt a smile bubble up, and he blew his air out his nose in a horsy snort—he wanted to cry and yet did not want to wake Pia up, and this dilemma was the thing that brought a smile to his lips. It did not last; instead he quietly sat and let the tears run out of him, and tried not to sob, and wondered if he had begun to love this woman, and if so whether he was prepared for it. Whatever that might mean. And so he sat, and listened to the sounds she made while sleeping. This was another Pia to that delightful creature, so profane, that he had known the night before. The coldness in the room came slow upon him, and told him that the night was nearly spent and the new day soon to come, and only then did he undress, and found a corner of the bed in which to sleep. He did not curl up close, as if this would allow some minor buffer for their privacy. Just once, and lightly then, did he allow himself to kiss the back of her neck. He was listening to the early songs of birds and closed his eyes and thought, Perhaps this is one night when I won't sleep. And did not think one other thing, for then he slept.

# A Worm

Arriving home from Pia's the following afternoon, Costa was about to open the door when a more immediate need distracted him. His nose was blocked, and so he tweaked his proboscis while breathing in, to clear his nasal passages. Catching the lingering waft of Pia's perfume that mingled with another, darker, sexual thing, the smells their bodies made when making love.

They had been lying in her bed that morning when Pia popped the question.

'Have you ever made love in a garden?'

Costa thought on this. Yes? No?

'Does one tree make a garden?'

'That might depend on what kind of tree. Not an apple, I hope?'

'It was a laurel.'

'What was her name?'

'Laurel.'

'If it was a cherry tree, would you have said her name was Cherry?'

'Even if we'd made love under a fig her name would still be Laurel. Not Cherry. Or Fig.'

'Where is she now?'

'I've no idea.'

'Oh. A quickie underneath a tree?'

'Not quite. We were married at the time.'

Costa chewed his bottom lip and looked away. He was seeing a man and woman underneath a tree, making love as the horses grazed and nuzzled. The memory of it was making him feel sad and awkward, uncomfortable to hold.

143

He rolled onto his side, pretending that he needed to stretch his arm while staring at the wall.

'You have a very beautiful hand,' Pia said.

He expected to find that she was laughing at him. She was not. He heard himself laughing instead.

'Pity I've only got the one.' He laughed again, though he could have cried just as easily. 'Would you mind if I told you you have a very beautiful leg?'

'I wouldn't mind at all. Would you like to touch it?'

'Yes,' he said, and ran his hand along the inside of her thigh. Then stopped. 'I can't go through with this.' Somehow the memory of his wife had come between them. He had shrivelled.

Pia was confused and angry. 'What a shithouse time to stop!'


Costa had not wanted to make love to Pia while thinking about his wife. They'd separated seven years ago, she had remarried and begun a family with the best man at their wedding. The last time he'd seen Laurel they had been breaking up the house, deciding who would keep the blankets, who would keep the bed—the usual agony of the final separation.

They'd done their best to remain civil, though as he packed Costa was seething with an anger he didn't dare express for fear that he'd become violent in the rage of his distress and heartache.

When at last the job was done and the house was empty, they'd shaken hands. He permitted himself one small remark that he'd regretted ever since.

'If it had been anyone but Constance,' he'd begun. 'Losing my wife and my closest friend . . .'

His wife had smiled then and squeezed his hand, and as she squeezed it seemed to him she made a point of smiling too sweetly, and she closed their conversation with a tender parting shot.

'Well, I guess he really was the best man after all.'

Costa stood at the door, lifting his fingers once more to his nose, somehow mixing Pia and his wife and all the other women in his mind.

Cursing himself for his indulgent stupidity, Costa opened the door and put himself to bed. Unconcerned that it was too early, crawling under his blankets, closing his body like a fist, and sobbing with his head under the covers.

When he woke it was already the next day. He decided to go for a walk. He got as far as the gate, stopping before he opened it. He was exhausted. Impossible, he thought, he'd only made it to the gate. Surely he could walk further than that? He felt defeated by this simplest task, turned around, and went back to bed. This was the shortest day he'd ever known. A kind of personal winter solstice? He drifted off, thinking about the planets and their rotations.

When he woke, another day had already arrived. He didn't dare go for a walk. Scared that once again he'd be unable to make it past the gate. He could not bear to face the gate and be defeated once again. Falling asleep, waking again. The effort needed to throw the blankets off.

He finally hauled himself out of bed. Walking down the hallway he felt he was dragging himself through the gizzards of his house. Standing outside, he saw a shovel on the ground and picked it up. Poking at the ground, feeling voided of all strength. He saw a worm and cut it in half. Shocked by his action, feeling his head was filling up with noise, he began to swing the shovel around his head, screaming as he did so. He was unable to do conduct in the world. Was he having a nervous breakdown?

His palm had sweated on the handle of the shovel, it flew out his hand and soared over the gate.

I've lost my grip, he thought, and squatted on the ground. He could see the two halves of the worm trying to wriggle away. Feeling a repulsion deep in him, weeping as he contemplated his self-disgust. He wanted to go back to bed, yet felt that even this was now beyond him.

# A Scraggly Mob

Rumour had it that next week in church Emile was going to remove his eyes and then replace them, as an example of his renewed trust and faith in his own god. The fact that his eyes were still dark and bruised from his strange theatrics the week before did nothing to lessen the curiosity that we felt. Did no-one try and dissuade him? The fact was no-one believed that he'd attempt to follow through, and the attraction was the chance to see him back down. The way we love to see another's final humiliation—their failure always makes it easier to make peace with our own defeats.

Emile was eyeing the scraggly mob who'd come to church, a smaller turnout than he'd expected. He looked at them and felt a degree of scorn.

Perhaps he needed to preach a harder sermon?

'I look at you, and what do I see? I see some of the most pathetic people that ever walked this earth.'

He fell silent. He was unsure how to continue. And so he held his tongue. And waited.

After twenty minutes Emile still had no idea what he'd say next. The silence in the church had become unbearable, and was replaced by fidgeting, coughs, and the sound of buttocks rubbing wool against the wooden pews.

Emile blinked. He could feel a clot of mucus building in his throat, he sniffled and for the first time spat a bolt of phlegm onto the sleeve of his gown. It brought the fidgets to a dead sort of silence that fell a little short of calm.

Then Emile spoke.

'Amen,' he said. And departed. A model of economy. Including the spit and his amen, he'd managed twenty-four words. Even by his own standard of brevity this was a record. Yet he was not pleased.

That night, as he was about to sit down on his bed and take off his shoe, Emile had a sudden thought. Things happen in threes. Three births, three deaths, three broken plates. He'd seen the eye of God, he'd seen God's Mother. Was there a third miraculous visitation that awaited him?

He wasn't sure that he'd look forward to it. They were troublesome things, these visitations. Or were they visions?

He could not split this hair while standing up, and so he sat down on his bed. He could feel the sharp point of a broken spring, and quite enjoyed it.

What would it be, this third image of his sacred eye? Might it not be the Holy Spirit itself?

Or might it be the devil, personified? Emile swallowed hard then, thinking on it. An hour later he was still sitting on his bed, he'd taken off one shoe and held it between his hands. The slight waft of his sweat rising off the leather. He had stopped moving, though he hadn't yet stopped breathing. But he was too scared to go to sleep, too scared to dream, too scared to go down to the kitchen, too scared even to take off his other shoe. He had no idea what to do, he was stuck in his rut of indecision, and his fear. And so he stayed just as he was, shoe in hand. As if somehow he could freeze the routine evolutions of this world merely by stopping still in his own tracks, like a lizard on a rock.

His mouth was dry and a white flaky spittle rimmed his lips. He was terrified, and yet elated. Perhaps it hadn't been God after all who had shown his face: perhaps it had been the devil, and for all these years he'd been in the confused service of the wrong master? That would make sense, he thought, of the turmoil in his breast. Of course his god was diabolical. That's why his lust had hurt him so and led him on: a benign servant of the Lord would not feel such a painful throbbing in his loins. He'd always known his cock could never lie, the lie had always been some thing inserted by his brain, that held him back. He needed to let himself go. You only live once, he thought, and it's a crime if we don't live it to the hilt.

From then on he was determined to act on whatever impulse came to him. What if I am discovered? he thought. What if I am killed? His cowardice began to filter back into him. No, he thought, they can only kill me once. And, until then, I'll do exactly what I please.

# Porcellana

Sylvana was appalled. She had been admiring a vase she'd just mended, made of a porcelain so fine it seemed transparent when held to the light. She'd dropped the vase and it had shattered into seventeen shards.

Cursing her ineptitude, wondering what she could say to the owner. Could she repair it? Was it better to tell the truth? Fiddling with the pieces, telling herself she could put it back together. Sweeping up the fine splinters of porcelain and porcelain dust. The owner had impressed upon her the fragility of the piece, it was over three hundred years old, and the only surviving relic of the family's great-great-great-great-grandmother. It had been a wedding gift.

She distracted herself with the recollection that porcelain was so named because it resembled a cowrie shell, which had first been named *porcellana* because it looked like a sow's vulva. She wasn't sure the recollection cheered her, thinking about the moment some man or woman had handled a cowrie shell and seen the similarity between the shell and a pig's genitals. Her mother had been known by that name, Porcellana. Sow Cunt? One of the many unwelcome things she had been told, or overheard, following her mother's premature demise. One of the joys of moving to a town where she was unknown—being spared the stories and whispers she didn't want to hear.

Bringing her attention once again to the broken vase. There'd never yet been a piece she'd been unable to repair, and she was not going to be defeated, even if the task seemed hopeless. Humming to herself in an absent way, she began toying with the pieces in her hand, slowly seeing how the things might fit back together, and where she might make a small paste with the porcelain dust to conceal the damage she had done. Employing her subtle arts of subterfuge as she recalled once more that porcelain owed its name to a shell that looked like a pig's vagina. Porcellana. Her mother hanging by her throat in the chicken shed.

Setting the pieces back down, feeling dry-throated, somehow emptied except for the remorse she could not shift deep in her guts. Refusing the impulse to weep, unaware she'd begun to bite her lip as she gazed at the broken vase with a stubborn concentration, lifting the smallest pieces with a pair of tweezers, determined she'd not stop until she had the puzzle of the breaks clearly established in her mind.

When she first heard that her mother was known as Porcellana she'd assumed it was because of a delicacy of build and temperament. Not realising then that her mother was being called Sow Cunt. It was not till much later that she'd wondered if it was a compliment: she'd taken time to look with tender eye on a sow's vulva, and she had to say it did look a little like a cowrie, sculpted and pinkish.

Sylvana held the vase to the light, handling it with great care. Astonished to find that she'd been able to repair it. Cursing herself for the time she'd taken, yet feeling a glint of something she could only call admiration for herself. It was a fine job.

But her elation at having been able to mend the vase only served to highlight some aspect of her confidence that had been broken. When had this happened? She had always been bold, determined to meet life head on, refusing to give her doubts free rein. She recalled the ease with which she'd once turned on her heel and walked back into La Tarantula, and seduced the baker with an ease that made her feel powerful and canny. Barging into his life, not thinking there might be things she had no business meddling in. Francesca had eyed her jealously, this intruder, and Sylvana had been surprised that Francesca had been so guarded: somehow she thought they'd be like sisters. Perhaps they were? The more she chastised Gianni for not being more present in Francesca's life, the more she knew she was blaming him for something she too was guilty of. Why had she not been to see the girl? Yet she was never home. Why had Francesca not come to visit? Clearly she was happy living out of town, in the gentle hills, some aspect of necessary privacy having been discovered. Sylvana could understand those satisfactions. She'd felt the same when she'd left home, and she had only been a few years older than Francesca. People grew up at different speeds—clearly the girl was a fast developer.

# Her Childhood Now Ending

Pestoso loved pruning trees. Around the house with his shears, trimming the hedges. His father had once painted a picture of the garden of Pestoso's childhood, a pine tree growing in the yard. One branch of this tree had disturbed his composition, so he left it from his picture. Later he'd sent Emile up into the tree with a small axe to chop this branch off, so that his painting might then stand uncontradicted. A rigour in his logic that the young Emile admired, and had somehow made his own. Uncompromising.

He felt Francesca was sucking the life out of him. As she grew bigger, he grew smaller. He foresaw a time, not far off, when he would be small as the flea he'd once crushed between his fingers. And Francesca's thumbnail it would be that squashed the life right out of him.

In a funny way, of course, he was absolutely right. The splendid way life has of confirming our worst thoughts, usually in our darkest moments.

Pestoso was out pruning. The sounds of the shears clipping had woken Francesca. She looked outside her window. He was engrossed, his back turned to her as he admired his handiwork. He had cut off every branch of the apple tree and left a bare trunk. He was making a little clucking sound in his throat, in this way voicing his approval.

Clipping the small buds off, the errant branches and dead wood. This satisfaction.

Emile's uncertainty had been replaced by something worse, a certainty so terrible that it would more correctly be called a dread. His certainty was this: there would indeed be a third vision, and this third vision would bring him face to face with the diabolic force.

The terror that he felt was much worse than the anxieties of doubt that he had previously known. If he had the choice he would have chosen to remain in doubt for every moment of his life, rather than to know with certainty that this third visionary encounter was going to occur.

Emile was too scared to sleep, too scared to stay awake. Too afraid to move and too afraid to stay still. In the end he tended to a kind of inner paralysis. Cataleptic, perhaps, rather than catatonic.

If one were going to know the manner of one's death, it would be no minor thing to know as well the time and place. One could then make plans. So too with Emile's nocturnal intuition of a pending meeting with Diabolus; and yet he had no idea when or where this would take place. He only knew that it would happen, was unavoidable and inevitable.

He had a bad case of diarrhoea and an upset tummy, his bowels had turned to water. Fear is such an inelegant emotion, and Emile was shitting himself with it.


Emile was sprawled in his chair, horribly drunk. What a monster he'd become. Had he not been a good man, once? Where had his virtue gone?

His saintly desire all bled from him. Knowing that he was embarked on another path now. Scared that he was going to meet the devil, and not realising he was become the very one himself.

Emile, tormented by his sexual fantasy, wanting to make it his reality. Not daring to, and wanting to drive it from him: how could he dispel it? If he stopped drinking, he thought, he might find some greater peace. Knowing he lacked the courage for it. His essential torment. Feeling his sex was a delirium he could not control.

Pestoso's drinking cup was one of a pair. They had been wedding presents to his mother and father. The night his mother died his father had thrown one against the wall and it had shattered. A reasonable thing, perhaps, given the distress he'd felt. Bringing the baby home, he'd been at such a loss, having lost his wife and gained a sickly son.

The foulness of temper had passed from father to son, and Emile often struggled to keep control of his. Struggling, but not succeeding.

Emile had never forgiven his mother for dying in labour. He felt this as the absolute rejection: she had spurned him at the moment of his birth, denying him all access to her. No warm teat would she place into his mouth, no suckling would be his.

He felt an immensity of anger, of a purity he'd never known. He was young and old, his father and himself, their combined anger driving through him, staking him, and all his rage and fury directed at his mother's cowardice in death.

His mother's name was Emilia. Emilia Frances Pestoso. In his delirium his hatred for her was absolute. It was not something he based on logic, and he gave no thought to the fact that his mother may not have chosen the moment of her death. He was full of a terrible infatuation, utterly immersed in a self-pity that contained no gleam of self-awareness. Or was he too aware of his own self, and unaware of any other?

Closing his eyes he was at peace, an angry peace but he preferred it to the numbness of his doubt. A terrible certainty was better than a blessed insecurity. He could see in the dark, with his eyes shut tight, a pair of lips, was it? His mother's mouth. His anger growing, his eyes shutting tighter, his lips pursed hard between the enamel of his teeth. He hated his mother. He had not let himself taste such strong hatred before, and as his mind's eye slowly curdled he tasted blood inside his mouth, his anger grown into a rage. He rummaged round inside his head, wanting to find the precise image of his mother. Finding nothing there, his anger firing him, and the taste of blood grown more intense.

Seeing then the image that he sought, his mother's features coming clear—except he recognised the face as his dead father's, transfigured though, the skin softer, the stubble absent, the lips perhaps a little fuller. His father standing in for the absent features of his ma. Opening his eyes, that he might banish this apparition. He'd ripped the labial linings of his mouth, his tongue now feeling out the ragged details, the indentations of his teeth, and the seeping taste of blood. His fingers curling round his drinking cup, he stood and hurled it at the wall. To his surprise it did not shatter, but merely broke in half.

Staring then, his anger muted by his disbelief, he had expected to see the fragments of his cup explode across the room. For a moment his disappointment sobered him, but this was a fleeting sobriety, quickly flooded by his thirst and rage. Drinking from the bottle, as if his thirst could not be quenched, and gagging as he tried to swallow, spraying the wine over the floor and himself, and hurling the bottle, which burst in a pleasing shower of sharded glass.

Now that's more like it, he thought, and for the first time that day he felt a tiny thrill of pleasure pulsing through.

Picking up the broken halves of his drinking cup, feeling the sharpness of the break, he cut his finger and watched with a curious satisfaction as the blood began to seep, the great crimson of it. He licked the blood and watched as it seeped again, and licked and watched it seep. For a moment he wondered if he might not sit back and drink and watch as his blood flowed until he too was nothing more than an empty bottle. But this cut was a puny thing, it was no gash. A little prick and nothing more. 'That's what I am,' he said, 'a little prick in a bleeding world.'

He gave his chair a mighty kick and was not prepared for the pain that shot into his foot. He'd thought to kick the chair apart, but the throbbing in his foot dissuaded him. Instead he threw the chair against the wall, but it was an awkward throw and the chair hit the wall with a moderate force, bounced off and landed back on its feet. Emile was staring at the chair, he felt it had somehow defied him, mocked him even. I am defeated by a chair, he thought. Even the furniture is stronger than I am. Am I so weak?

He was about to answer his own rhetorical question with

a whimpered yes, when some stronger impulse whipped him round. He picked the chair up with both hands and bashed the senseless thing against the wall, as if to knock all life out of an object that was already inanimate—unless we affirm once and for all that even the particles that whirl inside a chair are living pulses.

Emile was not concerned right then with the finer points of the possible inner life of his household furniture. He bashed the chair against the wall, knocking small chips of plaster to the floor, and heard the wood begin to seize and split. Every time he bashed he felt himself grow in stature, and every cracking of the wood and every indentation in the wall confirmed it—he had at last begun to grow to a dimension, a magnitude of being, that he'd always known resided deep within him.

He'd wrecked the four legs of the chair but the back and seat were still intact, and so he kept up this odd battery and assault, and felt his pulsing blood was like some thrilling fire now burning. He longed to smash the windows with his own bare fists, but was too cowardly, or too sensible, for that. Instead he hurled what remained of the chair at the pane of glass, and missed. 'Fuck your mother!' He stood, bewildered, unsteadied, and then he swung out of the room, misjudged the angle of the curve he'd need and knocked his face against the wall. 'I'll knock this whole damn house out of the earth,' he muttered, sure that the objects in his sight were now conspiring against him.

He rubbed his nose and was surprised to see the blood staining his fingers. He wondered if he was losing his wits. No, he replied to himself, I am only now beginning to find them. He didn't bother to staunch the flow of nasal blood, and the more the blood dripped from him, the more potent he became. He wiped the blood onto his hand and smeared his face. The great delirium of his anger felt like such a confirmation, he hadn't felt such animation in him for so long, he needed a drink, and as he went to get some wine he felt a curious elation. He'd teach the bitch a lesson she'd never forget, not in her life. For a moment Emile wondered if he'd pass out, he was overwhelmed by the flooding emotion, his head dazed and crazy. Thoughts of needles, catgut and prongs. Somehow a great confusion taking over, his mother lying in the shed, he'd sew her up, she'd never force him out of her and then abandon him to the foul humours of this world.

He threw up then, and it was a mighty pity that his delirium was not purged as he did so. He let the spasms wrack his guts until he felt that he'd been emptied, then stepping over the soppy puddle he continued on his way down the hall to his room.

He could see the Lips of Aphrodite curling at him. Those sneering lips. He'd trim that mouth, and clip the bud. At once more cleanly and more godly. He steeled himself for this, drinking from the open neck of a fresh wine bottle. Her childhood was now ending, and it was best the thing were done. Cut the spider's fangs off her black body with his knife.

He felt his cock uncurling in his pants, unwinding and nosing roundly, the swelling head, the blood that flowed now in the stem; his cock was hard and hot, and it felt good.

The pagan lips of Aphrodite would sneer at him no more.

Walking on his own up to the piggery. Quickening his step. His mind was made up, no question of it. Loving the certainty he felt right then, clutching his little bag of implements and the sharp edges of his broken drinking cup.

Emile was staring hard at the darkened images on the wall. A legless woman with a hairy cunt. The woman's head in the basket, staring at him. This profanity. His dreamy madonna had been well-clothed, not this naked legless scrabbling. She was making all the world a dirty place. His eyes then drifting to the other images, these crazed designs of copulation, bestiality, and a man with a wine bottle stuck halfway up his arse.

She was not there. He could smell her though, in this pighouse. In the darkness he saw a low shape against a wall. A mass beneath a blanket. He could hear her sleeping sighs now, the breath passing through her lips and nose.

He took a long draught from the bottle's neck, knew that he was ready and equal to the task ahead.

Francesca wept. Each time she thought she'd wept enough she caught her breath and wept again. She wept and her head grew light and her body seized just like a crab claw on the ground. And she lay and could not move, and thought there was no justice in the world, that the world was wrong if such evil could occur, and she felt cold and numb. She was not angry then, she felt ashamed and violated, she felt unclean and she felt she'd been betrayed by all the goodness in the world.

The drunk man cutting her clitoris off, drinking as he cut deep into her, then cutting at the lips and coming in his pants. This terrible apparition. The worst of all, it was no apparition.

An eye, big as insomnia, staring at her. When she awoke, it was already the next day.

PART FOUR:


# THE HEALING POWER
# OF THE GREAT UNWASHED

# A Pleasing Satisfaction

Pestoso was terrified. He could not believe what he had done. What had got into him? The diabolic pulse beat in his chest. Or did beat, yesterday. And today? How could he atone for such an act? He tried to shut the whole thing out of mind. The miracle is this: that he succeeded, if such a thing might be a miracle. He fell asleep, and when he woke he'd wiped his own slate clean. If he was asked he could deny, with conscience clear, any knowledge of the thing at all. A miracle of sterile amnesia?

If pushed, he might suggest that this was part of the girl's obsession, and her contorted relationship with her father. Had he not seen her with a needle sticking into her own skin?

Her hands were red and swollen, and somewhat raw. She had scrubbed now for three days and still felt dirty. She had stood under the shower for an hour and then Pestoso, troubled by the constant spill of water in the house, had called her out.

The house was spotless—every crack in every tile had been scrubbed and groomed, the scunge expunged and the slime and grime purged. Pestoso smiled when he walked into the kitchen—the mottled, marbled surfaces were shiny, the floor was washed and its old boards rubbed. There were still small spots of discolouration where the water was yet to dry. The tablecloth was soaking—he'd spilled some wine, Francesca had put a clean cloth on, a fine starched white, while the red spot of the wine was soaking out.

Throwing the filthy suds out on the lawn brought her a pleasing satisfaction. The vigour as she cast the sullied water out. The oily slop that ran in a thickish tide on the grass, its greasy lip run right up to the trunk of her napkin tree. Would the crab-apples be greasier this year?

She turned to walk inside. Now she would clean the pantry. Shifting the ancient grit of moulded bread, stale grains of salt, eliminating the poisons in the cracks, digging them out with a metal pin. The antique snots of the pantry's nose.

She'd throw away the jars and bottles that were unopened after years, and heave the tubes that held a last clot of old anchovy paste. She was going to give the house a thorough going over, and when she'd finished it would be clean, and then she'd have to start again, world without end, she'd clean and scrub and poke and shift and rub and sweat and still and still she felt the filth of Father's finger poke inside of her, and knew that she would never feel clean again.

Francesca had not told a living soul, and yet she felt no-one believed her. She could not speak about it. It defied the possibilities of her tongue. She felt her betrayal was total, then. Certain Pestoso had that power over her—that his voice was believed while her own would be distrusted. The certainty of it brewing in her, poisoning her blood. And so she held her tongue.

Pestoso's god was a male god, that much she knew. She was surprised to find herself wondering if there might be another god, a god for women. A god for girls.

# Lemon Tea

Emile never spoke about the man he'd been before he became a priest. Nor, beyond the fiery, watery tale of his conversion by hurricane, did he provide detail on how his priestly state had been attained. He grew quite meek and pious on this point, lowered his head and smiled in a way that made him look shifty.

'I was a sinner. God found me out and brought me to this town. The man I was died at God's hands, I was reborn.'

This was his answer. An evasion? Or a moving homily on the root of his conviction? What was his conviction? Had he ever been a thief? Had he ever known a life among 'the fallen'? And was he pushed, or did he jump?

He was falling downstairs. When he had fallen to the bottom he was surprised to find that he still kept falling, he'd fallen through the bottom of the floor and was now falling through the earth. It was an odd sensation to accommodate. But the earth was like black air, that was all, and held no substance for the fallen.

Emile woke from this earthy apparition and was, for a moment, intrigued. Still in the world of his dreaming, he had not realised he was back in the land of solid earth. He lay. Outside, the muffled world of animals making noises brought no comfort to him. He was reawakening, and did not enjoy it. His back hurt. He took some little comfort in it, but the little comfort that he took was little comfort to him.

His courage had fled. His convictions? He sincerely wondered what they were. His doubts returning, his certainties

163

grown distant. He felt angry. He wasn't sure what the target for his anger was. Was himself? His doubt? The fact that he was unsure of this made him angrier, as if his doubt had such control over him that he even doubted his doubts. A maddening proposition, one which gave him no purchase, and which may have been the trigger for his falling dream of an earth without substance.

Emile decided it was time to get out of bed, but he was worn out by the intense speculation of his recent days and for the moment was not sure where he was. He half expected to have woken in his father's house, and felt sad. The sadness mixed with a little guilt. Emile had been quite glad the day his father died. Had felt relief instead of grief. At the funeral he had had to clamp his jaw, jamming his teeth into their bite to stop the smile he felt in his innards from spreading up into his face. Knowing it would never do, yet not quite succeeding in keeping the smile off his face.

The dazed look in his eyes, staring off into the middle distance, or, if he turned towards the coffin that contained his father's bones and meat and water, he focussed not on that wooden box but at a point somewhere beyond, as if he was looking through the coffin down into the earth. The relief spreading through him, an odd light in his eyes, and the dopey half-grin on his face. The priest who read the service assumed the lad had lost his wits for all his grief, and didn't know the lad was suffering, if anything, from the intimations of a delirium of joy. So many strange secrets are harboured in the family.

It was only after his father died that Emile realised how much he hated the man. He'd always thought he was a model of filial devotion, but his devotion was riddled with fear. He assumed this was the natural bond that existed between the father and the son.

The idiot grin that stuck to his features, abetted by the clamping of his jaws, was the beginning of a delight and liberty that Emile had never known.

How he'd make use of this liberty was something he'd not begun to navigate. The realisation was happening in his body, which knew that it would not be locked up in a cupboard ever again, nor beaten with a tightly braided cord, the knots hard enough to break the skin and bruise the flesh. His body was breathing its relief. But Emile's mind was slow to catch on, the terror with which he'd regarded his father had frozen his mental assets. The strange thing was that in due course he treated his own body with the same contempt his father had doled out to him. He was his father's son.

And the hatred for his father, called love, turned into guilt which fermented and brewed into a terrible hatred for himself. Had he not become such a foul man he might have been an object of our pity. Or a subject? The truth, complex as ever, remains this: Emile was a man deserving of our pity, even as he was worthy of our supreme contempt.

Emile's father had died quietly in his sleep. Emile had gone to bring him tea in bed, something the lad had been trained to do from an early age, his father claiming he had no gift for mornings. And so Emile would rise and put the kettle on, his cold breath in the kitchen. Lighting the gas ring, and warming his hands by the flame as the kettle began to crack and rumble on the stove. His father drank a weak black tea with a fine sliver of cut lemon floating on the top.

'The citrus is good for circulation and is proof against heart attack and piles.' His father's claim. Though he'd suffered from piles throughout his life, and a heart attack had claimed him in his sleep.

On the morning of his father's death Emile, aged seventeen, had carried steaming tea into his father's bedroom on a silver tray, along with two pieces of white toast smeared with orange marmalade. He had done this for so many years he could not imagine that a day might begin when this would not be the case. His feet were cold, he'd been unable to find his slippers and so had trod into the kitchen on bare feet. The cold brown tiles of the kitchen had quickly numbed his soles, and rather than go and find some socks he'd settled on one foot, until that foot became so cold he'd had to spare it by placing his other foot on the floor. His feet so cold they burnt.

He quietly called out, 'Father! Father! Your tea. It's day.'
This was his usual refrain. His father was settled on his
back, the blankets tossed off his torso. The black hairs of
his father's chest were clear to see above the upper button
of his flannel shirt.

Once a week the shirt was washed and hung by the
open fire to dry. This task was one of many that had fallen
to Emile. He was his father's housekeeper. This might have
been why, in later life, Emile eschewed the satisfactions that
come from doing work around the house, the joys of
washing clothes or bringing a steaming cup of tea to one
who sleeps in bed.

His father had not stirred, and Emile made a quiet cough,
hoping this would rouse him. Then he quietly left the room.

The rug beside his father's bed had given his feet some
reprieve from the chill, but his morning vigil by the stove
had caused his feet to ache. His bedroom was across the
hallway from his father's. He was surprised to find his
slippers underneath the bed, where they always were.

He was tempted to let his father rest but knew his
father's anger if he let him oversleep. Emile walked back to
his father's room. The tea undrunk. A single plume of
swirling steam drifting slowly up towards the ceiling before
achieving a pure invisibility of vapour. The aroma of the
lemon now spread around the room. He shook his father's
shoulder and was surprised by several things at once: the
inert body; the lack of heat; the waft that came up from
his father's bed, the reeking wind of his father's last lament;
the cold feel of his father's lip, which he felt with the
knuckles of his right hand.

Emile, unsure what he should do, sat down in the small
wooden chair beside the bed. His father's coat hanging on
the chair's back. His father's shirt folded in half over his
trousers. His father's shoes and socks beneath the chair, his
father's underpants and singlet on the seat of the chair.

Emile, sitting by the bed, sitting on his father's underpants and singlet. Numb to the world. Then he stood and
pulled on his father's underpants, the singlet; he adorned
himself with the vestments his father had worn.

He felt warm now, and took a sip of the tea. Biting the lemon to get the goodness from it, the taste of lemon in his mouth. Looking into the favourite teacup of his father, he could see the outline of a single bird flying in the tealeaves.

The smell of lemon kept alive the memory of his father's dead body, in its last repose, from that time on. He would not let a lemon in the house and he often offended with his refusal of lemon tarts and pies and other citrus-flavoured sweetmeats. The smell of lemons and the smell of shit forever mingled in his mind.

The loose-fitting clothes of his father were an inappropriate costume, making him look foolish. He sat in silence, glum to the world, a hapless copy of his father, wondering what would become of him, confused to find the sweet fragrance of the lemon had become an essence of decay.

He'd never had to face a death before, meet it roundly with his eye. And so he sat. He heard a dog barking in the park across the street, and listened to the chattering of birds in trees. Thought he heard the distant mewing of an infant, or was it the harsh serenade of a cat demanding food? He swallowed and felt a tightness in his throat. Knowing he would be called upon to act, and knowing he had no idea what he should do. Feeling his toes wiggling in his slippers, their motion quite involuntary, as if his toes were telling him he could not sit all day, the time had come to act.

He shoved his feet under the chair, a habit of his when he was feeling insecure—he'd lock his feet around the legs of the chair as if to give himself a firmer footing to face the world. Bracing himself.

As he drew his feet back underneath the chair he felt them bump the creased black leather shoes his father wore. Reaching down he pulled the shoes and socks up and held them at arm's length. The comforting smell of old, worn leather, and the sweaty scent that came from his father's socks. Throwing off his slippers and slipping his father's socks on. Working his feet into his father's shoes. They were too big, a clumsy footing. He bent to tie the laces.

The second lace was worn and broke as he strained to get the tightest fit. A momentary lapse into hopelessness as he sat beside his father's corpse, clutching the broken lace.

Not wanting to look upon his father's flesh, not wanting to think or act, knowing he would have to do both. He stood up, felt the largesse of shoes too big for him, and walked out of the room.

He did not look back. He felt the shoes move around his feet as if they were animated by the spirit of his father, and had not yet grown accustomed to their new owner. A ghostly pair of shoes. Emile's desire to dispel this ghostly fantasy of shoes led him out of the room, made him walk with measured step and close his father's bedroom door.

He wondered if he might not just leave the house and never return. Someone would find his father's corpse, and they'd take care of it. He found this path of action attractive. And so he left the house. Walking down the steps he wondered what he should do next, and stopped. He knew he could not leave his father's body there. Could he? He knew that if he stopped to contemplate his actions he'd not find the motive for anything.

He kept his back to the house and walked across the street, into the middle of the park. He stopped and felt the formation of a pair of blisters from the dead man's shoes. Perhaps it was the shoes that pulled him up, the shoes that made him turn around, and led him back into the house. 'Father is dead,' he said out loud. 'Father is dead.'

He was afraid to let his feelings open up, fearing they'd engulf him and he'd be washed away, and as he thought on it something in him softened. It may have been the prospect of annihilation in the face of his emotions that let a little relaxation in. The thought of being swept away by forces he could not control, requiring from him no act of will, no decision—in this he found some comfort, and he wished he could obliterate himself in a cascade of remorse, that he might throw himself down on the floor and howl and weep and feel bereft.

Instead he felt bereft of all feeling, there was no grief nor other animating spirit in him. He felt unfit for this new chapter of his life, and so he walked back outside and sat down on the steps. The infant had stopped wailing. Emile joined with the birds who were silent in the trees as he sat and pondered, and felt absolutely nothing of this world. He was still clutching the broken shoelace in his hand. He put the relic in his pocket and rearranged himself upon the step, and discovered a single bone of feeling in him. Remorse. It was no great thing, but for the moment he would have to make the most of it.

It was odd, he told himself, the way that people died. What if we lived forever? He contemplated a world where no-one died, a world still populated with the all-who'd-ever-been. There'd be no room to move, he thought, all of those living souls crowding in. It made him feel claustrophobic, and reminded him of his father's habit of locking him in a cupboard. Perhaps it's just as well that people die, he thought, and make room for those still living. Something in him shifting then, he began to make his peace with death. He stood and stretched and went into the house. He'd have to face his father's corpse some time.

He tried to avoid the dead man in bed, yet could not take his eyes away. He was surprised by the relaxed features of his father's face, and by his own detachment. Already this dead thing was not his father, was just an object he'd have to help dispose of. He left the room, he put the kettle on, and made himself a cup of tea, strong tea with milk, no lemon. I can choose my own way now, he thought, and this brand new prospect filled him with apprehension. He drank his tea.

He'd tell the neighbours, they'd coddle him and tell him what to do. They'd make the right decisions, and he'd be spared the need to make hard choices now. He was pleased with this decision. He left the house once more. The large shoes of his father leant a curious shuffle to his gait, he gained comfort from the pathetic edge this gave him.

He walked up to his neighbour's house, in his father's too-large suit and shoes, announced, 'Father is dead,' and felt he had at last fulfilled his filial obligation. Events could now take their course.

His neighbour recognised the suit yet had trouble placing it on the body of the young man standing there. She did not react. And so Emile announced once more, 'Father is dead!' He watched her mouth open and her tongue lick the fine moustache that lined her upper lip, the little slick her tongue left behind. He was waiting for her to take control and could not understand why she resisted. Then she said, 'Oh dear, you'd better come inside,' and with relief he shuffled down the darkened passage of her house.

'Where is your father now?'

'He's in his bed.'

'Your father was not a happy man, perhaps he's happier now. I never liked him, I'm sorry to say, but I never lie about the dead. Have you made arrangements for the funeral?'

Emile was stunned by her outburst and shook his head.

'Well then,' the woman said, 'we'd best begin with that.'

At that moment Emile felt like a sheet of plain glass. All who looked would see right through him.

'Are you sure he's dead?' the woman asked.

Emile had been so sure he hadn't even questioned his assumption.

'How do you know he's not in a coma?'

Emile did not.


Emile was scared to go inside, half expecting he'd find his father sitting up naked in the bed, or else already starting to decay.

The old woman took a small pocket mirror and held it over his father's mouth. The glass did not fog up.

Emile, looking down at his father's shoes, had the feeling that his body belonged to somebody else. He saw his father's feet, his father's suit, he was wearing the burial suit of his father.

'I'll have to take these clothes off. They were his.'

'They'd make a lovely suit of clothes for burial. Slip them off and I'll help you dress your father.'

The woman sorting through his cupboards. Surprised to find a rack of girl's clothing.

'I didn't know you had a sister.'

Holding the clothes up to him.

'I must say, these are a perfect fit!'

Bunching his long hair then, and noticing the boy had black curls. Imagining a small red ribbon. Something that came from lower down, the voice of intuition.

'Put this on.'

The old woman was surprised by the transformation, and knew that a truth had come clear to her. Something about Emile and his father upon which she'd speculated, but never recouped her investment. Her neighbour had not just one son, he also had one daughter.

Pestoso wasn't a trained priest at all. The only training he'd had was when he was tied to a tree. Somehow the idea had formed and from then on he adopted the habiliments and mannerisms of a priest. He bought his vestments in second-hand shops.

It's hard to know what intuition led him to our town, the church had been closed for years and the small house with it. He left his bicycle on the edge of town and made the last part of his journey on foot. He felt it conveyed a more priestly impression. How did he find out there was a vacancy?

As he walked down the road the dust made his throat dry. His face blasted by the heat. All of the moisture in him rising to the surface. A small pebble caught in his shoe. The sharp pain each time he stepped. Something in it he quite enjoyed. The little flagellations of life as we pass by.

Arriving in town he saw a sign. He couldn't have been more pleased if it had said Holy Water, or Welcome to Heaven. It said Amaretto. The door was open, he slaked his thirst, and was well disposed to take a closer look at this small town. What he saw was most pleasing to his eye.

The articles of his faith were revealed soon enough. One doesn't ask a priest for his ID, he looked the part. He was just passing through. By the time he left, our lives had changed forever.

# An Unpaid Debt

Pia had not heard from Costa. She felt a little heartsore, told herself the sex was good, missed his company, and decided to get on with her life.

She felt she had an unpaid debt to Luigi, and wondered how she might repay him. Luigi protested that no such debt existed. She agreed that the debt was by no means one of financial obligation. It was a modest debt of gratitude. He'd been there and taken care of her. In his own bizarre way he'd helped her find a target for her determination.

She'd been deflated in the wake of her dancing premiere, and it was only her exhaustion that kept her from profound despair. She had left her flat only to buy food and the small essentials of her life. She began to see some humour in the whole affair, even if the joke was at her expense. The one-leg skittle of her, flat on her butt.

To tell the truth, the exuberant response to her dancing had terrified her, and she'd secretly agreed with those who'd seen it as the awkward perambulations of a recent cripple. She also knew that she'd achieved a momentary grace, and was not sure how to resolve the tension between these conflicting points of view. She felt there was a truth in both of them, and wondered if she might find room within herself to accommodate these extremes.

She wanted to send a message to Luigi, she thought a picnic would be nice. A simple way of giving thanks. Where could they go? There was a small stream not far from Luigi's stable. She'd never been there but she'd heard Luigi talk about the way he'd tried to catch fish as a child, with a piece of string to which he'd tied some cherries. He hadn't bothered with the hook, he was unaware that a hook was a prerequisite for fishing. He'd thought the point was to feed the fish by lowering food down on a string, and had felt dismayed when the fish refused his cherries. His dismay disappeared, though, when he sat and ate the cherries himself.

The creek was small and muddy, and Luigi felt perplexed as he and Pia sat down on the bank. There was a disparity between his memory of what the stream was like and the reality of the brackish water full of leaf mould, broken branches, and here and there a small brown fish nuzzling the algae that floated on the surface. He was embarrassed that they had come to this place that he had praised, only to find an ugly little waterway covered with scum.

The day had held a promise of warm light, but by the time they arrived the sky was covered by thin grey cloud, and the warmth of the sun was obscured.

Yet Pia didn't seem to mind. 'Well then, we're here,' she said. 'Let's eat!'

Later they had gone in search of firewood, the day grown cold. They'd thought to light a fire and get its warmth onto their skins. Much of the wood was damp, and there were splendid orange fungi, Log's Ears, Luigi called them. They peered at the fungi, Luigi feeling awkward, distracted as he was by his admiration of the lovely contours of Pia's bum. He was relieved when he heard Pia's voice. 'Oh look, a wasp!'

The wasp had a black body with red antennae, red legs, and a fine pointed red sting. Clear wings, with a black spot in the middle of each one. Their transparency was patterned with a fine lattice, like the skeletal structure that remains sometimes when leaves have dried. These lattice lines were also black, except for those that ran around the outside of the wings, which were red. It was a beautiful creature.

'Did you know,' Luigi was saying, 'that the wasp has been for thousands of years a symbol of divine intuition? Hermes was a wasp. Though that was in an earlier metamorphosis.'

Pia was about to ask him what he meant when the wasp began to stir, flexing its fine red legs. Luigi rattled on.

'I've always thought the beauty of the wasp is contained chiefly in its sting, while the beauty of the spider resides in great measure in her fangs. Wouldn't you agree?'

Pia was quite unconvinced of this assertion, but before she could answer him the wasp took off. It flew straight at her. She swiped and clipped the beast, regretted it in an instant and forgot her regret an instant later as the wasp swerved and circled back and bit her on the bum.

Perhaps it was the wasp that truly set her free. The pain of its sting was now a source of animation. Pia was not just hopping while giving voice to an agitated scream, hopping was not the word. If it is possible to run on one leg, she was running. As if this new pain in the arse had released her from that primal pain of her severed leg, and released her as well from the grief she'd felt as she mourned its loss. The wasp sting shook her body with bright life, and she was dancing.

When the pain had settled into a throbbing ache and Pia had collapsed onto the ground beside the scurfy stream, belly first, Luigi felt assailed by a sense of guilt. The fault was surely his for this waspish bite.

But he was also intrigued by a curious phenomenon: the frenzied movements of Zanetti, once she'd been stung, had perfectly resembled the buzz and motion of the wasp. As if, Luigi thought, woman and wasp were joined in the one ecstatic dance. He didn't mention this to Pia—the intensity of her screams was not the stuff of ecstasy at all, and yet the image of the woman and the wasp somehow had joined in Luigi's mind.

Pia was trembling, a strange excitement thrilling her. She turned to face Luigi.

'I moved,' she said. 'You saw it! I really moved!'

Despite the pain, she felt an immense satisfaction; she had embraced once more some deep part of herself.

She reached a hand out to Luigi. He grasped her hand, thinking she wanted help now to stand up. Instead she pulled him onto the ground and kissed him once, so very firmly on the mouth. And then she thanked him. Luigi felt a great confusion in the wake of Pia's kiss, and had no idea what he should do or say. He was relieved when Pia spoke again.

'Like Lazarus. I was bit by that wasp and I sprang up from the bed of my poor self! And, bugger me, that biting thing has proved I can still move my butt.'

As she lay there an image came to her, of a woman dancing on one leg. A woman dancing like a wasp, or a dancer who was somehow half woman, half wasp. A wasp dance, she was thinking, is that the thing that I'll be doing next?

# The Healing Power Of The Great Unwashed

No-one knew what had happened to Francesca. And so life went on as usual, if usual is the word for the kind of life we were all living.

It's hard to say just when she decided to stop washing. As if she had abandoned hope in water and now truly embraced the earth. Her hands were always filthy, and not just the black rims of her nails, her palms were often black, with a white trail where the sweat had etched the dirt away. Her hair was clotted with dirt and bits of autumn leaf, though one could say her hair was clothed in these same things.

There was a time when we were all more fond of dirt, and saw the earth as something healing and sacred. So that rubbing dirt into a wound was a kind of poultice. Perhaps Francesca had found her way back to this old custom and belief? Putting mud onto her groin and her wounded vagina. It was as if she were slowly turning herself into the image of that most strange and holy ikon, The Black Madonna.

Needless to say, her devotion to the cleanliness of Pestoso's house had also declined. The good Father was disturbed one day to find her mopping the kitchen with a bucket of dry ash and soil. If the truth were known, she frightened him. She was, he thought, acting most strangely. He had forgotten the strangeness of his own actions. The way that we forget and then invent a memory, that great convenience.

Francesca's infibulation was the axis—or, if you like, the axle—on which the wheel of the town revolved. But we didn't know this then. We didn't know what had happened.

# The Wasp Dance

Luigi was flattered when Pia asked him to speak before the dance began, but as he looked out at the many faces in the hall he felt flattened. Pia had chosen a small room at the back of the town hall, no more than a hundred and fifty people could fit inside. Luigi was quite happy that Pia was there, but he felt unsure about the other one hundred and forty-eight.

'Just tell them about the picnic,' she had coaxed him. 'Tell them about the stream, fishing with cherries. Talk about Hermes and the wasp. Then get out of the way.'

Luigi stood there blinking in the light. He couldn't see the faces of the people, though he could hear them shuffling in their seats, and he could not recall what Pia wanted.

'The sting of an insect is like a kiss that passes between the species,' he began. 'It is an act of love. The moment of the sting is an act of holy penetration with the divine. Our pain is simply our fear in the face of this revelation.'

The silence that now gathered in the auditorium was not unlike the one that follows when you've been slapped in the face by one you love, or by some hard and ineluctable face of logic. Pia, backstage, was amazed, and then had difficulty as she tried hard not to laugh.

'I received this intuition while gathering wood with my colleague, Pia Zanetti.'

He had been going to talk about the picnic but felt that it would be more impressive if he said they were gathering wood, it was somehow more industrious. Unable to stop himself, he pressed on into this unknown territory.

'The frenzied movements of Zanetti, once she had been

177

stung, resembled perfectly the buzz and motion of the wasp who stung her. Wasp and woman joined in the one ecstatic dance.'

Pia took a deep breath and prepared to launch herself. Just as she felt she had the vital élan she needed to begin, she pulled herself up with a jolt as she heard Luigi blundering on.

'Wasps have a different sense of time to us. They are fast on the outside and slow on the inside. Relative to us, time passes slowly for the wasp. From the wasp's point of view we look like we are moving in slow motion. But that's not the reason why we're here. Or perhaps it is. What forces now bring us together? If Pia had not been stung by that wasp—but wasn't that wasp moved by God's own trembling hand? Perhaps God merely meant to stroke her bum, but having neither finger nor feather with which to stroke, the task fell to the passing wasp?'

Pia was waiting for him to pause and take a breath, that she might cut him off. But he didn't pause, he merely gulped, she'd missed her chance. Or had she? Luigi had started to make a buzzing noise, like a wasp, or bee, and the audience in their boredom or disbelief had started buzzing back. As they buzzed so did Luigi, and the buzzings of the audience were growing louder. Luigi and the audience seemed to be competing with each other, hard to say who was the first to start screaming. People were laughing and standing on their chairs, oblivious to anything it seemed but this chance to ventilate their lungs.

As the screaming peaked Luigi stood back and tried to make himself heard above the crazy throng, 'Ladies and Gentlemen, Pia Zanetti!' And she was on.

Compared to how she moved in this second dance, her previous work was limp. Her dance recreated, at the start, the events that led to her unintended meeting with the wasp. The extraordinary thing was the speed and levity she acquired once she'd been 'stung'. It really did appear that she was running on one leg, and leaping, catching her balance and running on one leg again.

She gave a potted history of her recent life; she came

on with a wooden leg, it seemed she was the woman she had been. And then she popped the false leg off. That caused a shock, and there were some who felt she was obscene when she did that. They were the ones who got a greater shock when she undressed, so that we were confronted with the vital image of a naked woman standing on one leg; and who, of course, only had one leg to stand on.

She was not completely naked. She wore once more her pink tutu, and her dancing slipper with the pink ribbons that wound round the great Pietra from ankle to thigh.

Not everyone thought she was obscene. Others merely let their jaws drop, and from the moment she popped her false leg off the place went quiet—one reason why she'd chosen this as her beginning. She knew from then she'd have their full attention.

Pia's bottom was not a small thing, though she herself quite liked it. She flaunted it once she'd tossed off her leg, turning her back and bending over to give the audience what she liked to call the wasp's-eye view. She flaunted it not for the sex but just to say, A woman's got a bum, her body's centre is here, centre of gravity and levity both at once.

She bent and showed her arse and straightened up and bent again, making a passage from the back of the stage to the front. Picking up sticks, she called it. When she could go no further, the sting went in. Perhaps Luigi's strange incantations at the beginning of the night had set the scene too well, for as Pia made her backward progress, picking up sticks, some clever bastard began to buzz again and people being what they are, creatures of the herd, everyone joined in, and when the buzzing peaked so did Pia—she shot up, clutching her rear, and the house was screaming on her behalf. It was a curious spectacle, to say the least.

She kept her hands clamped to her bum to help keep balance, and to provide the added muscle that she needed. Once she started to pick up speed she could take her hands off her cheeks and start to swing her arms. She was beginning to travel at a fair speed, for a cripple, and won a grudging admiration from the crowd. The screaming had stopped but there were sporadic bursts of clapping.

Pia was lulling them into a false sense of security, and to her ears this paltry clapping was the sort you gave to some poor soul who never stood a chance. It made her angry.

The anger was a bonus she hadn't counted on, and the anger acted on her like a spring. The most difficult part of her strange wasp dance was now to come. She took in hand two metal balls attached to ropes and began to swing these weights around her, using them to help create some kind of centrifuge. They let her spin much faster than she otherwise could.

Between the anger and the ability she'd gained through sheer hard work she attained a great speed, and all this balanced on one leg. She'd had a metal cap placed on her dancing slipper, and for a moment it seemed that she'd bore a hole through the wooden stage, and if she kept it up she'd fall right through and disappear from sight. This was a false impression. She was spinning at an awesome rate now, you couldn't see the balls or her, not in detail, just the dark metal blur, a blur of rope, and a pink spinning blur of Pia.

Did she really levitate? Who could swear to it with certainty? But as she reached her maximum speed, perhaps she jumped, perhaps she didn't, but it seemed for all the world that she now lifted off the ground, and as she did she took us with her, we were all suspended. And then the lights went out, just as she began to drop. The last image the audience had was of Zanetti tumbling gaily through the void.

Pia's Wasp Dance was short, twelve or fifteen minutes. She could not do more, and had decided not to charge admission. She needed to do it for herself, that was enough, to show that she'd bounced back after her previous disaster.

She didn't come back for encores. Nor did we applaud. As if somehow the night was running backwards. We'd started with the screaming and ended with a curious anticipation, and disbelief. It seemed she'd drawn her audience up into the air, lifting us out of ourselves, before she gently set us back in our seats. Strange hush as the lights came up. Blinking, leaving, almost floating as we found our muted way outside.

# White Feathers

Watching Pia dance The Wasp Dance, Amaretto felt that he was lifted out of the many things that plagued him. That she released him from a burden he hadn't even known he had been carrying. He felt lighter, looser, as if his joints had stretched the ligaments that held them firm. As he walked home it seemed to him he had a goosy-footed walk, that he was nimbler, suppler, that he could bend backwards and place his palms flat down upon the earth. He wanted her. He wanted to thank her. He wanted her. He wanted her.

Amaretto was stuffing a chook, bemused by the feeling of his hand as it rummaged round the emptied innards of the bird. Pulling the gizzards out, packing the herbs and breadcrumbs in. He was thinking about Pia. How did a man woo a woman? He could send flowers, write a sonnet, compose a song in her honour. Food. Didn't they say the way to a woman's heart was through her belly?

The bird was stuffed and Amaretto shoved it in the oven. He'd win Pia to him, that he knew. But how?

Obsession believes in one thing, which is itself. Obsession was a trait than ran in Amaretto's family. It's not an endearing quality, though it's certainly enduring.

Amaretto saw Pia with the fascinated eye that young men have for older women. The crow's feet around her eyes, which he was sure were there from smiling but in fact remained whether she was smiling, sad or angry, only confirmed to him the magnitude of her experience.

He was attracted to what he saw as the richness of her world, her inner life. The fact that he knew nothing of it did not deter him in his affections, nor affect his determination to woo and then seduce her. Perhaps if he had known her better, had been able to separate the woman Pia was from the fiction that assailed his eyes when he looked on her . . . but as it was he was unhampered by any such thing.

Amaretto had been in love with his mother. But then all children are. Watching her brush her long brown hair. The smell of her hair exciting him. Sometimes she let him brush her hair, he liked the smooth bone handle of the brush and the resistance as he tugged, and the release then as the tangled hair came free. The bud of an erection in his boyish pants. Brushing her hair, the boy full of adoration.

Amaretto's mother was not one of those who cuddle, stroke and fondle. She was happiest when admired from a distance. The more that Pia tried to keep Amaretto distant from her, the more she reminded him of his mother.

Amaretto shifted to a pile of chicken legs stacked on a plate. One by one he made a circular cut around the ankle and then pulled the bone out. There was a little sucking sound as the bone came clear of the flesh, and he liked this sound. Like a full stop at the end, he thought, as he tossed another boneless leg onto the mound of chicken flesh. Throwing the bone over his head, it hit the wall, and landed in the bin. He did it as a joke the first time, and got a shock when the bone fell straight into the garbage. He kept at it then, and had achieved a perfect record so far.

He was going to stuff the chicken legs with mushrooms that were marinating in red wine, pepper and mustard. One of his favourite combinations, he could not escape his love of it. Thinking that a gooseleg would really be the one to stuff. How many mushrooms could he stuff inside a gooseleg? His thoughts returned to his frustrated desire for Pia Zanetti and it put him off his stroke. He tossed a chicken bone over his shoulder, heard it hit the wall and then land on the floor. Missed. He tried again and once again he missed.

He was trying not to think about her, but the more he tried to put her out of mind, the more he thought about her, and the pile of chicken bones on the floor quickly outnumbered the ones he'd managed to throw into the bin.

Amaretto started shadowing Pia. He was adept at it, she never once caught sight of him. But she knew he'd been watching, certain that at the moment she turned around to catch him he'd duck out of sight. She wondered how she might surprise him, and catch him in the act. She also knew that to catch him once would not suffice: there was no law against walking behind another person. She herself would seem to be acting strange. Amaretto was watching her as she went about her daily business, and even when she sat at home brushing her hair she felt his eyes were on her. She'd draw the curtains then and sit in darkness, and grow angry, feeling he had made her a prisoner in her own abode. So then she'd fling the curtains open and feel the violation of his gaze come into the room.

She became edgy, the smallest movement apprehended in the corner of her eye made her jump. When she turned her head there was nothing there. She wondered if she was going mad; perhaps there was nothing untoward happening at all, beyond the fact that she was lurching towards some kind of lunacy. It was not a comforting thought. She wondered how she could deflect Amaretto's attention. Perhaps he just needed a girlfriend? Perhaps she needed to turn the surveillance around, and spy on him? This was an attractive proposition. Except that it would mean making the boy the centre of her world, and then she'd know she'd lost her wits.

# Amaretto Takes A Gander

Amaretto was sitting in the almond grove, watching a gander trying to mount a goose. He wondered if the goose would let the gander into her. She waddled away. Amaretto found that he was blushing.

He wanted to give himself to Pia. He felt that she would know just what to do with the gift he'd make of himself. He'd cook for her, he'd clean her house, he'd carry her over the mud in winter, he'd feed her up. He didn't stop to wonder whether Pia might desire these things herself, his stubborn and selfish imagination made it clear to him that Pia would, given the right circumstances, be all too willing to share her life with him. Was he not an excellent cook? He was skilled in the arts of love and music.

The gander had not given up his attempt to mount the goose. Amaretto rummaged in his pocket and found some corn. He slowly walked toward the gander, who advanced, thinking that he'd protect the goose from this marauder.

Amaretto had been wondering what to do with all his geese. Sometimes he felt that he was running the cafe just so he could afford to buy their feed. Yet he baulked at selling them: something of his dead father's desire, his dream of geese and a great white wedding, lingered still. As if the geese were a massive bridal veil and gown and train, and instead of a wedding ring on his bride's hand would perch a gosling . . . it was an eccentric point of view, but no less valid for that.

He fed the gander with the corn from his pocket and then he grabbed it by the throat. With a skilful twist of the neck he silenced the gander's honking.

Settling back in the almond grove he began to pluck. The late sun shining on his face, he inhaled the moist cool air, plucking feathers as he did so. A small piece of down caught in his nose and he sneezed. Life was good.

Slowly he began to squeeze the life out of his geese, giving them the liberation of a tight-wrung throaty death. Each day he'd kill one bird. This was his plan: a goose a day. But just as children play with daisies, pulling out the petals as they declaim, She loves me, she loves me not, and, if that flower loves them not, pulling another out and starting again—in the same way, Amaretto played with his geese. If, when the goose was plucked, the verdict was she loved him not, he'd kill another goose.

He'd woo her with his art, a goose stuffed with prunes and armagnac, but not a goose that loved him not. He was killing an awful lot of geese, and each day the feathers, which he plucked only to find that still and still she loved him not, were left outside her door. It was a futile, strange endeavour. He fantasized about her nipples as he plucked; his fingers plucked while in his mind he sucked. He was besotted with her. A dangerous affair.

Someone kept leaving feathers by the door. Pia found it quite unnerving.

It took her a while to realise who had left this trail of feathers at her front door, and when she realised she could not believe she'd not divined the thing at once.

Her room was filling with white feathers. She began to sneeze. The feathers shuffled every time she sneezed—that stirred the dust mites up and then she'd have to sneeze again. She was caught in the eye of a terrible season.

She started to make a pillow, a pillow and then a quilt. After the pillow and the quilt she decided to make a feather mattress. After the mattress, another three pillows, and another quilt. She settled into her downy mattress with its quilts and feather pillows, and thought, This is luxury!

185

True, it made her sleep a little hot. Her dreams took
on a fevered aspect. She would not have said that the bed
was infected with the germ of an obsession, nor that the
more she slept in it, the more she was exposed to this subtle
germ.

# Francesca Makes A Sweeping Statement

So many things remain unknown. When did Francesca start collecting sticks? And why? She'd see a stick and stop, pick it up and add it to the bundle on her back. It must have started with one stick, and then a second, the third and fourth and fifth were quick upon. How many sticks does it take to make a bundle?

You'd have to say that she was aging quickly, she didn't look the thirteen years she was.

It didn't happen in a day, nor did it happen overnight. Yet she had grown old. And the pile of sticks upon her back had grown as well. Almost you'd swear that pile of sticks upon her back was a pile of years. If that were true she wasn't any age you'd normally compute. She'd become ancient.

Francesca started sweeping the streets with a giant broom made from the sticks she collected. As if somehow she'd clean the whole town. She was always there, with her brush, its long wooden handle bound round with twigs. You could speak to her but she would not answer. Who knows if she could hear us? And to bang her ears with platitudes, to talk to her about the weather, this would clearly be a nonsense. Nor could she be engaged with any deeper notions, and a solicitous 'Hello, Francesca, are you alright?' would not even be met with a glance from her eyes, could not stay for a second the sweep and swaying of her broom.

She swept and swept, and when she'd reached one end of the town she'd start again, sweeping now from the other side. She always worked her way towards the centre, where the church stood in the open square. The church doors were shut against her, she'd tried to sweep her great broomloads of dirt into the church itself. Having been thwarted in this, she seemed happy enough to sweep the mess into the square outside the church, leaving it there.

At first she'd swept the square clean and continued with her broomload toward the large portal of the church. We'd thought her civic duty was clear. It was only when she began to sweep the dust and grit inside that we began to feel there was some other indication. It was an odd thing to do. We made no connection then with events we knew nothing about. We did not interpret her actions as a sign. What might we have deduced? She was behaving a little strangely, that was all. In another time we might have said that she was schizophrenic.

Francesca's cleaning urge did not abate. She had already spread a thin carpet of dirt right across the square. Yet she showed no signs of stopping. If anything, her grip upon the broom was now firmer, and her strokes grew more determined. You would see her in the distance, sweeping up her little clouds of dust. Her eyes were always focussed on the dirt in front of her. If she lifted them, they focussed on some distant point—the far horizon, the end of the street, a wall across the square. No-one could remember when she'd last looked them in the eye. No-one tried to stop her. We didn't ask her if she wanted food or water. We were afraid of her. It was not a noble thing, to be afraid, and yet we were. We told ourselves she had become unapproachable. The simpler truth was that we didn't dare approach, and as long as she did not ask for our help we were glad we didn't have to give it.

When the carpet of earth across the square had grown to a depth of half a foot, we wondered what Francesca had in mind. What would she do next? There were various hypotheses. She was going to plant a garden, using the dirt from the town's streets as its seeding bed. This seemed a good idea. Others claimed that she was going to build some kind of underground bunker, though it would have been easier, surely, to start somewhere that had earth already and use a shovel, not a broom?

And why would she want to build a bunker? Or might it be some kind of burrow? Then again, why would she want to build a garden in the centre of the town? We had no answers to these questions and so we left her to it. She was not doing any harm. Given that each day she swept the town from end to end, you'd have to say in fact she did some good.

Emile was growing agitated, however. He acted as if Francesca had not changed, and if he saw her out sweeping the streets, or depositing yet another load outside the church, he'd say, 'Good morning Francesca! You're looking well today! Keeping busy, are we?' He no longer stood in front of her while speaking. The first time he had planted himself before her, trying to make conversation, she just kept sweeping, and swept a great load of dirt onto his shoes, and as he stood there protesting she swept on, brushing past him. For a moment Emile had imagined that he would be swept along, part of the garbage she propelled before her. He found this disconcerting. He still kept up his short, one-sided conversations, but he never tried to block her path again.

Francesca grew quite dusty of visage. Where she'd had fair skin you'd have to say that now her skin was dark. Whether this was from the dirt or from the fact that she was always out of doors and had begun to weather, you couldn't say. You didn't need to, and it was most likely a combination of the dirt and the sun, mixed with her sweat as she swept and swept.

She also grew a quite pronounced black moustache. She certainly had no intention of shaving, just as she seemed to have abandoned all thoughts of washing. It's true that this was a dirtier time, we didn't wash with the frequency that people seem to now—we didn't feel the need. We quite enjoyed our sense of smell, and you're healthier when you wash less. So there was no precise time at which we would have said 'Francesca needs a wash!' We were all a bit unwashed.

There comes a day when you know that summer's over and winter's on its way. In that same way, which isn't any precise thing, just the slow accumulation of days as they pass by, we realised that Francesca had stopped washing long ago and that her skin had grown quite dark. She was not black but she was a good browny hue, though as she flushed with her exertions you could see a certain pinkness underneath the dirt.

The first of Francesca's obsessive drawings appeared not long after her sweeping began. It was a circle, or perhaps more an oval shape, drawn in rough charcoal, drawn round and round and round. An appealing volume, in its way. Was it somehow emblematic?

They started appearing in different places around the town.

Turning a corner, on an abandoned wall it caught your eye. The first time you saw it you saw nothing much. The second time seemed coincidental. The third vision confirmed the series and after that you knew you were the beholder of somebody's bright obsession. And though the obsession was bright, if by bright we mean something that holds a promise, they caused a disturbance to the eye, these darkening eggs of the girl's young self.

A dark eye looking at you. As if this eye could see the darker aspects of yourself. A troubling glance. This dark eye was a mirror, from which the eye recoiled once it had seen what was revealed. And yet there was an attraction, as if our diabolical counterpart had just revealed itself. The deformed reveries Francesca's blackened scrawls provoked.

I may as well tell the truth. Her oval scrawl was a vagina.

It was a reasonably accurate portrait of her organs. Pestoso had clipped her wings, her bud, or, put more bluntly, he had, inspired by God knows what darker god or knowledge, cut off her clitoris and hacked at the lips of her vagina. The savage strokes with which Francesca made her sharp oval designs represented vividly enough the lacerated scars Pestoso left.

Infibulating her infundibulum, his retina focussed on the retinaculum.

Francesca's crude diagrams were her way of announcing what Emile had done. He'd sewn her up. It stopped her period and it took her half an hour to piss.

# PART FIVE:

# A RIOTOUS PATERNITY SPRUNG FROM HIS LOINS?

# A Riotous Paternity Sprung From His Loins?

Francesca's diagrams had one terrible power. They made people want to tell the truth. Only the amnesiacs were safe, though whether this was true for those whose amnesia was self-induced is another question. The sadness her drawings provoked made people blurt out the oddest things. The sense of loss contained within those charcoal holes, those dying cunts, called up the very thing the onlooker had lost within themself.

No-one ever saw Francesca drawing her vaginas. They just appeared, like posters sprouting overnight, but what was being advertised?

Those dark mirrors of Francesca's held a terrible fascination. They were dark wells of negative sympathy. They filled the onlooker with the apprehension that the worst had happened, and still worse was yet to come. A most unsettling disposition. Like the giddy thrill that overtakes one standing on a cliff. That strange desire to jump. Taking one step back, instead. And falling deep into themselves, quite unprepared.

There was a time when women would drown themselves in wells to ruin a family's water supply, their revenge if they'd been slighted in some catastrophic way. Were these dark wells of Francesca's her way of poisoning the local water? The water of the self, muddying up?

Perhaps the thing they reflected most was this: that essence of violence at the very centre of the world. The town was haunted by their gaze. People started looking over their shoulders while chatting to friends, feeling they were observed. Feeling that eye's gaze on their back. It needled them, pricking away at a tender spot, lifting the scabs, so that the old wounds were reopened.

Gianni was afraid.

This was not his daughter. When Gianni saw her then he nearly died of fright. And at the same time had an odd flash of déjà vu. For what he now beheld, when he saw his daughter, was the image on the postcard his dead wife had sent when she'd announced to him that she was pregnant. Even if the girl who had become this awesome creature had been his daughter, this ancient woman was no more his child. A riotous paternity sprung from his loins? No question of it.

Gianni saw the black eye clear enough. It's a black cunt, he thought, a great vaginal eye, like the eye of The Black Madonna. He was unaware that the author of these disturbing works was his daughter.

They were beacons of a profound inner sadness. Sadness is a potent drug of addiction. Once you've acquired a taste for it you want it more and more. And your appetite remains unchecked, and that cup of sadness flows and flows. Gianni was drinking more and baking less.

Francesca had become completely withdrawn. Sylvana tried talking to her, but Francesca just nodded then walked away.

Francesca was no longer really with us. It was hard to say that she was still human. Not that she was inhuman, but you'd swear she'd become other—something more, not less, than us.

Gianni was perplexed by this strange vision of his daughter and he felt a great guilt as well. He had failed her. He wondered how he might redeem himself, both in the eyes of his daughter and himself. And yet he dared not approach her. Why had he been so incompetent when faced with his daughter's menstrual blood? He felt he'd been party to an elementary betrayal. The paucity of his humanity, despite the complicity of his mammoth paunch.

# The Hooves Of A Mare

Sylvana, walking home and feeling short of breath, found herself immersed in the darkened eye that stared at her from a doorway. Remembering something she'd forgotten from her childhood. Sitting with her father by an overgrown bed of tomatoes, the red juice oozing from the fruit that ripened then burst under the late summer sun.

To her surprise her father had said, 'You'd almost think the hills were bleeding with you.'

Both silent then. An embarrassment they shared. Her father left and Sylvana had picked one of the split fruit and sucked the juice out. There was an odd comfort in her father's image of the hills and herself bleeding together. Propelled by a curiosity, she'd fingered her bloody cunt then, tasting the sweetness of her blood. Finding a mustiness as well, some essential ferment and fertility. The breeding ground of her? Taste of blood and tomatoes in her mouth.

Thinking about it she felt a new respect for her father. He was not a man of words, yet in his way he'd been staunch. And Gianni? He'd failed in his primary duty, and Sylvana felt angry at his inability to deal with what should have been a simple thing, his daughter becoming woman. Francesca had been orphaned by a bakery. Sylvana knew that like Francesca she would always come after La Tarantula in Gianni's affections. Gianni was good with bread and good in bed but it was not enough. Telling herself, 'I'm making love to the bakery, not the baker!'

She was attracted to the smells, the textures, the sense of purpose she gained from being there. The sex was a delight but she was using Gianni. Glad of the reprieve from mending broken plates, the smell of glue. Telling herself he was not the King Dick of her dreams. Confused as she wondered then who was the abuser and who the abused?

She knew a decision had been made. She'd once watched a stallion trying to service a mare; at each attempt the mare's hooves thumped against the stallion's chest. Sylvana was amazed the stallion's bones did not crack. Yet she was not too concerned for the stallion and had begun cheering on the mare. Something had broken in her, her patience and sweet feelings for Gianni had become tempered by disgust. Unsure whether she was disgusted with Gianni or herself, yet unable to check the feeling that Gianni's betrayal of Francesca was also a betrayal of herself. Muttering to herself, 'It's over.'

She swallowed her saliva and felt some odd confirmation of her decision in her guts. Blinking, she felt momentarily stunned as she realised she was still standing in front of the crude scrawling on the door. Feeling she'd been away and then come back. Turning her back on the dark eye that stared out from the door, she felt a confidence come into her stride as she headed for the bakery. No point avoiding it. Better break the news at once, before her confidence faltered.

Pausing at the back door of the bakery, taking a breath, seeing once again the brisk power of the mare's hooves beating against the stallion's chest as she knocked on the door, then entered.

She was not sure which thing surprised her more, the hardness of her voice or what she felt to be the veracity of what she said. Gianni looked up from his flour, but before he could speak, before he'd even decided what to do with his face, Sylvana said, 'Gianni, you're the most disgusting human being I've ever met. If I ever have to smell one of your farts again I'll kill you with my hands.'

And then she left.

# Costa's Inkling

Stefano Costa sat at home. Before him a table. On the table was paper, and *il mano finto*. The false hand. In the hand he placed a fountain pen filled with ink.

He sat in his chair and gazed at the hand that held the pen. Closing his eyes he created a picture of it in that special zone in the centre of his forehead. The hand appeared for a moment, then faded. He opened his eyes and gazed once more at the plaster hand.

Now, with the care of a fond lover, he slowly brought the stump of his wrist up towards the plaster hand. He nestled the stump into the perfect fit of *il mano finto*. He was reminded of the sensations of making love for the first time. He felt the hand enter him.

He closed his eyes. There, in the centre of his forehead, was the hand. His hand. He tried to move the pen. It felt awkward, clumsy.

He could feel a cool sweat on his forehead. He took a deep breath and opened his eyes. Fastening his gaze on the plaster hand, the point of contact between hand and pen. He closed his eyes. This time he succeeded in making a single downward stroke on the imaginary page. It seemed to take forever.

He was reminded of a time when, as a younger man, he had walked from his apartment to his landlord's house. Walking with his appendix exploding in his belly. The pain had been crippling, and he remembered this walk as the longest in his life.

199

He had made a single downward stroke. 'I'. It was a beginning.

'I.'

It's the vertical plane: it connects the earth to the sky. In physical terms it represents the spine, with the anus at one end and the brain at the other. The 'I' explores this vital contradiction, our life is the conflict and resolution between these zones. One so exalted, seemingly unattainable; the other so base and basic, a world of bums, of earth, of dung and weight. The result of this conflict—that is 'I'. The world of idea, pure, and the world of pure shit.

Costa read back what he had written and then he grunted. Not bad for an illiterate farmworker, he told himself.

His first cycle concentrated on the vowels: I, O, A, U, E.

They are the heart of utterance, he thought, the cry, the moan, the orgasm, the sob, the wail. The essential utterance. The consonants give definition, rhythm and form. But the vowel is the inner ear of the song of language.

# Costa, Bent And Trying To Straighten Up

Costa needed to get out of the house. He'd shave first—he hadn't shaved for a week and his beard was stubborn. He enjoyed the feel of rough stubble, rubbing his hand around his face before he lathered up. The bristle was long, the razor blunt, and by the time he'd finished the water had gone cold. He sustained one small cut under the chin; apart from that, no major damage, though his neck and face felt red and chafed.

He splashed cold water on his face to stall the flow of blood. Rinsing the black stems of stubble down the drain, he felt a sense of liberation then, and couldn't wait to see what the day had in store. It was already late afternoon but he had a great desire to go to town, and was not concerned by the thought that he'd have to walk home in the dark.

When he reached the front gate he flipped the latch up with his thumb and gave the gate a solid kick. It swung quickly round, and Costa had just enough time to slip through before the gate came whipping back and locked into place. Kicking the gate gave him a particular satisfaction.

He was feeling brisk, almost dainty, and decided to forego the pleasures of his yellow bicycle.

He loved the feeling as he began to lengthen his step, and swung his arms, though the feeling of air on the wrist that wore no hand was something he'd not grown used to.

It was dark when he reached town. He wandered round, encountered no-one that he knew, and started feeling sorry for himself. He had expected there would be some kind of welcome. It was ridiculous, he knew, and yet he felt deflated. He noticed for the first time the soft earth beneath his feet and wondered why he'd never noticed it before.

Gianni was not home, and Costa was avoiding Pia's. Afraid to face her after the excess of intimacy. He felt cowardly. After walking round the church and past La Tarantula three times, he headed off to Amaretto's. He'd drink, he'd eat. And then? Kicking himself now that he'd left his bicycle at home.

He could see the cafe as he turned the corner, and already something in him had grown calm.

Three hours later he was still at Amaretto's. He'd eaten beef, he'd eaten mushrooms, he'd drunk red wine, a bottle to himself, and followed it with whisky. Life was fine, and the world had just been emptied of all pain. He was wondering if he might permit himself one more drink before he left, or if this would tip him off the edge of delight and nudge him towards stupor.

It was a complex question. He could not decide whether that final drink was to be or not to be, and surveyed his options. He could order a drink, and drink it. He could not order a drink, and not drink it. He could order a drink, and look at it, sniff it, but not drink. The very fact that he'd begun to indulge in these confusing speculations was sign enough that he did not need to drink again. He found this logic worth entertaining, yet how could he entertain his logic without a drink to hand? No, he thought, that does it. If I can think as straight as that, then I don't need another drink, I need to sober up.

He was relieved that he'd resolved this tricky question, and then surprised as Amaretto appeared from behind his shoulder, put a clear shot glass in front of him, and poured another whisky while patting Costa on the back, murmuring, 'This one's on me.'

Amaretto did not like Stefano Costa. Stefano was taller than him. Amaretto preferred to talk when Costa was sitting down. He felt this gave him some slight altitudinal advantage.

Costa thought Amaretto was a conceited little gobshite, but was happy to drink his homemade booze. And happier still to drink his whisky on the house.

# Sylvana And Her Room Of Broken Plates

At first she hated living on her own, she'd never felt so lonely. Or was it that living alone she realised just how lonely she had felt throughout her life? Slowly she had made peace with herself, and the terrors of loneliness were altered by the joy she found in her own company. There was a special happiness that came, the joy of knowing she could cope. It was enough.

There were times she didn't recognise herself. She'd grown up in a rural slum, and the stirrings of an intellectual life had cut her off from these country roots. At times she wished she could become a country girl again, milk the cows or strain the water from the yoghurt in the muslin cloth. She told herself that life was simpler then, and yet she knew that it was not.

She had begun a strange invention—the invention of her self—and while she felt afraid, there was a strength and peace there too.

Her craft of repairing broken plates had been the result of an accident. She'd been dining with a friend when she had dropped a plate onto the kitchen bench. The plate had broken rather neatly, almost in half. Despite her friend's protestations she had taken it away, and had found the break was easy to repair. She'd taken time on it, and was surprised how much she enjoyed the simple task. It was an act of meditation. On what? It was the joy of bringing back together some broken thing. She laughed and smiled to herself. If only families were so easily repaired. But then her smile sank and a pain resurfaced. She focussed on sanding back the glue until no trace of it was visible. It was a job well accomplished, and she knew it.

As did her friend, who turned it up and down and could not find where it had broken. Her friend had then enquired whether she would repair two plates of that same set, which were badly chipped. She still had the chips, had kept them for three years and never gotten round to fixing them.

Somehow this simple thing had become an occupation— word got around from friend to friend, she never advertised, and she was embarrassed to charge people as much as her time was worth, so she kept herself underpaid and busy in one stroke. And yet this thing had brought a self-respect, and a modest income. Enough to pay the rent and feed herself and have a drink in a late cafe when the fancy took.

Getting high on the vapours of the glue tin as she mended broken plates and vases. Bringing a subtle harmony once more to the victim of a marital dispute, a treasured plate thrown hard against the wall.

Pestoso had once brought a broken drinking cup. He looked furtive and embarrassed while making a display of everyday good manners. He explained it was a trifling thing, no consequence, but if perhaps she could just . . .? Well then, I'll leave it here and when it's done you'll be in touch?

While Sylvana was a gifted worker, one thing worried her: some jobs never seemed to get done, whether because she was too good and so people flooded her with requests, or because she was too slow, or because she was just losing her mind slowly to the glue.

The pieces would lurk for months in a box in a corner, or underneath her bed, she'd never get them out. These were mostly the requests that came from friends, the jobs for which she said, 'No payment, labour of love!' Misbegotten phrase, quickly resented when she realised how much time she would lose in the task. Her friends became embarrassed to ask if the work was done, too coy to request their broken pieces back, and too polite to make it clear that they would pay for time it took.

The broken fragments seemed to be growing at a rate that outstripped Sylvana's capacity to put them on the mend.

She wondered if more plates were being broken than at the same time the previous year. Was there an invisible equation between the harmony of the town and the rate of breakages? And if so, was the proportion direct or inverse? More broken plates instead of broken noses? Or was the shattered glass just the beginning, the fragmented portent of the violence yet to come?

Her room was filling up with fragments and fractures, some fine as hairs and others coarse and cracked. She imagined herself sitting in the room with just her head protruding, the room become a giant urn made of the ruptured homeware of the town, encasing her. And no matter how fast she worked, for every plate she mended another three were brought to her.

# A One-Night Stand

As she walked down the street she happened to observe a solitary man sitting in Amaretto's, a singular man with a singular hand and a singular stump. It was late at night and she decided to go in.

Sylvana liked the look of him. She sat at a table with her back to him, where she could see his reflection in a mirror behind the bar. As she sat down she was already smiling to herself. She looked into the mirror just in time to see him look away. She turned her head as he started to glance back at her reflection. She swivelled now to face him. He was smiling.

One pleasure Sylvana had not known was that of breaking glass, hurling some precious vase at a wall or ducking head while screaming. At times she was sorely tempted to fling the piece she was working on, but she restrained herself, squinting her eyes and bringing the tiny chips into place like a fine jigsaw puzzle. For her, this moment was sublime. Something that Costa, when they spoke of it, was quick to accept. His experience with walls had held a similar fascination and delight. He'd never thought there might be a connection between their vocations, a unity that embraced a dry stone wall and a broken plate.

When he'd mentioned that to Sylvana, she'd looked at him, not knowing what to say. She was tempted to ask if he would like to come up to her room and—and what? Look at her broken fragments?

Costa had joked that she might glue his hand back on

and they had laughed. She wasn't sure what to say, instead she took his hand and gave it a tiny squeeze, their hands resting on the table. They looked at each other and smiled, and then she said, 'It's been good to meet you.'

'Would you like a whisky before you go?' replied Stefano.

'No', she said, 'it wouldn't do if I got the shakes while trying to glue the pieces back!'

She stood and thanked him and left, feeling confused, kicking herself and wondering why she'd run away when she found herself most attracted to this handsome one-hand man.

She turned and saw him watching her as she walked away. She waved and he raised one finger, his hand still resting on the table. She stopped, and smiled at him. She felt contrary and didn't know what to do. Rooted to the spot. The desire to take that man's root into her, a frisky feeling. Oh God, she thought, he's seen me shuffling from side to side and knows I don't know what I want and knows exactly what I want.

Stefano had not moved. She stood in the dark light of the narrow road. A decision came. She took a breath and prepared to walk back inside. She mentally rehearsed herself saying, Oh what the hell, the broken plates can wait, on second thoughts a whisky seems a good idea!

This reverie was ruptured by the sound of someone calling out her name.

Terremoto. He was some streets off, but approaching. She walked quickly into the bar, and said to Costa, 'Come with me and have a drink, I'd love to talk but I can't stay here.'


He was momentarily surprised to see her hands clutching the soft cheeks of her bum. He placed his own hand there and gave a squeeze, their hands joined in this cheeky embrace.

'Oh God yes,' she said, 'if you want to squeeze my arse like that I'll come. But slow, sweetheart, slow.'

They came at once, although this took some time. One of those delightful conundrums of the flesh. A physical enigma, that the fastest way to come may be the way that is most slow.

# Bread Roses

Terremoto wanted her back, and he wanted her badly. He wanted her front as well. Moulding the dough of rolls was a torment and a grief, and they kept turning into phallic-looking things, phallic and limp if such a thing may be. He was an unholy cocktail of grief, self-pity and sexual longing. Getting longer. He'd win her back, sure of it.

Without knowing why, his hands began to wring a wreath of roses from the dough. Too funereal, perhaps too apt. He punched it up and kneaded once again, and made a bunch of roses out of bread, complete with thorns and petals, and then he baked his bunch of roses in the oven.

He'd glazed the petals a curious baker's red, and the thorns were sharp and overcooked, almost but not quite burnt—strangely realistic. A nice effect. He wondered why he'd never thought of it before. The green tint of the leaves and their fine serration was something else of which he felt quite proud.

For a moment he wondered whether he would take them to Sylvana or leave them in the shop—placed in the window they were sure to generate a lot of interest from passing trade and regulars alike. But they were made for her, a token of love, perhaps he could win her with his art and show he was a kindly man who loved her well. He ignored the darker voice that muttered She's a fucking bitch! That voice he didn't hear at all, just shrugged his loaf and bent down to smell the flowers that he'd baked. He'd wait until they had cooled a little so they'd be firmer and travel better, but not completely cold so that their fragrance would still reach out. He'd win her back, yes, yes, of that he could be sure.

The sound of humans making love is like so many other sounds and like no other sound at all. When you know that's what you hear, you know as well your ears don't lie. It's not the sound of water gurgling down a bath and it's not the sound of dogs and bitches running in the night; it is at times almost but no, is not the sound of cats clawing the moonlight as they rut, nor is it the sound men make while carrying a new piano. It may be that it is never the same sound twice, but like a saxophone you know it when you hear it.

As Gianni climbed the stairs up to Sylvana's place he heard that sound and laughed a little to himself. A friendly sound, he thought, those neighbours on the floor beneath Sylvana's were a passionate couple. He mounted the stairs and chuckled, and his chuckle made his legs feel lighter as he hoisted his bulk up all those stairs.

He'd brought the fresh-baked roses, still smelling slightly. The short detour he'd had to make to Amaretto's had taken longer than he'd thought and it was getting late, he might have been a little drunk but amaretto only made the breath smell sweet. His lips and mouth felt thick and sticky. He climbed the stairs, taking a rest by the front door of the copulating neighbours. His ears were playing tricks, the sound had stopped, perhaps the sound had not been there at all? Perhaps his own desire had led his ears to make that carnal chorus as a comfort to him? Just one more floor and he'd be there. Would she let him in? He hoped so. After all, he had his gift of flowers.

He reached the second floor, which was the top floor in this small block. He stopped to tuck his shirt into his pants and smarten up, placing the fresh-baked roses between his legs while he completed this delicate maneouvre, and was just about to knock when something stopped him.

The sound of humans making love is like so many other sounds and like no other sound at all. It's not the sound of compressed air rushing out of a bladder—or is it?

Whatever it is or was or might or might not be, the sound Gianni heard did not deceive his ears.

What should he do? He didn't know. He was in shock. He sat down on the top stair. He'd knock the door down, he'd leave the roses where she'd find them, he'd call her name . . .

But of course he then did nothing of the sort. He wept quietly for a moment, then shuffled himself together, picked up the roses and slowly made his way back down the stairs. The sounds of humans making love and enjoying a fine and well-made climax followed him out the door into the street. Then it grew quiet. Mmmmn, he thought, the roses will look good in the shop window.

As Gianni walked home he tried to put the sounds he'd heard as far from him as he could. The more he tried to not think about them, the more he could think of nothing else. Wanting and not wanting to know the identity of the other man. Feeling an outrage burning in him, and a strange, belittling shame. Eavesdropping in his mind on the fevered motion of their copulation. Wondering which was worse, if it was someone he did or did not know. Trying to convince himself that his ears were playing tricks, and sure there were two people in Sylvana's room. He could hear the bedstead thumping hard against the wall as he listened with his mind's ear, the bed thumping hard against his cranium.

Gianni couldn't sleep. He had another name for her now. Slyvana. It didn't make him feel a whole lot better, but it helped. He wondered if there might be a way to use the window of the shop to his advantage. He didn't know how. Perhaps he'd go and have a chat with Amaretto. It was a hazard, having a friend who was a barman. Whenever he went to say hello he had to have a drink. Well, didn't have to. Was he a drunkard? He was a social drinker, and it just happened that his best friend owned a bar. He knew there must be something with the window, but he didn't know what. Yes, he'd go and have a talk with Amaretto. Between the two of them, over a drink, they would work something out.

It only took a word from Amaretto next day to clear

the whole thing up. Gianni didn't know if he was happy or sad to learn the identity of the man who'd fucked his love inside his head while he'd tried to sleep and failed. He didn't know what to do, and wondered how he might react when he saw Mr Stefano Costa again.

He could imagine a haughty silence and a withering eye, trying to provoke his guilt. He felt a fresh wave of jealousy wash through him, and quite enjoyed it.

Slyvana. Bitch. How he wished he'd never met her! He cleared out the window and left the roses on their own as his display. They looked quite elegant and just a little bit pathetic. For the nonce he was quite happy with that effect.

# Gianni's Second Coming

He decided to take himself to the whorehouse. He'd only been there once before, quite drunk, he'd needed that false courage just to step inside. He had drunk tea with a young woman who was saving money for a trip. They talked about bread and prostitution, the flour and the flesh. The girl confessed she did not know why men would come to such a place, that appetite was foreign to her. Nor could he explain it.

Still, they came to an understanding, he paid his fare and spent an hour naked in her company. She was gentle with him and he was satisifed with that. She kissed him on the lips, something he'd heard a prostitute would never do. And she had rubbed his forehead with her thumb, on his third eye, this was the thing he found most touching.

She said her name was Amy. He wondered on this. Was it true, or was it just part of the role she left behind when she left work? It would be that, he thought, yet even so he fantasized about their meeting once again after her shift. And knew this was a fantasy.

It was a rite of passage that he'd made. Something a man was expected to do, and until that threshold had been crossed his manhood was provisional, and unconfirmed. It was a different confirmation to the wafers and the wine. Or was it?

But this second coming was a curious affair. He'd felt an innocence, almost a surge of adolescence, when he'd entered the first time. That was gone. The place looked busier now, the women were working in the rooms, and the men who waited watched a woman who was speaking to a wall. The woman was telling the wall that she'd been orphaned when she was five years old, and she was wondering if this was why she now had sex with strangers to make her living. She turned and addressed the room.

'I don't enjoy it that much. I know I'm good at it. I just don't enjoy it.'

She began a demonstration of her art. Rubbing herself against a wooden chair, her legs straddling it. The small white shorts she was wearing rubbing up and down the back of the chair. Gianni looked away.

The whole thing made him feel uneasy. He drank his tea and noticed how the woman's voice rarely changed, locked in the tones of simpered service. He could not follow through this second time. The horror that he felt as he glanced up at the woman straddling the chair. The whole scene filled him with dismay.

Yes, he thought, he would love to spend time with a woman in her knickers, but not for the sheer mechanics of that joy. A woman who wanted to make love with him, and with whom there was a shared desire—that was the thing he'd come for, the very thing a whorehouse doesn't have for sale. The white shorts reminded him of his late wife, and the whole affair made him feel sad. He drank his tea, stood up to leave; a woman now approached, placing her hands to his lapel.

'You're not leaving now?' He was sorry that he flinched but could not help himself. An illusion had been shattered. He felt grateful for it. He fled.

Walking back home. The shops he passed in the early morning light seemed unfamiliar. He looked at them with different eyes to the ones he'd had as he walked briskly to the brothel. Perhaps he had sobered up? The coming blue light of the sky was a deep, deep hue, and he felt happy, walking home, to have seen this light.


Gianni's impotence was a direct result of his jealousy. He'd never been impotent before and didn't know how to deal with it. It didn't bother him at first, because he didn't notice it. He could only notice his raging anger whenever he thought about Sylvana, or when he began feeling up his doughs and remembered how once the touch of dough had filled him with desire for her body.

His breads were limp things now, his breadsticks made people laugh. He heard them snigger as they walked past in pairs, the laughter starting as the couples passed beyond his window. Out of eyesight, but not earshot. That's when he'd hear the remark, and then the pair of them giddy with their little laugh. There were times when he thought that he might rush out into the street and accost the passersby for making lewd remarks about his limp breads sagging in the window. He caught sight of his reflection in the window one night and thought, It's a bad job!

His anger receded and he was thinking about sex, and he had to say he'd lost his appetite for it. He'd lost his appetite for food as well, and he was shrinking. He no longer ate while he was on the job and he had no desire for eating after work. Worst of all, the job he dreaded most was looming: his annual humiliation at the hands of the Easter bun.

# In The Wake Of Their Brief Affair

In the wake of his tryst with Sylvana, Costa was feeling even more tremulous than he had before. He'd found such solace in her arms. He wanted to feel gleeful, bright and sprightly, and instead found that he was full of guilt. Convinced that he had betrayed Pia, Sylvana and himself. The more he thought about it, the worse he felt, and the more he avoided thinking about it, the more his cowardly nature was confirmed. Deciding that he'd not venture back into town, and he'd abstain from sex.

He'd made that vow yet found it difficult to keep. Invariably he'd find himself full of a vital animation that led in short time to the sweetly smelling spilling of his seed. He started masturbating with a frequency that alarmed him, and the more he tried to curb this aspect of his vitality, the more he seemed to bring himself undone. The yeasty smells wafting up from underneath the sheets. Telling himself there was one consolation in sleeping on his own: there was no need to argue over who got the wet patch.

Immersing himself in his alphabet, convinced it was the way to regain some sense of his self-worth, and calling it an occupation. Was it an occupation? It was something he seized at, in the hope it would bring a stability, or at least give him enough ballast to help him make it through another day. Puzzling over the implication of the letter F. A broken ladder. Would he ever reach the letter Z? And if he did, what then? Might he not begin to write a dictionary? Closing his eyes, imagining once more that his plaster hand had become flesh. Feeling himself grow teary, becoming disgusted by his self-pity. Wanting to propel himself into some greater action and discover once again a sense of purpose he felt that he had lost. Diddling round the house, cursing himself for laziness and fearfulness, yet feeling he'd become broken and could no longer function in the world. He was spending more time inside than he'd ever done in his life, wondering why he felt frightened every time he left the house. Telling himself it was just a stage he was going through, and only half aware that he'd become utterly reclusive.

Sylvana, when she hadn't heard from him, got a surprise to realise she didn't even know where the man lived. Reproaching herself briefly for being slutty, though finding it hard to achieve a convincing tone. She'd enjoyed their night together, yet was relieved when Costa was gone. Glad they'd made no promise to each other, feeling undesirous of further complication in her life. At least it had helped get Gianni out of her system.

Or had it? She was wondering why she'd cut Gianni off. Had she made the right decision for the wrong reasons, the wrong decision for the right reasons, or had she not really made a decision at all? The ripe quandary of it.

Now that she'd set the horns upon his head she found it hard to believe she'd ever loved that fat baker. He was an object of ridicule, no less. Surely she'd just felt sorry for him? Or for herself? Someone to break her solitude? And yet she missed his gentle warmth and the rituals of the bakery. Still, she had sworn she'd not go back, and that was that.

She felt a dismay come in her as she contemplated a simple fact. Perhaps she'd made the right decision, for the right reasons, after all. Could she and Gianni not be friends, at least, leave it at that? The overwhelming memories her body had, the pair of them floured up and flowering on the bench. Her body missed the ripe comfort of his flesh. Was she just too proud to go back to him? Missing the way they'd talk of bread and bakers, the mental fit they had, as the bakery filled up with aromas.

For some reason her thoughts drifted to Francesca. A frightening transformation. She seemed so out of reach. Sylvana knew then that she'd keep her distance from the bakery, and felt her jaw clamp hard, as if her teeth were joined with glue.

# Terremoto's Day And Night

When Gianni lugged the big bags of white flour on his shoulder and let them flop onto the bench, a fine spray of powdered flour drifted up into the air. He caught the ripe whiff of sweat that ran along his arms from his underarms, and sweat stung his eyes as it dribbled down his forehead. A sharpness that made him think about the knife he'd rip along the flourbag. He didn't like to think of himself as a butcher but the image caught his mind, of the knife that ripped the flour sacks and opened them like a belly on the bench. More powdered flour then, drifting in the air like a baker's mist, making the webs white. The spiders ate this flour—he wondered if they were becoming vegetarians, evolving into white floury creatures, damp white jewels that glowed out of the darkness. Watching the delicate way they wove their webs, leaving little spider tracks of white along the strands. Sometimes he wondered if he drank too much.

I'm sweating like a pig, he thought, and then stopped. He'd never seen a pig sweat.

His water pouring out in beads that fell from his nose, other drops trickled down his neck onto his breasts, shaking as he shovelled the hot trays of newly baked bread out of the oven. A small spray of water as he shook his head, then shovelled another tray of loaves into the oven.

Gianni felt a sadness in him. The water in him preparing to burst out. The blubbernoodle of his body bouncing as his diaphragm contracted and released, his jiggly body's jig, and the weeping sounds, and the hugging of his knees, the whole caboodle wobble of it. He had failed his daughter.

Why had he not seen Francesca for so long?

He wiped his face with his handkerchief and blew his nose. He had just time enough to go and have a drink before the loaves would be browned off in the oven. He drew his breath, prepared himself, and then stood up.

The smell of bread followed him out the door like a friendly dog come for a walk. He felt tired. Had he ever felt this tired before? A weariness that filled the very water of him. He didn't have the strength to walk. He decided to squat down, the exertion justified by his paunchy comfort once this descent was achieved. He felt the ripe cheeks of his arse spread under his weight. The solid pudding of him, a squatting ball of flesh.

He didn't know he'd fallen asleep, but the nightmare smell that came into his dream was prolonged by the smell that came into his nose and woke him up—the nightmare smell of burning bread.

Gianni was in shock. He'd never burnt a loaf before. The smell was everywhere, he had to throw the lot away, the fine creamed buns and cakes, the fresh-baked loaves, the lot. I couldn't feed that to a pig, he thought. In a smoky daze he wandered off to Amaretto's. He didn't need a drink, he needed a bottle. He'd burnt the bake. The shop stank of his stupid error.

The first drink washed his throat but the smoky taste remained, so that the amaretto had the taste of burnt almond. The second glass filled his mouth with a sickly sweetness, a brief reprieve before the smoke was back inside his throat. The smoke of burning bread down in his lungs and in his belly. He smelt like a burnt and spoilt loaf. He drank again.

He knew he would keep drinking until he threw up, somehow the prospect cheered him. He smiled an odd, defeated smile, the next two glasses disappeared at once. He was well underway and braced himself, knowing that he was equal to the task.

He felt quite ill. He didn't really feel like throwing up, he wished that he could sleep.

He was lying in his bed, staring at the ceiling. Trying to stop the thing from moving round. He closed his eyes and felt worse. A whirlpool in his guts that dragged the whole of him into its orbit, all of his solids gone to fluid.

He opened his eyes and fixed them on a corner of the window frame, as if by holding on with his eyes he'd stop the room from whirling round. To his delight the whole thing stopped. He let himself take a deeper breath, and the game began again. Trying to hold on with his eyes as his stomach too began to whirl. His saliva turned to bile.

A mighty peristaltic fit like a great *tsunami* surging through his body. A small backwash of triple belches, the bitter gas up in his mouth and down his nose. A second surge driving through the centre of the whirling stuff he was.

He hauled himself out of the depths and sat up, and then a third surge grabbed hold of him, as if he'd been punched in the guts, except he'd been struck this mighty blow from the inside, and this hard fist was made of air and water. He brought his weight forward, sitting on his bed and felt the gushing mass of him spilling out into the night.

He would have sworn that the next day would bring a measure of relief, and was surprised when he found that if anything he now felt worse.

The violent fit had passed, but in its wake there remained some vaster poisoned thing, the whole of him. A muddle of smoke and amaretto and burnt bread and stale sweat. If he had any appetite at all it was an appetite for sleep. He stayed in bed. All of life felt queasy. The queasy song of birds, the queasy light of the sun behind the curtains, he was the queasy centre of a queasy universe.

He felt in need of irrigation. He gagged some water down his throat and felt it slurry down. He washed his face, the shock of it against his skin. He drank a second gulletful of water, the greengall taste so profound in him. Another thirsty gulp, squilling round inside. He'd need to scrub his innards bare and start again. How did you scrub your guts? He'd done that sure enough last night, scrubbed hard and raw, and with a toxic wash right through him. He felt some slight improvement, with an odd result: this clarity of water let him find out just how rotten he felt.

He let his eye fall on the mushy puddle on the floor. He'd need bucket, rag and mop.

Rubbing the boards. Bemused by the disgusting things of life. He'd once helped a friend kill his first pig, a handy beast where nothing goes to waste. They'd had to boil it in a bath to get the skin and bristle off. They left it in too long, and when they went to lift it out the whole damn hog came apart in their hands. Eyes meeting with the shock, each one holding an arm or leg, the poor hog's hock.

They had to lift the pig out bit by bit, a piecemeal pig, and no choice but to set the jaw and get on with the job. Trying to think of something else, hard though when the reality of the thing was so strong, a boiled pig come apart at the seams.

Galling thought as he wiped his own gall off the floor. He smelt like that poor pig, the common gall and bladderb-ile. Musing then, Is there a difference between a man and a pig?

A riddle there, though the answer eluded him.

They'd eaten the poor porker, too, it had become a thing of honour. How could you kill meat that you weren't prepared to eat? They had eaten the pig with reservation, and as they chewed they avoided the one thing they knew rejoined in their thoughts—the floating bits of pig around the bath. They chewed and ate. It made a good bacon, that pig; after the first meal it had become much easier to eat, and they'd traded off the other parts in place of wine and oil.

He didn't feel like eating now. He'd have a lie down on the bed. Open the window. Cool breeze blowing. Perhaps just pull the blankets up.

And then he was asleep.

He was floating belly up in a big white bath. Hands reaching in. He came apart as they tried to lift him out.

Blinking his eyes. Too bright out there, keeping them shut brought greater comfort. He had seen a pig sweat. The pig they'd butchered, boiled and sweating in the bath.

There was a difference between a man and a fine white pig. With the pig you could make use of every bit, the bristles and the bones, the snout and hooves and skin, the whole damn hog. Yet with a man, it seemed, the pity was so much of him was left to waste.

He thought of the expression on his friend's face when the pig's leg had come off, and started laughing to himself. He was, perhaps, just starting to feel okay.

# Luigi's Contemplation Of An Infinite Illusion

What of Luigi? Where had his attempts to glimpse an image of the divine left him? He rarely went out of doors, convinced that the experiment required a closed environment—a photograph must have borders. If there were no borders, then it would be an infinite thing, of no use to the human eye.

The eye can observe the infinite, but the brain cannot cope with it. Trying to divide an infinite illusion into a finite number of parts.

An impossibility, Luigi thought. He kept the stable door closed at all times. He painted the windows black and The Filing Cabinet became a darkroom.

How would he know when the photograph had finished processing itself? If he threw a window open prematurely, might he kill off the experiment at a vital stage of development?

See him sitting in total darkness, contemplating his photograph of God. Impossible, of course, as it is too dark to see him. Hear him, as he moves while sitting on his three-legged stool, the creaking of the legs a confirmation that Luigi is not yet dead.


He was grappling with a difficult question. He'd always assumed God must have eyes. But as he sat in his darkroom he began to doubt this proposition.

Was it more preposterous to propound a blind god than a god who sees everything? And seeing nothing, is this god less deserving of our love? Might this god be an object of pity, or our compassion? God, Creator of the Known and Unknown Worlds, creating landscapes full of awe and wonder, and God has no eyes to see it. Instead God knows the whole thing as a lizard knows a stone—that knowledge you get inside your belly as you crawl along the ground.

Luigi was flummoxed. Was this why there was such tactility, things oily, greasy, muddy? So many different kinds of smooth—the smooth of glass and marble, smooth of silk and velvet; the kind of smooth an eyeball has, different inside from its out, smooth jelly of the aqueous humour.

In the land of the blind god, might it be true that the blind are closer than the seeing to God, in all God's darkness? Is this why, at the beginning, God said, Let there be light? To know the thrill of creating something that even to God would be unknowable? So that God might have some mystery in an existence that's Divine?

Luigi's head was hurting from these intense speculations.

It was not a sharp pain, more a dullish throb that occupied his occipital lobes, his medulla oblongata, his whole aching brainbox.

His cerebellum was caput. His brain strained by the heavy weight of thoughts he was not accustomed to lifting.

Would his brain explode, implode, or just capsize? The verb and action eluding him, each thought battering the last. His head stuffed full, then overstuffed, and still his senses and his thinking cramming him with information, and all the while the jellied coils recoiling like a lizard being beaten with a stick.

When Luigi came to, he was relieved to find the great pain in his sconce had subsided. Deciding he'd attempt to draw no conclusions, and fearing that this thought might be the tiniest impulse needed to set the machine in motion once again.

He wondered how he might stop himself from thinking, and caught himself, and ceased this briefest wonderment before it could properly begin. He heard the fowl gurgling in a clucky sort of way as they roamed and ranged around

The Filing Cabinet. Picking up a bowl of vegetable scraps, the remnant of his midday meal, banging the metal bowl with a battered fork with crooked tines. The birds eyed him darkly, and he desisted from the tempting speculation of how the sights a bird's eye sees might differ from the sights of man and woman, of dog and lizard.

Setting a different course, he opened up the mighty stable door and felt a gush of clean air washing through the musty smell of the overladen stable. The light hurt his eyes.

He cast the kitchen scraps before him and watched as the hens rushed past him. Their dirty feathers that were once white had become a quasi-grey.

Putting his hands behind his head, rubbing the bones of his sorry skull, content to do just that and nothing else as he watched the birds go at their feed.

He wandered over to the tank to take a look at his rocks and frogs and photographic papers. The water was stagnant, and as he dipped his hand into the murky liquid he was dismayed.

A brown and green scummy mess. He could not believe that a photograph of God could look so apprehensive to the eye, nor smell so foul.

There was no sign of the frogs. They must have grown, he told himself, and simply hopped out of the tank. A pang of jealousy running through him as he wished that he could do the same, abandoning his hopeless task.

Staring at the wall that he might enjoy some small reprieve from the sight of so much mess. Wondering why he'd ever begun the misbegotten enterprise he called his photograph of God.

He turned his back on the foetid tank and looked around the room. He felt like kicking something.

Three large hessian sacks appeared to be the perfect target and he gave each one a kick. He could not recall what was inside, and with relief he saw a small puff of powder lift off the bags each time he kicked. Remembering the origin of these sacks—three bags of flour Costa had sent to thank him when he'd made *il mano finto*.

The chaos of The Filing Cabinet had ceased to be a source of wonder and had turned into a source of aggravation and dismay.

'I'm going to clean the whole thing out,' he spoke aloud. 'How can there be a photograph of God when there is so much clutter?'

Doubting that he'd have the strength to do it. Panicked by the thought of standing in an empty room. As if the mess had become his anchor.

No point rushing things, he tried to reassure himself. Perhaps if I begin with just three sacks. He felt placated by the clean aspect of his logic. What would he do with these three sacks? Rye flour, Stefano had said. If he started baking bread again the stuff would last him for a year.

He kicked the nearest bag again and watched once more as a puff of flour escaped the hessian. Like three fat bellies, he told himself, and was amazed by the clear and easy answer to the question of what to do with them.

Gianni was delighted by the gift. He put his arms around each bag, and couldn't help but think it was somehow like a woman.

# Amaretto's Ritual

Amaretto loved to play the small harmonium in the church, the soft bell tones and fluting sounds, the urgent mumblings of the bass. He had sweet fingers. Sweet, and bitter. Whether he made music or made food, that bitterness and sweetness was always there. As you listened to him play you wouldn't know if you were feeling happy or sad.

He had begun a ritual of his own. He would walk slowly down the centre aisle of the church, hearing an imaginary music, a bridal waltz of his own composition. In his fantasy this was his wedding day, and at any moment now he'd hear the rustle of a bridal train made from the myriad feathers of plucked geese. He stood, full of his adoration, waiting, surely waiting.

The longer Amaretto stood before the altar, the younger he became. His years began to slip away, until he was a small boy again.

He felt like a child prodigy when he approached the sweet machine. He'd never had a lesson. As a child the sprightly sounds had danced out of his fingers, and his music was gay of heart. But as he aged his sprightly touch faltered, and became more leaden.

He seemed too young to have such sadness in him. His music had become more chromatic, as well, and the curious intervals that he imposed as his fingers slid along the keys were quite disturbing.

Lifting up the lid of the harmonium, he placed his fingers on the jaundiced ivory keys. There was a moment now when he felt clean, or perhaps he merely felt that he was empty.

The sadness and the futile aspirations disappeared, and for this moment you could say he was at peace. He smiled then, and began the task of composing his bridal hymn. It always started as a waltz, yet the more he played, the more its lilting quality would be lost, and in its place there'd come the numbing tones of a lament. And as he played he was slowing down, until after some twenty minutes had elapsed there were long delays between each note, and each chord was sustained for one whole breath. Every time you thought he'd stopped he'd start again.

He sat sit there immobile, hands over the keys. He knew that his music had come out all wrong. He was convinced that if he could perfect his bridal waltz he would attain the woman of his dream. He could not see that he was launched into a dreaming most corrupt, and that what he sought was something he could not attain, because the thing did not exist.

It was a curious affair, and while he sat at the harmonium with an expectation of happiness, he always closed the lid on it feeling sad.

# Cafe Zanetti

When Amaretto had exhausted his supply of white feathers he was at a loss how to keep his odd obsession on the boil. He did not see it as an obsession, of course, obsessives never do. The frame of their own world is clear and stable, and if Pia Zanetti preoccupied him—occupying as it were the foreground, middle ground and background of his view; if she filled the entire frame of his imagination, of his reason and unreason—he saw this as something normal, and nothing untoward.

He was in love, that was all, with the most beautiful woman in the world. Woman of his dreams, woman of his fancy. Amaretto would not have said that he was a sick man. If he went to sleep each night thinking about Pia Zanetti, there was nothing odd in this. If he helped himself to sleep by fantasizing that he was slowly taking off her clothes, or that she accosted him quite boldly in the street and stuck her hand down his pants; if he woke in the middle of the night and felt a tongue licking his lips and thought, It's hers! only to discover that it was in fact his own; if he awoke to pee in the early hours and had trouble getting started with the flow because he'd just been making love with her; if all of this had become the condition of his waking, dreaming life; if he thought only of her, whether he was washing potatoes or scrubbing the floor, whether in an idle moment wondering what she was doing right then; or if when walking he noticed a long white cloud and thought It looks like a woman dancing on one leg—if all of this was now the main condition of his life, he knew that there was nothing wrong, perverse or aberrant in his behaviour.

It was just the prime condition of a man in love.

How did he love her? Had he not killed and plucked a thousand geese in her honour? Had he not bestowed on her each of their feathers as a token of his love, esteem and his devotion? Was he not a maniac? Not in his own estimation. But now that his supply of feathers was at an end he was unsure how to express his true feelings for the woman he loved.

He thought of Pia lying on a bed of goosefeathers, with her head on a large pillow of goosedown, her naked body covered in a quilt of feathers from his geese—he assumed that Pia slept naked, but had not had the chance to familiarise himself with the habiliments of her nocturnal attire. He could think of nothing else. He was convinced that in her he had found the embodiment of all the graces, and all the necessary vices. His essential life partner was revealed to him, and she rebuffed him utterly.

Not that he had declared his hand to her. He assumed it must be clear to Pia that this feathery tribute was his own. Who else could have such access to a legacy of geese, and could shower her with white goosefeathers? Surely in this his standing was unique? Perhaps there was a sign that he could give, that would make it clear he was her goosy champion? Perhaps if he wore a white goose feather in his ear? No, he would need something more emphatic. But what? It wasn't long before the idea revealed itself most clear to him.

He carved a prototype out of butter. He would not have said he was a monster. He carved it with a love so all-consuming it was obscene, and had the weather not been so cold the butter would have curdled as he ran his blade and spatula through it.

The cafe was closed for three days. Behind its doors, great activity. Knocking of hammers. Rasping of metal, beating of iron. At Amaretto's something was brewing.

On the third day, at nightfall, one might have seen, had one been standing across the street, or even, like Costa in a previous life, suspended from a rope and dangling from the spire of the old church, Pia Zanetti dressed as she'd been when she'd performed The Wasp Dance, naked from the waist up, and tied with a long pink ribbon from ballet slipper to thigh. One would have seen her being hauled by a rope up in the air, suspended by her neck. One would have sworn that she was being hung, and so she was. Or at least an effigy of her, which Amaretto had now installed as the figurehead of his new cafe.

Amaretto's was no more. His new cafe? Cafe Zanetti. The entire decor featured Zanetti motifs, and everything stood upon one leg: the chairs, the tables, the bar, and suspended in the air—although to tell the truth she was bolted to a pair of metal brackets, but even so, above the entrance to the bar—there she was, Pia Zanetti.

One small detail Amaretto had not reckoned on: when you walked inside you would look at Pia overhead. You'd look straight up, and unwittingly you'd find that you were staring up her dress. Most disconcerting. Not only that. In the mind's eye of Amaretto it was clear that Pia wasn't wearing any knickers.

Cafe Zanetti was the last straw. Pia's anger rose from her gizzards, curling through her. When she first saw the ikon of herself above the cafe door she had mixed feelings: there was a momentary sense of flattery, before her anger reasserted itself. She looked inside. The cafe was empty and the door was locked. It was 7.00 a.m. and she'd not slept that night. Had attempted sleep, but her insomnia was more persistent than her somnia.

Pia started to lock herself indoors. She had sworn off amaretto. Feeling, when she was out walking, as if she had grown a pair of antennae. She was afraid, and could feel her fear fizzing in her. It had changed her chemistry, she was too conscious of every small detail. The movement of a bush by a gust of wind drew her full attention, things that she would once have blinkered out now absorbed her totally. She was finding it hard to get through a day, and felt depressed. She was unfamiliar with the feelings. Fighting off the agitation and despondency.

# Papaver Somniferum

Gianni was a frustrated musician, and he envied Amaretto's musical abilities. He wondered if a baker might not play his tune upon the belly of the town, so that the populace might dance or sing or weep with the same response that music could provoke. What was the range of his instrument? Might one bake a bread that was tinged with sadness, remorse, melancholy or despair? What of jealousy? Was there scope for a truly tragic bread? He was reminded of the loaves Luigi's father baked before he died. Might one bake a bitter bread that still beguiled and tantalised the eye? And what of comedy, delight? What access did he have to the sublime? Was there scope for a bread that provoked mirth? He wanted to make a bread that surpassed the limits of his trade. A bread, a cake, he placed no limits on the form.

He started by thinking about the passions: anger, hate, love, jealousy, despair and joy. He wasn't sure if they were the only passions, but it gave him some tacit starting point. He'd have to choose with care the avenues of his research, or suffer the calamitous consequences that might result. What would happen if he perfected a bread that bred hatred within the town? Or an anger bread? He would do best to stay within the realm of the more hospitable, some kind of angel bread, a joyous loaf. Though the possibilities of all of them intrigued him. Jealousy.

He discovered his powers by accident. A bag of valerian had been labelled basil, and he'd been too drunk to notice that bass fragrance of the herb. He made focaccia, selling it hot from the oven. People took it home for lunch, followed by the longest siesta in their lives.

He started his experiments with much caution. He decided to work with only two subjects. He was the first. The second was Emile Pestoso. He hadn't told Emile of this, it had evolved of its own volition. If that's an admissable assertion.

'Gianni,' Emile had said, 'do you mind if I have a word with you, in private?'

And so Gianni closed the shop door and slipped the latch, pulled out a stool for Emile while he spread himself over a bag of flour that was propped against the wall.

'Gianni,' Emile had continued, 'I'm having trouble sleeping. I've tried everything. I've tried drinking, but it only makes me ill and I sleep for two hours, no more, and wake with an awful heachache. I've tried drinking warm milk before I go to bed. I've tried herbal teas and lying on my back for half an hour, I've tried counting sheep. But nothing seems to work. What should I do?'

Gianni nodded. There was an immediate suggestion that came to mind, it sometimes worked for him, but he didn't think it worthy of a man who wore the cloth, and so he made no mention of it. He knew two other things for making the wakeful sleep. Valerian was one. *Papaver somniferum* was the other. He'd discovered the powers of valerian. Here was a perfect chance to further his researches.

'Well, Emile, that is a right brat of a problem. A man needs to sleep. That is God's will. If a man can't sleep he can't eat, and if he can't eat he can't think straight, if he can't think straight his world falls off its axis. There is one thing but I don't have it handy. Give me a week, and don't mind if I suggest that, should you find you're feeling randy, then just do the natural thing. You know. It might help.'

Emile pulled a sodden handkerchief from his pocket, blew his nose, and quickly left the shop.

Gianni acquired a batch of poppyseeds, from the poppy known as *Papaver somniferum*. Prepared correctly they have a range of powerful medicinal effects, among them the ability to induce a deep sleep, hence the *somniferum* of their name.

If the dose is extreme they can act as a narcotic poison, which was not Gianni's intention. But he thought they might induce some very pleasant dreams.

Emile walked into the shop just as Gianni was pulling these curious cakes out of the oven.

'What smells so good?' Emile asked.

'It would have to be my armpits!' Gianni replied, then laughed, lifting his arms above his head. As he laughed drops of sweat fell from his arms and trickled down his shoulders.

Emile smiled, trying to humour Gianni while masking his repugnance for this kind of jocular vulgarity. Were it not for the fact that Gianni's cakes were good, and that he was never asked to pay for them, he would never step inside. But his tooth was sweet, and as it was he could not stay away.

'Perhaps you mean these?' Gianni added, holding up the hot baking tray on which his new creations were steaming. 'Poppyseed cakes. From a very old recipe. An insomniacs's treasure.'

Gianni decided to withhold any other information. He certainly wasn't telling Emile that the *Papaver somniferum* was better known as the opium poppy.


Emile, hovering on the edge of sleep, was thinking of Gianni. For a moment he saw the fat man smiling at him, and then the eye of his sleep descending focussed on Gianni's mouth. Out of Gianni's mouth crawled a small black spider, which grew and grew. He recognised La Tarantula, the spider that resided over the entrance to Gianni's shop.

This was not a comfort, for the spider had grown large, it overpowered his vision. He could no longer see the spider, could only see its eye grown huge, his face reflected in the round bulb. He saw himself distorted, and wondered if this was a true image of himself, this gross misshapen thing.

Yes, he thought, some truth in it. Was this the eye of God come to stare him down? He was awake, and it was no comfort to think that he had been asleep.

# Emile Falls In Love

Something rising out of his sleep. At first he couldn't put a name to it. When he could, he wished he hadn't. There was a new terror in him. The terror he had known in his life till then had been, he thought, a dress-rehearsal for the terror that now came naked to him.

An infestation of spiders is not a pretty affair, unless you find a revelation of spiders just one more manifestation of the sublime. Emile did not find it so. He was not merely appalled, he was scared out of his wits.

He wondered if this was the demonic presence he had been expecting now for weeks. Something in him muttered, No, there's worse to come.

The spiders were small and black, quite cute really. But they had no intention of remaining small, they grew, and the black spiders quickly assumed a stature that exceeded any notion of the cute. He squashed them underfoot, but as he broke the beasts, where there had been one spider two now rose. The more he stamped the creatures underfoot, the more he became an instrument of their proliferation.

His bedroom was awash with spiders. The speed with which they moved around the floor, onto his bed, up the walls, onto the ceiling, seemed a fluid motion to his eye. He wanted to make a quick bolt for the door, yet he dared not, as that would mean crossing the growing lake of spiders that stretched between his bed and the door.

There was a solid carpeting of spiders now, the floor no longer visible, the walls and bed and ceiling all become a textured black. The whole room filling with the beasts.

236

They'd soon occupy every cubit of the room. They'd find a way to enter him, he would be no more than a holding ground for this dense arachnidan mass. He closed his eyes, plugged his ears with his fingers, and stopped his nose as well, hoping to bar entry to the creatures.

He was sure that if he took one breath he'd inhale the spiders. Too scared to open up his eyes, too scared to breathe, too mortified to scream as that would give the spiders the vital breach they sought. His head was bursting, his lungs clamouring for air.

He wanted to pass out, this was his prayer, and to his relief his prayer was answered.

When Emile came to the first thing he knew was that his head still ached, and he was glad of this meagre continuity. Something tickling his nose. A nasal hair, or a spider's leg?

When finally he dared glance through one eye, barely opened, he was convinced the fine hairs of his eyelash were spider legs. Opening his eye a little further he felt a hint of dismay as he surveyed the room. An empty bottle of red wine, his drinking cup. A strange disappointment came upon him as he wondered if he'd begun to lose his mind.

Emile, when he thought about it later, was surprised to find that he'd enjoyed the spidery animation of his bedroom. Perhaps enjoyed was not the word, as he'd been terrified. And yet there'd been an animation, an exaltation, that held a fascination for him. He struggled to put his thoughts into words, because the thought was difficult to accept.

He'd enjoyed the arachnidan infestation of his room because, while he had succumbed to its terror, he had also felt so overwhelmingly alive. He'd never thought that fear and dread might be such positive emotions. The thought rubbed against him, chafing him.

He didn't like to tease the fine gossamer of this argument. Permitting himself instead a glass of warm red wine.

Emile had fallen in love with fear. Why couldn't he have

237

fallen for a more benign face of love? He was enchanted by the life-enhancing properties of terror. That rush of adrenaline, like a liquid spike in his veins. Each time he thought of the seething carpet of black spiders he felt his glands spiking his blood.

Could he not, through the controlled use of his fear, keep himself in this exalted and hypermanic state? The terrifying face of his new lover filled him with apprehension, itself not an unpleasant sensation. He decided he'd better have another glass of red.

The thrill of terror had Emile in thrall. Like any drug, once you've acquired a taste for it you build up a resistance. How could he keep the thrill sharp? By inducing greater peaks of terror. It was a bad business, and not the kind of pursuit for a man with a constitution as delicate as Emile's.

# PART SIX:

# THE BREADMAKER'S CARNIVAL

# Gianni's Humiliation

So often what is good in life comes disguised as something bad, and our success is only revealed in the depths of failure. One thing that made Gianni feel distraught was this: every year he was subjected to an annual humiliation due to his inability to bake a hot cross bun.

His hot cross buns were lamentable creations. He tried to convince his customers that the shrivelled, burnt things he offered were holy interpretations of his art, the only thing that would respect the mortal sufferings of a man who'd been nailed to a cross, and who had only vinegar to drink.

'It would never do,' he explained, 'to have some moist and luscious thing when we're confronted by such suffering.'

It was a contrary logic. Emile tried reasoning with him, asserting that Easter was a time to celebrate the Ascension of Our Lord, it would make sense to match his feat with a hot cross bun that also rose. Gianni would begin to grow angry, though the source of his anger he never revealed. He was ashamed that he could not make his hot cross buns rise.

The truth is, his heart wasn't in it.

Gianni was of another calling. He worshipped at the altar of an older god, and a woman too. Perhaps that's why his hot cross buns would never rise.

Each year as Easter approached, Gianni felt a dread begin to mount. Each year he felt the dismay as he picked his buns off the tray. His heart sank in direct proportion to the heaviness he felt on his palm. In disgust he'd toss his heavy little buns that never rose and always burnt, they'd bounce off the walls like rocks hurled in scorn. He should have accepted the inevitable long ago, and just stopped trying.

For the simple truth is this: you can't cook hot cross buns in a pagan oven. Was this the reason for Gianni's annual humiliation at the hands of a bun? A stupid figure of speech, as a bun has no hands—though who said that speech ever had a figure?

# An Early Spring

The Breadmaker's Carnival has become a popular event—it features in tourist brochures, and tarantellini have become regular apparitions in cooking magazines every Easter, though not with quite the same recipe that was first used.

Gianni Terremoto was the inventor of these curious little cakes. It has been suggested that he set out quite deliberately to sabotage the Easter services. Others claim it was an accident, or that he was simply trying to compensate for his terrible buns. The fact remains that after eating these Easter cakes the town went mad, and this communal dementia lasted several days.

As Gianni Terremoto was the baker of the cakes responsible for this communal fit, it seems fair to acknowlege him as the Father of The Breadmaker's Carnival.

The daffodils had sprouted in their bulbs. A hot early spring had blossomed overnight. The jasmine flowering on its trellis, its fragrance wafting in the air.

Was it a visionary temperature? What is the priming heat for a human brain? The heat at which we start to hallucinate, or see visions?

The flowers started sweating. Fresh-bloomed roses drooped their heads and gave up, expiring in a falling cloud of petals. A heat to flush poisons from the body. A heat to ferment milk. Fermentation is a curious process in which a transmutation occurs. Some would say that it's the transmutation of the profane into the sacred. Others would say the reverse is true.

You would have said that heat was unseasonable, except it brought some of us into season, a funky heat that melted inhibition.

Ergot is a naturally occurring disease of cereals and other grasses. It is caused by ascomycete fungi of the genus *Claviceps*, especially *Claviceps purpurea*, in which the seeds or grain of the plants are replaced by the spore-containing bodies of the fungus.

The essential attribute of ergot is this: it is a naturally occurring hallucinogenic. And ergot blooms most often during times of great heat.

# His Poor Hope

On the eve of his fiftieth birthday Gianni Terremoto woke up feeling foul. It was not only the rotten mouth he had from too much drinking. And it wasn't just the bilious feeling that he got when he thought about Sylvana entwined in a fundamental embrace with Stefano Costa.

He looked at his calendar. It was almost April Fool's Day. And this year April Fool's Day coincided with Good Friday.

It is not usual for Good Friday and April Fool's Day to coincide—this happens only once every two hundred and thirteen years. It's an incidence the church has never liked.

Tonight is All Foole's Eve, Gianni was thinking. His mother had gone into labour on All Foole's Eve, and he'd popped out, ripe as a melon, the next day. So he was born an April Fool.

The reason for his lethargic depression became clear. He had to bake his Easter buns. Tomorrow there'd be a mighty queue, some people wanting to buy their Easter buns, others come to see how badly burnt his buns would be this year. That they might mock him.

The whole thing filled him with apprehension. He'd always told himself that if at fifty he had not succeeded in his aim to make a cake or pastry or other delicacy worthy of history, he would give the game away and accept defeat.

He cast his eyes around the bakery, looking for some inspiration. He felt confronted by the immense poverty of his materials. Flour and water. Eggs and butter. Miracles have been made with less, he muttered. The thought only made him more depressed.

He had just got up, and already he wanted to get back into bed. It was not an auspicious beginning to his day.

He caught sight of the three bags of rye flour Luigi had left as an early birthday gift. And next to them, a large jug of mead. A birthday gift from the same Luigi three years earlier. How quickly those three years had passed. He'd still been confident, at forty-seven, that he had time to perfect his creation and place his name in the ledger of famous bakers. Now, aged forty-nine and three hundred and sixty-four days, he'd run out of time, and inspiration, and the thought made him feel insipid. He needed a sip of mead now.

After the first glass Gianni felt some slight improvement in his condition. Looking once more at the three bags of rye flour. He'd never heard of a sweet bun made of rye. He felt a resentment and wanted to kick the flour bags. Instead he waddled over and with a grunt hoisted one of the bags off the ground, holding it tightly to his chest.

He couldn't walk with the heavy sack, and so he made a curious waltzing movement as he wheeled himself and the sack of flour over to the workbench, the sack settling into the curve of the ancient wood.

He felt an immense weight of failure in him, mingled with a determination to make one last attempt. He took a knife and made a small split in the hessian. Tasting the flour on his fingertip.

He decided to make a small batch of rye buns, just to get the feel of it, they'd do for breakfast and might inspire him to some greater achievement. This was his poor hope, on the eve of his fiftieth birthday.


The blobs of dough had barely risen, something stifling their elevation. They bore an unfortunate resemblance to certain types of dung. He sampled a morsel. The texture in the mouth was thick and chewy. Passing by the oesophagus into the stomach it left a doughy coating on his inner tubes. A sensation not considered pleasant.

They would take days, Gianni thought, to pass through

the body, leaving it in much the same form as they arrived, just uttered by a different pair of lips. Before this salutary event, the dough fermenting in the stomach and intestine would result in the brewing of a lethal gas. He baptised them Fumet Breads. They looked like deer droppings, after all. He'd have to throw the whole lot out.

# Bathing In Figs

Luigi had been wondering what to give Gianni on the advent of his half-century. He'd thought the bags of flour might do, but as they'd been a gift from Costa to him, they were really Costa's birthday gift to Gianni. Luigi hadn't mentioned this to Gianni. He was feeling guilty. He'd need to make another gift.

He was about to make himself a cup of coffee when he stubbed his toe, and stumbled on the very thing he needed. A gift that would inflict a little pain upon the giver, and so alleviate his guilt.

His coffee drunk, the decision was made. Three years ago he'd helped Amaretto fuel the still for a batch of fine amaretto. He'd also picked the almonds, and his payment had been an invitation to pick figs from the trees that grew behind the almond grove. Luigi had considered it a mixed blessing at best. He'd already done a week's work, and to collect his wages could take another week.

Luigi decided to pick every fig from Amaretto's trees. It had taken a day to pick the fruit from each tree, and on the seventh day he felt like resting, but the figs were ripe and he was faced with a new dilemma, how to preserve the fruit before the lot turned into a ferment of fig mush.

He hauled the fruit home, and bought five gallons of brandy. He was stuck on one detail—the container he might use to hold the figs.

In the end he did the only thing that was obvious, or at least it was obvious to him.

He placed an empty bathtub on a long metal trolley that had three wheels, two at the back, and a single wheel at the front. And then he set to work, cleaning the figs and tossing them into the bath.

He was surprised how easy the work was once he'd settled into it. Though he'd yet to solve the riddle of how to seal the tub. As a precaution he decided to pour a thin layer of olive oil over the figs and brandy.

What happened next might have been an accident, but if it was it gained Luigi's seal of approval. He didn't want to drown the figs in oil, just create a thick film, and so he balanced a candle on the edge of the bath to help him see. It was delicate work, and as he poured the oil he knocked the candle with his elbow. Surprised by the rapidity of his reflex as he snatched the candle in mid-air, but not before a drop of wax had fallen onto the figs. To his amazement the wax was floating on the oil, and the simplicity of the answer to his problem took his wind away.

It was almost dawn when he had finished. He had perfected his technique so that by night's end he was working with a candle in each hand. The thick wax lid had made a perfect seal.

And now, three years later, he was going to give his figs away. The gift had stature. It was worthy of a man who'd lived for fifty years.

Luigi made a curious sight that afternoon as he slowly wheeled the bathtub into town. He didn't want to break the wax and so he didn't dare rush. Seeing the green moss on a stone, and catching the chirrup of passing birds. It took five hours to get to town. He'd had the sense to bring fifty white candles.

When he was almost there, he stuck his candles onto the waxy surface of the bath. This was an intricate job, and it was getting late. He lit his fifty candles.

As Luigi continued on his way he saw, in his mind's eye, Gianni's mother labouring through the night. A floury baby birthing from between her legs. Luigi, pushing the bath along, careful not to push too hard, not wanting to extinguish any of his candles. Trundling along.

It had not occurred to Luigi that brandy is a flammable liquid, and that with fifty candles burning on top, he had sufficient firepower to set the thing off. Oblivious to this he wheeled the bath of figs along. He was almost at the back door.

Sylvana arrived at the back of the bakery at the same time as Luigi, surprised to see him rounding the corner. Even more surprised to see him pushing a bath with birthday candles. She knew that Gianni smelt ripe, but would not have said the obvious present for the man was a bath on wheels. And what had she brought? A cake of scented soap. She had been hoping to mend fences, but now Gianni would think they were conspiring. Though she'd also brought a bottle of amaretto.

Nothing could have prepared them for what they saw when they silently opened up the back door of La Tarantula, hoping to spring their birthday surprise.

Gianni was in his birthday suit, lying on a bag of flour, chafing himself. The three of them, Gianni, Luigi and Sylvana, all caught with their pants down. Then they were laughing. It was too preposterous, or too human.

Gianni was crimson. He struggled to his feet and pulled his pants on. 'A man has to scratch an itch, you know. Would you like a drink?'

Sylvana cut him short. Handing him the soap and bottle. 'Happy birthday, you disgusting creature!'

Gianni's thirst rendered him oblivious to all insult. He wanted to get three glasses, but Luigi placed a rope between his hands.

Gianni was dumbfounded when he realised he was berthing a bathtub of candles. He saw the way the candles made the shadows in the roof bob and duck, and he saw Sylvana dancing naked on the roof, and wished that when he brought his eyes back to earth she'd be standing naked beside him. Flushed then, shaded with grief and guilt and a rush of lust.

The candle stumps had burnt low, and the lowest of

them had reached the wax that sealed the bath. As Gianni hesitated, the candle sputtered and broke the wax seal. Gianni took a deep breath and was about to blow out his fifty candles when the naked flame hit flammable gas, the top layer of the brandied figs. There was a bright blue cloud of flame.

Gianni had singed his face and eyebrows. There was an intoxicating aroma of figs and brandy in the room. Gianni was rapt, Luigi somewhat entranced. It was as well that Sylvana had her wits.

'Gianni,' she said, 'if I was you I'd blow those candles out before this bakery explodes!'

The urgency of their situation now finally understood, they took a deep communal breath and blew the candles out, coughing in the smoke that came from so many simultaneously extinguished candlewicks.

'Here's to a man who's lived for half a century.' As soon as she'd said it Sylvana wished she hadn't. It had sounded good in the privacy of her head, but the look Gianni gave her made her feel stupid. It had never occurred to him that he had lived for half a century. It made him feel ancient, and underlined a simple fact: he'd had ample time to achieve his goal of making baking history. Beaded by his failure.

This bitter reverie was interrupted when Sylvana prised his lips apart and inserted one of Luigi's brandied figs into his mouth.

'I've always thought figs the most sexual of fruit,' Sylvana said, as she popped a fig into her own mouth, and then Luigi's. The three of them sucking and chewing the figs. They were exquisite. The way the figs seemed to undress the palate, making it open and vulnerable to sensation. It was a complex taste, and as they swallowed the three of them were satisfied.

There followed a moment of uncomfortable silence. Gianni was glad that he'd thrown away his prototype buns, spared at least this small disgrace. Sylvana wondered if she dared ask how his Easter buns were progressing. Gianni opened the amaretto, drank and passed the bottle to Sylvana, who drank and passed it to Luigi. Luigi drank and passed the bottle to Gianni, who drank again. Sylvana refused his offer of another slug from the bottle's neck, then changed her mind and drank again. Luigi had reached into the bath and was sucking another fig. There was a maudlin feeling come on them.

Gianni was wishing Luigi would leave. He wanted to be alone with Sylvana.

Sylvana was recalling the tradition of All Foole's Eve in the town where her mother grew up. At sunset people would congregate in the cemetery, shedding tears over the graves of people they knew, and over the graves of strangers. Weeping on a stranger's grave was one of the prerequisites, the beginning of All Foole's. The weeping and lamentation would go on for several hours, though people could come and go; there were sausages cooked on an open fire, and at the entrance to the cemetery was a barrel of onions. People peeled and ate raw onion to stimulate their lachrymal abilities. On their knees by a stranger's grave, the onion in hand, and the burning onion fumes to lubricate their eyes.

One grave with an unmarked headstone was the focus for all who came to All Foole's. This was the grave of two young children, a brother and sister, who died of hunger during a time of famine. Their parents had left them to forage for food but had not been able to return. The bodies of the brother and sister were found in a barn, their mouths stuffed with straw.

They were known as The Twins, even though they were not twins. They were buried in the local cemetery, and as no-one knew their names, they were buried with a blank headstone.

People paid respects to anyone they knew who was buried in the cemetery, and then assembled by the graveside of the twins. There would be hundreds of people pressing in, all of them weeping. The curious thing was that at some point the weeping would change, and lose its ferocity. The great fit of weeping would slowly turn into laughter. This was the night the living came to laugh at death. Not at the dead—that's why the night began with earnest weeping. But it ended with the laughter of the living. There was always music, people dancing on gravestones, clapping their hands; people would begin to make ribald jokes, the drunker men would drop their pants and flash their cheeks while standing on the grave of the two dead children. Look! Here are The Twins.

After midnight some said it was prudent to hurry home. Others claimed that it was only then that All Foole's began. It was considered an auspicious thing to copulate in the cemetery that night, assuring a long life and a happy year to come. Sylvana had lost her virginity in that cemetery.

Rousing herself from these thoughts, Sylvana noticed there was nothing baking in the oven. The distractions of her arrival with Luigi had concealed the fact from her. Gianni guessed what she was thinking, for he nodded and said, 'The bakery is closed tomorrow.'

She heard herself say, 'Oh dear.' She wanted to say more, to change his mind, and all she could manage was another 'Oh.'

'Let me give you some figs,' said Gianni as Sylvana turned to leave. He was looking for something to put the figs in. He wanted to prolong the inevitable moment of her departure.

Sylvana was growing more animated as the alcohol made her innards glow. Luigi handed her the amaretto. She took a long draught from the bottle.

Leaning forward to take another fig from the bath, she slipped and plunged her arm and shoulder in. Her shirt dripping with fig brandy.

'Too good to waste,' she said. She pulled her shirt over her head and wrung the drops out as she tilted back her head. Luigi was distracted by the sight of her breasts, and was not sure where to look as Sylvana walked to him and squeezed a few drops of brandy out of her sleeve into his mouth.

Gianni walked over to the bath, cupped his hands, and took a long drink of birthday brandy. He plunged his hands into the bath and came up with both hands full of figs. The liquid streaming through his fingers. He offered them to Sylvana, she laughed and pushed him away. Gianni lost his balance.

For a big man he began to make an elegant recovery, as if he was sitting down in mid-air. It was a pleasing illusion that lasted but an instant; his body continued its great descent and Gianni was spreadarsed in the bathtub with the figs.

Luigi felt Sylvana taking his trousers off and did not resist, and lifted his shirt off himself. Sylvana now naked, the pair of them undressed Gianni, who seemed in no haste to leave the bath. The three of them sitting in the bath with Gianni's figs. The brandy making their eyes sting. It stung the pizzles of the men, as well.

It seemed they had begun to laugh and cry at once. Luigi fell out of the bath and hit his head on the floor. Gianni and Sylvana clambered out to help him.

Luigi was shivering. 'I'll light the oven,' Gianni announced, and threw some wood into it. When the flames began to flicker, the three of them were grateful for its warmth.

'You have to laugh into the oven,' said Sylvana. 'That's the secret to baking buns on All Foole's Eve. You have to open the oven door, squat, make a sound like you are shitting, and laugh into the oven. That's the tradition. It's what my grandmother used to do. She said it makes them rise. Have you got anything to eat in this shithole of yours?'

Sylvana was poking Gianni in the chest. Her finger sinking into him each time she poked. 'And you call yourself a baker!' Sylvana laughing at him then, and Gianni felt relieved she had stopped poking.

Sylvana walked off, and returned with a quarter-loaf of bread, a piece of cheese and two apples. She bit into the cheese, then stuffed some bread into her mouth. She chewed as if nothing could distract her from this business of eating. Gianni swung open the oven door and pretended to shit and barked a baleful laugh into the oven's mouth. Sylvana almost choked from trying to chew, swallow, bite the cheese and laugh at once.

She strode to the oven, pushed Gianni out of her way,

then dropped into a powerful half-squat. She began to push her hands against her thighs, and as she pushed she began to grunt. She turned her head to face Gianni and he was surprised to find she'd begun to sweat from her exertions. Her stomach muscles were tight and quivered with the effort. 'You've got to do it till you sweat some poison out,' she said.

Luigi and Gianni watched, spellbound, astounded, and a little frightened. They were waiting to see if a turd would appear between her bare cheeks. They were distracted from this posterial perplexity by the sound of raucous laughter bursting from her, somewhere between a wail, an orgasm and a sob.

Luigi was enthralled by the way her ribs could expand and bend as she breathed deeply, right down to the pubic bone, and let her body fill with air, the great accordion of her then wracked with the effort of laughter. Sylvana slammed the oven door shut and stared at Gianni.

'I don't know if it will work for you, but that's what my grandmother used to do. Though only on this one night of the year.'

Gianni, stunned, had no reply. Sylvana was rubbing her arms, and began to dress.

'Happy birthday, Gianni,' Sylvana said, and kissed him gently on the mouth. Gianni would have put his hands onto her hips, or wrapped his arms around her, but before the kiss had properly begun it had ended, and he watched in dismay as she walked across the room and closed the back door behind her.

Luigi was feeling awkward. The expression on Gianni's face once Sylvana had departed made him uneasy. He took his own leave shortly after.

Sylvana did not feel like going home. She didn't know what she felt like doing and was surprised to find she'd thrown herself out of La Tarantula. She had thought she was just settling in, about to make a night of it.

She was hungry. Would Amaretto's be open? She doubted it, but with the endless hope of the hungry she set off to see if there was any joy to be had in his kitchen.

# Gianni's Creation

Gianni was mulling over Sylvana's strange actions, and the sight of the three of them in bath together. He had a terrible night ahead. Could he not just run away? If he failed this last time, then tomorrow he would run. Promising himself that small remission. He could say it was his own April Fool's joke. Though he, more than anyone, would know that all along the joke had been on him.

Sylvana's presence seemed greater in her absence than when she'd been naked before him in the bakery. Where was she now? Gianni felt certain she was with Stefano Costa, the pair of them entwined utterly. His jealousy was of a magnitude that rivalled the dimensions of his belly.

Sylvana and Stefano coupled in a kama sutra of variations in his mind. Gianni stumbled across the floor, tripped and banged his head against the wooden bench.

He was thinking about a violent bread that he could bake for Costa, spiked with darnel and sour beans. A severe dose of food poisoning would be the least result of such a concoction. How he'd love to see a whole population of Costas and Sylvanas writhing in the grip of it.

When he sat down and had a swig of amaretto though, he felt his rage soften. He thought he'd smelt Sylvana come in through the back door.

He paused then, and it might have been a mistake. His thoughts had turned to aphrodisiacs. Something he could bake and eat with her. Oysters? Yes, but an oyster bread was not inviting to the eye. Perhaps if he placed it in a small pastry boat, surrounded with bechamel and pepper? No, Gianni thought, she'll think I'm making oyster fannies.

The most potent aphrodisiac he knew had been given to him by Sylvana. Distilled from the sap of an African tree and used to bring bulls and cows on heat. In men and women it caused blisters to erupt on the skin. But used in moderation? Just a small drop? She had given him a tiny phial of the sappy distillation. He'd wanted to try it with her, but Sylvana demurred. She was not sure how they'd avoid the blisters.

Might he bake a batch of conciliatory cakes for the pair of them, Sylvana and Stefano, they'd come out in terrible rashes and foul itches as the blisters surfaced on their skin. Gianni found this notion appealing and decided it deserved further consideration, aided by another tot of amaretto. The bottle nearly empty. But the bath of figs was full of brandy. And he had his jug of mead as well. He swigged the amaretto and realised the vital flaw in his logic: while Sylvana and Costa might be covered in blisters, this would not occur until the aphrodisiac had taken effect.

The first consequence of his labours would be to incite the pair to ever more fervid copulation. Back where he started, with a population of Costas and Sylvanas copulating in his head. He put the bottle down and farted once.

His mouth felt oversweet, cloyed and sticky. Perhaps he needed to rinse it with brandy?

He walked unsteadily towards the bathtub, then stopped. He didn't feel like brandy at all. He scratched the back of his head. There was another notion starting to ferment under his skull, unless ideas ferment lower down, perhaps in the gizzard-tubing wrapped about his belly. He scratched his skull again. He was trying to stop himself from swaying, and not succeeding.

His thoughts returned to the task at hand, his Easter buns. The night was passing and he had not begun. Perhaps he should do the honourable thing after all and run away? Though he could not run, and would have to make do with an amble.

He smiled as a pleasing idea came into view, pleasing and wicked. An Easter tribute with a difference. He'd bake the pair of them in a carnal embrace and put it in the window. This would be his revenge. He didn't pause to think the plan through in any detail, nor did he stop to consider possible consequences. He had a clear task, and a way to vent his anger. His legs seemed to hold him more truly to the floor as he embraced this happy purpose. He'd put the fuckers in his window.

He needed to be drunker than he was. Wondering if he'd find a way to beard his fear if he had enough to drink.

The figs floating in the old bathtub looked like dark eyes, staring at him. Making him nervous.

He dawdled over and plunged a hand into one of Luigi's sacks of rye flour. His saliva combining with it to make that most elemental dough, flour and human water in the mouth. He liked the taste and ate a little more. He couldn't help nibbling the flour. It appeased his nervousness. He ate a handful of it, washing it down with fig brandy. The fig and rye and brandy flavours were quite appealing.

He was exhausted. He had not abandoned all hope, he might yet bake his way out of his Easter dilemma. But he felt so tired. Perhaps a little nap was needed? And so he gently lowered his bulk, lying against the flour sacks. He felt at peace.


In the halfway state between dreaming and waking he was muttering to himself. He needed to get out of the bakery. Those spidery eyes, and the eyes of the figs, made it hard for him to concentrate on the task at hand.

He was walking down the street. He hadn't bothered to dress. He'd thought he'd just amble to the back door, take some air and clear his head. But at the door his feet kept going. With each step his body shook, and as it shook he felt the earth tremble under him. The slower he walked, the better he felt. A strange elation filling him.

He was standing in the square outside the church. The soft earth underfoot as he marvelled at the world in his birthday suit. He walked into church and was surprised to hear the sweetest music. He stood at the back of the church, lost in his rapture. The great bag of his wind inflating and deflating. He thought Amaretto must be there, but when he walked down the aisle the organ seat was empty. The music had stopped.

As he gazed beyond the altar he found that he was staring at a woman made of bread. Why had he never noticed it before? A bread madonna. He approached and was surprised to find that she possessed an animation. She was poking her tongue out at him, and then she bared her teeth. It did not occur to him to question why this woman made of bread was in church, nor why she was naked.

He was kneeling before her, and she pulled her lips apart with the gentlest movement. She had a clitoris made from a fig. He saw an eye staring back at him from within her glossy red vulva. It was a strange awakening.

Gianni blinked then. He was lying on a sack of flour, and there was a moist corner of the sack that was wet with his saliva.

The central image of his dream came back at him. Kissing the lips of her vagina as he nuzzled at the gateway to the world. It was a strange altar at which to worship, though who could say that it was worse or better than another?

Gianni blinked again. He had wanted to take a bite of that sweet fig. The doughy lips forming a mouth that held the fig like a fleshy jewel. And he *had* bitten, felt the satisfaction as the mouthful slowly travelled down his pipes into his belly. To his surprise the holy fanny was intact. A magic pudding unlike any there'd been before.

He had kissed the doughy lips of her vagina and he had seen the eye of God. This was his vision splendid?

He didn't know the flour he'd sampled from Luigi's birthday sacks was starting to affect his reason. He would not have said that he'd begun hallucinating. The *Claviceps purpurea* made short work of him.

His jealousy was gone, and had been replaced with an alarming altruism. He imagined all the crosses in the world turned into fannies. The fanny as holy relic, an ikon shaped like an eye. Seeing all, and nothing.

In his stupor Gianni saw Pia Zanetti's bottom blossom from a bun, and hills made of dough, and houses of hard-crust pastry. The trees were made of cake, and on the hills and in the fields his buns were turning into haunches that copulated, and the landscape was transformed into a world of generation and regeneration. All the stories he'd heard from Sylvana. Aphrodite and her lips, the ancient carnivals. Éostre, the antique goddess of dawn, her festival at the vernal equinox. Giving her name to Easter.

The moon was high, and so was Gianni. He was struck by a fact so simple he was stunned he'd not paid it heed before. Aphrodite was Venus, and the festival of Venus was always held on the first day of April. Not only was he an April Fool, he was also a child of Venus and Aphrodite.

Standing in his birthday suit, he belched and farted, rubbing his hands as he stood before the oven, and decided he'd have another birthday toast. A notion lumbering through him. His fiftieth birthday would be celebrated by one and all, and they'd celebrate in the name of Venus Aphrodite.

A birthday cake baked in her honour. He'd turn the clock back for one day and forget about the hot cross buns that never rose. He'd confect some other sweet delight. A profane thing? Perhaps. But La Tarantula was outside the church, and so he felt the thing would be alright. A birthday party they'd not forget. It made him laugh, albeit nervously.

Rubbing Luigi's flour with his fingers. He'd need white flour to lighten the rye. In what proportion? Half and half? One third to two? He wanted the rye to dominate but not overwhelm the palate. Needing a light texture, even so.

His thoughts crowding with buns and muffins and pastries.

His desire to make a copulating couple for the window had altered. He was going to make a woman of bread. A centrepiece for his window. A woman with dark rye skin. This woman of dough was calling to his fingers. He tugged his palms and joints, as if the flesh of his hands were the first dough he'd knead this night.

Grappling with a sack of white flour and going back for another bag of rye. Tasting the blend of flours unadulterated, if that might be said of something that had such adulterous consequences.

# A Woman Of Bread

He was surprised by the ease with which he'd begun to sculpt this female form. She was complete, except for her left leg, and the detail of her sex.

Gianni was moulding the bread woman's cleft, puzzling and toying with this most delicate of tasks. Wondering then if he'd not make a modest prototype, with the dough and figs and mead.

It certainly looked good enough to eat. He refrained from his desire to pop the uncooked morsel in his mouth. Instead he picked the fragrant sweetmeat up, cradling it with his fingers.

As he fitted the morsel snugly in place and smoothed the edges with his fingers, he knew something else had fitted into place. The little pastry boat nesting in his imagination—Gianni knowing he'd just confected the very thing he'd sought. Wondering how the pastry would fare inside the oven. Wanting to have it cooked and burning in his mouth.

How to craft her pubic hair, that she might be a grown woman? He wanted her to have red hair, and added cochineal to the dough. He began to make long trains of fine pastry, laying them out around the shop as if they were festive ribbons. A strange red web he wove. His hands covered with cochineal, looking like they were covered in blood.

This way he passed the night. Making her pubic hair, hair for her armpits and legs, fine nostril hairs, hair for her head and ears and bum. Had he succumbed to a vice of literalness?

His mouth looked red and gashed where he'd rubbed

261

it. Looking like a debauched transvestite in his floured black apron, with his floppy breasts. A strange apparition.

He hadn't meant to mould a menstruating woman, but it was clear he had. The red dye stains in her groin left no doubts.

He'd forgotten about the bread woman's other leg, and now it was too late. He placed her in the oven as she was, a splendid monoped with fig-jewelled sex, the sight more pleasing than any figleaf.

He was about to close the oven door when he remembered Sylvana's strange routine. He leant forward and felt the dry heat burn the air inside his lungs, choking him. His stomach muscles contracted and he was surprised as a little turd shot out of him, he had meant to imitate the pose but he'd surpassed himself, and the shock of it caused his laughter to reverberate inside the oven. It bounced back out and hit him in the face. He slammed the oven door shut then, and told himself with great relief, The thing is done.

He wanted rest, wanted drink, but he would not pause until he'd baked his tarantellini. He'd set before the hungry eyes of the townsfolk an Easter bun the like of which they'd never seen before. He pushed the bath of figs up to his workbench. And laboured through the night.

Gianni sprinkled poppyseeds, inserted figs, rubbed in mead. He put some of Sylvana's aphrodisiac in the mix. He used too much. The phial was empty.

He'd never known his hands to work so quick and true. He was amazed by his prolific fingers, and the veracity of his pastries. A pastry bellymouth with clitoris and lips and jam—rich, ripe and bloody. His own stunning confection. Yet felt anxious as all hell. He sat out the back lingering with the smell of his little cunny cakes, nervous and agitated, assailed by moral questionings and doubts.

This was, he told himself, a holy war. The tree, the egg, the glowing lips of Aphrodite, the loaf of bread, the wine. They'd stripped the village cupboard bare.

This was his own crusade, except he didn't have a cross, he had his cunty little cakes. It was, he thought, a farcical revolt.

His mind spinning and reeling. He settled back into the bags of flour and let his own flopped flesh hang out. The white spiders on the roof were such sweet creatures to behold. Above his head a small spider was building its web, wonky, woozy, asymmetrical. An eccentric liberty of line.

And what of Gianni's buns? To call them buns seems a disservice; how do you draw the line between what's cake and what is bun? They were cataclysmic cakes. Gianni's cakes were a combination of some of the most powerful aphrodisiacs known. Not even Gianni realised the full force of his creations. He'd used the seeds of the *Papaver somniferum*, mead from a jar of honey that had naturally fermented, and his little phial of African sap. He was unaware that he'd combined these ingredients in rye flour which had been exposed to the *Claviceps purpurea* fungus, which the Germans call Mother Corn. Some say its mental lever was the thing that witches used to make them fly. After eating Gianni's spiced tarantellini any one of us would have felt quite able to orbit the moon.

So to call them buns or cakes seems a little underdone.

No-one in their right mind would make such a thing on purpose. But Gianni was not in his right mind when he made them. How was he to know the flour had been contaminated?

# The Day Begins

When Gianni came to his senses the next day, he was surprised to see what he had made. The blessed eye of his creation, lined up in rows along the windows. He'd fallen asleep after he'd made the whole display, and was woken by the sound of someone tapping on the window.

At first he thought it was a continuation of a gorgeous dream. Venus Aphrodite had been to see him in his shop, he'd shown her all about the place, upstairs and down. She was about to reveal some great secret, and as a prelude had starting knocking on his head with her closed fist, *tap tap tap*.

He woke up and his head was hurting, and he saw a small woman tapping on the window pane. It was Pia.

'Gianni! Are you open? Oh, I'm sorry, were you asleep? But you were sleeping on the floor? I thought you must've dropped something underneath the counter. Oh well, I've woken you up. Gianni, are you open?'

The day had broken. Gianni could have sworn that it had broken on his head, such was the poor condition he was in. Feeling somewhat contrite.

His enthusiasms of the night had ground him down and left him feeling bruisy. Gianni groaned, shook his head, and waved Pia away.

'Go to Amaretto's and get two coffees and I'll let you in.'

Amaretto and Sylvana had kept each other up till late, and it was Sylvana who first heard the sound of someone knocking.

'Don't get up,' she said, 'it's too early. It's only someone wanting milk.'

They cuddled up, and after a few more knocks the silence came upon them like another sleep. She hadn't meant to have sex with him. She hadn't minded, though, in fact she'd enjoyed it. She hadn't come but she'd come close, and the tenderness between them had been ample, a soft bosom that enfolded both of them. Grateful for this, and quite content.

Baffled by her feelings for the man. Did the fact that they'd made love mean they were already having a relationship? Or was this an aberration? He had a strong body odour. She didn't mind the manny smell of him. Reminded her of the way her mother's goats would get a randy smell that came off them in a funk.

Amaretto's fixation on Pia had not declined, though this was not a thing he felt comfortable speaking about. Nor did he see a contradiction in the pursuit of his ideal, his quest for Pia, while spending time with another woman in his bed. They were merely finding ways to comfort one another.

Amaretto had a gift for consolation. Sylvana, Francesca, they'd both been comforted by him. And later on had spent time with their discomfort.

Pia returned to Gianni's. Gianni hadn't moved. He looked like a beached whale on the wooden floor. He was staring at the window and the cakes, he was counting and mumbling. He looked dazed, even a little worried.

'Gianni? I'll come back in an hour. Amaretto's still in bed and it looks like you should be too!'

'No, no, Pia, I'll shift my arse. It's been a strange night.'

Gianni hauled himself up slowly, grasping the wooden leg of the counter to help steady himself. He decided not to bother about standing up, all fours would have to do. He lumbered over to the door on his hands and knees like an overweight dog, slid back the bolts and opened up. He was looking at Pia's leg.

'Is something wrong?' she asked.

He wondered if he dared tell her of his encounter with

a woman made of bread. He hadn't yet been out the back, he wondered what, if anything, might be there. Or was it who, if anyone? Would he find a woman made of dough? Or had he put her in the oven?

'Gianni?' Pia's voice again. 'Are you alright?'

'To tell the truth,' he said, 'I wouldn't know. Let's make that coffee.'

Pia was a permissive soul. She'd never reconciled herself to monogamy, though she'd once been engaged.

'I'd always meet some man and want to stick my tongue right down his throat.'

Some days before the intended marriage she discovered that she found the groom repulsive and cancelled the wedding. She had a high tolerance for the eccentricities and vagaries of human life: nothing surprised her. Even so, Gianni came close when he confided to her what had inspired him in the making of his little Easter cakes.

Gianni had made each cake by hand and, like snowflakes and flowers, each one was different. There were bigs ones and little ones, bloody, sweet and bruisy figolinas. They all had figs but some were fleshier, or fruitier, had wider lips or narrow mouths. They all looked kissable, at least in Gianni's eyes.

Hard to know who was more surprised, Gianni or Pia, as they looked upon the woman of bread who lay upon the wooden bench in the bakery. A splendid monoped, with two ripe figs for eyes, her fine red hairs, and the figolina pastry nestled in her crutch. She looked like a goddess of bread. Gianni wondered if he'd dare to put her in the window. He swallowed then and didn't hear the small winds breaking out of him.

Pia was too polite to comment on the winds, and didn't know what to say about the fat man's woman of bread. Gianni handed her a coffee and Pia wrapped her fingers round the cup, enjoying the warmth that spread now to her hands.

They were sipping the coffee when there was another knock at the door. Gianni groaned. His quirky cakes had great powers of attraction, a small queue was forming at the door to La Tarantula. Gianni was wondering how he could put the impatient pastry eaters off. His head aching, he groaned again and resigned himself to the fact that his day had begun, and knew there was no end in sight.

'Well,' he muttered to Pia, 'this should distract them for a moment!'

Together they lifted the breadwoman off the bench, carried her into the shop and set her down among the cakes in the window. Faces peering in at them, pressing their noses against the glass which then steamed up from the onlooker's exhalations. Gianni opened the door and stuck his head out.

'Five minutes,' he said, 'I'm opening in five!'

Closing the door quickly, he walked out the back. 'We'll finish that coffee yet,' he said to Pia.

Pia could feel her heart somewhat aflutter, the curious cakes, the woman of bread . . . She heard herself laughing nervously. Was this Gianni's April Fool's Day prank?

'It's a rather different Easter bun you've made this year,' she said.

'Yes,' Gianni answered, and then fell silent. He was wondering if it was going to be his last.

# A Groggy Bear

Costa wanted to go to church that morning, though when he thought of the events the last time he'd been, he hesitated.

He was feeling stroppy, and had forgotten that he had once given thanks for losing his hand. He was not sure that God existed, and certainly not a god that would have Emile as a representative. He felt like having an abusive word with the Creator, and felt inclined to assert that there was no creator, just a destroyer.

This was his stubborn sense that morning as he crawled out of bed and shook himself awake, feeling like a groggy bear.

One thing he loved about a well-made wall of stone was that it could last for hundreds of years. He had seen a wall that his great-great-great-great-grandfather had built. He'd seen walls that were over five hundred years old and still standing. He'd also seen the way wild pigs snuffled round and toppled stones, and he'd spent a morning repairing one small corner before he'd given up, realising that to repair the whole could take a year, and still the pigs would come and snuffle round, dig out roots and knock down walls as they burrowed, ate, rummaged and shat. He liked the fact that a wall had a lifespan greater than any man or woman's. It made him feel that the wall was superior—and yet it only existed through the ripe intelligence and hard work of the ones who'd built it. No matter how long it lasted, the day would come when the wall would fall.

He was feeling restless, and didn't know if he felt like knocking something down or building something up, or both.

As the grogginess sloughed off his body and he splashed water on his face, he felt less grumpy. He was hungry. He didn't want to eat stale bread. His appetite would keep until he got to Gianni's. He filled his gullet with water.

When he was dressed he stood outside, looked up at the sky and felt his feet planted solid on the ground. He spat once. He was about to head off when he was distracted. Two clouds travelling in opposite directions had collided and were forcing through each other. It looked like a clenched fist. He spat again, his belly rumbling. He had intended to walk to town but his belly was impatient.

He lay his hand on his old yellow bicycle, pushed off and started pedalling. The thought that he'd get there quicker made his belly rumble with greater haste. It was, he thought, a bastard logic: that his belly would become less patient as the time needed to satisfy its craving was reduced. His stomach contracted, squeezing his juices round. Hard pedalling then, that made him sweat and brought his hunger clear out in him. He took deep breaths of air, and enjoyed each breath so much you might have thought that he was feeding on it.

He saw something then that quite disturbed him. A dog with a piece of rope caught round its head and neck. The animal was in a frenzy, trying to free itself. The dog charged out of some bushes, crossing his path, and knocked him off his bike.

He wanted to free the animal: yet no sooner had he seen it than it was gone.

Stefano wondered if the dog was some kind of omen. Perhaps it would be better to avoid the Easter service? He'd had his day in church. Yet something called on him to go. Or was it just his hunger?

And so he pedalled into town, feeling a twinge as he passed Pia's, determined not to look up at the windows of her bedroom, and looking up. Noticing only that the curtains were open and the windows closed.

He leaned his bicycle against a wall at the backside of the church, and walked around the block to Gianni's. He could smell the fragrance of La Tarantula, the waft led him by the nose as the saliva gathered in his mouth.

When he reached the shop, he saw a milling throng, some waiting in a ragged line as others ate with great abandon.

He felt the heat coming off the bakery, and the sight of so many people eating with enthusiasm made his innards contract again. He saw a small sign above the doorway, nestled in the fangs of the great spider—'No Bread Today, Easter Cakes Are Free'. The spider sitting over the hungry queue, and the feeding throng.

# Sylvana Shines

Shortly after being woken by Pia's knocking Sylvana had risen, walked home, had a shower and decided that she'd better dress for church. She hadn't known what to say to Amaretto, so kissed him on the forehead, gathered her things and left.

She was wondering what she'd wear, and whether she would or wouldn't go to church. She hadn't lost her faith—she doubted she'd ever had it.

Pulling on her boots, pulling them off as she decided they needed polishing. Sitting on her bed, rubbing brown polish into the leather and buffing the hide with rag. Pondering what on earth had got into her, that she'd eat beans with Amaretto and stay the night. Was a knowledge of country customs a bad thing, sometimes?

As she descended the flights of stairs she was thinking about eggs, it being Easter. It reminded her of gathering eggs from the chicken coop, and hunting round the yard for eggs the birds had laid while foraging for food. The way the eggs were spackled with chicken dung and straw, and the way her mother looked when Sylvana found her hanging by the neck inside the chicken coop. She lost all impetus to keep walking down the stairs. Sitting on the steps, feeling the cold come through the cotton of her pants, chilling her bum.

Remembering the anger she'd felt at her mother's death, the great betrayal, and yet it seemed that this had happened to someone else, not her, Sylvana, sitting with a cold bum on the stairs. Telling herself she'd made her peace with it, though when she closed her eyes she could see once more

271

her mother strung from the rafter beam, and the way the wind made her mother's body swing like a pendulum.

A certainty came into her, she'd go to church. As if she might lose herself in the crowd, and find some common pulse to set against the image of her mother's body as it ticked at her, devoid of pulse.

Hauling herself up slowly, making her way down the stairs. She thought about Gianni's paltry record with his Easter buns and the thought distracted her, and made her laugh as she contemplated his failures.

Feeling some greater animation in her steps as she took the stairs three at a time, breasted the doorway and arrived on the street. The fresh air bathed her as she made her way to La Tarantula. She bit her lip, and to her surprise began to run, feeling a surge of energy. As she ran she saw, just for a moment, the way some days her mother would smile when Sylvana came back from gathering eggs, placing the soiled eggs in a chipped porcelain bowl.

She wondered if she'd not run straight to church and say a prayer for her poor departed mum, but before she'd managed thirty paces she found she'd slowed again, the heavy breathing in her.

Joining the queue outside the bakery she found herself staring at her boots, admiring the deep brown shine she'd brought to the old scuffed leather, and in this simple thing she found a glint of admiration for herself.

# Later That Morning

Costa's hunger was making him impatient. He was only metres from the door. Eyeing off the big black spider as he prepared to walk beneath her.

The window was blocked from view, such was the power of attraction of the bakery, as if the entire population of the town was trying to fit inside. Around the window was a great press of the hungry, the vital and the curious. Costa found that he was thinking of all those bellies and their juices swimming round, and the great peristalsis of this hungry herd, the acid juices and the bile, and the ability of this mass to devour the entire contents of the shop, feeding on the corpus of the great black spider.

His contemplation broken by his first glimpse of Gianni's window. A naked woman made of bread cavorting in the flour, her hair red and her body streaked with blood. Unsure what feelings this provoked, taken unawares by this strange display. His belly tightened in him like a fist, just for a moment, then relaxed, and then tightened once again. Held fast and firm in the grip of his hunger. A delirium in him, he was so hungry now, hungry with the exertion of riding into town, hungry with his hunger. Hungry with the sight of the bready nude that beaded him with her eyes.

He was underneath the spider, standing at the entrance to the shop. He looked up as if he might peep under the skirts of La Tarantula, felt a twitch of guilt and impropriety, and told himself it was a stupid thing to be embarrassed about, peeping up at La Tarantula. He expected to find the mouth of her sex stare back at him, and gave himself a mental kick—he had no idea about the genitalia of

273

arachnids, he'd certainly never tried to make his own inspection. He was struck by a curious thing: viewed from underneath, La Tarantula looked like a black church with flying buttresses to help lift the mass of her body.

He hadn't realised the queue had moved ahead, and was jolted forward by a hand that pushed him into the shop. He stumbled and fell, a flash of anger subsided as a voice muttered an apology. He recognised the voice. Sylvana's.

Both of them lost for words. Stefano relieved to find he had no need to speak as Gianni's voice commandeered the room. 'Stefano! You treasure! Get out of here!' And as he spoke, three cakes appeared in Costa's hand. 'See you in church,' Gianni's parting shot. As he brushed by Sylvana Costa felt an embarrassment. He nodded and echoed Gianni's greeting, 'See you in church,' and walked outside.

He hadn't bothered to look at the cakes that Gianni thrust into his hand, he'd already stuffed the first into his hole to appease his hunger. About to pop the second cake into his mouth, his eyes pulled him up, a disbelieving sort of gaze. He made a slow perusal of the cake. Shit and damn, he thought, I've never seen a cake like that before. He went to bite and found that he was sucking instead, so that the fig juice came out slowly.

The church bells were ringing, and there was a vein of discontent as those who'd yet to taste Gianni's wares began to fear they'd miss out. Their fears assuaged by the sight of Gianni appearing at the door with a long trestle and setting out a mound of cakes. It's true there was a jostle and true some cakes were squashed by the grasping throng, yet no-one was trampled. The hungerpanic reached a crescendo before it ebbed, and the crowd quickly thinned as people made their way across the soft dirt of the plaza, eating cakes as they maundered into church.

Gianni blinked, a mixture of surprise and disbelief—he'd satisfied this massive hunger. A moment's peace, before he thought, I'd better stir myself, because today the church is full and I'll be in it.

He farted once and felt his head go clear. He was exhausted, and so immersed in the what-he-had-to-do he hadn't noticed that nobody had thrown a cake at him, nor had any of them burnt. No-one had complained about the woman of bread. They'd been too busy stuffing themselves.

Pia was sitting quietly in the shop, playing with the top buttons of her blouse. She hadn't meant to stay and help, but she hadn't had the chance to leave either. The need to alleviate the great hunger for Gianni's Easter cakes had asserted itself, and she'd found herself dispensing his quirky fare. Glad now of the chance to sit and fiddle. She'd buttoned and unbuttoned her blouse forty times while Gianni swept the floor. She would not have said that she was acting oddly. Utterly absorbed in this banal action. The pleasing reverie, and the sounds of Gianni's broom stroking the floor. Gianni was being very meticulous, he'd never been so thorough.

There seemed to be no hurry. Gianni set the broom down. He'd thought to change into his Easter best—he was still wearing the floured apron, streaked with cochineal, and the black sweatshirt he had put on when the morning dawned. But he didn't want to change, deciding he'd go as he was, a tradesman to his harvest feast, in his old workclothes. He'd wear his best leather shoes, though. His small concession to Easter. The cochineal stains on his hands would not scrub off and so he left them there, like the bloodied hands of a butcher's boy.

Pia looked again at the woman of bread in the window. Gianni's bread madonna was not black, but the rye and the baking had combined to make her a deep, deep brown.

Something was troubling her. Then she began to laugh. Gianni turned to her, his eyebrows pointing to the roofbeams.

'You've put her vagina on upside down. Or is it back to front?' And she laughed again.

Gianni was confused. He became defensive. 'No I haven't.'

Pia could not help laughing. 'Oh, yes you have!'

Gianni was taken aback by her audacity, the ease with which she lifted up her skirt and proved her point. Perhaps his great fatigue had inspired such an elementary blunder.

He felt foolish and clumsy. The church bells had stopped ringing.

They walked out into the daytime air, feeling light, a little heady. The day came rushing now to greet them like an enthusiastic puppy. They felt the soft air, their bodies pushing through it, it seemed that they could feel each dark and sweet sensation. And in this way they slowly walked across the square into the church. A strange pair, the baker with red hands and the one-legged ballerina. The pair of them embarked on the path of their delirium.

Gianni's shoes were pinching his feet and he slipped them off before entering the church, a shoe in either hand. Pia content and smiling at the world as she hopped beside him.

Where would they sit?

The church was full. Stefano raised a hand in greeting and pulled them down. The neighbouring buttocks on the pew squeezing along to make some room. Gianni felt his cheeks begin to spread like a plump cushion full of air and water. Settling in and sitting back.

Noticing a gentle buzz in the atmosphere. Emile was not in church, perhaps that's why the room seemed to be breathing so easily. Gianni had not forgotten Emile. When Luigi arrived in the middle of the hungry throng Gianni had given him one of the little fanny buns to leave in the vestry for Emile. But Emile was not in sight. The happy hum of whispering voices all around settled over Gianni like a sacred fog.

# A Sacred Fog

Truth is, that sacred fog was settling over everyone, and unsettling us as well. Our tastebuds tingling with the tantalising tastes of Gianni's Easter cakes.

Perhaps it really was a sacred fog, and sheltered in its misty depth we could reveal the hidden parts of ourselves. The kind of licence we were granted then. The strange and terrible liberties we took, and granted one another.

Profligate is from a word that means to overthrow. Our desires then were profligate indeed, and truly surfaced.

Gianni was feeling overwhelmed by a spirit of great benevolence. Gazing at the stone walls of the church, he'd never noticed how well they were fitted. The fact that they fit at all, that walls could stand and not fall, seemed something approaching the miraculous.

Costa was feeling similarly benign. He heard someone whispering and laughing about the cakes. Costa closed his eyes and was surprised to see *il mano finto* doing a strange freehand scrawl. Behind him he could hear somebody humming, and recognised the tune. He too began to hum. The little ditty spread and within seconds the church was resounding with many voices singing 'Happy Birthday' to Gianni. Gianni was delighted.

Just as quickly as it began the singing ended. There were titters around the church. Gianni felt called on to respond in some way. Emile had still not arrived and there was a feeling in the church like schoolchildren when the teacher is not there. A stupid liberty that invites pranks and foolery.

Gianni was feeling unrestrained. He had in mind to

preach a sermon. He'd often thought he'd like to be a preacher. Perhaps a mounting inebriety fuelled his misbegotten intention.

He shambled down the aisle, feeling giddy, and the front of the church seemed an excessive distance for his ambulation. He turned into a pew in the middle of the church, making room for his feet between the pew-bound buttocks. He wavered a moment, and enjoyed the fleeting sensation that he was about to topple backwards. Regaining his poise he took a deep inhalation, and began to speak.

'A long time ago, when it was still dark, God was sleeping, and when God awoke in all that dark God felt alone, and scared. This continued for thousands of years. Through all that time God was sure that something was moving in that darkness, but did not know what it was. Even if God had known what it was God had not yet invented language, and so could not have given the thing a name.

'God slept, and each time that God awoke in that fearful dark God's fear was greater. The more God's fear grew, the more God was convinced that something else, some other and ungodly emanation, was moving in the darkness.

'After many more years went by a spark of light lit God's first fart, and for a moment God could see the water, and the subtle play of light on its surface, and only then did God realise that the water had been there all along, was the thing that moved in the darkness, and God was comforted. But the illumination vanished, and the play of light on water vanished with it, and God wondered if God would live to see such a beautiful sight again. And God drifted off to sleep, and the sadness that permeated God's celestial atmosphere was greater than any God had ever known.'

Gianni stopped then, surprised to find that he was standing on a pew addressing his congregation. The eyes staring at him were unsettling and he lost his balance. He fell forward, burying his belly in the unsuspecting face of some poor soul. He clambered to his feet.

He wondered what to say next to this common herd,

and began to sing a strange ditty, intoning it like a liturgy.
Lord of misrule, preaching his *sursum corda*?

> If you haven't been kissed
> while the priest has been pissed,
> then you've never been kissed
> in your life.

> There's a bit of a lurch
> in the old stony church
> and the priest has got drunk
> and he sways.

> There's a reek on his breath
> that smells like a death
> and the priest wants to
> get his away.

There was laughter in the church. Gianni paused and
looked around him. Then he sniffled and wiped his hand
along his sleeve. He flinched his shoulders as he did so,
and the sniffle and flinching made him look like a swollen
parody of Emile. There was another flutter of laughter.

Gianni felt untroubled and unhurried. He pretended to
drink from an invisible bottle while mimicking Emile's more
intimate gestures. The laughter inspiring him to an escalation
of excess.

Some defining moment had arrived, a birthday indulgence; he'd fill the void created by Emile's absence.

# An Habitual Ambiguity

Emile enjoyed the ambiguity of his habit, the pleasing fall of the cloth. Going about his day frocked up. His fingers found the hem of the long cloth and raised it above his knees in a pleasing skirtiness. Catching sight of himself reflected in the window of his bedroom. Feeling coquettish. The confusion in him made him blush. Needless to say he had been drinking.

Trying to skirt around his confusion, and finding instead it hemmed him in.

They'll want a special sermon, he was thinking, perhaps a few sheep frolicking on hills. The thought of sheep made him recall that once he'd clipped off tails in a dream. The time had come to construct his parable about the god who made the dog, and the devil's flea. He was feeling giddy and sat down on his bed.

He saw himself appear to his congregation in some finer image of himself, a strange apparition of the womanly priest that he might be. Wishing he could make of himself some new invention, and escape the one he was.

He felt a thread of anticipation that was undercut by a more familiar impulse, and the only word he had for it was dread.

Emile was scared to leave the house, and yet the prospect of the adrenalin rush his terror would provoke was far too tempting. He edged towards the front door, and beyond, making his slow and fearful way to the church.

The closer to the church he got the more terrified he felt. The more terrified he felt the more ecstatic he became, the chemicals his fear let loose spiking him up. The more exalted he became, the more rapturous he felt he could become, propelling him forward.

He was in a shocking state, not fit to be seen in public. He was getting a little gibbery, and then he'd calm himself down, permit a little laugh and straighten up his clothes. He'd cough and start to walk a little quickly, then stop for a moment before taking off at double speed. And so on.

He stumbled on his hem, fell onto the road and banged his head. He grazed his forehead, and as he checked to see if there was blood on his fingers he recalled his vision of the headless madonna and the way he'd plunged his fingers deep into his eyes.

Awash in the dubious sea of his uncertainty. What on earth had possessed him? How could he dare set foot in church again?

Had he been drunk? He felt a fool. He thought about the old Lenten service when a pair of ass's ears were set upon the head of a novice, who held an orange in one hand while reading backwards from an upside-down bible. One of the old traditions.

He was unaware that a new tradition was being born as he ran and fell and stumbled to his destination. The carnival was already in its labour and the contractions were coming deep and regular.

Emile, arriving at the vestry door, dithered for an alcoholic moment, and was just about to rush inside when his eyes clasped hold of something that gave him a physical support, the sight of it so very tangible. A strange beguiling little tart—or was it a cake?—with a moist and juicy fig right in the middle.

A gift from Gianni, that angel man. The ripe fig a little Easter egg, thought Emile. He sucked it up and thought of a sheep's eyeball in his mouth and blinked and swallowed. The fig tasted sweet and fizzy, perhaps a lingering sourness that made its presence felt, then faltered, leaving a pleasant aftertaste of fermented sweetness in the mouth.

Emile, dispatched.

# Carnival Breads

'Aphrodite is a dangerous god to worship. There are some who say she's the goddess of infidelity, worship her and you might provoke great instability in affairs of the heart. A goddess of carnal love is not the same as a goddess of conjugal fidelity. Rather than in the heart, the problem might lie a little lower down. If one was crude one might suggest the problem lies between your legs. Or that you are lying between somebody else's.'

Gianni had no trouble capturing our full attention.

Did Gianni really worship Aphrodite? He knew she was portrayed as a goddess of bestial appetite, but Gianni had another vision. He saw the mouth of Aphrodite as an emblem of the essential mystery.

Gianni was talking in a confidential whisper, we were transported.

'I have a terrible confession to make. I have betrayed you all this Easter morning. I've put an aphrodisiac in the cakes. I'm sorry. We've all eaten them. It was my foolish April birthday present to us all. Perhaps I've earnt your stern rebuke and consternation, your condemnation.'

Gianni stopped to mop his face profusely with his sleeve. He was sweating, and saw once more the piecemeal pig come apart in the boiling bath, and saw his blood-red hands stained with cochineal, like some demented and exhausted butcher-priest who's slain the beast. An astonished silence in the church. Nobody laughed.

Then of a sudden Gianni was taken by a powerful idea and waddled out of church, intent on one thing only, to find his red woman of bread and bring her to the altar. An unreasonable and ludicrous aspiration, and Gianni was the right fool for the job.

He lifted the bread madonna out of the window, cradling her in his arms, and carried her in her pink splendour to the church. He could hear the sweet music of Amaretto at the harmonium as he strolled with his Venus Aphrodite.

Walking with her down the aisle, Gianni felt a déjà vu of his vision the night before. Now he'd re-enact his dream in the light of day.

Amaretto was in thrall. His bridal waltz had come out clear. He was wedded to his song, at one with himself, his music, and that old harmonium. Realising then that the battered instrument was the thing he loved most in all the world. It had been true and faithful, whether he was bitter, upset, or maudlin. No matter how disturbing the atonal and polyrhythmic distension perpetrated by Amaretto's feet and fingers, the harmonium always struggled to comply. He was in his heaven. He did not know that Harmonia was one of Aphrodite's daughters.

Who knows why a brioche woman, rubbed with mead, could exert such an attraction? Gianni did not know the answer to the question. She had a pink glaze in the light, daubed as she was in such a quantity of cochineal. As Gianni walked her down the aisle small waves of onlookers drew near, this curious tide. Gianni didn't want to slice her with a knife, instead he plucked off one of her toes, and then the next, handing her out piecemeal to the human tide that surged around him. He was quickly relieved of his burden, as people helped themselves to his splendid effigy, popping a toe or finger into their mouths, sucking on it, chewing, and venting approval with their sighs.

The level of intoxication in the church was increasing all the while, as the digestive juices began to break the Giannicakes apart, and the sweet fermented chemicals and additives began to seep into the bloodstream. Not only were we poisoned, we were overwhelmed, elated. Such was the hastening degree of our inebriation.

When Emile finally appeared he was startled by the uproar and commotion. It was unusual for any day, let alone Easter. All that remained of the woman of bread was the last of the Gianni cupcakes, which Gianni cradled in his hands like some queenly insect with fragrant wings. Gianni offering this sweetmeat to Emile. Something in the gesture that seemed right—they had all eaten, even the tiniest portion of her arm or thigh or belly, pieces of her travelling ever smaller round the church till everyone had some morsel. And now here was Emile, come lately to their improvised harvest feast.

Emile knew all eyes were on him, so he accepted the gift from Gianni, put his nose to it, and thought A little marycake has come into the world. He smelt again and inhaled the aroma. He'd gobbled the one he'd found in the vestry, and like Costa it was not until he eyed his second one that the canny magic of the thing beheld his eye. Emile faltered then, something nibbling his amnesia.

He sucked the juice from the pastry mussel, and then bit it in half.

All mouths chewed their silent cud in unison with Emile. He closed his eyes and swallowed. The many apples Adam, and apples Eve, that rose and swallowed with him, unseen in his personal darkness. And then opening his eyes.

Emile was chewing with animation when his eyes lit on a most disturbing sight. The old joke says the only thing worse than finding a worm in your apple is finding half a worm. Imagine Emile's dismay as he saw half a spider sticking out of the marycake, neatly fringed with the indentations of his teeth.

That's why some people called them 'tarantellini'— because one of La Tarantula's own had been smuggled in, whether by Gianni or La Tarantula herself. Emile swallowing his pride, and another bite of spider, as he took the rest of Aphrodite's Lips into his own. Emile looking at us all, closing his eyes, and then the simplest words, 'Let's pray.'

Here's the oddest miracle, a miracle of infamy and joy: when Emile said 'Let's pray' and everyone closed their eyes, what did they see? They saw the little cakes Gianni had made. All of them nuzzling together at the gate. What happened next?

A commitment to the truth can be a horrible prescription. Trying to put the details in, without a blush. A recipe for persecution . . .

# Costa's Eye-Witness Account

father Pestoso's service began quite normally, after such an abnormal beginning. Or was this a lull that beguiled us into thinking that normalcy had been regained?

I could hear a high-toned buzzing in my ears. I tried to dismiss it but it gradually gained in force. I closed my eyes to hear it better. In the middle of my forehead I had the vision of a pair of lips, and then a mouth opening. The high-pitched sound I heard was coming from this mouth.

As I listened more carefully I could hear within this sound other sounds, some higher, some lower. A series of pitched harmonies which encompassed all sound and all music. I was surrounded by this strange music.

I opened my eyes, and to my amazement found myself standing in the middle of the church, mouth open wide, this strange call coming from my mouth, ringing inside my head, rising up from my stomach.

I looked around and saw the entire congregation was on its feet, joined by some strange impulse, all standing with mouths wide open, the strange ringing harmonies pouring out.

I closed my eyes once more. The mouth was still there in the centre of my forehead. The lips began to quiver, my guts were trembling. I started to shake with a most terrific laughter, as if my whole body was one giant mouth. It was like an epilepsy of mirth. Once again I opened my eyes and could not believe the scene.

The entire church was shaking with laughter, the priest was trying to support himself on the altar rail. Every time he looked set to regain his composure he would take a deep breath and collapse to his knees again, laughing on the verge of tears. This triggered successively deeper waves of laughter in the congregation. It was as if the priest was some divine comedian. We were in raptures, we were ready to explode.

The priest was now in tears. He could no longer stand, and was rolling on the ground, sobbing. A giant wave of sadness swept over us, the priest's tears were our tears. A terrible moan pierced our lips, everywhere people were wailing, beating their breasts, hugging their neighbours in consolation and some deep-felt need for human contact.

Then suddenly, shots rang out around the hills and valley, thunderbolts that broke the sky and struck the ground. A mighty rain began to fall.

The people in the church had started singing and swaying slowly forward. A curious, hypnotic state, the rhythms interlocked, a pulse of cross-beats and cross-rhythms that slowly scrambled up the brain.

It's hard to say when the swaying turned into a step, or who was first to take that step. Perhaps it happened all at once, or by degrees, or by some strange kind of decree, it's impossible to know. Slowly we walked and swayed right down the central aisle, where brides had walked to meet their grooms, and as we made our way we sang a song that wasn't any hymn, was just the sound our voices made when they were joined.

When we reached the altar we continued on our way, until we reached the back of the church where the man hung on the cross. Someone reached out, they were too short, other hands joined in and lifted the ikon from its wall and brought it back, as one of us, and with the ikon at our head, still singing and still swaying, we made our way to the baptismal font. The statue of the woman with her child was taken from above the font and came with us, our quickened step, as still we circled round the church. The tempo of our feet increased, the walk became a gentle run, a slow stampede, running in circles round the church. The sound our voices made had changed, a rhythmic stamping noise now came out of our guts, and on we ran, around and round, speeding up, the ikons held high in the air, until we ran out of our breath, all in one corner at the back of our church. We collapsed.

You could feel the heat that came off all the bodies so close and so exerted, hear the heavy panting of the breath, smell the raunchy sweet-lipped smell that came from under-arm and groin, coupled with sighs as we got comfy. Finding a belly for a head, or a shoulder, we accommodated each other, we arranged and rearranged, till we found a way that we could fit together like a giant puzzle of the village on the floor.

The storm overhead had gained in intensity, and a cold wind was blowing through the church. The portal banged against the wall as if someone was knocking, demanding entry.

It's a frightening liberation when you lose yourself in the mob, become part of the common herd and the herd is running, changing direction, stampeding and charging down things that stand in the way. The impossible momentum. Cavorting like a pack of drunken gods in our pursuit of pleasures and sensations hitherto unknown. Breaking the bounds, dismantling the laws. To know, for one day, what that was like.

Everyone closed their eyes, our common thought was of a gateway made of flesh. A common herd, born of the woman with the mammal's teat. We were of this earth, not separate from it. This was the thought those Gianni cakes induced, the fortune in the cookie.

I found myself in the arms of Pia Zanetti, both of us sobbing with great passion. Over her shoulder I could see strange couplings forming all over the church: farmers' wives with farmhands, altar boys with school teachers, the priest was joined in a profound religious embrace with young Amaretto. I could feel the hot tongue of Pia Zanetti in my ear like some terrific promise. At which point, let me confess, I was on the point of losing all control.

I forced myself from the embraces of Pia. I decided to leave the church and let my head clear in the fresh air. No sooner did I stand outside the church than I was drawn back inside. Pia's hot tongue had taken hold of me. I took a deep breath and plunged back into the church. I could not believe what I now saw.

Some couples were openly copulating on the pews. Others were grouped in circles. I was reminded of the carnival tableaux of Breughel. The church full of people jumping and spinning and tossing each other in the air, or sliding between each other's legs.

They looked like sheep frolicking on a hillside in spring. It seemed appropriate for Easter—a time of rebirth. Even the copulators seemed free of shame, as if they were performing some deeply religious act, a profound communion of the flesh and spirit, giving themselves utterly to some higher task. They took on a burden, exposed themselves to ridicule, because theirs was a religious role. They bore witness to our origins. They were women, they were men, they were Pro-creators.

A great silence settled over us. We found ourselves drawn into small circles around one or other of the copulating couples. We bore witness to their labours. Somehow their daily identities slipped from them. Before us lay a man, a woman. Even so, I could not help a pang of recognition in seeing Pia amongst this holy flock of improvising priests and priestesses.

Emile looked at Pia and saw Amaretto, a most feminine aspect of the lad that Emile embraced. He could not believe the tenderness he felt right then, as if something that had been denied him all his life was at last presented to him. He was on his knees and had adopted a profound attitude of prayer as he sucked on Pia's nipple, and did not give any thought to the mysteries of how this gorgeous Amaretto had grown fine breasts, delighted as he was to participate in one of the gentler mysteries.

Pia felt undone, and opened herself to him. Surely, she was thinking, as I live and breathe I swear that God is swimming in my waters.

Without being aware of it the breathing of the onlookers—The Witnesses—and the breathing of The Pro-creators (as these roles were later designated) became synchronised. We who Witnessed became as One with the Pro-creators.

Their sighs and moans became ours, and as their Orgasm approached so did Ours.

One of the men, it was Emile Pestoso, though I blush to reveal this information, began to mouth, 'Oh God Oh God Oh Oh Oh God!' He became our choir master, we answered his call, we were joined in this ecstatic hymn, the call and response of procreation.

One of the women made her reply. I could not help noticing her voice—it was Pia—and despite my holy intention I confess I felt a pang of jealousy, though in such a holy state it was a most unworthy emotion. Above the chants of 'Oh God Oh God Oh Oh Oh God' which now welled throughout the church with a commitment and intensity that far outstripped our usual singing of the hymns, above all this Pia could be heard intoning in a high soprano, 'I'm coming!' and once more we took her chant, took her experience for our own.

The entire church shook as she shook, we shook, trembling on the threshold of exaltation, one vast imminent Arrival, a true Coming. Each felt it was they who were on the verge of Be-coming; as if the gift of tongues had entered into us; we were penetrated and received the holy spirit, on the blink and shudder of some holy moment. We were babbling and screaming.

Truly, truly we were at that moment Divine, Godly, free of sin, free of guilt, we were naked and blameless. We had reinvented religion, reinvented the church, reaffirmed the root of its origin. In some way we knew we had been blessed. The children born of this day still hold a special place in our village.

The church heaved like a belly in childbirth and was still, except for the work of our lungs as we laboured to catch our breath. We were exhausted. Looking around the church it was as if we saw each other for the first time. Eyes were bright and clear, they shone, cheeks were red, lips were full and mouths were gently open. There was an overwhelming sense of love, coupled with our amazement.

# PART SEVEN:

# A CARNIVAL MARTYR

# A New And Terrible Tarantella

The smell of Francesca cutting through the other wafts and odours brought proceedings to a halt. The dark penetration of her body's ripe aroma. She looked like an old humpback, arched to one side, and the way she limped implied that walking could be painful. She kept her head low to the ground, eyes following the earth. When did she stop to look up at the sky?

Francesca felt an immense pity for the dirty mob she saw. She had moved far from us long ago. Who was she now, if she was no longer the baker's daughter? She felt she'd become a stranger to herself. She'd never felt more at home in herself, either. She did not feel ugly, though she knew she had become a startling creature.

The roof was leaking and there was a steady drip of rain falling on Francesca. The slates needed repairing, and the conspiracy of wind and rain was showing the extreme of disrepair the old church had achieved. The rain began to fall inside the church as we gazed up, unblinking. A drop of rainwater, and another, falling on Gianni's eyelid.

Francesca turned and slowly looked at each one in the church. It was an intimidating gaze, making us feel inept and dirty as we stood beneath her admonition. We were quelled, and stood mute, returning her gaze. Finding some new communal vision, watching Francesca. The rivulets of water streaming off her, the thick matting of her hair losing its mud and sticks and dried leaf.

Francesca was the only one of us who was clothed, and we felt most naked as we stood before her. We did not expect her laughter. Nor did we hear it. The humpbacked crone of her, this battered revelation. The rain had washed her dirt away. Not only was she the only one among us who was not naked, she was the only one among us who looked clean.

And then Francesca found her tongue. It started with her weeping, a gagging sound like a fishbone catching in the throat, as though she were giving birth to her tongue, coughing it up, delivering it herself, and in this way finding the power of her voice.

And yet she did not speak for long. She pointed to Emile and said five words. 'I wish you were dead.'

It was enough.

No-one had heard Francesca speak for so long, the fact she spoke at all was a shock. It seemed no-one had heard her words, no-one reacted. Distracted by the sound that issued from her lips. Then her message struck. We were dumbfounded, silenced by our lack of comprehension. Francesca had our full attention, however, and quickly moved to make her message clear.

The church was still. Francesca, standing on a pedestal where once a statue of the Virgin and the Child had stood, slowly lifted her skirts to heaven.

There's a bawdy brothel dance called La Tarantula that Lola Montez once popularised on a goldfield in Australia. I don't know that Francesca had ever heard of it, and in any case this was not the brothel dance that bore the spider's name. The brothel dance requires a slow cascade of yells and whistles, combined with stamping feet, while the dancer shuffles and slowly lifts then drops then lifts again her skirts, until that fine and hairy mouth of hers stands revealed beneath its web.

Francesca's actions called to mind this bawdy dance, but there was no hint of titillation. What she revealed was the trigger for a profound sadness. She stood on the pedestal, lifted her skirts and showed herself. She had shaved her pubic hair to make it easier to see that her genitals had been horribly mutilated.

Lips gouged and then an attempt to stitch them together. The horror of it filled us with despair. Emile Pestoso had turned quite pale, as had we all. But his pallor had that guilty, furtive hue, so that before we had the time to think on it he had already fingered himself. His crazed paternity, this brutality. Before a word was spoken, before the church erupted, before all this, the blighted man paused briefly to stare at us, then fled.

We were surprised to see Emile disappear into the shadows at the rear of the church. Nobody thought to chase him. Our immediate concern was for Francesca, yet she had already moved out of our range. We were stranded in our not knowing what to do.

Grappling with this horror, trying to make some sense of it. Perhaps it was then that the seed of the Carnival began to germinate. So that out of this horrid thing we might find a way to build a greater sense of purpose, and a light of goodness.

The tragic motor that propels the human herd is a potent force, and may be more potent than any other. Which is the greater, the power of sadness or the power of mirth?

Could it be that laughter burns out quicker, like magnesium burns in acid? That the pains of life burn with a stubborn fuse? When mirth subsides and the tinge of sadness starts to form. As if our pain is the thing that gives us shape and substance. The very idea is a pessimist's delight.

The tears that followed in the wake of Francesca's revelation did not arrive at once. We were too stunned. There was no immediate uproar. We had seen too much and could not accommodate this appalling and final revelation. But the tears did come, and the rain still fell, and the roof slates kept leaking, and the water kept finding new cracks in the ancient roof, and the tears that washed our faces with the rain gave us the taste of salt, reminding us of our mother Sea, the amphibians thrown onto the beach and walking on it, the unstoppable forces of the world moving on.

There was a gentle quality in the way that people started holding hands and clasping bodies, and in the rocking motion that was triggered by the tears, the diaphragm's tight contractions. Our anger had not arrived, was on its way, and when it came another of our primal faces would be displayed. The shocking knowledge of ourselves we gained that day.

The effervescent delirium provoked by Gianni's cakes had been replaced by a shocking sobriety. The beacon of Francesca's wound illumining our disquiet.

You would have thought we'd go rushing out of church with tins and sticks but we were all of us, in one baleful vision, become victims of trauma. Nobody left the church. Except Emile. Who spent the longest night of his life huddled in the cocoon of his damp bed. The living daylights shocked out of him, and the horrid nightlights charging in. Every noise provoked a dread, was someone there? He was too scared to leave the bed, and hid under the blankets in a perfect coddle, the muffled sounds of trees that creaked with groaning trunks, the sounds they made were now his own.

Emile waiting for the worst. When it came it exceeded his expectations.


It was night-time. Bodies were scattered around the church. Some people had not moved for hours, though there was not the usual sense of time, and minutes might have been days, hours minutes. No-one had gone home. There was a kind of daze, or stupor, that followed in the wake of our strange day.

Francesca moving among us, but not reacting to us. As if we were vehicles for her curiosity, or her confusion. She was etching one last giant oval, blacked into the wall, her final emblem. Others joining in, executing her design upon the wall. It was the one part of the old church we left standing. We wanted some memorial, a reminder of where we'd been and where we'd travelled, even as we stayed at home.

We got cold and burnt some pews, and little fires scattered round the church. It looked much bigger without the pews. There was more room to move, we quite liked that. You could stretch out on the floor,

It did get smoky. People marking the walls with burnt sticks, Francesca among them. The lot of us scribbling and making marks on the grotto our church had become. Huddling in our cave. Knowing the meaning of 'company'.

# A Dismal Intuition

Emile went straight home. He didn't know where to hide and so he hid inside his bed, and thus we knew exactly where to find him when the time came.

It may have been some older impulse, a game of hidey-ho with his dear papa from years ago, that made Emile try and lie inside his bed yet cast no form, as if the bed still held an empty promise. That he could vanish into air. A dismal intuition, as it was all too clear that Emile was huddled up and the bedclothes covered him.

Emile's amnesia had vaporised when he saw Francesca's wound. In its place he was left with another terrible certainty, an image of his own monstrosity.

The abandonment he felt was total then. His folly all-consuming. So many aspects of himself felt foreign to him. Even his thirst for drink had deserted him.

Huddled under his sheets and blankets, the lamentation coming from his lips, 'Oh help me, God!'

Pestoso remembering in a flash of shocking intuition the abuses of his childhood. Knew it was true yet could not face it, did not dare believe it might be so. His father standing over him. His father's hand beneath the sheets. Oh God, let it not be so, and yet he knew that it was so.

His memories demanning him.

God the Molester, leaning over the bed. The poking of him, the fondling then, as if his body was not his own. Become a toyful thing for the potent one who had his way. God the Defiler. His father's too familiar love. The hand that's come to feel him out.

298

Emile making his denial, and knowing in the heart of his denial that his denial was untrue.

A rather brutal nativity. No rams or sheep or hay, and no wise men. Emile's father, standing on his own. The weird light in his eye.

Emile wondering what set off this unwelcome flood of memory, hearing again his own poor plea, 'Oh help me, God!' The words his father used as he stood over the bed.

Together they'd make a prayer of forgiveness for their coupled sins of the day. Another prayer for Emile's dead mother. Emile's father would then kiss the boy too firmly on the forehead, cheek or mouth, as a hand slid underneath the sheet.

In short, Emile was abused by his father on a regular basis.

Emile curdled in his bed, unable to comprehend the veracity of something he wished could not be true, while knowing the truth had finally found him out.

Some say the curses of the father are bestowed upon the son, and those who are abused abuse. Something Emile did not consider as he lay in the mouldy darkness of his bed. Not that he would have found much comfort in it.

When he thought about the violence he'd committed on Francesca, he could only groan, and said once more, 'Oh help me, God,' and again his father's hand was there to find him out, and the cycle of his memories and guilts played through him again. And so he spent his miserable night.


Emile was confronted with a terrible vision. His head was sticking out of his mother's vagina. His collar was too tight and the blood was pulsing in his head, throbbing and chafing. He tugged his collar and felt the muscle of his mother's nativity organ fasten tightly around his neck. The more he tugged, the more the fleshy necklace throttled him, cutting his breath off. He was appalled to find that the circulation, cut off in this way, made part of him protrude, even as he screamed in terror for his life.

# The Rain That Fell That Night

The rain that fell that night fell in sheets, and more, it fell in quilts, and entire closets of bed linen—a glory box of a gale that spat down vats of moisture. Washing the dung and dust downhill, into the open square outside the church.

The water might have cleansed the buildings but as it did it gathered a mass of dust and dirt and dung, and by the time it arrived in the square it had turned into mud already. The mound of Francesca's dirt joined by this breeding, fertile mass.

The next day when the sun came out the town began to sweat, moisture oozing out of every pore. With the heat and moisture came another intimation, a sprouting thing. It wasn't just the painful blisters that had blossomed on our bodies. There was worse to come.

Nobody was spared. This was an outbreak of food poisoning on a scale not previously known. The whole town was scared of dying. Lover's canoodles were disrupted by a foul burp, the prescient gasses of a dark-brewed inner storm. The bowels and gizzards in their tempest. A tumultuous disruption in the lower ear and inner eye.

Had the entire vat of figs gone off, so that while they tasted sweet it was the bittersweet of poison?

By mid-morning a sullen lethargy had come over the town. You'd swear the sun, after rising, had begun to lower itself, as if the sun itself was thinking of going back to bed. A drowsy sun in a drooping sky.

People no longer walked. Where there was an attempt

made at independent locomotion it was more a lurch or stagger than a stroll or bustle. We were stumbling. There seemed to be a greater frequency in the number of heads that bumped into walls, or shelves, or other heads. There was a growing tendency to just sit down, letting one's neck go slack, jaw loose, just staring.

It wasn't long before the groans began. Clutching our bellies, we found that Gianni's cakes were not as fit for table as we'd thought. After the groans, the retches, and wretches that we were, our groans were profound. A depth of peristalsis, our gizzards reaching down like hands to wring the lower body like a dirty sponge.

We started throwing up, and it was some relief, though we were far from cured. Pickled, the better word.

A mass evacuation was taking place. The tempest of the night before had started again, only now it raged inside us, and our internal environs were the zone of tumult.

The fresh fig tarts, so golden and beholden to the eye.

Clutching our bellies, the writhing gizzard was a lizard in revolt, we spewed and heaved and groaned and thundered. We shat the skin off our arses till the shit stang raw flesh, and the arse was a red ripe wound.

One started, and everyone went off. The sound of vomit spattering against a toilet bowl is not an enigmatic sound. And then we puked.

Was it Gianni's fault? Was it Luigi's? Or was the fault our own, punished for our lack of abstinence? The repudiation of our heretical appetites?

And then it passed, this gizzard storm, leaving in its wake a bitterness of mouth and dullness of palate, and a bruised feeling around the abdomen. Our internal muscles strained from such exertion. Some people ventured out of doors, those who'd spent this second storm outside considered crawling to some safe refuge, others had begun to dig their way into the soft earth, as if like worms they sought some more benign environ. The sun was high above us now, its rays were sharp like needles. The steamy heat coming off the earth into our nostrils. Our throbbing heads.

The great evacuation provoked by this virulent outbreak of foodpoisoning acted as a purge. Cleansing ourselves from the inside. Leaving us dazed, emptied, yet curiously hopeful. It seemed at last the worst was over, and there was promise in whatever lay ahead.

That gentle voice of optimism. And how wrong we were.

# One Remarkable Assertion

In the wake of this communal nausea nobody noticed that the bakery was quiet. We were glad of our new fasting. We had so much to digest, and the bitter taste that remained once we expelled our rumble bile turned our thoughts to anything but food.

It was not long before a new hallucination started. We were as vulnerable as maggots.

A communal hallucination is a strange fact of life. There have been many of them, and together they make an unsettling history of humanity. Towns joined in the delirium of communal guilts and fears and aspirations, their poverty of mind and body conspiring to overthrow the communality of reason. This bizarre social disease. Such, then, was our condition.

During the night Francesca had dropped a bundle of sticks around her, some kind of casement. She would not sleep in the church. Instead she settled in the open square, on the muddy earth. Untroubled by the flooding rain and the tide of earth it carried. Sleeping like a stick insect in her cocoon.

When she emerged, we wished she hadn't. Her head was the first thing visible. This was still Francesca's head, but awesome to behold. She could freeze you with her eye. She had grown eight legs, so that hers was a spidery presence. She walked on all eights.

There was a commotion. At first we didn't recognise her. This was some curious oddity, a frightening, disgusting thing. But then a voice called out, 'Look! It's Francesca!'

This spidered woman rotated her eyes and drew up on

her back legs to look at everyone. We couldn't take our eyes away, caught between our fascination and our revulsion.

We were stunned. Somebody threw a stone and wounded her. Then she recoiled. It looked as if she would now be killed. But Sylvana stood between this strange Francesca and the rest of us. Don't kill her. Please don't kill her. And we didn't. It was that simple.

After a while you can get used to anything, and we grew used to this new Francesca. She stayed in the square, and had begun to spin a web. We assumed it was a web. Her mouth bent deep over her crutch, her front legs teasing out a gossamer.

She'd woven a curious codpiece in her groin.

Perhaps it was the desire to respect her privacy that saw the square begin to empty. People withdrew to the church, or slept in a lane, some ventured to their homes to rest. And yet no-one could rest. Returning timidly to the square. There was no sign of this strange Francesca. We wondered if we'd done the right thing, letting her be instead of killing her. We wondered if we'd seen what we thought we'd seen. We didn't know what to think, to tell the truth, and did our best to put the event out of our minds.

# Emile's Death Rattle?

The time had come to go up to Emile's. This shabby business. And how shabby we felt, so that we were fit specimens for the job.

When we finally arrived Emile had no trouble knowing we were coming. I don't know why the sticks seemed so magnetic.

No-one was talking. Bits of tin appeared in other hands, people started hitting sticks on rusty metal, a rotten clang it gave, but that seemed to be the music our ears demanded. Making our racket as we walked up the hill.

The hill was getting steeper, we were dreadfully hungover, and this was a sorry, difficult business to transact. We didn't really want to march in the name of justice, each of us feeling the thorn of our mortality, and the conundrums of morality, freedom and responsibility. Our true desires were monosyllabic. Eat. Drink. Sleep. Instead we laboured up the hill with our heavy thinking, and when we'd finally overcome the steepest gradient the sounds of wood on metal began once more to riffle through the air.

The sound of Emile's death rattle?

When we were outside Emile's our certainty faltered, and the atonal music of our sticks and tin died in the air. A more humble mob we were then, and when we approached the front door we stood around, hesitant. Somebody knocked on the door and we all went filing in.

Emile was in bed, his eyes wide open. He looked appalling, but perhaps that was apt, in our eyes he had become a most appalling man. He had that startled look of rabbits in a spotlight just before the trigger's pulled. Wishing that he might stand with his accusers and repudiate the man he'd been.

A voice began to pray. 'Our Father . . .' Emile watching with shiny eyes, his mouth trembling at the edges. As the prayer concluded he watched the shapes made by the mouths and lips as they pronounced, 'Amen.'

Then the covers of the bed were peeled back and Father Emile Pestoso, with hairy legs and chin, was revealed like a fresh pupa with its cocoon stripped away.

He made a small sound, then coughed a clot of green phlegm onto the sheet. His spit-gob somehow acted as a trigger. A tension in the air unleashed.

There is no law against going berserk. Not when you go berserk communally. There's no-one then inclined to press charges. Who threw the first stone? It was raining stones from heaven and we all spat upon the man.

We couldn't help ourselves. That's what we said, and so consoled ourselves. We spat on him with gusto, phlegm and gristle. Venting the produce of our gall and spleens.

There's a special humiliation that comes when someone spits on you, and you meekly wipe the spittle off your face and acquiesce.

Emile, to his surprise, found a glimmer of enjoyment there, though confirmation might have been the better word. As if, for a moment, his worst intimations of himself had been confirmed. Finding some small peace in that. The peace vanishing as the reality of his predicament came flooding back at him.

He wished that spit could wash him clean, and knew it could not. Wished they'd spit rocks and knock him out. The curious thing is that they didn't.

He wouldn't have minded being stoned. He wondered if there was an ecstatic state attained before or as the rocks began to hit. He found the idea of it oddly attractive.

They led him out into the garden and handed him a length of rope. There was a strong tree there. It seemed clear what he should do. He looked at the tree, at the rope, and at the faces of his congregation. One head nodded, the rest had eyes and jaws set hard. There was no forgiveness, perhaps some pity. He knew what he had done, he now knew what to do. They left him to it, that he might find whatever grace or dignity remained in this, his final act.

Emile knew the game he'd played with fear and terror had been a paltry thing. A perverse parlour game. Now he was confronted by something that truly terrified him: himself, perpetrator of his actions. And the clear task at hand, that he must now make an attempt upon his life.

He was the living face of Evil, and the thought overwhelmed him. He was abhorrent in his own eyes. He hadn't known, till then, that he was Diabolus. He had expected so much more from his third vision.

He had betrayed his god, he had betrayed himself, he had betrayed them all. He was wicked beyond salvation. Into the hellbox with the other broken type.

Emile was handling the rope and could see the justice of his predicament. Trying to make some sort of noose, his hands shaking, the rope refusing to obey his fingers. Or were his fingers avoiding the truth held in the rope? Telling himself he'd never been good at knots.

When they came back one hour later he was squatting at the base of the tree, holding his knees and rocking himself. He had fouled his clothing.

# Revelations

Sylvana was not prepared for the revelations of the piggery when she set foot in there. She was alone, and had wandered past the old crab-apple, noticing the bright green shoots of new growth.

The wooden slats of the piggery's door. She called then, 'Francesca,' to respect some kind of propriety.

She could see nothing, the room was dark, she stepped down into the piggery and lost her balance. She squatted on her haunches and let her eyes adjust. Slowly the patterns of the room came clear. Francesca's murals. She muffled a laugh as she saw the bottle sticking up Pestoso's arse.

The woman straddling a fat baker could only be herself. How had Francesca seen her? Eyes rolled into her head, a grimace of pleasure on her face. The sight of a goat called Amaretto made her forget her role in the tableaux, particularly the innovative way this he-goat was being milked. Filling up the comepot, she thought, and was alarmed by her profanity.

She noticed another diagram on the opposite wall. A young girl's face, which was also the moon. The moonlight fell into an old church and lit the altar. A young woman lay, back turned, so that her face was obscured. A delirious priest held a bottle in the air, while in the other hand a drinking cup dripped blood. One of Francesca's black ovals had been branded into the wall. As if, where there should have been a crucifix, a crueller emblem took its place.

Sylvana was feeling sick and turned to leave the piggery.

She could hear a group of people making a commotion in the garden by the side of the house. In the distance she could just see the top of the church spire.

She heard a noise of bells. The music of a martyr newly born? Or of retribution, swinging through the air like a dumb and rusty axe?

# Old Testament

Pia was surprised by the curious purpose she felt as she walked into Pestoso's bedroom. Lighting a match and setting fire to the sheet, her heart pumping as she waited for the flames to catch.

The flame was tentative. There was a paper on Emile's bedside table. She picked it up and read, in Emile's poor hand, his curious epigram. 'God made the dog, but the devil made the flea.' This had been scribbled out and another text scratched in. 'There is no such thing as evil, just the gradual removal of good until none is left. Saint Augustine.'

She crumpled the paper in her hand, her nose assailed by the dank smells of Emile's room. The flame still foundering. She fed this paltry fire with the crumpled paper.

The flame took hold, and the cotton sheets began to singe and burn. With a calm hand she gathered the sheets into the centre of the bed. She put Emile's chair on the bed and was happy to watch the flames singe the legs. The fire burning into the mouldering mattress. The smoke was making it hard for her to breathe. She retreated to the doorway, confident the deed was done.

The fire would spread and engulf the house. Though not, she found herself muttering, his memory. A figure so corrupt that when he died they burnt his bed.

The crackling sound of flames made her anxious for her safety. She left the house by the back door, and could see soft plumes of smoke rising in the air and disappearing.

Pia braced herself for whatever sight would greet her as she rejoined the small crowd in the garden. Emile was crouched on the ground, he seemed to have lost all power of speech, unless the ability to blubber is still some kind of rude articulation.

She watched as Costa handed Gianni a rusty axe, and saw Gianni's jaw trembling as his hand closed around the handle. His eyelids blinking. Pia struck by some strange awe, or was it just a lack of feeling?

Emile was weeping. The smell of smoke caught in Pia's nostrils. No eyes had turned her way, they were oblivious to everything except this horrid business now at hand.

Gianni was ghastly pale. He looked like the ghost of bread, with livid hands. An unwholesome and unwelcome apparition. Emile screaming as he watched Gianni pick the axe up and lift it slow above his head. The ancient ritual, so oft repeated. The bloody butcher with the axe held high up in the sky, the axehead grown large in his eye, yet so much larger in Emile's.

Hard to say who felt the worst right then, Emile or Gianni.

Gianni wilted, and let the axe drop to the ground. The horror and the shock you feel when you discover life can still become Old Testament.

Gianni looked at Emile, the way his tongue flickered at his worry wart. Seeing Emile in the shop, panicking as he strove to decide what he would choose. Bomboloni or cannoli? Cannoli or bomboloni?

Confronted by Emile's poor humanity. Dropping the axe as an audible expulsion of hard breath caught his ears. Emile had shat himself again. Gianni felt this was no way to kill a man, and any certainty he felt about this terrible affair had now departed. There was a strange relief for all of us in this brief caesura. Costa picked the axe up and handed it once more to Gianni. The finality of the gesture was at once welcome and perplexing.

He's a fool to hesitate, Pia was thinking, and wondered if she'd take the axe out of his hands. Perhaps this was a woman's job. Women seemed to make a better fist of the awkward features of this life. Sorting out the living from the dead. Her reverie ruptured by the moment of decision as Gianni swallowed and with an air of resignation brought the axe down quick and hard on Emile's skull. She looked away. Justice is done, she told herself. Was it justice, and was it truly done? Perhaps some things are inevitable, she answered herself, and felt a great confusion.

She closed her eyes, wanting to say some kind of prayer, and found she could not. May God forgive this frenzy in my soul. Was that a prayer? It would have to be, for now. The image of Gianni with the axe held high was forming in her mind. Would she ever again see Gianni as she'd seen him yesterday, a friendly baker, or would he be for all time this fat man with an axe held high?

Distracted by the heat and smoke of the fire, she could see the house begin to blaze. A hand on her shoulder. She knew that it was Costa's.

Their eyes met briefly before they chose to look away.

After the great grunt of Gianni's as he brought the axe down there were no other angry cries.

It's strange the power of attraction some things have. Emile lay at our feet, ebbing away. Embarrassed then, we turned our backs on him, and no-one spoke. Left to our private shames, our private angers and disappointments. Night was falling and the shadows coming down. We felt less righteous. We couldn't even raise a shuffle, and so we shambled back to town.


After the striking pain of the blow's impact Emile had been surprised and then relieved to find that his pain had subsided into a dumber kind of ache. He was in pain, but it was bearable, and even brought some kind of solace. As if, somehow, his pain confirmed him.

Lying on the ground, his poor lungs clutching at whatever air they could, Emile wondered how many breaths he might have before he died. Wondering what chance, if any, he might have to atone. Or was it too late, too late too long ago?

Every breath can be a prayer, he thought. He took another breath, and then stopped breathing.

Or at least attempted to. And was defied by the

automatic reflex of his abdomen. The vacuum he wished to create of himself was denied. Feeling another peak of failure in him, that he could not even keep his breath out of his body.

# Francesca's Last Moments

Who knows what Francesca was thinking as she walked up the hill and saw the burning house she'd once cleaned and scrubbed? Or how she felt when she saw Emile fouled, broken, praying to the god of wind under a tree. The great congealed gash. Her ministrations to him. Bringing him water to drink. How did Emile feel, to be confronted with this spectral vision of himself, and his accuser? Francesca did not linger in his company.

Returning through the darkness full of smoke and the glowing embers of the ruined house. Stopping to stare into the remnant flames, before continuing to the fusty piggery. Gathering her things in a small wooden handcart and wheeling the pathetic trolleyload of worldly possessions behind her.

Pausing to stare at her images on the walls. Stepping out of the piggery then. Feeling tired by the prospect of her journey back to town. Ready to find some ultimate relief.

As Francesca walked, with Pestoso's house behind her, an ease came into her step. She felt a burden had been lifted from her. Her spine felt straighter.

I could do anything now and I would be unstoppable.

The thought brought her to a standstill. Realising she'd stopped herself before she'd done a thing, and finding some humour in it. Walking to town, with a sense of danger joining her liberty. The danger was nothing that she minded. Reaching the top of the hill, the whole town below her. Enjoying the view, wondering if she'd ever see it again. A vital impulse in her hips as she kicked off, and quickly strode downhill.

# Some Magnetism

The next morning a strange silence settled over the town. The usual early morning bustle was not there. Gianni was exhausted, collapsed against a flourbag.

Feeling penitential. He hauled himself up, and pondered once more the miracle of hydraulics that let him elevate the great bag of water that he was. Fiddling with flour on the workbench, adding water to make a dough. Little figures now appeared between his fingers. A miniature landscape made of dough, with men and women, a tiny replica of his fannybuns, the church . . .

Colluding with the dough, that he might distract himself from an excess of contemplation. He groaned. The unwelcome memories coming to him. Was it time for a drink?

The thought of amaretto made him feel ill. He lumbered over to the sink, drank some water, and put his head under the tap.

He was awake, the water told him that, but he felt shocking. He didn't want to think about his strange birthday and stranger Easter. His present to Emile of an axe blade in the head. He'd never killed a man before. Nor was he sure there was a virtue in it.

Trying to keep Francesca out of mind, desperate for any distraction from a reality he could not comprehend. He could not help seeing once again the festive copulations, and then the sight of his daughter on her pedestal. Feeling an anger in the soup of his confusion. Clenching his hands, the handle of the axe fitting snugly in his mind.

Gianni looked out the window. Francesca was bathing in the square. Washing her hands meticulously, then her arms and face. Scrubbing her skin with a rough cloth that made her glow quite pinkly as the blood came to the surface.

Performing her own rite of absolution with her ablutions. As if her long personal drought had broken at last.

No-one had seen her drag the little trolley behind her. No-one noticed it until, her ablutions complete, Francesca started emptying the trolley on the mud-pocked earth of the open square. Making her little worldly pile. Some brushes, a bottle of ink. A black woollen coat that had been twisted into a surprising form by her distorted body. It seemed to lean of its own accord.

She began to build a pyramid of sticks, teasing this puzzle in her fingers as she stacked and rearranged the kindling brush. Perhaps this was the first stroke of another kind of painting, one that would be her last.

Francesca's actions seemed to hold some magnetism. Others wanted to wash, and rinse their mouths. And leave some token of themselves on the ground. A mounting desire for repudiation. Who was the first to drag a pew out of the church and set it down on Francesca's pile? Why did others follow suit? Who cut their hair and threw it on the growing mound of cast-offs?

We were creatures of a strange freedom. Were we discovering some new form of existential theology? Or had we achieved a new level of barbarism, setting back the cause of enlightened humanity by centuries?

# Clearing Out

Something was wrong. Costa sensed it as soon as he opened the stable doors. The Filing Cabinet was no more. Luigi's room was in a perfect, commodious order.

It seemed devoid of life. No mouldering mounds of newspaper, no anthills—so much order in place of the chaos of Luigi's world made Costa feel inestimably sad.

He heard the church bells ring. It was a Sunday morning.

Francesca was standing in the square. A ring of people nearby. No-one was talking. Nor did any approach her, or address her. We'd become circumspect? Her eyes were closed. Arms folded, her legs apart that her foundation might be most solid.

When she opened her eyes it was as if we were not there. She slowly walked into the church.

Who knows why we followed her inside? The gravity of her being that drew us in her wake.

Yet she did nothing, apart from staring keenly at the walls and portal arches.

Outside, Luigi was unloading the contents of The Filing Cabinet off the back of a truck, tossing them onto the growing mound of detritus in the square.

Costa had his own concerns. Fingering his treasured plaster hand. He was wearing it on his neck, with its fine red cord, wondering if he might make a present of it to Luigi. He could see Luigi throwing giant bundles of yellowed newspaper, boxes of cloth fragments, and the little harnesses he had once placed on his chooks. Luigi did not look up

317

from his work and Costa did not want to intervene. He'd never seen Luigi look like he was working, and this was a revelation.

Costa weighing his plaster hand with his good hand, trying to discern which was the heavier. Grasping the plaster hand and throwing it with all his might into the pile of throw-outs. It hit one of the church pews. Costa watched the hand shatter, and saw two fingers make an obscene gesture. His plaster hand had given him the finger.


Amaretto could not remember when he had last felt so disgusting. Emile had jilted him for Pia. No, he thought again, it was Pia who jilted me for Emile.

His hands plunged in the washing up, some kind of solace, the dirty plates and cups bringing a pleasing tangibility. But thinking about Pia and Emile was a mistake, he learnt, as he grasped the nearest object under the hot and soapy water. Remembering too late you never left a sharp knife in hot water. He felt the metal slice his index finger to the bone.

He ran the cut under cold water and could see his finger turning blue. He dried it with a clean towel and bound it with some rag.

There was a mighty din outside. The sound of metal scraping stone, and of metal snapping and wood breaking.

He was unprepared for the ruction he now saw.

A giant, unweildy obelisk had begun to spiral out of the ground in the plaza. Furnished with chairs, bed springs, coffee cups, armchairs, gilt picture frames, the works.


Gianni wanted to clear himself out. Instead he picked up some empty flourbags, carried them round the corner and tossed them onto the rapidly growing mound of half-scorched pews, abandoned clothing, old and leaking workboots, this odd pile that was already not a pile but had become some awkward tower rising out of the mud of the square. Gianni wondering what he'd throw out next.

Would he drag the old workbench out of the shop and cast it onto this unwieldy and improvised tower? So much history, so many loaves and rolls. He and Sylvana had made love upon that bench, the pair of them floured up and flowering.

Gianni felt relieved as he dragged the hulk of the baker's bench into the square. Upending the bench with one last great push and watching as it toppled forward, propped against a broken pew. Heading back into the shop, wondering what next, with no thought of consequence or regrets.

The smell of burning feathers drifted across the square. Pia had set fire to the quilt, pillows, mattress and other objects made from Amaretto's feathers. Amaretto was watching as the flames consumed the pile in vigorous gusts. The smell was foul. This was Zanetti's addition to the tower. Amaretto was in tears, perhaps it was some necessary catharsis.

Pia knew her next destination: she was going to Cafe Zanetti, she'd take that place apart with her own hands and toss the ikon of herself, and the chairs that swivelled on one leg, they were all going and she would be the happier for it.

As she turned to walk to the cafe Amaretto divined her intention. He grabbed at her. To her surprise, and his, she grabbed his hair, then pushed him to the ground. She gave a kick of her mighty leg and felt a sharp pain in her foot as it connected with his teeth. She didn't stop to see what damage she had done, and continued hopping on her way.

Her foot hurt like hell. She had to stop and lean against a wall. She'd gotten quite a lovebite from Amaretto. Her foot looking ragged and swollen. The bluish veins rising to the surface. She didn't mind. The pain was worth her satisfaction. She forgot about the pain and hopped on.

Yet Amaretto quickly found himself caught up in this new mania. Perhaps Pia's kick had been a blessing?

Doing his best to ignore the pain in his jaw, he began to help Pia, and to her surprise she let him. Amaretto held the ladder while Pia grappled with the bolts that held the ikon of herself above the cafe door. Together they carried

319

the ikon over to the square, and without a word they threw
the fetish onto the growing tower. Wordless they turned,
they would gut the cafe now, amazed to find some helpful
bond had formed between them.

Gianni was wrestling with the old wooden spider outside
the shop. The metal hooks had rusted to the metal of the
frame. Giddy from the force he needed to wrench La
Tarantula off her wall.

He made a funny sight, the waddling bulk of him, with
a huge black spider on his back. He pushed his way through
the bustle of the square and stood on a makeshift platform
that had been erected so that people could add their detritus
to the growing mass. Gripping the spider by her front legs
he thought for a moment of how he'd been a skinny boy
when he'd made the beast, admired her fangs, then cast her
off into the wreckage.

# In Immobility, Perfection?

Francesca was pulling up the stones of the old church floor. Levering them with her fingers. Then she began to dig into the earth. Scratching away, grubbying herself as she dug and dug. She made a trough a metre deep and a metre long. When she'd made the trench she turned.

In a corner of the church a small ikon of a mother and child was leaning against the wall. Francesca picked the battered ikon up, and with a slow step walked back to her little trench. On her knees then, gently lowering the ikon into the hole and covering it with earth. Patting the earth with her hands and laying a small ring of funeral stones around the mound.

Then she walked outside and stood utterly still. In her immobility it seemed she had at last achieved perfection.

No more additions were made to the giant tower of cast-offs. It seemed to hold a kind of promise, but what promise was that? Looking to Francesca for an answer. But she had withdrawn into herself, consumed by some great silence, or stillness, and her stillness froze us all.

The last sight we had of Francesca that evening was of her standing quiet in the square. In the morning she was still there and it seemed she had not moved. She did not look tired. It appeared that she had gathered strength, and the enormous stillness she was garnering within her was an aspect of this force. It attracted us and yet repelled, no-one came too close.

We were curious to discover how this strange power of Francesca's would be harnessed, or unleashed. Immune to our intrigue Francesca kept on with her vigil.

When at last she moved, many hours after she first took up her pose, she seemed to have acquired enormous strength.

What did she do? At first, barely a thing. Yet it was clear her pose had altered, some subtle shift that indicated she was coming out of her long trance. She was standing with her back to the church, arms folded across her chest, legs wide apart, anchoring her.

It was some time before one could say with certainty she was moving, such was the slowness of her motion. It tricked the eye into believing there was only stillness, and yet she was not facing in the same direction as she had.

After three hours had elapsed she had turned an arc of some 45 degrees.

From then she must have speeded up, because it only took another hour and a half for her to turn the other 135 degrees. At last her slow rotation was complete, and she stood, arms still folded on her chest, staring at the old and leaky church. One might have been forgiven for wondering if she was trying, merely with the power of her thought, to tilt the structure and bring the whole thing down. Or was she preparing to fill her lungs in one slow and massive inhalation, so subtly powerful that it might loosen the church's foundation, and then in a short, sharp exhalation blow the thing out of the ground?

It was impossible to tell if she was still breathing, there was no apparent movement of the ribs or lips or stomach. Yet she was clearly still living. It was equally difficult to tell when she began to uncross her arms.

She stood with her arms by her side, slowly opening her hands and closing them again into fists. They resembled in some way the gills of fish. It's true some people were convinced she'd begun to breathe in through her hands.

To our relief and amazement there was an audible intake of breath, and Francesca began a long slow laugh that came first as a rumble from her belly and slowly spread through her. Before we'd had the time to accommodate this new vision she rushed at frightening speed, and disappeared into the church. It was as if a wall had finally come down, the quietude Francesca's mighty stillness had provoked was ruptured, and we joined in that mad dash into the church.

She had dragged the heavy pedestal she'd occupied two days ago underneath the portal archway of the church. She had a rock in her hand and began to pound at the keystone in the arch.

Francesca was possessed. Or was she merely inspired? She knocked out the supporting stones and stood panting heavily as at last the portal's keystone fell to the ground. She'd take the church apart with her bare hands, and we joined her then, because the sense was plain and clear, and her conviction fuelled our own.

Francesca preaching now her difficult lesson to us all. As if she had taken Emile Pestoso at his word, his sermon of a headless madonna, and the renunciation of the flesh. And in due time we then renounced the body of the church, which had itself become corrupt, that we might start again.

Why did we not try to intervene? She was so close to us, and yet so out of reach. Who would have dared to lay a hand on her? Her strength of purpose so much greater than our own.

Francesca now of a superhuman strength, unless that strength was supernatural.

Gianni could see her climbing onto the great rubbish pile, which now included the keystone, outside the church. Giving it a monumental aspect as she stood on it, like a guy ready for a bonfire.

Francesca was standing in the middle of the tower, some ten metres or more up in the air. A fire began, and the flames were soon crackling up near her feet. What use our incantations then, or even the action of running to fetch water? There may have been some attempt to liquefy the flames, but they were too late. Francesca had set fire to herself, and fired herself in our imaginations at the same time. Preserved in our living memories as the flames consumed her.

Some say that Gianni Terremoto spontaneously combusted, that this was the spark that ignited the tower. Some say this is untrue, that Francesca struck a match and simply set the thing alight. Certain it is the thing burst up in flame and with that burst the baker Terremoto caught fire and exploded. A curious thing. He didn't even have the time to scream, just burnt up in a flash.

The most irreverent claimed Gianni had farted as Francesca lit her match, and the wry rye wind that billowed from his arse was all it took to set the great explosion off. A tempting theory, the symmetry of it, and the stuff of legend. Some stranger things have happened in this world.

What was spontaneous was Gianni's decision to run into the flames and retrieve Francesca. He burnt, and yes he did seem to explode. And yet Francesca did not. That was the odd and canny thing. Francesca stayed just as she was. Immobile. Her body did not burn.

The blazing tower consumed our full attention. Singeing our eyebrows, making our faces tight, and yet we could not look away. Joined in our fascination, and our dismay. The sickly smell of Gianni's cinders curing our appetites.

It was a long, slow fire and burned with an intensity that forced us from the square, to avoid the excesses of heat and radiation. Burning through the afternoon, through the evening, into the night.

Francesca somehow still standing, still not burning, her perfect posture untouched by the flames. She was just a dark shape in the burning eye of so much flame. Gianni had gone up in a burst of foul-smelling smoke and gas and the smell repulsed us, and yet our disbelief was greater than our repulsion. Our need to look into those flames so much greater than our need to look away. We gazed, in stupefaction, and contemplated our delirium.

# Emile's Unholy Ghost

Emile was shocked when he realised that he was not going to die. He had already made his peace with it and felt a little cheated. Yet his shame and disappointment were tempered by a glimmer of gratitude, and a strange thought was passing through him.

What happens when we meet at last the moment of catharsis?

He was alive, and wanted to get on his knees and pray. He did not want to say 'Our Father'.

'Dear God,' he thought aloud.

He stopped. He didn't know how to continue. He could hear the chirrup of a single bird. The pain of it made him wince.

Emile had become sensitive to sound, as if it perforated his eardrums. Any vibration in the ear made his head throb. He'd never realised there were so many sounds. The whistling sounds of wasps' wings, the hissing of leaves in trees. The source of his distress was also a revelation of a resounding cosmos, but like so many revelations it brought no comfort. Worst of all was the sound of his own voice. If he spoke, he was in pain.

When he stopped his ears with his fingers he heard a dull roar, the throbbing, humping noise of his heart, the whoosh of blood and sounds of his inner reticulation.

He wanted to be deaf to the vital sounds of himself, and wondered how he might stop the very Ache he had become.

As Emile finally struggled to his feet he felt something in him had died. Or been knocked out of him. An awkward resurrection as he attempted to walk and felt again the searing pain in his cranium. He wondered then if he was truly dead, and had become one more lost soul, stumbling through its limbo.

Perhaps that's why the first apparition of Emile that night was recognised as his own unholy ghost. A splinter of the man he'd been. Muttering apologies to everyone and everything. Whispering 'I'm sorries' to each closed door, to the rusty hinges of each gate, attempting to broach the subject with anyone who crossed his path. Surprised to see people scurrying out of sight like roaches when a light's turned on. What kind of light was this, this apparition of Emile? The great wound in his head had sealed, the blood streaked on his face and neck, the bloodsoaked cloth of his cassock and the mighty crust of the gash in his forehead. Surely that pathetic skull had been stoved in? Crushed like an insect's shell beneath a foot? This shuffling ghost who walked, the very phantom of Emile.

No-one dared believe this was not a ghost but the man himself, cloaked in his wound. The foul man begging for redemption, looking for a soul to hear him out, that he might make his last confession and die in peace. No-one would stop to listen. Instead we clapped eyes on him and fled.

Emile mumbling 'God is love' to the passing shadows. Not realising that God might also be fear, hatred or loathing.

Surely there is no truth to the rumours that Emile Pestoso was hounded through the town, pelted by a ragged mob who chased and hunted him, hitting the ground with sticks, ringing bells, and striking metal onto metal?

Emile was hunched up in the dark, sobbing uncontrollably, his back against a wall. It was hard to feel pity for a man who'd been such a monster. It was hard to hear him sobbing in the night and not feel pity. What should one do? Throw stones, as one might those nights the cats claw the roof and mew in the delirium of their heat? Our hearts were closed to Emile, even if our ears were open. We were hoping that by morning he'd be gone, or else have come to his senses and hanged himself. He would not go away, and so the dilemma remained firmly on our minds.

What dilemma? It was as if the ritual of the axe onto his head, up on the hill, had absolved us from any further action. We thought we'd killed the man. But he lived on. In the chaos that followed Francesca's revelation and subsequent immolation, we were only half aware of Emile. He was on the periphery of our vision, broken, we were convinced that he was slowly dying. None of us wanted to put him out of his misery. I don't mean that we sought to prolong it. Did we? We were not that conscious. It would be truer to say that Emile began to itch at us. His continuing presence. Were we still responsible for him? Must we instigate some formal process, a prelude to a hanging or other form of execution? And as we hesitated, caught in the delirium of our lives right then, as we swung out of control and swung back in again, the wreck of Emile was living proof of something we would rather forget, and could not afford to put out of our minds.

What was our primary dilemma? It was to do with the nature of forgiveness. Could we forgive this man? Did we have any basis for it? Didn't justice cry out to be done? Had justice not been done, and God or some law of chance had spared him? Strange questions came into our minds, bringing no answers, just a profound unrest.

It might have been some older lesson that had been preached. Who among us could cast the first stone? An eye for an eye is such a sweet and easy doctrine. That way the ledger is kept clear. Should we castrate him, and be done? But of course by then Emile had beaten us to it. So many strange truths. In a clumsy attempt at some kind of redemption—one might say an act of restitution, except this act of restoration demanded another terrible removal—Emile had cut his genitals from his body, flinging them away from his person as if somehow his generative organs had been at fault. Was this not a most cruel and terrible face of innocence, a naïve thing, this answer to a problem we'd not begun to comprehend?

There was one unintended consequence of Emile's actions. Or was it his primary intent? Suffice to say the poor and blighted man had bled to death.

We were confused, angry, ashamed, embarrassed—and profoundly sad. Something was nagging. A seed of doubt?

Each of us felt responsible in some way, or could see a part of Emile within ourselves, no matter whether large or small.

It seemed too easy to demonise Emile and raise Francesca onto her pedestal. We felt the need to embrace the two of them, even if we had to hold close to our hearts something we found reprehensible.

How should we deal with the monstrous presence in our midst, and might we yet accept that monstrousness as part of all of us?

# Her Rock-Hard Gaze

The town was famous for its storms, they'd fill the southern sky with dark grey clouds that travelled quick until they blotted out the sun and the sky was black.

It looked as if the sky was indeed setting for a storm, but the sky was wrong, these were not clouds, and they were coming from the north. Somehow the heavens had been scrambled; instead of cloud the nose detected smoke, and a fine rain of ash was falling.

The town was burning. The fire had spread from the tower to the church and nearby buildings. Gianni's bakery. Amaretto's bar. The old heart of the town.

People sat on the damp earth of the hills around the town. The strange grey-yellow light made the grass and leaves appear unnatural. Watching the rivulets of smoke that poured out of the church, and the tower still blazing in the square.

And then the fire spent itself. The old church was still standing. Oddly enough, so was Francesca.

The great blaze had raged, and when the firestorm had subsided, she was there. She had settled into the earth she had once swept into the square, the earth and ash had been fired in the flames and made a paving stone, one single rock that now covered the square.

Her own self planted firm in it, her feet under the surface.

Our new chthonic martyr?

The old church smouldering. The pews all gone to ashes. There was an echo of the smoke up at Emile's, where the last cinders of his house were gasping.

Francesca standing alone. She'd taken possession of the square. Bits of stick and ash had melted down and stuck to her. A dark black and purplish hue, a lumpy shape of her. Francesca had turned completely into stone, and there she stands unto this day, our dark madonna.

You'd like to say that it couldn't happen. And yet so many stranger things make up this world. Have you never seen the church of Santa Chiara? Her body never decomposed. After more than seven hundred years she lies there still, in the dark crypt of the church they built for her. It's hard to see her through the gauze, her tight-stretched skin. She didn't rot, instead she chose to mummify. Perhaps she didn't choose at all, strange things do happen.


Which is greater, the joy of demolition, or construction? Or are they part of the one deep pleasure? We attacked that old and suffocating church with our hands and hammers, our hearts hard at it. It was a huge job, we laboured without caution, and there were some near misses.

Perhaps it was an inevitable labour of renovation. Buildings have their lifespans; like a human body they grow tired, and they decay. There were no lengthy meetings, no formation of committees. The thing was clear to us, and we began it on an instant.

The dust got up our noses, congealed into thick snots that we blew out onto rags. The black soot a relic of that defunct church. Setting to it with a strange optimism. Knowing we were going to rebuild.

Costa had never thought he'd see the view from the top of the old spire again. Somehow it had survived the blaze. Had he not repaired these very slates? It seemed that that was in another lifetime. The perplexity and confusion of his thinking. Remembering a stream of piss that flowed, and he the fountain, dangling from his string.

Glad of the hammer in his hand, he smashed into the broken spire, cracking the slates. Enjoying the sound as they broke through and fell into clear space. He struck again, settling into his rhythm. Sweating and swearing as he swung the metal hammer, finishing what the fire had been unable to achieve.

We began to see the demolition of the church as a necessary purge. Through rage, purification. Three men were struggling with one of the few remaining pews, using it as a battering ram to pound a wall. Sylvana joined them, bracing the pew into her shoulder, the dull thud as the wood hit stone seemed to hold some kind of promise.

Her shoulder was aching, and the four of them had made little impact on the wall. The wall, however, had made a big impact on them. They were panting and sweating, and needed to put the pew down and rest. Once they'd put the pew down it seemed obvious that they should sit on it. It was so good to rest that Sylvana wondered if she'd ever stand again. Around them other bodies toiling. A whoosh of dust, some glad cries, as in another corner of the church a wall was holed and you could see right out to the rose garden. The vestry had been gutted, the charred remains of the wooden doors pulled off their hinges.

Sylvana wondering if she'd ever get the burnt smell out of her, it seemed to penetrate her skin and pores. Wondering where she'd find a good sledgehammer.

We scrubbed each stone, setting them in the sun to dry. Pulling the old church down, scrubbing it clean. And then the monumental task of rebuilding.

Every one of us helped to build that church, and it was Costa's steady hand that guided us. When we'd used up the old church stones we started picking cobbles off the street, as if the streets were now demanding that they had their noses cleaned. Scrubbing away at the grit and dirt and foetid accumulations. Placing them into the growing membrane of stone this new construction had become.

It wasn't in our minds to build a circled, spiralled thing, it simply happened. Only later did we see that we'd built a church that, in some lights, looked like a breast. As if this new church might suckle us, and give us succour, and restore the damaged capillaries of our belief. When it rained this breast dome shone, and when the sun rose or went down it glowed a gentle pink.

As we laboured, the germ of a strange idea was breeding in us: that what we needed was not just a new church, but a new religion.

It was a marvel, the structure had been built in such short time. The line of helpers and assistants stretching like ants. The mighty dome slowly lifting from the ground. One of the old dilemmas, how to make the transition from rectangle to dome? We dispensed with the rectangle, and so the problem disappeared.


Costa was exhausted.

So many people wanted to slap him on the back, wanted a part of him for themselves. He was becoming weaker, as if with each hardy backslap some little piece of himself was knocked away.

He began to wonder if he should cultivate some foul habit, to deter the enthusiasm that strangers had for him.

# A Paving Stone

Sylvana had been unable to throw the boxes of chipped plates and fractured vases onto the mound of cast-offs in the square. Wondering now if she had missed her chance. Wanting to see the end of it, her life of fragments. Feeling she had seen and done too much to comprehend it all. Francesca's immolation and Gianni's expiation too spectacular to contemplate.

She felt like breaking something. Without further contemplation she picked a plate out of a box and broke it on her knee. She was surprised how easily it snapped. Looking round the room then, eyeing her boxes of oddments. Her eyes gleaming with the joy of demolition.

Sylvana hurled vases, plates and glasses one by one against the wall of her small flat. The satisfaction so profound she wondered why she'd never done it before. She enjoyed the way the plaster shattered and small shards of glass landed at her feet. She threw and threw, until she'd emptied every box and every cupboard.

Sylvana looked at this curious carpet that now covered the floor. A small pocket of sunlight illuminating the shattered fragments. She was exhausted, squatting on the floor, her knees jutting out.

She thought she might burst into tears, but found instead she felt quite calm. Letting her air out in a rush, closing her eyes before she took her air back in.

The pieces on the floor now rearranging in her mind's eye. The subtle logic of the scattered fragments. Opening her eyes, she couldn't get the image of Francesca out of mind, Francesca's tarantella in the church, and the image of Francesca in the flames. Not crying out, just swallowed whole.

The sunlight made the colours of the fragments more intense, reds and greens and blues, this mottled tapestry. She began arranging them into hillocks, separating the colours.

Laying out some kind of palette made of the sharded fractures of the town's domestic life. She couldn't say just when the broken relics started to arrange themselves into shapes and patterns. There was no flashpoint of revelation.

Sylvana was sitting in the middle of the church on the soft earth floor. Staring at the circular wall. Her eyes travelling right around the church and coming back to where she had begun.

She'd carried seventeen boxes of shards. They'd covered the floor, her bed, the kitchen, but against the expanse of the church's wall her boxes looked puny. How many would she need?

Word got out that Sylvana wanted to make a mosaic for Francesca. People started turning up with broken china, cracked teacups and the like. Hurling them against the wall of the new church, as if this was one way to baptise it. It felt good, hurling the china; in no time at all there was a pressing throng of people in the church, laughing, hollering, getting hot and sweaty. Unable to stop themselves, such was the liberation.

The fragments building up in hillocks by the walls. The raw stuff from which she'd make her mosaic. All the images coming to her then, in a running stream.

It was a rather shocking tribute. She replicated Francesca's murals in the piggery. Adding her own details. Francesca as she stood now in the square. Gianni's woman of bread, and his crazy sweetmeats, those instruments of delirium and frenzy.

When the church and the mosaic were finished, it was a mighty thing to finally walk inside. Humbled to find we had made something that took our breath away. As if it celebrated some kind of stasis we'd achieved, after the years of diastole and contraction.

That's why there's a small reliquary devoted to Emile. It has two shutters on the front, and when they're opened a light automatically shines forth. This light falls on Emile's favoured drinking cup, and on an old razor blade that folds into an ivory handle inlaid with mother-of-pearl. His initials on the handle. It isn't much, but does it need to be? It is enough to remind us that those parts of ourselves we hide away are the very things that need to be brought out into the light. It's the only way, perhaps, that one can be truly free of shame—by acknowledging those things that seem to be the essence of our darkness.

Perhaps the essential question Emile's reliquary asks of us is this: can there be hope left in the world if we set limits on Compassion?

One could talk of freedom, responsibility and the like, yet such concepts seem so bald, and our inner life so hairy.

# Saint Francesca?

The immolated presence of Francesca exerted a benevolent influence on us all. Odd thing. There was a solidarity in her presence. She kept us company, and we were the better for it. It seemed our luck had changed, and people started calling her Fanny, while marvelling that she'd achieved an afterlife.

To be a saint you must perform a miracle. What miracle was Francesca's? Perhaps, most simply, that she survived the worst. And so she became our carnival martyr. Some say we have no right to call her actions saintly. We're a heretical lot these days. She took her life? And yet she's living with us still.

Who knows how or why she became our female deity. Perhaps it was the accumulation of her pain that fired her? In a way it seemed that she had borne that pain for each of us, or known in a major key the pains that we all felt. And so, in elevating her, we elevated each of us. That bruised and battered child each of us harbours, this was Francesca. Our Black Madonna. And of course she isn't really elevated: there is no pedestal, and with her feet sunk in the earth she is lower now than she ever was. The earth's become her pedestal, and she's a part of it.

It's said that one day Francesca will hatch out of her dark cocoon, with her whole self intact, and to see this image of a woman come whole to us will be a marvel. And so we live in anticipation of this miracle, never knowing if we will live to see the day, and happy for it, even so.

# Epilogue

To tell the truth my grandfather looked shocking. He had not eaten for three days, at least nothing more than tea and biscuits, a little fruit. Some rice with an egg yolk mixed through it. As if he, and not Francesca, was the one who aspired to live on air. The hot wind of his voice blowing through me.

There were so many questions rising in me, and challenges I wanted to make—yet every time I tried to speak he stilled me with a gesture of his hand. A funny winding motion of his thumb and forefinger. I took this as a sign of a man winding his wristwatch, and that it was my grandfather's way of telling me he was running out of time, to let him speak. Or was he merely winding me instead? At times I caught a glimpse of something in his eyes that gave me pause, some darker knowledge.

I wondered if he'd read my thoughts, because he beaded me then with those bright blue eyes of his.

'The time has come,' he said. To my surprise he hoisted a wooden leg from underneath his bed and handed it to me.

There is no protocol for such a thing. I sat awkwardly with the leg across my lap. It was much heavier than I expected.

'Don't ask me what to do with it, just promise me you won't burn it.'

I nodded dumbly.

He coughed then, and he looked a little fidgety.

'I was spawned at that bastard ritual they call The Breadmaker's Carnival. It's a bastard ritual because each

337

year it throws another litter. These days they give them all the town's name, and call them Bacheretti. No doubt the time will come when everyone will have the same surname. But we are not Bacheretti.

'I am the only child of that first carnival of bread. The original descendant. Emile Pestoso was my father. Pia Zanetti was my mother. That's her leg you're holding. It's full of holes, just like this story.'

I looked at the old man. I was determined not to look away or blink. I wanted to hit him, or weep. I felt dumb, and numb, and sat there staring at him. He looked away and coughed again.

'I wanted you to have this from my lips, and no-one else's. Give you my account of it, spill a family secret in your ear. Costa raised me as his own. He said I had Pestoso eyes. You've got them too. Welcome to the family. That's why we go by the name of Stoopes. Who'd be a Pestoso in this life? The painting was done by Sylvana. She gave it to me when I turned thirteen. It was my coming of age. The year I first went to the carnival.

'I had thought to tell you of that time, and how it felt to walk through town as The Pestoso, pelted by the women with rotten fruit and ripe tomatoes. I had thought to tell you of the service in that church, and the ritual copulation in the name of poor Francesca, how we celebrated her fullness, having mourned her fully for a year. But you've come too late, and if you want to know what the carnival is like these days, you'll have to go yourself, find your own way to Bacheretto.'

The old man stopped speaking. He looked terrible. He seemed to be making some final effort.

'I may have been born outside the church, but at least I was conceived inside it!'

The old man started to laugh. He looked at me, his eyes were shining, we were both laughing then, as if his laugh infected me. He put his arms around me, and we embraced. My laughter capsized then, and I was sobbing on his bed.

Of a sudden he began to cough. I thought to slap him

on the back but he shook his head. He lay back down, he was pale now, and staring straight up at the ceiling. Then he nodded once and spoke gently.

'I don't expect you to believe a word of this, but if you do believe, I won't think the less of you. And that's God's truth.'

He began to chuckle once again. The end came quickly. A sudden spasm, it was done. I heard a click, and noticed that the Sony's batteries had died just as the tape had ended.

I sat there for a while, looking at his features, composed in their parting gesture. I don't know how the old bugger did it, but he died with a smile on his face. And those last words, 'And that's God's truth.' Wondering if I'd not heard some other sibilance in there—a simple 'Strewth!'

# Acknowledgements

A number of literary debts need to be acknowledged. Discovering Piero Camporesi's *Bread of Dreams* in 1989, having just completed an early draft of this manuscript, was uncanny. The major debt was the confirmation that no matter how strange or exalted one's invention, it will rarely exceed the limits of what human beings have already done to one another, or experienced. Sylvana and Gianni's conduct on All Foole's Eve owes something to Camporesi's *La Terra e La Luna*. His *Rustici e buffoni* was also fascinating.

Paul Celan's poetry has long been an inspiration. The corpse that ticks at Sylvana owes a debt to Celan's 'The Straitening', as translated by Michael Hamburger.

This work was commenced in 1988. A great number of people have helped this writer. My thanks, foremost, to my parents Hilarie and Phil for their unstinting support. Thanks also to my sisters Christine and Philippa, their excellent men Russell and Colin, and their fine offspring, Adam, Philippa, Annabel, Ingrid and Ivor. Nor should June be overlooked. Nor the splendid memories of Johnny.

Thanks Trish, you typed the first version of the shortstory. You knew when to get out. Thanks Eduardo, for recognising the beast. Thank you Peter, and Petar, you were both inspirations and good friends. Elias, you and I will always drive each other mad, God be praised for this small mercy. Mr Laszlo, more power to your bass and brewing. May your brewer's elbow never fail. Leisa, thanks for the Collins Dictionary that has been my mainstay. Fifi and The Rez, and Lula and Dawn and famille, and the many other Canberra friends, not forgetting those of us who have done

# Acknowledgements

time at Rocky Crossing; nor Gloria, Chris, Kika, James, Stephanie, Claudia, and etcetera.

Thanks. The same goes for Ann, who has long been an inspiration, George who has been a perpetual enigma, James for the fine stimulating discussions and strong coffee, Don and Meme for an early appreciation, Graham Pitts for an observation about rhythm, Matthew and Melody and the many others who were making music that summer. And in the years since.

In Melbourne thanks to Jocelyn Harewood for her good judgement, and her support, including careful reading, writing space, and the loan of scanning and computing gear to enable the last cut to be made.

Thanks to Bob Clutterbuck and Terry for considered responses. Thanks to Sandy and Scotty for their humour and intelligence. Thanks to Sylvia, Suzi and the choir folk. Thanks Sarah, and Sara, and particularly to Carolyn who more than anyone has had to live with it.

In Italy I have many debts, including those to Patrizio Lloyd and Il Lanternone, Nicoletta Boris, Stefano, Marina, Sebastiano, Caterina and Margie Buscaglione, Giorgio Donati, Tiziana, Paulo, Ted Keiser, Jacob Olesun, Marni and Gigi, Franco and Raimonda . . . . . .

Thanks to Gaby Naher, Sophie Lance and Jill Hickson; Kris Hemensley; Michael Heywood. Also to all at Allen & Unwin and Meredith Rose, who edited the text.

This work has been completed with the assistance of the Australia Council.

This book is dedicated to
Hilarie and her love of language
Phil and his love of story
' ' who showed me a face of courage
Carolyn who lived with it.
It is also dedicated to the memory of Carolyn Joy Wood.
Gloria.